MICHAEL DOBBS

Michael Dobbs has been at the right hand of political controversy for more than a decade. He was at Mrs Thatcher's side as she took her first step into Downing Street as Prime Minister, he narrowly escaped from the Brighton bomb attack on the British Cabinet, was Norman Tebbit's Chief of Staff during the 1987 general election, and was recently appointed by John Major as Deputy Chairman of the Conservative Party. He has been called 'Westminster's baby-faced hitman'.

His first immensely successful novel, *House of Cards*, was made into an award-winning BBC TV serial, featuring Ian Richardson as unscrupulous Chief Whip Francis Urquhart. This was followed by two more bestselling novels: *Wall Games* and *Last Man to Die*. In 1992, he published *To Play the King* – the highly controversial sequel to *House of Cards*, in which newly appointed Prime Minister Francis Urquhart came into conflict with the new King. A *Sunday Times* No. 1 bestseller, it also became a major BBC TV serial. *The Touch of Innocents* continued Michael Dobbs' remarkable bestselling success when it was published in hardback, remaining in the *Sunday Times* bestseller list for eight weeks. A TV serialization of *The Touch of Innocents* is planned for Autumn 1995.

Michael Dobbs lives in Dorset with his wife and two young sons. His new novel, *The Final Cut*, the third and final Urquhart novel, will be published in hardback by HarperCollins in January 1995.

THE TOUCH OF INNOCENTS

'Michael Dobbs enthralled us with the dastardly Francis Urquhart. Now he has invented a new and even nastier political villain. It adds up to a tremendous chase and battle of wills – and wiles . . . wickedly captivating.'

Daily Express

HOUSE OF CARDS

'This blood-and-thunder tale, lifelike and thoroughly cynical, certainly carries the ring of authenticity . . . a great triumph.'   Anthony Howard, *Independent*

'Here is a political thriller writer with a marvellous inside track knowledge of government. *House of Cards* is fast-moving, revelatory and brilliant.'
Daily Express

TO PLAY THE KING

'Michael Dobbs has an uncanny knack of forecasting the future. A fascinating read and a conclusion that would send a chill through Buckingham Palace.'
Sunday Express

'With a friend like Michael Dobbs, some might say, who on earth needs enemies? His timing is again impeccable. A good romp, and gloriously cheeky. Dobbs' books grab because of their authenticity – the man knows his stuff.'   *The Times*

LAST MAN TO DIE

'Truly the great escape . . . quite simply, a good old-fashioned adventure that rattles along to a cataclysmic finale.'   *Daily Mail*

'Thrilling escapism . . . what a corker, with a cunning twist in the tail. After this, the last moments of the war will never seem the same again.'   *Daily Express*

WALL GAMES

'An expert on erring political shapers of public destiny. Dobbs is the sort of operator who seems to be precisely where the action is at various moments in history.'
The Australian

'Merits a medal.'   *Independent*

MICHAEL DOBBS

The Touch
of Innocents

HarperCollins*Publishers*

HarperCollins*Publishers*
77-85 Fulham Palace Road,
Hammersmith, London W6 8JB

Published by HarperCollins*Publishers* 1994
1 3 5 7 9 8 6 4 2

First published in Great Britain by
HarperCollins*Publishers* 1994

ISBN 0 00 647594 9

Set in Trump Medieval

Printed in Great Britain by
HarperCollinsManufacturing Glasgow

To the memory of my Mother.
Who had to fight harder than most.

ACKNOWLEDGEMENTS

Writing encourages curiosity. I have been so fortunate in my own life that it would be too easy to grow narrow-minded, self-satisfied, all curiosity crushed, yet that would lead to nothing but autobiographical novels for which I suspect there would be an even smaller market than for my memoirs.

So I have always chosen to indulge my curiosity and include in my books groups of people against whom there is extreme discrimination – politicians, kings, homosexuals, prisoners of war. Until now, I have lacked the courage and certainly the experience to write about the largest group against whom there is widespread discrimination – mothers. Particularly working mothers.

As my various careers have flourished I have watched female colleagues being torn between maternal instinct and professional ambition, conscious of my own male advantage rather than their dilemma. Perhaps, with the help of this book and of many friends, I now understand that problem rather better – and the conflicting, often tormenting, emotions of which it is composed.

I owe an enormous debt of thanks to many people for their help. Most of them have shared deep confidences, either personal or professional, and do not wish to be directly acknowledged, but they know who they are and I hope they feel, when they have finished reading *The Touch of Innocents*, that their time and unselfish efforts have been well spent.

Therefore I shall restrict my specific acknowledgements to the two most important women in my life: my late mother, Eileen, and my wife, Amanda. The only truly wretched part of my life has been that I was unable to share more time with my mother; Amanda has been by far the best compensation. The two of them have been, and continue to be, an inspiration.

MJD

ONE

Her eyes were distracted, dazzled. One moment the country lane had appeared anonymous and empty in the swirling night rain, the next it was a blaze of incoherent light which screamed of danger.

The brain responded immediately, but inadequately. It could not tell that the fool on the tractor, suddenly aware he was blocking the path of an oncoming car, had panicked and switched on all the headlights; there was only that state of alarm that sends the senses cartwheeling, freezing the mind, where instinct rather than intellect takes control.

Isadora Dean would never remember what happened next, the confusion and sense of fear as the source of light came closer, the clarity of understanding that ahead lay disaster, the struggle with rubber and brakes which seemed to adopt a logic of their own as they danced and pirouetted amidst the leaf-strewn mud of an English autumn, the numbing slide away from light into darkness and the unknown, a feeling of weightlessness, of being in space, spinning off into another world, eternity.

Eternity. Death. *Her* death. Damn, what a waste.

She had already crossed into the underworld, it seemed. The car had left the road and was carving a tunnel of light through the tangle of wood that pressed around. Skeletal, leaf-stripped branches leapt out from the darkness to snatch at her, to drag her to disaster as a kaleidoscope of images flashed past faster than the eye could capture or brain decode.

Fear began only as her mind turned to the children. Benjamin. Little Bella. She released the breath caught in her lungs long enough to begin a strangulated cry. 'Hold tight!' How absurd. The boy was still soundly asleep, comprehending nothing, and how could a six-month-old baby hold tight to anything other than a mother's breast?

She saw the bole of the gnarled oak but barely; it could have been a rock-face, a bolted door, the bottom of the deepest well. But she knew it was Immovable Object. Disaster. The End. Izzy felt nothing, not as her body began to lift from the seat and tear against the restraining belt, not when the inertia lock snatched back at the belt and threatened to carve her in two, not even when her head hit the roof of the hire Renault as it began to roll and the windscreen exploded into a thousand pieces of razor-tipped stardust.

And she would remember nothing. For as the point of her head just behind her hairline came into contact with the pressed-steel frame of the car, a shock wave like that of an earthquake passed through her brain, shaking it, stretching it, causing the cells to vibrate and become microscopically displaced. The damage was at first subtle, but decisive. As the cells twisted away from each other the chemical balance of the brain was disturbed, turning the neurological pathways from a running track into a synaptic slough, tangling and entrapping the electrical messages which perform the brain's work.

She lost consciousness and when, in a while, she came round, she would still lack coherence and focus because many of the higher functions of the mind remained lost in what had become the ensnaring tar pit of her brain. She was unable to assist the terrified and penitent farmer who ran to drag her and her children free from the wreckage, found it impossible to respond to the concerns of the paramedics who tended her, didn't notice the shrugs of the firemen who arrived too late to save anything from the burning metal carcass.

Yet there was still worse. Even as her body gave the impression of making some revival from the initial assault, the bruised and insulted brain was swelling.

And would continue to swell.

A small vein inside the inner brain had burst, spilling blood, creating pressure under which the nearby brain cells and their surrounding nerves would no longer operate, so reversing that original revival and pressing down her senses ever more deeply into the pit of tar.

The eyes opened but did not see, the ears heard but could not comprehend, the senses drifted away on a moonbeam until all coherent memory of the scene would be gone.

Of the crash.

Of the fire which brought terror to half the night life in that usually tranquil Dorsetshire woodland, and of the sirens and flashing lights which did for the rest.

Of her arrival at the Weschester General on a desperately busy night in A&E with its confusion and barely controllable clamour after some drunk had pulled a fire alarm.

And of the rush to get her to the intensive therapy unit as the medical staff began to realize that, instead of recovery, something with their patient was going devastatingly wrong.

*　　　*　　　*

Sunrise in San Francisco. A tantalizing purple and pink cast stretched across the horizon, the mist obscuring where parched hills stretched up to kiss the Californian sky, with only the lights of Oakland flickering their daily welcome from across the water to indicate where earth met heaven.

The first Boeings of the day stood out like angry fireflies against the still-dark clouds while two endless lines of automobile traffic swarmed across the Bay Bridge, mimicking the relentless march of worker ants; another half hour and the march would be but an agonizing crawl.

He stood by the open window, a salt-brushed breeze snatching at the smoke from his cigarette as night gave way to the lighter, noisier tones of day and the dawn chorus of streetcars called for their first passengers.

It was like no other city on earth, he thought; at the very frontiers of paradise. So relaxed, so uninhibited, so unlike the bureaucratic jungle of DC where the women didn't even wait until winter to freeze.

Over the Bay the early-morning flights were beginning to stack up; he'd be catching one back in a few hours' time. It brought him yet again to pondering how long it would be before his own baby was up there with them. The MPAA. Conceived by computer, gestated in committee, and about to be delivered unto Congress. The lightweight Multi-Purpose Attack Aircraft, the state-of-the-art fly-by-wire variable-geometry radar-reflective Mach-3 aerial acronym that only required a pilot, so they said, to tell it when to go home. The collaborative brainchild of trans-Atlantic aerospace firms which was supposed to solve most of NATO's and all of his own problems for the next twenty years. Project

Sure Hit, as it had originally and less than tactfully been known. Project Shit, as it had been immediately redubbed.

So the President, angered by the sniggers of a sceptical press conference and eager as ever to shower himself in righteousness rather than ridicule, had on the spot rechristened it Project Dust. 'And Thine enemies shall lick the dust,' he had thundered, not textually entirely accurately. But who amongst the reptiles of the White House Press Corps would ever know?

So, the Duster was expensive, but what did they expect of the most technologically innovative piece of military hardware in a generation? So it was already a Cold War cowpat, a weapons system in search of an enemy, a huge and wasteful distraction in a world where the term superpower rang like a ghostly echo through the lengthening dole queues, bread lines and back-street abortion clinics of Middle America. But, after years of recessionary compromise and Congressional gutlessness, it was the last chance, the *very* last chance, to glue back together the design teams and production lines that had saved the West a hundred times over when the liberal pedlars of compassion had prematurely announced 'peace in our time.'

The Duster would get built – had to get built. For Joe Michelini there was no alternative. No prospects, no job, no future, no understanding finance company, not for a forty-three-year-old planning director with a lifetime of service in an industry that would effectively cease to exist.

So it *would* get built. Even if it meant his kissing the backside of every procurement officer in the Pentagon and sucking the toes of anyone and his mother who had the vaguest connection with the Senate Armed Services Committee.

DC made him think of Izzy, home. If you could call it home, with a wife who – more often than not – wasn't simply in some other city but on an entirely different continent. She didn't even use his name.

He glanced at his watch. It was Sunday; over in Europe it would be early afternoon, surely she had to be home this time. Once more he picked up the telephone, listened to the ringing tone; once more it remained unanswered, another of his messages that seemed lost in space. Not just a different continent, another planet. The story of his married life. And this time she'd disappeared with the kids. Nothing, for more than a week.

'Bitch,' he snapped quietly, patience and cigarette finished. Through the open bedroom door he could hear the rustle of sheets and saw an elegant, bronzed thigh protrude from beneath the covers to hang limply over the edge of the bed. He shrugged. Somehow, here in California, there seemed to be no ill winds.

He dropped the phone back into its cradle and with the fingers of one hand rearranged his rumpled hair; it was thinning, a few years ago he would have needed to do battle armed with a brush. But so many things had changed in these last few years.

With his cigarette stub he made a slow, deliberate mess in the ashtray, taking a deep lungful of fresh air to fill his chest and flatten his stomach. Then he went back to bed.

They had laid her out on the bed in the far corner, where it was quietest, to die.

The mass of monitoring equipment suggested that the major body functions remained normal but the scan had revealed the problem. The offended segment of the brain had swelled, the white cells and the surrounding grey-coloured nerves which should have stood out sharp and distinct had become blurred, sucked into the neurological mire, and now even the lower physical functions were beginning to decay.

The teaching sister shone the beam of a pencil torch into the patient's opaline eye; the pupil reacted, but insipidly, not as it should, and not as much as yesterday. She unclipped the pulse oximeter from the tip of the middle finger and pinched the soft part of the nail which would normally produce an irritated flexing of the digit.

Nothing.

The brain was no longer responding to the stimuli of shocks, commands, smells, noises, pressures, pains. The sister, Mabel McBean, a woman of middle age and generous girth whose hips rolled and shoes squeaked as she crossed the vinyl floor of the ITU, who had half a lifetime's experience of the self-destructive tendencies of others yet who managed to retain the innate Tayside compassion of her childhood, glanced across at the student nurse and shook her head.

'I wonder who she *is*,' the student nurse, an Australian out of Wagga Wagga by the name of Primrose who carried her birthright with shy fortitude, mused for the fifth time that week.

'Extraordinary. I've never known a lass like this to be so anonymous,' the sister responded. 'It's no' as if she's a tramp or been living in a cardboard box.' She picked up the hand once more. 'Manicure's expensive.'

She gave the nail another pinch. No response.

She replaced the oximeter and like a fussy mother hen readjusted the cuff which monitored the blood pressure, looking once more into the handsome face of the patient, a woman in her thirties with fine bone structure and rich, fox-red hair.

'Bonny make-up job, too.'

The bruised lids of the eyes had turned a vivid purple and pink as though treated by a trainee beautician taking her first tentative steps at colour coordination, and there was a tiny nick below the left eye caused by the fragmenting windscreen which looked angry but had needed no stitches and would have left perhaps only the faintest of scars. If only it were granted the time to heal. Otherwise the face seemed at peace, resting, not dying.

It was a compelling face, handsome if a little too expressive for McBean's traditional eyes, broad around the eyes and tapering from elevated and faintly oriental cheekbones to pointed chin with a finely carved nose and full, expressive lips. Loving lips. Contemporary cover girl rather than classical beauty, particularly with the carefully cropped hairstyle. The skin was fresh complected, out of doors, the orthodontics out of this world.

Yet there was also a suggestion of suffering, McBean thought, an overdose of experience that had etched a little downward crease at the corners of the mouth as though the woman had made a deliberate choice not to live off her fine looks but instead to compete, to join the daily struggle with the rest of the world. Beneath the battered eyes the skin had the stretched, pale mauve hue of fatigue and the red undertones which mark where tiredness turns to exhaustion and starts eating away inside. More than the strains of motherhood. Implying . . . what? Stubbornness? Pain? A certain lack of fulfilment? McBean sighed; it seemed they might never know.

Primrose interrupted the sister's thoughts. 'Can't the police trace the car?'

The student nurse was seated at the head of the bed, brushing the hair as she had done every night of the last week, trying to remove fraction by fraction the large clot of blood which had matted and tangled and ruined its deep red lustre. They could have cut out the clot, of course, and destroyed the carefully created short style, but there would be so little chance for it to regrow. Even in death there should be dignity.

Sister McBean shook her head. 'Renault. Left-hand drive. Could have come from any one of a thousand places in Europe. And the fire destroyed everything, even her identity, poor girl. Got out wi' nothing but the clothes she was wearing and they were precious little help. Italian silk, American denims, a rain-forest wristband and sneaker shoes they reckon might have come from somewhere east of India. Upper class Oxfam.'

'What about the little boy?' Primrose persisted.

'Osh-Kosh. The bairn was wearing nothing but Osh-Kosh which is as common as an English Duchess. The poor mite's too young to talk properly, they reckon no' even three, and they can squeeze no' a thing from him. May be suffering from shock, although he seems to understand English. And a smattering of French.'

'And the baby?'

'Perhaps I should try a little Gaelic on him. I wonder if they've thought of that?'

'The baby,' Primrose insisted, but found her answer in McBean's sad eyes.

'You'd have thought that the father or some other relative might have enquired,' the student nurse murmured. 'Surely someone must be missing them?'

'If I had the looks of this lass I'd expect half the men I knew would be missing me.'

'So where are they, then . . . ?'

'What the hell you mean, "she's gone missing"?' Grubb hissed down the phone. The foreign editor of World Cable News looked in agitation around the noisy Washington DC newsroom, anxious about who might be eavesdropping, uncertain what was hitting him. Excuses, for sure, but close behind excuses usually came a heavy shower of shit.

'She left no number? No contact?' Grubb couldn't believe what he was hearing. It had never happened before, one of his foreign correspondents simply deciding to go walkabout, leaving no means of contact, simply gone missing from the most important foreign beat they had, covering the whole of Europe. Izzy was one of the best but now the stupid bitch had landed him right in it. Already he could hear the shower head beginning to splutter. And it was not the time to be smelling of anything other than roses, not with the cable news network on its financial uppers and looking for more cutbacks.

He groaned as the young producer, three thousand miles away in Paris, tried to explain. 'Not those damned kids again? Chrissake, we gave her six weeks spawning leave and she's only been back a few months. How much more blood does she want?'

The young producer was reassuring; it had been a difficult time for her, she had wanted to get away, clear her head; she was under a lot of domestic pressure, personal things to sort out. For just a couple of days. Yes, he knew it had been more than a couple of days, more than a week now, but he could handle everything, it was all under control. No need to panic.

Grubb, a short and fleshy man of uncertain middle European descent with razor burns on his dark cheeks and a chin that sagged like a feeding bag, demurred. He thought it was an excellent time to panic. When the piece he needed from London came over the following day fronted by the producer rather than their top foreign correspondent, there would be no hiding place, only retribution.

He decided to get his retribution in first. He glanced across at the managing editor's door, which was ajar. The feeding bag shook, his voice rose to a shout.

'I don't put up with this sort of crap. Damn it all, I pay you to give me results, not excuses, and you don't go letting her out of your sight without she gives you some means of contact. Jesus H. Christ, there's a major Government reshuffle in Britain and you tell me she's off changing nappies. What am I running here, a newsroom or a nursery? If you can't find her in the next couple of hours you're gonna have to do the piece yourself – you better make it good, boy, right on the button, d'you hear? Heavy-duty stuff, something that'll sandbag those bastards over on the networks while they're still checking their zippers and fiddling their expense sheets. My show's the best in the business, and that's how it's gonna stay!'

Grubb glanced around furtively. His raised voice had attracted the attention of the entire newsroom and out of the corner of his eye he could see the managing editor standing at the door of his office, brow wrinkled and mouthing obscenities as he investigated the commotion. It was time for the full effect; he stood up, the full five and a half feet of him, to deliver his *coup de grace*.

'And then you find her, pronto. Dig her out from

under whichever stone or stud she's hiding, and you tell her from me that she's got her lily-white tits caught in a wringer this time.'

He slammed the phone down, not needing to act the role of outraged editor, before looking around the newsroom to wave away their rapt attention. He could handle this one. And if he couldn't he'd made sure that everyone, and particularly the managing editor, knew it wasn't his fault.

On the other side of the Atlantic the producer of WCN's European bureau smiled to himself. He was twenty-eight and about to get his first break on screen. If he did well, really well, they might continue to let him fill in, avoid the unnecessary expense of flying over another foreign correspondent, at last recognize his true talents rather than condemning him to the mindless fetching and carrying of coffee cups and arranging satellite feeds for others. This was his big chance and he had no intention of letting it escape. Perhaps he ought to be contacting someone to report a missing person, making enquiries; on the other hand he had a job to do, a flight to book and not a hell of a lot of time. From their Paris base in a matter of hours she could have disappeared to any of a dozen countries; who was to know which? And he needed a haircut.

Already in his mind he was writing the intro to the piece he would deliver to camera from in front of the great black door at Ten Downing Street.

He didn't mind if she never turned up.

Nobody had noticed the problem with the spleen. The buffeting caused by the pressure of the seat belts just below the ribs had caused the smallest tear in the soft surface tissue, no more than half an inch, and it had been oozing blood ever since. Not enough blood to cause a major physiological problem, indeed, scarcely enough to register any change on the monitors, just a slow, steady drain on the oxygen supply to the nervous system which had begun to degrade even the basic autonomic responses and which everyone attributed to the gradual dysfunctioning of a swollen and chronically damaged brain. But the bleeding had weakened the tissue surrounding the tear until, as spleens sometimes do, abruptly it ruptured. Spleens are the washing machines of the blood, designed to produce white corpuscles and break down the worn-out red corpuscles; they are not intended to haemorrhage and squirt blood into the abdominal cavity. When they do, patients normally have no more than a couple of hours to live.

Primrose was flustered. Less than forty minutes had passed since the grand parade of registrars, house officers, anaesthetists and physiotherapists had swept through ITU on the thrice-daily rounds, rushing around with their earnest faces and silly jokes, treating the nurses around them with as much consideration as uncomfortable pieces of furniture. Particularly student nurses. Yet now the anaesthetist, the one with the blond hair and salon tan, was on the phone, summoning her. She hadn't even realized he knew her name. What did he want; had she fouled up?

The other nurses exchanged knowing smiles; after all, he had the tightest and best-known *glutei maximi* any of them had seen in or out of surgical trousers.

So that was it. An emergency, he explained, of a distinctly non-clinical nature. These emergencies she'd been handling since she was fifteen. Patiently she explained she couldn't, not this week when she was working nights, trying to phrase her refusal so he wouldn't be unduly deterred, wondering how far the tan went beyond the forearms, when the air-conditioned calm of Weschester General's intensive therapy unit was shattered by the shrill insistence of an alarm. Alarms in ITU may sound if a patient rolls over and disturbs a sensor, or when a monitor is switched off for a bed bath or some other treatment. But patients in comas don't roll over, and there wasn't a nurse within twenty feet.

She cut off the anaesthetist without explanation and rushed for the bed, but already McBean was ahead of her and checking the monitor. Blood pressure dropping, catastrophically. The breathing, once so serene, abruptly shallow and rasping. Now the alarm on the ECG monitor joined in the drama as it detected a heartbeat beginning to race. The body was in shock; death was calling.

'Not so soon, not so soon, my lovely,' McBean breathed quietly. It was too sudden, too unexpected to give up the fight just yet. 'Hold on, a wee while longer. Don't go giving up on us, not now.'

Even as she called for the doctors to be summoned back the sister was making a further inspection of the patient, using her trained eyes, probing with her fingers, letting her years of experience block out the wailing of the monitors while she searched for the cause of crisis.

And quickly it was found. A distended abdomen, taut, a drum.

'Get a theatre ready,' she snapped across the ward. 'We'll be needing it in a hurry or I'm too old for this job.'

Calmly, she turned to the patient and began

stroking her hand, which was trembling in shock. 'We'll maybe get you through this after all. And then we can find out who you really are.'

The pavement across the road from the famous doorway was cluttered with the paraphernalia of modern news gathering which, in spite of the microprocessor revolution, still seemed to consist primarily of middle-aged men, each more dog-eared than the next, raising their voices to hurl baited questions in the direction of passing politicians. They stood like fishermen crowded along a river bank, overweight, overcoated and many thermally underpinned, hoping to lure their quarry into a sound bite.

'This is a traditional British game called a Government reshuffle,' intoned the producer-turned-novice foreign correspondent. It was the hour of day when the minds of most journalists descend to their stomachs and they begin the detailed process of planning lunch, but the twinges of hunger were deadened for the young American by the knowledge that it was peak breakfast viewing time back home, and he had it live.

'Into Ten Downing Street behind me in the past few hours have passed Britain's most able, and most ambitious. For some the door is the threshold to still greater fame and preferment; for others, it's the open jaws of the political crematorium. The game for us is to guess who has got what they want, and who has just joined the living dead. One junior minister has already let the cat out of the bag. When he left Downing Street just a few minutes ago, he was in tears. Others react differently. When he reappeared after his chat with the Prime Minister, the much criticized but usually voluble Defence Secretary could utter nothing more than a strangled "Nothing to say", while the Transport Secretary seems to have vanished completely. He went in through the front door of Downing Street some time ago, but it seems he must have left from the back.'

The correspondent turned to glance down the narrow Georgian street which, as though switched from the studio, became bathed in late autumn sunlight. Behind him one of the heavy net curtains at a first-floor window was disturbed by a shadowy figure – a curious secretary enjoying the fun, perhaps. Or the Transport Secretary seeing if the coast were yet clear. But the correspondent's attention was turned to a tall figure striding towards him from the direction of the heavy wrought-iron gates that shielded the entrance to Downing Street.

Even at a distance the bearing was notable. Many of the visitors to Downing Street that morning had appeared skittish and overflowing with nervous energy, others had been cautious, prowling, like stalking cats. This visitor seemed relaxed, self-confident, as though walking in the country, which, indeed, frequently he did. Yet his three-piece suit was all town, immaculately tailored and showing scarcely a trace of unintended creasing, the gold watch fob accurately suggesting an heirloom from a long line of distinguished and wealthy ancestors, while the highly polished shoes which caught the pale sun announced that this man was both meticulous enough to require they be polished daily, and of sufficient means to ensure he did not have to bother with such matters himself.

As he drew closer to the cameras the image of good grooming and close attention to personal detail became enhanced; the spare frame, the face healthily weathered rather than lined, a controlled expression difficult to read and suggesting a man who did not share his emotions lightly. Perhaps with his masculine manner and evident self-confidence he did not feel the need to share his emotions at all. The thick hair was laid straight back from the temples, its mixture of black ink and steel grey implying a man in his early fifties. A man, like a good malt, improving with age. And moist, pale blue eyes. He had the women of his local party association dangling from his Jermyn Street belt.

'And here's a man who seems to be relishing the game,' the young American continued brightly, but failing to realize that the name he offered viewers was being swept away in a sudden deluge of shouted questions. 'He's arriving not by car, but on foot, in full view of the cameras, denying himself any hiding place when he leaves. He's either very bold, or very optimistic. But this is a man hotly tipped for promotion.'

The politician turned his face to the cameras on the far side of the street and gave half a wave, but did not smile.

The correspondent held a hand to the side of his face to guard his earpiece; a voice that sounded very much like Grubb was bawling indecipherably at him. Something about an unnamed bastard.

'In his previous job at the Employment Ministry he made his name as a political tough-guy by defeating one of the most bitter rail strikes in recent memory, while in his current role as Health Secretary he's established a reputation as a radical reformer . . .'

More squawking in his earpiece.

'. . . whatever he's doing tomorrow, in many people's view this is a man who could eventually go all the way and one day be working on the other side of that Downing Street door.'

On cue a duty policeman saluted, the door swung open and without a backward glance the politician disappeared inside as Grubb's voice echoed across the satellite link, at last intelligible if deeply inelegant.

The young broadcaster drew a deep breath, no mistake this time, the words mouthed with almost excessive precision.

'We are likely to be hearing a lot more about Paul Devereux.'

The senses were stunned, literally. A blast of sheer white light had entered the eye, which had been unable to cope. The pupil struggled to exclude the glare but had found it an impossible task; the light beams felt as though they were tearing around the skull, harassing the brain like a pack of mongrels let loose in a school yard. The olfactory nerve, under assault from a powerful and nauseatingly pungent odour, jammed in revolt; the nostrils flared in disgust, but found it impossible to escape. A sharp pain shot up through the nerve tendrils of the left arm from somewhere near its extremity, travelling through the brain stem like an angry, malevolent wind, blowing away cerebral cobwebs, rattling closed doors and throwing open the windows of the mind as it passed. The sensation it created was intense and unpleasant, yet in response her body could manage nothing but a slight, almost contemptuous curling of the little finger.

Around the bed, the reaction to pain generated smiles. 'You were right, Sister,' the consultant neurologist, Arnold Weatherup, sighed. 'Once again,' he added with feigned reluctance. 'I thought this one had passed us by, but it would seem the main problem was a leaky spleen all along. You have a sixth sense about these things; not so long ago women like you would have been burned at the stake.'

'And no' so long ago, Mr Weatherup, doctors like you were robbing graves for anatomy specimens.'

The consultant laughed. There was always much laughter in this ward; it helped to ease the distress of frequent failure.

'The medical profession has always required its sacrifices,' the anaesthetist joined in, staring intently at Primrose.

'I don't think we need to prod or poke around any longer, Sister McBean,' Weatherup concluded, examining the fresh scar on the upper left abdomen through which the leaky spleen had been removed. 'I shall leave it to you to weave your charms and spells and hope that this recovery might continue.' He smiled. 'By the way, Burke and Hare, the grave robbers – Scots, weren't they?'

'No, doctor. Only the corpses they sold. Nothing but the best for the medical profession.'

None of this banter registered within the damaged brain, which was still dazzled and largely blinded by the unaccustomed light. The tar pit, although drying out, still delayed and frustrated the reawakening army of neurological messengers. They leapt from stepping stone to stepping stone, trying to find a way through. Most still failed and some, like those bearing short-term memories, would perish entirely, but others were more persistent, reinvigorated by the blood's fresh supplies of oxygen, trying first one route, then another, until slowly they came nearer their goal. The stepping stones were growing larger, more messengers were getting through, yet many still arrived out of sequence, jumbling their messages and confusing the brain.

Of the several hours before the accident and all

the many days since there would be no coherent memory, nothing but a dark void. Only through dreams, which have their own unscrambling process for memories, would she be able to revisit any fragment of the torment she had endured, and one fragment she would touch only in her nightmares. A meaningless, unconnected and untranslatable memory but one which was insistent.

The memory of a face.

Pale. Gaunt. A young woman with exhausted eyes and drained spirit. A face of parchment skin and the pallor of an aged, extinguished candle. Split across by chapped and shrunken lips. A haunted demeanour squeezed dry of humour, of hope. Trembling.

The face spoke only of despair, a despair that was to haunt every one of the nightmares which recurred both during the period of wakening and after Isadora Dean had woken from her coma.

For in every one of those nightmares, the girl was running off with Izzy's baby.

Michelini couldn't identify the precise moment he had made up his mind. Perhaps it was because the decision hadn't been made by him at all; others had made it for him. Maybe it was that weekend in San Francisco spent humping the chief policy adviser to the Californian Congressman who occupied the chair of the House Science, Space & Technology Committee. No sooner had she seen him off at the airport with the promise of the Congressman's ear – she seemed to control most parts of his anatomy – than he had caught the eye of a United stewardess as she kneeled down to retrieve the linen napkin he had dropped from his dinner tray. It was one of those looks practised by world-weary adults which leaves nothing unspoken. When she returned with a fresh napkin, it had her telephone number on it.

He knew he had only a few years left before he fell firmly into the category of middle age, when stewardesses would regard his appetites as primarily gastronomic, when they would see only the sagging flesh beneath his eyes instead of the suggestiveness within them and start asking him if he took medication rather than home phone numbers. He couldn't deny – didn't want to – that he was fascinated by sex, new conquests; it had been inculcated upon him at his father's knee and in those days the women simply turned a blind eye and got on with housework and motherhood. At least in first-generation Italian-American families.

Times changed, women changed. And he, too, had changed. He was no longer the *bandito*, the sexual athlete of his twenties, yet what he nowadays lacked in stamina he made up for in technique. He loved women. Not just one woman, many women. And he was on a roll, maybe the last one he'd get. Marriage, at least to a wife like his, had just been one of those rotten ideas.

At the start they had seemed so compatible. She was no innocent maiden but a professional woman in her thirties who knew what it was all about when he had invited her back to his apartment in the Watergate. He had learnt as much as he had taught. As she had mentioned later, it was not the view outside the window that had drawn her there, she'd seen that many times before.

They had seemed to share similar interests: a defence contractor and a television correspondent both headquartered in the American capital, both used to the frequent travelling and separations of business, both physically relishing their reunions.

Marriage had been the great mistake. It was a commitment she seemed incapable of honouring. She had promised to settle down, stop the globetrotting, the foreign adventures, assignment after successful assignment.

'Just one more year,' she would ask. 'It's going too well to walk away from it right now. Just one more year and I'll get a Stateside editor's job. Or maybe a slot anchoring my own programme.'

Then a year had turned to eighteen months, the promises had fallen like last year's leaves and she had been posted to the European bureau in Paris as their top foreign correspondent, taking the kids with her, flying back every three weeks. Vowing this would be the last time.

And he realized he was burned up with it all. Not just the absences, although that was difficult enough to deal with. 'How's the wife?' they would ask. 'How the fuck would I know?' he had begun to respond. Now she had been out of contact for more than two weeks.

It was more than the absences. More even than the frustration of reunion when she would arrive back exhausted, emotionally drained, too tired even to cook a proper meal let alone light fires in his bed. It had hit him at the cocktail party in Georgetown the other night. As her professional success had grown, increasingly he came to feel as no more than an appendage.

'Oh, you're married to Isadora Dean. How wonderful!' yet another breathless matron had exclaimed. Not 'Joe Michelini, how nice to meet you and tell me all about yourself' but 'Mr Izzy Dean' all over again and twenty minutes discussing her career before he could break away and grab another Scotch.

She hadn't even taken his name – 'for professional

reasons'. Used to be there was a clear division of responsibilities within a family, the man as bread-winner and the woman as breadbaker, not these end-less arguments about where and when they might be able to meet and who should do what and screw whom.

It was killing his self-esteem. Now it was on the point of killing his career.

'Joe, we have a problem,' Erskine Vandel, the president of Fox Avionics, pronounced in a manner which left not a shred of doubt that it was not he, but Michelini, who had the problem. They were in the presidential suite overlooking a wind-lashed Potomac, the early bite of winter adding exaggerated emphasis to the overcast atmosphere within the room. The president was seated in considerable pomp and splendour on one side of the desk, leaving the planning director stranded in space on the other, entombed in a chair that was deliberately four inches lower. It made Michelini feel uneasy, inferior, by design.

'You know that the MP-Double-A means every-thing to this company,' the president continued. 'To you, Joe. To everyone else who works here. Without it we're about as much use as a fart in a wind tunnel.'

Vandel had a strong anal orientation – 'I'm a seat-of-the-pants guy,' he would explain to new female acquaintances. 'You get no bullshit from me. Noth-ing but the real thing.' Yet behind the foul mouth there was an astute technologically based mind which had managed to build one of the most suc-cessful component supply businesses in the military aviation industry. It was scarcely his fault that the industry itself was less than half its size of Cold War days and was threatened with being permanently grounded. 'Know how to run a successful small business?' he would offer to any Congressman within hearing. 'Build a successful *big* business, like avionics. Then let the Government piss all over it.'

'So we have this problem, you see, Joe.'

Joe didn't, not yet.

'Wilbur Burns, that half-ass who owns WCN, has got it into his mind he wants to run for President. Not one of us, Joe. He's the sort of moralizing bastard who'll step out of the shower just to take a piss. Intends to use his station to trail his conscience like a stuck pig trailing guts and, so's he can establish his credentials, wants to offer up a sacrifice. Us. The MP-Double-A. You. Me. The whole show. And all the while pretending that the funds needed to develop it will pay for the dreams and votes of every mother between here and hell. Horse shit,' the president snapped.

Like an affectionate father he began stroking a gold-plated model of the Duster which occupied pride of place on a desk top littered with executive toys and silver-framed portraits of his three daughters. 'Joe, how long you been with this company?'

The voice was softer now and Michelini felt the prickle of sweat beginning to foregather on what used to be his hairline. He'd entered difficult territory and did not yet know which way to jump.

'Nearly twelve years,' he muttered.

'Eleven years and eight months on Friday,' his president stated. 'And in all that time no one has ever had cause to question your loyalty. Done a damn fine job for Fox Avionics. That's why I made you planning director. Gave you a great salary and an expense account twice as big as my own. Surprised you haven't put on even more weight than you have.'

34

'I work it off. On your business,' Michelini responded defensively.

'Never any doubt. You kiss ass over on the Hill like those Senators have got mistletoe dangling from their belts, and get laid so frequently I sometimes think you must be running for President yourself. Eh, Joe?' He started a laugh which echoed around the large office, but in return Michelini could offer only a taut smile.

'Never any doubt, Joe.' Vandel was leaning forward across his desk, the humour gradually subsiding. 'Until now. Trouble is, there'll be split loyalties. You here at Fox, and your wife the flavour of the month at WCN. Likely to get her own show soon, I understand.'

'Crap!' Michelini responded. 'Erskine, there's no way I would . . .'

But already the president was waving down his protest.

'Exactly what I said when some of the boys raised the matter with me. Capital K-R-A-P. Not old Joe, I said. But . . .' He flapped his hands in a gesture of helplessness. 'This is too big to take any chances. They said. WCN's the opposition and we can't afford the risk of having one of our top executives hanging out with them. Sleeping with the enemy. It's not as if this is the sort of job you can leave behind in the office every night, it's a twenty-five-hour-a-day commitment.'

Michelini bit into his lip, angered. 'If you know what's going on at the station you'll also know that my wife is currently based on the other side of the world. This is ludicrous.'

'And every three weeks she flies back here for . . . well, I guess, a marital update?' Vandel countered, trying for once not to take the coarse line before quickly abandoning the unfamiliar approach. 'Shit, Joe, it's not as if she's just another one of your casual pick-ups you can fuck and forget. Chrissakes, she's your wife.'

Michelini began to laugh through his nose. A hollow, scornful sound. Pillow talk! They were worried about pillow talk! Hell, what was he going to tell them? That he and his wife hadn't made love – had scarcely even slept together – since the moment she knew the second kid had been conceived. That the baby had been a last and desperate attempt by her to glue back the pieces of a marriage which had been falling apart. That it turned out to be a lovely baby, and a pathetic mistake. The marriage would never be put back together, and now there was an extra child to complicate matters.

'You don't need to worry, not about my wife,' he said.

'But I do, Joe, I do.'

'I don't even know where the hell she is. You do *not* need to worry. The chance of me and my wife having a meaningful conversation about anything other than the kids is absolute zero. Believe me.'

And then he knew it for certain.

'There's something you should know, Erskine. Tomorrow I file for divorce.' There. It was out. Already he felt better, in control. 'From now on, the only talking me and my wife are going to do is through lawyers.'

London was in for a meteorological mugging. Bursts of cold November rain from off the North Sea squabbled their way up the Thames estuary, annoying the seagulls and blowing them inland where they cartwheeled and complained before settling on the turbulent water, only to be disturbed once more by the river taxis forcing passage upstream against the ebb tide. The persistent rain had made the river angry; it scowled at the great city along its banks as it passed. A day for cancelling appointments, for crosswords, for drying out socks. A day when even Detroit seemed to have its attractions.

In his new office overlooking the Thames, Paul Devereux sat content. While others had been battered by the changing winds, he had flourished. He had the gift which all politicians crave yet which is accorded only to the few, that of luck. Others might have his natural abilities, some of them might even work as assiduously, but none in the last few years had enjoyed the favours of the press and the preferment of the Prime Minister as had he. From insignificance to Secretary of State for Defence in less time than it had taken even his own father.

He spun the ornate antique globe at his side, another Whitehall reminder of a bygone era with its profusion of exotic and extinct countries ablaze with the distinctive imperial red which coloured the old empire, the world of his stamp-collecting schooldays. Gossip had it that this was the globe the private secretary had used to explain to Devereux's predecessor precisely where was to be found the tiny colonial outpost of Belize with its small but expensive British military garrison and fetid tropical climate that rotted the turbine fans on the Harrier jump jets almost as quickly as it sapped the men's morale. Faced with the need for yet another round of economies, the Minister had sacrificed the lot, releasing the tiny Latin American country to the predatory clutches of its neighbours. As the story went, although the Minister couldn't find Belize on the map, neither could he find it on the list of critical Government-held constituencies . . .

With a sigh, Devereux turned once more to the unmarked leather-bound folder lying open on his lap which, in the most concise of forms, contained briefing on all issues of substance and urgency that his civil servants thought appropriate for the new Secretary of State.

'. . . *the SoS can expect renewed pressures from HM Treasury in the forthcoming expenditure round, in spite of recent assurances . . . These Treasury demands must be resisted at all costs . . . unforeseen scope of our commitment to the UN peacekeeping operations in South Africa . . . expected increase in threat from the dispersal of former Soviet nuclear scientists and weapons technologies . . . rising nationalist extremism in Germany . . . unpublicized visit last month of Joint Chiefs to Downing Street to discuss their growing concerns . . . hostile questioning can be expected from the Government's own backbenches . . .'*

Devereux smiled. It was a catalogue of horrors worthy of any group of civil servants about to go into budgetary battle with their sceptical and unimaginative Treasury colleagues, who were capable of sinking more aircraft carriers in an afternoon than an entire Nazi wolf pack.

One item was more specific than most, the language less florid.

'*23. In particular, HMG has undertaken to resolve its position on the MPAA, the proposed joint-venture fighter aircraft, by the end of this year. The project, much desired by the US Administration, faces considerable opposition within the Congress. It is unlikely to win Congressional approval without the full-hearted backing of the European allies. Most of our European partners are diffident, recognizing the military value of the MPAA in the increasingly unstable security environment but balking at the expected costs. Germany and Spain have let it be known that they will participate only if Britain does. On that decision will rest US approval itself.*

'24. Therefore the role of HMG and the SoS personally is likely to be decisive.

'25. The funding requirements for developing MPAA are significant, but spread over ten years. Moreover, we are in a strong position to negotiate a substantial part of the design and manufacturing work and consequent employment benefits for this country, which will give the SoS a powerful hand in bilaterals with the Treasury on development funding and other aspects of the MoD budget . . .

'27. Considerable public and international attention will inevitably be given to whatever decision the SoS makes.'

Devereux snorted.

'Considerable public and international attention will inevitably be given . . .'

Encouragement? Or threat? While there was no recommendation contained within the briefing, its positive tone left no doubt as to the desires of the MoD bureaucracy. The Duster was their virility symbol, the project which would redeem them in the eyes of their Whitehall colleagues after years of being squeezed dry by Governments in search of another billion or so with which to build a re-election platform.

Mentally he ticked off the three alternatives. He could refuse to back the project, thereby earning the gratitude of his hard-pressed Cabinet colleagues. Yet it would also earn him the relentless opposition of those powerful and privileged men within the defence establishment who had killed off more than one of his predecessors. Anyway, political gratitude, Devereux had learned, could be exhausted more quickly than a soda siphon.

On the other hand he could fight for the project in a public battle which would inevitably be bloody. But whose blood? In victory he would be cast as the most dynamic and successful Minister in the Government, an international figure of stature, a skilled negotiator, visionary politician and ever-rising star, the man most likely to. He could write his own accolade.

Yet if he fought, and lost, it would be a personal disaster. The successor shorn of success. The defence chief who retreated. Who came, who saw, who surrendered.

What would his father have done? Got drunk. Then beaten his wretched wife and disappeared to that end of the manor house where the housekeeper lived. The young housekeeper. There had been a steady stream of housekeepers passing through the manor house, all of them young, and all chosen by his father.

Devereux bit his lip. His father would have fought, and failed. But Devereux wasn't like his father. He wouldn't fail.

And, anyway, he had no need for young house-keepers.

In the blackness of her mind there was life.

She couldn't identify it as such, it kept changing shape, colour, intensity. But it was there. It was as though she and her senses were floating in the vacuum of space, approaching each other, recognizing each other, almost touching, with only the slightest nudge needed to bring them together but unable to find that final extra adjustment.

Frustration. Anger. I feel, therefore I am. More frustration.

The bundles of stimuli which were her inchoate thoughts passed by and were lost in the blackness or burned up like a lost body re-entering the earth's atmosphere.

She preferred those which burned. She took comfort in the light, and all the time there seemed to be more brilliance entering her world.

Then came the moment when the light turned into the recognizable colours of a rainbow and the dark veil began to lift.

'Mummie-e-e-e-e!'

The first time she had comprehended any sound, the first time Benjy had uttered any word, since the accident. Her eyes opened, were assaulted by the light but struggled and blinked and gradually found focus until she could see those around her – the diminutive consultant neurologist, Weatherup, with a constrained smile of professional triumph; Primrose, the student nurse, whose smiles showed no restraint at all; McBean, who radiated a quiet sense of privilege at having been party to another of life's minor miracles, and on whose ample blue-cottoned bosom wriggled the animated form of a young, dark-haired boy.

'B ... Ben ... Benjamin?' She formed the sound in the way a foal attempts its first step. Quickly they took away the cuffs and clips of the monitoring equipment so that mother and son could be reunited in an uninhibited and uninterrupted embrace. Soon Benjamin, overwhelmed, had fashioned a face like that of a latex troll and was tearfully expressing his pleasure and relief. Tears began to form in the corner of his mother's eyes, too, but as yet she had not found the strength or understanding to express her emotions.

'Where am I? What happened?' she whispered eventually, her hand reaching out instinctively to straighten the young boy's hair, but the effort proved too much.

'Och, so you're from across the water. American, are you?' McBean responded to the noticeable accent. 'And tell me. What's your name?'

'Is . . . Isadora Dean. Izzy.' The reply was tentative, sounding almost a question. But a start. 'My fath . . .' She started upon her habitual self-conscious explanation that she had been named after Isadora Duncan, the avant-garde dancer and teenage idol of her father, a Wisconsin dentist who hid a number of unpredictable passions behind the crisp formality of his dental mask, but the excuse was absurd and the attempt exhausting. She subsided and concentrated on trying to engage her thumb against her son's cheek to push away his tears.

'You've had an accident, lassie. Been in a wee bit of a coma. But you're a strapping girl, you'll pull through it fine. Won't she, Mr Weatherup?'

The consultant, who was gently checking the pulse in her wrist, nodded. 'Your spleen was giving you a little trouble, Mrs Dean, so we had to take it out. But that's not a problem. You won't even notice it's gone, apart from a very small scar on the left side of your abdomen. And you've been asleep quite a while, but I think you're going to be absolutely fine after a good period of rest. So long as young Benjamin here lets you breathe. Steady on, young man,' he protested with a chuckle, turning to Benjamin whose arms had locked around his mother's neck in a gesture which defied anyone to take her away again.

'He's . . . all right, doctor. Seems he's got a lot of hugging to make up for,' she countered.

'You led us a merry dance, Izzy,' McBean said. 'Until this moment we had no idea who you were. You *are* American, aren't you?'

Izzy nodded.

'Your son has been through quite a shock, too, was unable to talk,' Weatherup continued. 'It was something of a risk, bringing the two of you together. We hoped it might be just the thing to snap the both of you back into form yet we couldn't be certain how he would respond, if it might drive him deeper within himself. But I'm delighted . . .'

'My baby? Where's Isabella?' The voice, until now weak and hesitant, had taken on new strength.

'Mrs Dean, you mustn't excite yourse . . .'

The question came again, slow, precise, unavoidable. 'Doctor, where is my baby?'

The neurologist appeared suddenly uncomfortable, couldn't meet her gaze, buried his hands deep in the pockets of his white coat and cast his eyes towards Sister McBean. She sat on the edge of the bed, placing a hand on both mother and son. Her words were slow, softly formed, trying to wrap the hammer in velvet.

'I'm so desperately sorry, Izzy, my love.' McBean paused, fighting her own emotions. There was no easy way. 'I'm afraid your baby's gone. She didn't survive the accident.'

Hammer fall. Destruction. Inside something fractured, forever beyond repair.

Her face did not move, betrayed no pain, but in the flicker of an eyelid it had lost its flexibility and returning life, become a mask. With agonizing care, the lips sought for a response.

'Didn't deserve that. Not my poor Bella,' she whispered, then nothing more. Her eyes went to McBean, beseeching some form of denial, but there was only compassion. A noise began to grow inside her, from deeper within than seemed imaginable, torn out by its roots, which was to burst forth in a sickening wail of grief. And of dismay. Of lost love. Of recrimination. Of guilt. Particularly of guilt.

A cry for an innocent lost.

TWO

Grubb rapped on the door, hesitating fractionally before he entered. Characteristically he was a man who pushed his way around life ignoring the sensibilities and wishes of others and wouldn't think twice about barging into hospitals, funerals, bedrooms and even ladies' washrooms in search of his prey, but the managing editor had only recently taken over and was something of an unknown quantity.

Hugo Hagi, of West Coast Japanese-American stock via Wharton Business School and IBM, knew relatively little about TV news and had the good sense not to pretend otherwise. Instead of constantly watching television on one of the half-dozen screens which hid his office wall he would embalm himself in front of the computer screen which sat on the end of his desk. He was not, as Grubb would complain after a couple of beers, 'batting from the same dugout'. The whole industry was being taken over by accountants who cared nothing for the professional pride of a world scoop and the exhilaration of dumping all over rival channels but who got their rocks off by studying bottom lines. Maybe they didn't reproduce, didn't know how to, just split in two like amoebae.

The new man had the frustrating habit of switching off the screen every time someone entered his room, as if he were protecting some great secret with which others couldn't be trusted. Hell, there were no secrets in an open-plan newsroom where you had to raise your voice even to proposition one of the graduate researchers, but Hagi's office was alien turf. Behind his back they called him ET on account of the unnatural green glow of the computer screen which normally lit his sallow features, and because everyone wished he would go home.

'Hugi, got a minute?' Grubb enquired, using the foreshortened soubriquet the Japanese-American hated only marginally less than ET.

The switch was thrown and the green glow subsided. The alien emerged in human form with a thin smile on his well-groomed features. He was considerably the younger, a three-hour marathon man, lacking the rough edges and dusty aura which hung around the foreign editor. There were no family photographs on the wall, only his framed MBA and a signed photograph of Wilbur Burns. It left Grubb feeling both resentful and nervous.

'How can I help, Eldred?' Hagi emphasized the name, retaliating in kind, insisting on the formal version of the foreign editor's name rather than the more familiar Ed. How could you run a news room with people calling you 'Eldred', Chrissake?

'Thought you'd like to know ... Hugo,' Grubb added, withdrawing from the field of battle under cover of a smile. 'Problem solved. We've just heard from Izzy Dean, seems she's been in a mother of a car smash and got herself stuck in a coma in some hospital in the West of England. She's gonna be OK. Bad news about the kid, though. The young 'un didn't make it.'

Hagi seemed to be taking his time digesting the information, and by the vinegary expression on his face it seemed to have given him wind. 'Did you say the problem was solved?'

It was the turn of the foreign editor to wrinkle his

brow. 'Sure. I mean, we know where she is. She hasn't disappeared.'

'But is she back working? Is she gracing our screens, pulling in the viewers?'

'Hell, Hugo. She just lost a kid. Nearly killed herself, too. What's the friggin' problem?'

'The problem, Eldred, is that Izzy Dean is once more not doing the job we pay her for.'

The screen flickered back to life as Hagi checked the details. He always checked details.

'In May and June she was off the air for more than six weeks.'

'That was maternity leave. She was entitled. Hugo, she worked right up to the wire. Even had the baby induced so's she could get back in time to take the Paris posting. What more do you want?'

'And two years ago it was another six weeks maternity leave. Makes me wonder where her priorities lie, making news or making babies,' Hagi continued.

'She's a woman . . .' Grubb began to splutter, but subsided; he could see the direction in which his superior was headed. His tone grew suddenly more practical. 'She is one of the best.'

'Not if she's off screen, she's not.'

Vivid language came drifting through the door as a young female production assistant exchanged views with a supplier who had thus far failed to deliver the promised portable satcom system to a correspondent on the point of leaving for the civil war in South Africa. Newsrooms could produce as many casualties as a civil war, except in civil wars they were less likely to bayonet the wounded.

'Izzy's in line for a presenter's job,' Grubb continued, 'maybe even her own show. That's what . . .' He was about to say that's what Ira Weiss, ET's predecessor, had hinted, but Ira was yesterday's man and his name now dirt. 'That's what ... was thought.'

ET raised an eyebrow at the green screen. 'She's pushing forty.'

In fact she was thirty-seven, but Grubb wasn't going to contest the point.

'Let me put this on the table, Eldred. I think the strategy should be to present the younger face of news, not to be worrying whether our presenter is going to come out in a hot flush all of a sudden. Don't you agree?'

It was time for the foreign editor to join the game. He had considerable admiration for Izzy, it was impossible not to, but there was no shared personal chemistry. He found her prissy, and she didn't fuck. Not him, at least. And if someone's job was going to be on the line under the new management, sure wasn't going to be his. He rubbed his razor burn thoughtfully.

'You know, Hugo, there's no denying that this motherhood thing gets in the way. Not that she's complained. Apart from the maternity leave, she's never missed a day for mumps and measles and the rest.'

He wanted to be fair. It would make the betrayal so much more effective.

'She's very professional.' Pause. 'For a woman. But you know, Hugo, it's not easy. For us, I mean, you and me. We need to send our people into some of the toughest spots in the world, into the middle of wars, revolutions, natural disasters, you name it. She's never backed off, not that you'd know it. We even gave her some of the most difficult assignments, Gaza, Bosnia, the Colombia drug cartels — that's where they shot up her car and she got winged

– just to test her, to see if she was tough enough, had the balls for the job.'

He looked hard into ET's eyes, trying to calculate the mood.

'But that was before she got herself elected to the club. What are we gonna feel like now if we send her into some war zone, she gets her fanny shot away and we're responsible for two motherless brats?' He corrected himself immediately. 'One motherless brat. We've got to live with that. It just . . .' – he waved his hands – 'complicates things.'

'Getting pregnant once you could put down as an accident, one of those hormonal things. But twice looks like she's making a career out of it. Not, of course, that I'm against equal opportunities,' Hagi insisted, covering the legal niceties as if some federal agency had his office bugged, 'but going into battle with babies clinging round your neck inevitably . . .' – he nodded in deference to the foreign editor's own phrase – '. . . complicates things.'

There was a brief silence.

'So what d'you want me to do?' the foreign editor enquired.

'Why, Eldred, I want you to send her our best wishes for a speedy recovery and get our star foreign correspondent back to work, pronto. Doing what she's paid to do.'

'And if not?'

ET tapped a couple of buttons and the screen flickered. 'I see you're already over budget this quarter. There's no money to provide additional cover, nor to run a nursing service, either.' He turned from the screen, bathed in its eerie glow. 'If not, Eldred, as foreign editor you will have a sad and very painful decision to reach.'

*   *   *

She had just got to her favourite bit, where she always felt a tug of excitement even though she'd read it a hundred – well, possibly a dozen times, when the balloon is about to smash into the African mountain top and plunge the great adventure to disaster and death.

She had loved Jules Verne ever since she was a kid in bed with chicken pox and discovered that tearing round the world in eighty days with an intrepid Victorian explorer and his rag-bag of companions was far more fun than school. Somewhere at home she had a rumpled cloth-backed copy with her name written inside in careful, childhood letters, each individually and patiently crafted. 'Isadora Dean. Age $10\frac{3}{4}$.'

They had encouraged her to go back a little, to the things which had stuck and were important, which her memory could embrace with comfort and certainty, to build from solid foundations so she might begin putting into their proper place the scrambled recollections that lay strewn about her mind.

Of the accident, and of a significant period both before and afterwards, there was nothing but a void penetrated by occasional flashes of light which had disappeared even before she could identify the elusive images they illuminated. Why had she come here, to Dorset? Perhaps because her grandfather had been born in this part of England, somewhere in the Wessex of Thomas Hardy, but she couldn't be sure. Even memories of the days immediately after her recovery from coma were fitful and confused.

Most distressingly, much of the previous couple of years lay scattered like the shards of a mosaic attacked by vandals. Personal things, things of great value. The name of her godson. When she had last been back home. What she had given Benjamin for his birthday. Too much of the short time she had been given with Bella.

The process of recreating the mosaic was agonizing; she would reach for a piece only to find it had eluded her once more and she was grasping at thin, empty air. Often it was also humiliating. The previous day she had telephoned her producer in Paris, only to discover from his wife that he was no longer her producer. Had she forgotten they'd left both his legs behind on a mountain road above Sarajevo after he'd stepped on a Serbian mine while trying to take a piss, the trembling voice demanded in accusation.

Then it all came flooding back, the agony, the guilt, the shattered bones and screams, his own brave reasoning that he could have been knocked down crossing the Champs Elysées – a justification that somehow satisfied no one, not his wife, not even those who had shared the risks with him. Some memories she wished could remain hidden.

One image plagued her mind, lingering in its shadows, refusing to step into the light. She would attack, only for the image to recede deeper into the shadows; she would draw back in exhaustion and it would creep to the edge of the circle of light, tantalizing, mocking. Ghostly. Hollowed eyes. Shrunken lips.

Aged before its time.

The girl. With Bella. Always the two together. Inseparable. An image of death.

They had found a video player for her and every morning one of the nurses with access to satellite TV brought in tapes of the previous day's WCN coverage. Even though it quickly glued back together much of the missing mosaic – she'd even forgotten who was Vice President, but then, she excused, so had half the American public – it was exhausting for her to watch. It reminded her there was a world out there which was working and warring and getting along perfectly adequately. Without her. The reassurances of her new producer that everything was under control and that she need not worry had precisely the opposite effect; she found it difficult to fight her way through the mist of depression which settled around her.

They told her it was normal, to be expected, part of the recovery process after brain damage, a frequent side effect of the drugs, but she was not convinced. It was more than the medication. It was the guilt.

'You should call home,' Weatherup told her. He was sitting on the end of the bed, no longer in ITU but a general recovery room. She needed to share the pain, not lock it up, he encouraged, she needed the support of family. Izzy had insisted that she be the one to break the news to her husband, but wasn't it time?

'I . . .' she had begun, but shrank into the pillows. Something inside was holding her back. Made her uneasy.

'Look, Izzy, I know it must be difficult, but think of what you still have. You have Benjamin. Your family. A fine career. So much to look forward to.'

Somehow the neurologist's words didn't gel.

'Will . . . will I be able to continue?'

'With a career or motherhood?' he asked.

'Both.'

He smiled and reached for her hand. 'You're making excellent progress. Just three days out of a coma and you're reading, watching television, taking an interest, regaining your strength. You've nothing to worry about.'

'Doctor.' She beckoned him to lean closer so she could whisper directly in his ear. 'Bullshit.'

He gave her a long, calculating stare. 'OK, Izzy. If you want the full picture, I think you're strong enough to take it. The truth is no one can yet be sure. Your brain took an almighty beating inside, and sometimes there are lingering after-effects. Some memories may never return. You're bound to be emotionally unsettled for a while. It's possible – not likely, you understand, but possible – you may be susceptible to epilepsy in later life, but we have drugs for that. You might find some areas of your brain don't want to work as well as they did. We know there is some damage and brain cells don't repair themselves, but the system has an amazing knack of compensating, finding another way of getting the job done. You're in excellent physical shape, you're recovering remarkably well. I can guarantee nothing, but if you were a horse personally I'd back you in the Grand National.'

'If I were a horse you'd already have shot me.'

'You'll be fine,' Weatherup insisted, laughing. 'Climb Mount Everest. Have another ten babies. Just don't attempt it all at the same time!'

'Mothers don't always get a choice,' she replied, but the mist of depression had lifted a fraction.

'Tell me, Izzy. It's a personal question, do you mind?' he asked hesitantly. 'I've wondered about it ever since you were admitted. You have a remarkable scar, just . . .' He glanced down as though trying to examine himself, suddenly uncomfortable.

'Just here, on my breast.' She ran her fingers over her nightdress just above her left nipple.

'We had to examine you thoroughly, you understand,' he explained hurriedly, not wishing to imply that his thoughts were focused on anything other than sound medical practice. Even so, she was a remarkably fine-looking woman ... 'A strange injury. We couldn't decide what it was.'

'Bullet wound. Probably from a nine millimetre Uzi. Badly stitched. My car got shot up in Colombia by a drugs gang I was investigating. The head of the cartel promised me exclusive access for a week assuming I would sleep with him. When I didn't he took exception, for some reason didn't want either the tape or me getting to the airport. Wrecked the car but this hole was the only damage they managed to do to me or my crew. If only they were as pathetic with their other business operations.'

She made it sound matter-of-fact, as if she were reporting on someone else's problem.

'Good God,' Weatherup muttered in astonishment, sounding very English. 'We don't get too much experience at this hospital with wounds from machine guns.'

'Sub-machine guns,' she corrected.

'And that's what you want to go back to? My dear girl, you must be quite crazy. But very brave.'

'Not really. Screwing him would have been brave, but there are parts of me that even my editor doesn't own. Anyway, I was five months pregnant.'

'More crazy than I thought!'

'Not at all. I used the bump to smuggle out a world exclusive in my knickers and underneath my sanitary wear. The good Catholic border guards just wriggled, far too embarrassed to look closely.' She smiled, but his words had hurt. Had she been a man the doctor would have been not amazed but enthralled, excited by the challenge, relishing the danger, anxious to hear more. Instead, he had patronized her, unintentionally and nowhere near as badly as she was patronized in her own office, but still a grating reminder that already she was re-entering the world she had left, and all the contradictions and torments it held for her came flooding back.

Like the missed birthdays and broken promises which she hoped Benjamin was yet too young to understand or be hurt by. The searing pain when he seemed to treat the nanny as more of a mother than her. The games and rhymes she had so much wanted to teach him but which he'd already learned. From someone else.

The insanity of arriving back from the death camps of civil war scarcely three hours in almost any direction from Charles de Gaulle, in time to wash for Sunday lunch.

The anxiety when she discovered that from her 'happy box' of essential travelling supplies were missing the dozen clean syringes she carried to avoid the infected needles of a war zone, and the blind fit of anger with a two-year-old when she discovered Benjamin had taken from it the tiny compass without which she couldn't guarantee locking onto the satellite. On such small things might hang her life and the story, although she did not care to ask which her editor valued more highly. Gambling her own wits against snipers from Beirut to Bosnia for an audience she knew was so jaded by nightly overkill they might just as well be watching their laundry spin and who thought the Golan Heights were a suburb of Cleveland.

Waiting on the sandy beach outside Mogadishu as the execution by machine gun of two army deserters was held up, even as they stood blindfolded and bound tight against empty oil drums, trousers fouled. Held up, not by God or a quixotic judge, but by a BBC cameraman while he changed his clapped-out battery.

Returning to receive not accolades or understanding but a relentless demand for more, more, more, knowing they were pushing her harder than anyone else, waiting for the little woman to plead cramps or hormones or simply to break down and make a mess of her make-up. The pigs.

Balancing the lust for a story against the demands of self-preservation, conquering your own fear and crawling that extra exclusive maggot-infested mile before remembering you were a mother with responsibilities back home.

Home. It was time to call her husband. Her nervousness, for which she had no explanation – or, at least, none she could remember – came flooding back.

A ring. An answer.

'Joe?'

A silence. A long silence.

'Joe, it's me. How are you, darling? Have I interrupted you?' God, it was pathetic. Sunday morning, what could she have interrupted?

Another long silence.

'Where are you?' he muttered.

'In England, Joe.'

'I thought you'd disappeared to Mars.'

'Joe, please. I'm in hospital. There was a car crash. Did you hear me?'

He didn't seem to have made the connection. His mind was blocked, struggling to find the things he wanted to say. 'You gonna be there long?'

'I don't know. Maybe another two weeks . . .'

'Anything broken?'

'No, but . . .'

'Give me the address.'

'You're coming over?'

A silence.

'No, I can't. I'm up beyond my butt in work. Just give me the address, will you?'

'Joe, there's something I've got to tell you.'

'I've got something for you, too. Didn't want to do it like this, but . . .'

A pause while he struggled for the long-practised words and failed.

'Hell. I've had enough. Of you disappearing, of being left on my own, knowing that I come about as low on your list of priorities as root-canal work. I'm out, Izzy. Out. I want a divorce. I just hope we can make it quick and clean. Be mature, eh? For the sake of the kids?'

Perhaps he might have expected the silence that followed, but he showed no sign of it. 'Come on, Izzy, it can't have come as that much of a shock to you. Christ, it's not as if there's anything left between us. Let's just formalize it so we can both get on with our own lives. I've got all the details prepared for you to look at. Just give me the address.'

'You're trying to deliver divorce papers to me while I'm lying in hospital?' she gasped. There was a sudden avalanche of memories, of pain, exposing the hard rock-face that had become their relationship. She recalled it clearly now. The rows, his growing frustration turning to bitterness, a marriage that had become no more than an accommodation.

'What do you expect me to do?' he continued. 'You left me with no option; I haven't known where you've been for more than a month. Did you expect me to wait until you finished playing Marco Polo in your own sweet time?'

'Joe!' she pleaded, all the carefully considered phrases swept away. 'For God's sake, listen to me. Please. Bella. Our baby. She's dead.'

There was nothing from the other end of the

phone. The scalding of a man's heart makes no sound.

'Joe, she was in the back of my car when we went off the road. Benjy's fine but . . . Bella's gone, Joe. I'm sorry.'

The voice at the other end, when at last it came, had a strained, unnatural quality.

'You killed Bella?'

'Don't, Joe, please.'

'How did it happen?'

'I can't remember, I just don't know. Joe, come see me. Grab a plane. Let's not talk about this on the phone.'

'Where are you?'

She gave him the details. 'You're coming to see me, then?'

The voice on the phone was like the hissing of a serpent. 'The only thing you'll get from me are divorce papers. You killed Bella, you irresponsible . . . selfish . . . bitch!'

She did not know how long she lay back on her pillow, eyes closed, the tears forming twin cascades that soaked into her hair. She did not cry for her lost marriage; even with her scrambled memories she could not persuade herself she had lost something of irredeemable value. The tears were for the loneliness and sudden sense of vulnerability which settled around her like a marsh fog of autumn, for the frustration and anger as thoughts and memories collided within her head to undermine her sense of self-control, for the lack of familiar landscape in a world which in a few weeks had been shattered almost beyond recognition. But most of all she cried from aching guilt. The guilt which insisted that she might, after all, have been responsible for the crash. Her fault that Bella was dead.

Her eyes opened. She could look back no longer, not when it meant grappling with memories filled with so much pain. There was only one way – forward, no matter what, and build something new and brighter for herself and Benjamin, if she could.

She picked up Jules Verne. Her long-loved friends were still unrescued, on the very edge of disaster as they clung precariously to the balloon's basket. She threw them in the wastebin.

Devereux sat in the corner of the New York bar and watched with a practised eye. The bar was on the lower West Side on one of those blocks where the street language was Spanish and sunlight never reached the pavement. He liked these type of places, where he could get away from it all, the officials, the papers, the constant flow of formality and urgent business which dominated his other world. This was so different: classless, outgoing, utterly un-English. A challenge. And he enjoyed a challenge.

He'd flown to Washington on his first overseas trip to flex his muscles on the Duster. The US Administration wanted this project, wanted it badly. The hot breath of Congressional concern was gusting through the basements of the Pentagon; the project's proponents were anxious to embrace any good friend they could find and Devereux was one of the few. The deal was not yet done, there was still more juice to squeeze from the lemon, but already he had made his mark in the capital of the most powerful country on earth.

And now he had escaped. Some shopping in New York before he flew home, he had explained, letting slip the shackles, sliding away from the pathways of power to this bar, where he was no longer Minister but Man, where there were no middle class moralizers, Protection Squad heavies or Fleet Street hacks. Nothing but a good, old-fashioned challenge.

He watched as an elderly and hugely overweight woman entered the bar, dragging a plastic sack behind her and jangling a large bunch of keys suspended around her waist. She had come to restock the vending machines, wheezing as she crossed the room, pausing only to take a long pull at her cigarillo. Her jaw dropped like a fish as she gulped for breath before taking yet another pull.

Wheeze, gasp, puff, jangle, wheeze; the sounds punctuated her slow progress. In a querulous voice she announced that she had to have her back operated on again. She appeared to invite a general conversation but only the barman responded, and that after a delay of several seconds.

'Your back again, eh?'

Another delay. Like Ground Control to Mars.

'Not until New Year.' She began attacking the cigarette machine. Wheeze. Puff. Jangle. 'Not getting laid up over Christmas.'

The barman offered no response, forcing her to continue the conversation on her own. 'I guess I'm gonna go one of three ways. Lung cancer, cirrhosis of the liver or a broken heart.' She paused to catch her breath. 'Think I'll give up men. Too damn dangerous. Hell, I'm only sixty-four. Lotta life left in me yet.' The guppy jaw dropped several times while she hitched up her sagging support tights through the folds of her woollen cardigan. The barman polished glasses.

'They better have a cigarette waiting for me at the door of the hospital. And a drink. Going in and coming out.'

The barman raised an eyebrow; she heaved her

sack and her tights slipped once more. She paused to light another cigarette from a second pack in her pocket, not a cigarillo this time but menthol. Her attempt at safe smoking, cutting the risks. Then she dragged her sack in the direction of the condom machines in the men's toilet, barging through the door without knocking.

As her sagging frame disappeared, Devereux laughed inside. Not at her, but with her. She knew she was ludicrous, spicing her nicotine with the occasional menthol in the pretence of delaying or avoiding the inevitable process of consumption inside her lungs, but she was doing it her way and would go out on her own terms. Unlike most politicians. Unlike his father.

Know thyself, and thy weaknesses, the better to understand and if necessary to exploit the weaknesses of others, he muttered. The old woman was a hag, but no broken reed. His father, at his bitter end, would have envied her.

Devereux turned the whisky around in his glass. Life was full of challenges and risks; it took an exceptional man to confront and vanquish them and, in vanquishing, to become great. He was an exceptional man, and would become great. He wouldn't be his failed father's son forever.

But one challenge at a time. He finished off his drink, ordered another, and gazed with interest and anticipation at the two women who were arranging themselves at the next table.

Izzy was pissed off. Deeply pissed off, in the way that gets you out of bed in the morning in spite of hospital routine.

Every day she would find herself waiting with growing anticipation for the videotapes of yesterday's WCN newscasts, and this morning she'd set it up, punched the appropriate buttons and settled back in her chair.

And seethed. The tape had included a major slot from the new Mafia corruption trials in Palermo, the one involving a cardinal, an actress and two former prime ministers. Her territory. Now being squatted by that testicularly challenged little jerk of a producer.

She was jealous, hacked off with the producer, but mostly with herself, surprised that even from a hospital bed it could matter so much.

The door to her old world was beginning to open a fraction. Then K.C. Craven arrived and kicked the bloody thing off its hinges.

K.C. was black, doe-eyed and had flown in that morning from Washington DC. She was Eldred Grubb's assistant, by far the finest of his few redeeming features. In her first week at WCN, with innuendo sweeping the newsroom as to why the foreign editor had hired an attractive mahogany-skinned assistant who was both taller and graduated from a far better university than he, she had been asked to explain her name.

'Katherine? Connie?' a colleague had enquired.

'Why, bless you child. No,' K.C. had responded in a mock Southern drawl, lashes fluttering. She enjoyed being theatrical; the entire newsroom was listening. 'I was named K.C. 'cause my mamma said she conceived me during an unscheduled time-out with a basketball player during play-offs in Kansas City. Best time of her life, she said. So even if she forgets who, ain't never gonna forget where.'

Later Izzy discovered that K.C.'s father was a much-respected doctor in Minneapolis and her librarian mother had never been to Kansas City in her life, but Izzy was sworn to silence. K.C. was a good friend and the first enjoyable recollection to come alive for Izzy from what seemed like another, distant life.

'It's great you could come,' Izzy said, not for the first time, as they walked arm-in-arm through the gardens.

She was making her first trip outside the hospital walls and Izzy had found the air unexpectedly damp, her mind still unadjusted to the lost weeks and changing seasons. The last few days had been frozen crisp, clean, the leaves on the old oak guarding the hospital entrance hung limp in the still air. But a storm was on the way, heralded by a tumultuous sky that seemed as though Turner had thrown his entire palette of paints across the heavens.

K.C. wrapped herself more tightly in her cloak. She had been careful to explain that Grubb had sent her, she couldn't stay more than a few hours, yet to Izzy it was as though her friend had trekked alone across the Antarctic.

'You're the first thing from my life before the accident which hasn't brought me pain. The divorce. Bella. Watching Fido pretend he can do my job.' Even as she spoke she realized that her life was still a jumble of conflicting priorities. That, at least, had not changed.

'What do you feel about the divorce?'

Izzy shook her head. 'What's to feel? Not angry, just – empty. I've always known he was unfaithful, got his brain in his boxers and his privates forever on parade, but funny thing is I'm finding it hard to be bitter. The marriage was a mistake, I think I can see that now.'

'How a mistake?'

'I was feeling pressured. Well into my thirties. The

clock was ticking, the tubes beginning to get tired. Time was running out on me. I didn't know how to handle it; everything else in my life had been planned, set into neat periods. College, grad school, internship, climb the ladder, PA, producer, correspondent . . . but this wasn't going to be so tidy. The hormones were nagging away: do your bit for posterity, time to stretch the flesh. The job meant everything to me, yet suddenly . . . it wasn't enough. I wanted the job *and* the kids. After Gaza it became something of an obsession.'

'What happened in Gaza?' K.C. pressed, wrapping the cloak still more tightly around her. As the day and its more spectacular hues began to fade, the wind was creeping in to claim its place. The storm was gathering.

'It was during the Intifada, just before your time. The Palestinian riots had flared up again and I was over there with Dan Morrison from NBC to get an Arab's-eye view. Interviews with local leaders, mullahs, the teenagers who were causing the trouble, that sort of thing. Lots of pictures of the rioting from behind Arab lines as they were throwing stones, petrol bombs. Nothing we hadn't done a thousand times before.'

'Dan Morrison?' K.C. puckered her brows. 'Was he one of us?'

'That's one hell of an epitaph,' Izzy rebuked. 'But you're right. What do any of us leave behind? That's really my point. Dan was like a big brother to me, we'd covered so many stories together. Never once got out of hand, the closest I got to his bed was the times I laid him out on it when he'd got blind drunk. Which was pretty often.'

She tried to smile at the memory, but there was no joy in her face.

'Dan and I were shooting from pretty much the same location, great position where the camera could see it all over our shoulders, the Arab kids throwing stones and burning barricades right up to the Israeli lines beyond. Someone had to go first, we tossed a coin and he cheated. The sonofabitch was always cheating me, but only on silly things. Said he liked getting me riled, best entertainment he could find in a foxhole.'

She drew in a deep breath full of sorrow. 'So, he stepped out half a pace to give his cameraman the full perspective and started to roll. He was talking about religion, about how both sides invoked divine justice and from their knees proclaimed their devout interest in peace. So long as it was *their* peace, of course. Then, they shot him. Through the back of the head. A single bullet, he was still talking as he fell. I helped drag him back and he died right there in my lap.'

'Who were "they"? Who shot him?'

'Who knows? It was an Israeli rifle but the army said the bullet was fired from a stolen weapon, intentionally to stir up anti-Israeli feeling in America. Either way, didn't matter much to Dan.'

She sighed, there were no tears, she was too professional for that. Although sometimes tears help.

'OK, so it's the risk we all take. Could have been anyone. Would have been me, if Dan hadn't cheated. But it got me thinking, what do you leave behind? What did Dan leave behind after all those years of screwing and drinking his way around the world? Of finding the back doubles to every airport and putting his neck on the line so some armchair producer back in the States can fill in the airtime between the sponsor's messages? What? A better world? All Dan left behind was a grieving mother, a busted Chevvy and an empty apartment in Greenwich Village on which he still owed fifteen years' payments. And I didn't even have a mother to grieve, K.C., so I knew I had to get on and have those kids or I'd end up just like Dan. Does that make sense?'

'Does the sun rise, stupid?'

She shook her head wistfully. 'So I panicked. Married Joe. I'd known him for more than two years, although I realized later that in all that time we'd spent less than three months physically together. And I understand why he wants out. It's an occupational hazard in my job and his. And men change after kids, you know. The first one is a mystery to them, a mixture of fascination and terror; by the second it's simply a matter of mechanics. Your plumbing gets torn and twisted, you end up running on a damaged undercarriage and you find that once-passionate lover starts approaching you with all the sensitivity of a mechanical shovel.'

'And only one gear.'

'Joe was lousy about pregnancy. Resentful, jealous even. The baby had taken my body and his place beside it, and the more I swelled and the baby wriggled the more he simply moved away from it. From me. Like his life had been invaded. With Benjy he was bad, with Bella even worse.'

A silence hung between them. For the first time, as she found the words to describe her husband's reaction, she knew without doubt that it was over. A chapter now closed, one she had never dared read out loud before.

'But somehow I can't find the energy to be angry. Hell, I'm almost relieved. I've been trying to balance Joe and the kids and the job for so long I was feeling like a bridge too far, slowly cracking in a hurricane; this simplifies things, one less weight to carry.'

The frost-dried leaves were beginning to chatter on the trees like the dying rattle of the day, falling around the women like the tears Isadora had been unable to shed.

'How long are you going to be here?' K.C. enquired.

'Everyone seems delighted with my progress. Maybe just another two weeks. Then perhaps I'll take a month off to get Benjy straight, sort things out with Joe. He's bitter at the moment, but he's not a bad man, he'll come round. I need time for myself, too. I haven't even been able to say goodbye properly to Bella.' The voice, so used to talking of death, was steady but very quiet. 'No tears yet, no mourning. They cremated her, did you know that? An unidentified little baby, no claimants, so they cremated her. I can't even bury my baby.'

'That's . . . barbaric,' K.C. shook her head in disbelief.

'No. Just bureaucracy. Mindless bloody bureaucracy, as it is all over the world.' She fashioned a smile of defiance. 'Don't worry, Izzy Dean will be back, I shall insist on it. I need just a little time for the bruises to heal. New Year.'

K.C.'s eyes grew large and swam with tears. 'Oh, shit,' she stammered. Leaves rustled round their ankles like rattling leg chains.

'I've had a crack on the skull, K.C., but I haven't lost all command of my senses. The Great Grubb doesn't hand out trans-Atlantic air tickets like cups of coffee. You're here to do a job, his job, I've known that ever since you arrived and I'm sure you've come bearing more than our beloved foreign editor's best wishes. But you are also my friend, I won't forget that. What is it?'

K.C.'s eyes begged apology. 'You know the

pressure he's under. The money people have moved in, they've laid off another fifty staffers, the newsroom looks like the Alamo.'

'Before or after Santa Anna arrived?'

'Izzy, you're the best we've got, even Grubby has to admit that, but it also means you've got one of the best foreign postings we have and there are fifty people sniffing around to see if they can take it from you.'

'That's a compliment.'

'Even your little pimp of a producer has put in an official request to join the reporting staff, based on what he's done in the weeks he's been filling in for you.'

'How long is it now?' She furrowed her brow and tapped her forehead. 'God, there are still things in here which simply don't connect.'

'We're into December, Izzy. Nearly six weeks since you last had anything on air. And they're building up for a civil war in Ukraine. Grubby wants you in Kiev not . . .'

'Not flat on my back with my feet up in some part of the world he's never heard of.'

'You've got it.' She hesitated. 'You've also got this letter, Izzy.' She reached inside her shoulder bag and retrieved an envelope. 'It says three weeks. It says be back in three weeks, by Christmas, or they are terminating your contract. That taking off without letting anyone know where you were going was a hanging offence. That in the last three years you've clocked up more sick leave than anyone in the office.'

'Being pregnant is not an illness,' she replied testily.

'Izzy, I'm sorry.'

'I know you are.'

68

'You'll be back. Please say you'll be back. Don't let those miserable men with the clammy hands push you out.'

The night was silent. The wind had dropped as the rain began to make itself known, the storm was almost upon them. They were back beneath the great oak, but the leaves had stopped falling. They were all gone. The tree stood stark and bare. Winter had arrived.

'My baby. My husband. And now my job?' Izzy replied at last. She shook her head. The words of her award-winning report from Gaza, unscripted, the camera no more than a blur through the tears, the blood of her friend still damp on her hands, were forcing their way back into her memory.

In this land there are no victors, only victims. No children who are not soldiers, no difference of view which does not make enemies, no freedom which does not mean the persecution of others, no justice. In this land the utmost barbarities are committed in the name of God and love by extremists on all sides. And tonight they have claimed one more innocent victim. His name was Dan Morrison. He was my friend.

In a green and pleasant land many miles away from Gaza, the tide of personal injustice seemed to have become a flood and about to carry her away as just another helpless victim. The rain began to fall, heavily, trickling down her face.

'I'll let Benjy decide. I've still got him. I'll let Benjy decide.'

But it was not to be.

Michelini slammed full into the wall, the impact driving the breath from his lungs and forcing the taste of bile into the back of his throat. His heart hammered against his aching ribs, a searing pain like a razor-cut stretched from his left ankle all the way up to the back of his knee. He thought he might vomit. He was about to slump to his knees but knew that in doing so he would concede not only the game and the ten dollars but also his sense of virility. He would die standing up, not on his back. On second thoughts, dying on his back offered amusing prospects, but not during a game of squash. Instead of expiring, he settled for a slow and methodical retightening of his shoe lace. He had found himself retying his shoe laces a lot recently.

'Can't you afford new laces, Joe?' his opponent enquired with a knowing smirk.

'With what you lawyers charge? Gimme a break.'

'OK. Last game. You win and I'll buy lunch *and* new laces.'

'Yeah. And charge it back to me in your bill with a goddamned mark-up. Creep.'

'You're the one who's been creeping. You put on more weight or something?'

'Screw you.'

'We aim to please. But you know I charge by the full hour. Way out of your endurance league.'

Michelini decided to save his breath and responded with a gesture involving his little finger and its pinky ring before retrieving the ball from a far corner of the court. So he was a pace slower today; he was as fit as ever – well, would be if he gave up smoking once again – but he'd not been in the mood since he had heard about Bella. He'd been home most evenings alone, brooding, trying to work out the anger which had been growing within.

He felt cheated. He had scarcely seen Bella for more than a few weeks during her short life and then only at nights when he wasn't travelling or working late. There had always seemed to be plenty of tomorrows for catching up. He was too used to not seeing her; he scarcely knew her, his own baby. Couldn't even focus on what she looked like. And because he also felt ashamed that he did not feel her loss so very much more, he turned the sense of shame into anger aimed at his wife.

Then, last night, there had been a knock at his apartment door. A neighbour, a woman newly arrived in the Watergate complex with whom he'd exchanged pleasantries in the elevator about the turning of the leaves and the previous weekend had lent a hand with some bulky shopping. She had knocked about half eight, thanked him once again for his help and asked if he'd had dinner, would he fancy a hamburger and bottle of wine? He was about to explain that he'd already eaten and anyway was on a diet and didn't want to be disturbed when he noticed she was already carrying the McDonald's and Montrachet. She meant business.

He had stuffed two quarter-pounders and finished most of the bottle himself while, in between hamburgers, she had satisfied some of her own appetites. They hadn't even left the sitting-room floor and he could still feel the carpet burns. When it became apparent that she'd be going for more, both before and after apple pie dessert, he'd had to fake it, and he wasn't as good at that as he used to be.

This morning he'd felt like one of last night's french fries; no wonder he was a pace slower. And he still didn't know her name. Better ask the concierge.

It had been the first time he'd done it in the family home. He had a sense of family ethics that you didn't cheat on your wife in her bed or on her living-room rug, you kept that for elsewhere, separate from the family. But he felt that she – it was 'she', not 'Izzy',

71

he'd already embarked upon the mental process of divorce – that she had cheated him far more fundamentally than he had ever cheated on her. He was not even two full generations away from the old country concepts of family and vendetta; somehow it passed through the blood that there were no situations in which no one was to blame. This had to be someone's fault. Her fault.

Usually he'd announce some of the more adventurous details of his conquests to his lawyer, Antonini, just before they played an important point so as to consume his opponent with titillation and second-hand lust just when he needed all his powers of concentration. He decided against it this time; it might seem inappropriate and even incriminating on the day they'd agreed to extend the game into lunch in order to discuss his matrimonial problems. In any event, he felt invigorated by the memory and once again set about persuading himself that he looked, felt and played younger than he was. He pummelled the ball and started the new game.

They were towelling themselves dry when Antonini got down to business.

'You sure, Joe? About this divorce?'

'I'm sure. The marriage is going nowhere, doesn't really exist. She's never here, always off with God knows who doing God knows what.'

'Double values, Joe? You've been no saint, either.'

'All that counts is it's over. One big, fat zero.'

'Pity. I thought you two had such a good thing going. I'd hate to think you were – you know, simply going through one of those phases.' He'd meant to say 'patches', but now it was out. 'A lot of men do, Joe, and regret it like hell after.'

Michelini's eyes flared. 'What? You think I'm going through the male menopause?' His tone was aggressive; he was naked, suffering that feeling of inadequacy borne by many men in the locker room, and covered that inadequacy with belligerence. 'Thanks, Toni, but my hormones are working great – good enough to give you another thrashing on the court any time you want. No, I'm not going through one of those phases, it simply that my marriage is down the pan and I want you to help me clean the mess up.'

Antonini backed off, waving his hands. 'Fine, Joe. I hear you loud and clear.'

But Michelini was in gear, wanted to get it out of his system. 'It's never been much of a marriage. All she wanted was kids so she chose me as some form of farmyard stud. Rent-a-dick. "Is it your fertile time of the month, dear, or shall I roll over and reread yesterday's newspaper?" I've felt like I've been drowning in her hormones. She goes on about motherhood yet there she is every day trying to prove to the entire fucking world she's got bigger balls than the next man. I wanted a wife, a real woman, Toni, not some flak-jacketed Amazon who travels the world with a camera lens poking out of her knickers.'

He threw his damp towel bitterly across the room where it flopped into a large hamper. 'She wouldn't even call herself Mrs Joe Michelini. What's wrong with that, for Chrissake?'

The lawyer's tone was smooth, professional, but pressing. And once more inappropriate. 'Have you thought about the kids?'

'Kid, Toni. Kid. We've only got one now. She killed Bella, remember?'

Michelini, completely naked, squared up to the lawyer with his arms hanging stiffly at his side and his fists clenched. He felt guilty about Bella, wanted

73

to take a swing at someone. He was beginning to attract the attention of others in the locker room.

'Easy, Joe. I'm only doing my job, I have to ask these questions. You'll thank me for it later.'

'The kids should never have been dragged halfway round the world by a mother who even then would take off at the drop of a hat and disappear for a week or more. Kids need a mother, not to be dumped with a string of agency nannies who don't even speak proper English.' His chest heaved as he fought to control his own passion. 'They also need a father, yet because of her I scarcely knew them. Now with Bella I'm never going to get the chance.' He jammed a college ring back on his finger with a violence that must have hurt, but he did not flinch. Rather his voice grew quieter, more disciplined, the words like ice.

'She is a completely irresponsible mother, Toni, and in a million years I'll never forgive her.'

'Try not to make it all too bitter, Joe. That's the way things get messy. Expensive.'

'No worries. My company's backing me on this one, it's agreed to pay every cent of my legal costs. No expense spared this time around. Don't let it go to your head, you bastard. Just make sure I win.'

'If it can't be done neatly and cleanly, she'll fight. She's got to protect her professional image as Miss Clean, won't accept being pilloried as an unfit mother.'

'But she *is* an unfit mother. That's the whole point. And she may find it more difficult to contest than she thought.'

'What do you mean?'

Michelini turned to look into the mirror as he adjusted his silk tie. He was all control now. 'Because she's away so much she left it to me to sort

74

out the bills and family finances, that sort of thing. Gave me power of attorney in case anything happened to her.' He finished the knot with a flourish and turned to face the lawyer. 'I have control of her bank accounts.' He paused. 'Sadly, we hit a lot of unusual family expenses recently. When she gets round to looking into her accounts, she'll find nothing but a rainstorm of red ink.'

'You cleaned her out? But she can sue the pants off you for that.'

'If she wants all her dirty underwear spread out in public, sure. And if she can find a lawyer to work for her for love and no money. So I'll be reasonable, we'll compromise. I shall let her have a clean and quiet divorce. I won't drag her reputation through the mud. I'll even replenish her bank accounts. All on one condition.'

'Which is?'

'She killed my baby girl. I'm not going to let her have that chance with my only son, Toni, not if I have to fight her in every court in the land.' He slipped into his jacket, flexing his shoulders as though the well-tailored suit was his armour and he was once again ready to do war with the world. 'I want custody.'

She stared without comprehension at the face at the foot of the bed. Too much had collided in her mind that day and it had left her drained and disorientated. Shortly after breakfast she'd heard he was looking not just for a divorce but custody. War, with Benjy as the battlefield and her fresh out of ammunition.

There was physical pain, as though someone were wrenching out a tree which had its roots growing deep within her. She saw life through a haze of unreality, the sterile and polite conversations around her bed echoing like the hollow laughter of a cocktail bar, the walls drawing in, closing down her world, stifling her. While she was there, idle, they would be plotting to grab Benjy. She had to get out.

When she had raised her intention of discharging herself, they had not been unsympathetic. Her physical progress was excellent, her neurological signs improving, as long as she didn't overdo it the change of scene and stimuli might do both her and the child good. They had suggested – firmly, to the point of insistence – that she spend ten days as an out-patient in the neurology department and then, with fortune and continued progress, she would be free. Another check-up in three months, again six months after that, and they could pronounce her recovered. A minor miracle of the medical profession on which they could congratulate themselves.

It was only at the point when she began to focus on escape as reality rather than theory that she came to realize what a huge step it entailed. She was a woman in a strange land, penniless, with neither possessions nor friends, and a young child in her charge, lacking even a means of proving her identity. Such practicalities had seemed so unimportant – up to now. Where did she start trying to pull it all back together?

She was stumbling through an undergrowth of tangled personal details when out of the blue he was there, waiting to catch her as she fell.

'Hello. How are you getting on?'

She gazed at him in some bewilderment. 'I know you but . . .'

A hand reached out. 'Paul Devereux. Remember? You interviewed me, a few months ago.'

'Of course . . .' The soft, watery pale blue eyes, the clipped sentences. 'I'm sorry. It's as though you've stepped out of a past life. I don't associate you with this world.' She waved her hands around her, extending one to meet his greeting. The lights were beginning to switch on. 'You gave me an exclusive.'

'And you gave me a bloody hard time.' His expression implied no hard feelings.

'If I remember correctly,' she replied, tenaciously but not unkindly, 'you played the male politician and expected me to play the little lady. Foreigner, too. Easy meat, you thought.'

He took the challenge in his stride. 'Indeed, it hadn't passed my attention that you were both a foreigner and an attractive woman – if one is allowed to remark on such things in these politically correct days of ours.' He shrugged to indicate he was a hopeless case. 'And by the time you'd finished I felt in need of a visit to one of my own casualty departments.'

'Something like that,' she nodded approvingly.

'No need to worry. The scars have almost healed.'

'I wasn't worried, Mr Devereux,' she assured him, rejecting with a smile his appeal for the sympathy vote.

'No, I didn't suppose you were. I see you are regaining your strength. Practically fighting fit, I'd say.' He was enjoying the banter. 'I'm delighted.'

'Why?'

'I beg your pardon?'

'Sorry. I mean, why are you here? It's not every day a Government Minister drops in to check my vital signs.'

He chuckled. 'As Secretary of State for Health, hospitals were very much part of my world, and this hospital in particular. This is Weschester, my constituency, you see, and I make a point of dropping by every month.'

'I don't have a vote, I'm afraid.'

'Voters hold sway perhaps once every four or five years, Miss Dean. Chickenfeed compared with the power wielded by you and your colleagues in the media. But this is merely a social call. Heard what a remarkable recovery you've staged. Wanted merely to find out how you were progressing.'

She told him she was leaving hospital. He seemed dutifully concerned. She admitted that it was going to prove rather more complicated than she had realized. Should've asked K.C. for help, but hadn't thought . . .

'As your local Member of Parliament *ad interim*, perhaps I can help.' His smile was warm, well practised. A political smile. To be ignored. Yet in those remarkable blue eyes, where feelings can rarely be hidden, she thought she could detect more than a merely professional interest. Not entirely avuncular, either.

'I have nothing, absolutely nothing, but the hospital gown I am wearing.'

Aware for the first time that she was a shade underdressed, she moved across the room to her dressing gown.

As she put it on she couldn't help but feel self-conscious. She hadn't lost weight as quickly as she would have liked after the second birth, her breasts were heavier and she wasn't wearing a bra, and the muscle tone she'd been building to lift and tuck everything back to its former shape had largely dissolved with the extended bed rest. It bothered her that he was looking, but only because she wasn't at her best. The style in her dark red hair was gone and she felt dowdy, unattractive. Very post-maternity.

Once again she was left wondering if there could be life after birth.

By contrast he saw a handsome woman of above average height who, although still frail, moved with grace across the room and who even in her anonymous hospital cotton was unquestionably feminine. The skin was clear, fresh, the hair brushed lustrous and her green eyes bright, active, questioning, eyes that were not made up but which scarcely needed artificial highlights, eyes he had seen many times on reports from the danger zones of the world where make-up would have looked faintly ludicrous. Green eyes, his favourite. Eyes that had danced in the midst of a room crowded with grizzled correspondents and that had helped him pick her out for the benefit of an exclusive interview.

It was the first time a man had stared at her like that since she came to hospital, and he made no attempt to hide his appreciation; self-consciously her mind brushed over the tiny root-like veins on her leg which had erupted during pregnancy and which she had resolved to have cosmetically removed. When she had the time.

Suddenly her thoughts struck her as strange. She had been faithful to her husband throughout their marriage yet here she was already worrying about what other men might think of her, and she of them. Such sensations were smudged with sadness, yet she could not deny the kernel of excitement that was also there. At least she was starting to feel something again.

'And technically I have trouble in proving I exist. All my identification was lost in the crash.'

'No problem. If you'll allow me I'll kick some backsides at the US Embassy. Get someone down to see you.'

'You're very kind. Should have done that myself but, before today, I hadn't really given it a thought. Such things seem irrelevant when you're lying in hospital with your memory rattled to pieces. I suppose I'd better get hold of my bank and find some means of living and dressing; social services are finding a boarding house in the town for Benjy and me to stay while I sort things out.'

She was thinking out loud, not beseeching help, but he responded without hesitation.

'Look, you're trying to get well, not bury yourself in problems. Allow me to cut through all this for you. Please. Not often a politician can do anything about real problems, we're always too busy pretending we're saving the world.'

She was amused by his modesty.

'I have a house in Bowminster, about fifteen miles from here. Stacks of room, empty during the week while I'm in London. You and your son would be very comfortable, and very welcome. There's thatch and plenty of land and a gardener who can be your chauffeur and run any errands. Give you the time and freedom to sort everything out.'

'That's far too generous . . .'

'Don't make me out to be something I'm not, Miss Dean.'

God, how incredibly modest and English he was, she thought. For a brief moment she looked into his moist eyes, flecked with the strange upper-class confection of authority and inbred decay, and wondered if all those stories were true and he was an archetypal English fag, before she realized she was being revoltingly cynical. Still, if he were, it meant she had nothing to worry about by staying in his house . . .

'Since I have no family living with me any longer . . .'

OK, a closet fag. *Christ, Izzy, the guy's trying to help you!*

'. . . I hate the thought of the house standing empty for so much of the time. I'd be very happy. Telephone bill's already enormous so don't worry about that. And as for clothing and the rest, that's easy.' He plunged into his jacket pocket for his wallet. 'You have to be a good credit risk. Here's two hundred pounds to get you going. Give it back when you're on your feet.'

'But I can't accept money from . . .' – she was about to say a strange man but it sounded too pathetic – '. . . from a politician. The Secretary of State for Health.'

'Oh, but I'm not!' He clapped his hands, delighted to be able to overwhelm her argument. Unlike last time. 'You missed it. The reshuffle. I'm now Her Britannic Majesty's Secretary of State for Defence. And you, Miss Dean, are a foreign correspondent. If my attempt to help bothers you, simply treat it as a bribe.'

They both laughed; she felt desperately vulnerable, it was time to stop fighting. She thanked him, and he arranged for his gardener to pick her up at two that afternoon.

Only later did the realization dawn that this was the man in whose hands were now held the future of the Duster and with it her vengeful husband's fortunes.

A sense of well-being began to build inside Izzy as she collected Benjy and began to gather up the few items of clothing and second-hand soft toys that had appeared from the various streams of helpers and benefactors which trickle through any hospital. She had her son, whatever his father planned, and at last she was making a start on piecing her life back together again. She was no longer alone; things couldn't get any worse, she told herself.

The Devereux driver would be arriving soon and it was time to bid her goodbyes. She made the round between ITU and the neurology department and up to the toddlers' ward, all the places which had been her world for the last few weeks, shaking hands, receiving wishes, congratulations and gratuitous advice, offering her thanks.

It was in the toddlers' ward amidst the muddle of bright colours and overstuffed animals, at the cot next to Benjy's, that she came across preparations for another departure.

'Time for us to go, sweetheart,' a young black woman was instructing a small and very white child. The child, a girl, was scarcely a year old and protesting vigorously; the woman was of West African origin by her heavy accent.

Izzy felt a tug towards the girl, vigorously redhaired like Bella had been and not much larger, and her gaze wandered back and forth between woman and child.

The woman, noting Izzy's interest and confusion, let forth an amused whoop. 'No, I'm not her mother,' she beamed.

Izzy returned the good humour. 'Somehow I didn't think so . . .'

'I take her to meet new parents,' she explained, before realizing this was scarcely an explanation at all. 'I am from the social services. My name is Katti. This little thing is being adopted.'

'Poor thing,' was Izzy's instinctive response, but she was immediately contradicted.

'No, no, dear. She is lucky. Nice new home. Two cars. Loving parents.' Katti lowered her voice to offer a confidence. 'See, the natural mother is a single lady, only fifteen, from some place around Birmingham. Come here to have her baby. Lot of these girls come here, it's quiet, by the sea, away from friends and parents, you know. Very private. First she says she wants to give the child for adoption, then the silly thing changes her mind. But her parents won't let her back, see?'

'I see. But I find it difficult to understand.'

'Right. So the girl gets scared, thinking the baby be taken from her. Runs off and lives for months in squats, hiding, caring for the baby all by herself.' Katti's eyes, huge and encircled with dramatic dark rings, rolled in pain. 'And she starts thieving and doing God knows what else for food and baby clothing. By the time we find her, the little baby is like a scrap of paper, so underweight, sleeping in a cardboard box.'

'So you have taken the baby away from its mother?'

'Goodness, no. We talk with the girl, and talk and talk. No rush. We never do anything in rush down here.' She laughed at what was obviously a standard Dorset line. 'In the end she agrees it's best for her and for baby that she stick to the first plan and let the little one be adopted. No way she can cope. We don't blame her, poor thing, she tries so hard.'

At this point the baby, indignant at having ceased to be the centre of her minder's attention, threw up over the clothes in which only moments before she had been dressed. Izzy smiled and the black woman scowled in mock offence, but Benjamin pointed at the baby and gave a whoop of laughter.

'Baby thdick, baby thdick,' he gurgled. His eyes shone with impish joy. It was the first time he had laughed since the accident.

Still a month short of his third birthday, Benjy's speech had been in any event rudimentary and the trauma of the accident had initially destroyed his willingness to persevere, yet since Izzy's reawakening she had spent much of every day teaching him once again the basic lessons which fear had forced from his mind. For Benjy, and even more so for Izzy, every lisping phrase represented a major victory.

Now he was laughing, too. Fighting back. Growing again. Izzy's eyes brimmed with pride.

'Baby's leaving hospital, Benjy,' Izzy told him, straightening his collar. 'You and I are going to leave hospital, too.'

'Dake baby wid us.'

'No, Benjy, this little baby's going to go to a new mummy and daddy,' she started explaining, but Benjy's humour had instantly turned to petulance and childish frustration. Since the accident and her traumatic albeit temporary 'desertion' his emotions had become fragile, more clinging, impatient.

'Not dat baby. Dake our baby wid us. Baby Bella.'

She gathered him in her arms and smothered him in kisses, clutching him possessively as though someone were about to snatch him from her, hiding within the curls of his hair the tears that were beginning to form.

'Baby Bella can't come with us, darling.' The words hung bittersweet on her breath. 'Baby's dead and gone to Heaven.'

'No!'

'I'm sorry, Benjy . . .'

'No, no, Mummy. Bella nod dead,' he responded indignantly.

'What do you mean?'

'Lady came an took Bella away.'

THREE

With great tenderness Izzy sat Benjamin down, smoothed his hair, hugged him again, and gave herself time to recover. Patiently, with difficulty, she tried to explain to her son that he was mistaken. That he must have imagined things.

The boy would have none of it, sticking firmly to his claim. He had some concept of death, it was one of the first lessons that children picked up when seeing the scenes of suffering on which Izzy reported. Death was a child who went to sleep. Never to wake up.

'Lady dake baby Bella. An Bella cry.'

'Which lady? A lady like this, Benjamin?' she asked, indicating Katti, the black social worker who had begun to take an interest in the plight of mother and child.

'No, no. Different.'

'A lady like me, then?'

Benjamin studied his mother as if for the first time, concentrating. 'No.'

In an instant the image had returned to Izzy and, with it, dread. Fear burned a pathway up her spine, searing along the back of her neck and beneath the skin of her scalp until it had set her mind ablaze. In the flickering light cast by the flames she saw the same lurid mask as in her nightmare.

The girl. Eyes now full of terror. Melting away.

And taking Bella with her.

She grabbed a crayon and piece of paper on which

Benjy had been scribbling. She drew a face, thin. Long straggles of hair.

'Like that, Benjy? Hair like that?' she enquired, haltingly.

He nodded.

'An old lady, Benjamin? Was she an old lady?'

'No, Mummy,' he answered impatiently, shaking his head in disagreement.

'And eyes?'

She drew two circles, but he looked blankly at her work. Then she began drawing around the circles, roughly, unevenly, until the eyes had grown small and the surrounding shadows distended and dark.

'Yes. Dat her!'

And now Izzy fell silent, appalled, frozen in torment. It couldn't be true. Could it?

'Can I help?'

It was Katti. Izzy turned slowly, waking from a dream, part nightmare, part fantasy, but which nevertheless she felt certain was a dream.

'My baby died. Here in this hospital. A few weeks ago.'

Katti's eyes widened in sympathy.

'I know very little, really, haven't wanted to. Until now. Few details, no death certificate. But it's time to sort everything out. How do I do that, Katti? Do you know?'

'Your baby dies here in this hospital? Sad. But no problem. I tell you, I can sort all this out for you. Here, my card.' She thrust a flimsy card with her details into Izzy's hand. 'You don't worry. I find out everything, you call in a couple of days. OK?'

Weakly Izzy smiled her thanks and the torment began to recede. But, as hard as she tried, it would not disappear, for glowing in the embers of her torment was also hope. Pathetic, pointless, desperate new hope.

An idea struck her. A foolish one, she knew, but one which could do no harm, might banish the illusions and end the agony. Help make her certain. She left Benjamin on the ward, explaining she still had one more person to thank.

It was not difficult to find, though badly signposted. Those who needed it knew where it was. As she had regained her strength and begun to move about the hospital she had noticed the steady trickle of vans with no rear windows or apparent identification disappearing in the direction of the far corner of the car park.

It consisted of scarcely more than a prefabricated cabin. Above a set of large double doors was hung a small, unembellished sign, the only relief to its otherwise total anonymity.

'MORTUARY.'

She stepped inside.

She was in a room which acted as a corridor. Down the centre of the corridor ran a grille covering a drainage gully. In one corner stood a mop and bucket, in another a tubular metal trolley and behind that a large wall chart on which, in numbers from one to sixteen, were charted names and measurements. The wall opposite was dominated by grey metal doors some three feet high, stacked in double rows, with corresponding numbers. One set of doors had a hand-written placard taped to it.

'LONG TERM. DO NOT LEAVE UNLOCKED.'

The room was cool. From somewhere further within she heard a clattering sound, a metal tray being dropped, perhaps, and she followed the noise. She passed an open door through which could be seen a small wood-panelled chapel of rest, outside of which was arranged a row of cheap stacking chairs on which someone had left a pair of freshly washed wellington boots. As she turned the corner, the floor colour changed from grey to green; before she knew it she was through another set of double doors.

The room was considerably larger than the previous one, set out like a hotel kitchen with sinks and counters and plastic dustbins and scales and scrubbing brushes and spotlessly clean utensils of all sorts. Hanging from a hook on the far wall was a circular saw.

In the centre of the room stood two stainless-steel benches, each with a surface consisting of a shiny metal grille. On one lay a clutter of scalpels, hammers, saws, chisels, scissors, shears and other tools which would have made her late father, an enthusiastic woodworker, envious. On the other, under a spotlight which made the damp table gleam, was a small mound of material which was being attended and sorted by a small man in green overalls, apron, latex gloves and rubber boots. The floor around where he stood was damp. The strains of a Mozart symphony were being broadcast from a radio on a nearby counter and, as he leaned over the table, back towards Izzy, he clenched his buttocks in time with the music.

Pom. Pom-Pom. Pom-Pom-Pom-Pom-Pom-Pom.

While his lower body rose and fell with the rhythm, the rest of him remained utterly still, fixed upon his work. It was some time before he realized he was not alone.

'Hello, doctor,' he greeted from beneath his mask. 'Be with you in a minute.'

Her eyes shifted to her right where, along the wall, she found the identical grey metal doors with corresponding numbers, the other side of the refrigerator.

In front was another trolley on which, covered in a sheet, lay stretched the unmistakable outline of a body. Now she knew what materials the man, a mortuary technician, was sorting through.

She was used to death, but not like this, antiseptic and neatly numbered. And the stench was missing; there was no putrefaction, no singed flesh, only a slight tang in the air of – what? Formaldehyde, she guessed.

The technician finished his sorting and placed various items into small plastic jars. As he turned, she could see he had left on the table top a bright, pink, oozing slab of liver.

'Excuse me if I don't shake hands, doctor,' he chuckled, advancing towards her with soiled and gloved hands held high. He reminded her of her gynaecologist. 'How can I help?'

'I am not a doctor.' She found her mouth was painfully dry. 'I am the mother of a baby girl who . . . passed through here a few weeks ago.'

The technician was transformed into a bundle of agitation. His bushy moustache twitched and he began hopping from leg to leg. A flush began beneath his chin that stretched up to and then over his balding head.

'Oh, my! I am so sorry. But you really shouldn't be here. Please. Please! Wait outside.'

In ungainly fashion, with hands still held in the air, he ushered her out of the room and indicated she should sit on one of the stacking chairs. He then disappeared, closing the double doors firmly behind him. She heard the sound of latex gloves being ripped off, the clattering of metal trays, the gushing of water. And the sound of a grey metal door banging shut.

His face still glowed with embarrassment when

he reappeared. 'I do apologize. I thought you must be a visiting doctor. I had no idea.' He sat down on the chair beside her. 'You really, *really* shouldn't be here, you know, it's most terribly irregular.'

'But I am here.'

'Yes, well, I suppose you are.' A tentative, ungloved hand shot from beneath his cuff. 'Russell. My name's Mr Russell. Tell me, how can I help you, Mrs . . . ?'

'Izzy Dean. My name is Izzy Dean. And my daughter was six months old. A car crash. Her name was Isabella, but at the time you didn't know her name.'

'Yes, I think I remember her. You'd like to know a few details?' he enquired hesitantly. His moustache twitched once more.

'Yes.'

'Look, you go and wait in the chapel, while I go and fetch the register.'

The chapel was rudimentary. Veneered walls, plastic flowers, garish electronic candles. Part of the design specs for a facility to which the architect had forgotten to add soul. Not a place to find comfort, or anything else, come to that.

Then he had joined her, bearing a large leather-backed book.

'Here she is.' His finger traced across the page. 'Yes, I do remember her. I performed the autopsy myself – we have to, you realize, with every unexpected death.' His tone was full of sympathy. He had split and sundered hundreds of bodies; on the table they were to him just another day's engrossing forensic work, an endless stream of testaments to Man's folly, brutality, and plain bad luck, but he had never forgotten that behind every statistic and restitched corpse lay someone else's grief. Or almost every corpse. Occasionally there were those who seemed to have arrived direct from nowhere, like the baby.

'She's marked here as an Unidentified Female Child – approximately six months of age – the night of 1st November – she died of a sub-dural haematoma, I'm afraid. There was a little light bruising on one arm but no other serious injury. She would have felt absolutely no pain,' he reassured her. 'See for yourself, if you would like.'

He handed her the register. Her eyes wandered across the double page, halting at each entry, the details, medical terms, signatures, dates, before moving on. As they did so they left a trail, two small drops of tears which fell on the pages.

So it was true.

'I'm sorry,' she apologized, wiping the pages dry. 'I'll be all right.'

'Of course, Mrs Dean. I understand. You know, she was a very beautiful baby,' he continued, feeling the need to offer further comfort. 'I remember her very clearly. Her face was very peaceful. She had lovely dark curls, reminded me a lot of my own little boy.'

Izzy wiped her eyes and turned to face him. 'No, Mr Russell, she had red hair. Took after me.'

'But dark, surely . . .' he began to protest, before realizing it would serve no purpose. 'I'm sorry, I felt sure . . . Must be my mistake.' Yet his voice lacked the edge of conviction. He was humouring her.

'My little baby had red hair,' she repeated, voice wooden. A coil of chaos was beginning to turn inside her.

'Of course, you must be right. Foolish of me. I . . .' He hesitated, stopped. He found something important to study at the end of his fingertips.

Inside Izzy there was no more place for words, for

logic, for a man's explanation of things. She felt as she had that very first time she had known Bella. The faintest fluttering, deep within, a butterfly, a stretching of wings. Life. And from that touch of life a tremor of excitement and hope lengthened throughout her entire being.

'I'm sorry,' he said. 'I don't think I can be of much more help.'

'Mr Russell, you've been more help than you could ever believe.'

Unusually for a man whom others tended to hold in some kind of anxiety-based awe, the hospital psychologist was feeling perturbed. Already the therapeutic glow of his long weekend spent annihilating pheasants was beginning to fade as his systems re-engaged gear for another offensive against emotional and psychological incontinence. He had been summoned in peremptory fashion to deal with a patient he should already have got to know considerably better than he had, but, with the local health authority stretching resources ever more thinly upon the ground, how could he be expected to deal with every inmate? Particularly one who the clinical records showed was recovering exceptionally well, yet who was turning out to be no more than another overwrought woman clutching at unreality.

Izzy was seated in a utilitarian consulting room which was undersized and distinctly cramped. In front of her, perched on the edge of his desk and trying to look informal while at the same time achieving the height which would give him dominance, was the psychologist. Behind him in the chair sat her neurologist, Weatherup, while to her rear she could sense rather than see the hovering presence of a hospital administrator. They had her surrounded.

The psychologist waved his glasses at her. When he felt harassed he had a habit of repeatedly gesticulating with them to emphasize a point before ramming them back on. To assist in this process he had a remarkably flat and bony bridge to his nose which in wistful moments he thought tended to make him look rather owlish, but which to Izzy, looking up at his perch from the discomfort of her sagging and foam-upholstered chair, gave him the air of a buzzard at prey.

'Look, Miss Dean. Izzy.' He attempted a smile and leaned forward in what he took to be a confiding manner, but which to her was more like the buzzard reaching for its breakfast. 'Perhaps it's my fault; I should have got to talk with you more fully before now, but I wasn't expecting you to leave hospital quite so soon. You must realize that the feelings you are experiencing are entirely natural. Having trouble accepting the loss of your baby. Not being able to grieve properly. After all, one minute she's there with you and the next – at least the next as far as you are concerned – she's been dead many days and you've had no chance to say your goodbyes. We understand, really we do.'

He braced his shoulders and the spectacles were thrust back on his nose.

'But you must try to grasp the fact that in this country we don't make mistakes like that.'

He had the patronizing manner of any number of public men who conducted interviews while staring at her ankles or the bulges in her blouse, unable to accept that a woman could comprehend or even be truly interested in the depths of his answers. Oftentimes in their anxiety to act out what they regarded as the strong sexual role model they would fall off guard, giving up far more than they would ever have considered providing to a male reporter. But this one was giving up nothing; he had nothing to give, other than excuses and platitudes.

'We have systems for such things, you see,' he continued. 'Patients are tagged with a plastic ID bracelet from the minute they come into hospital and that ID stays with them until they leave. It can't drop off or be lost, it has to be cut away; there's no scope for confusion. You must trust us on this one.'

She didn't. 'I thought I read some while ago about parents being sent home from a maternity hospital with the wrong babies.'

'Wasn't that in America?'

'Bournemouth, I believe.'

'I'm sure I've heard about it happening – only very occasionally even there – in America, but never here. Not in England.'

'In Bournemouth,' she insisted.

'But not in this hospital, Miss Dean,' the administrator joined in. To question was to criticize, and it was his system she was questioning. 'There weren't two different babies in this case. Just yours. So it couldn't have happened, I'm afraid.'

'The confusion over your baby's hair colour was a simple error of memory, Izzy,' Weatherup intervened. 'After all, hair colour and the like aren't recorded in the mortuary register. It was just a stumble of memory. Goodness, you of all people should understand that.' He tried to raise a reassuring chuckle which became impaled and died upon her direct and very professional green eyes.

'I'd like to question the other staff. The nurses on duty that night.'

'You'd be welcome, of course you would. In fact, I'd recommend it as part of your therapy.'

'Therapy? To forget?'

'To come to terms, Izzy,' Weatherup continued.

'Gentlemen, I have no intention of coming to terms, as you put it, if that means brushing aside these inconsistencies.'

'There are no inconsistencies,' the administrator joined in with a protest, his voice rising a semi-tone in impatience. 'We're talking about nothing more than the confused memory of a technician whom you took by surprise in a part of the hospital where you shouldn't have been.' He was growing exasperated, he didn't care for anyone prying into the efficiency of his systems, least of all a foreigner and a patient who within minutes hopefully would be on his discharge list and no longer the hospital's responsibility.

'This isn't getting us very far,' Weatherup intervened, keen to get the conversation back on track. 'Izzy, talk to the nurses, if that's what you want. Find out how much they really care – and cared for Bella.'

'But remember we've had perhaps a thousand patients through the doors of Accident & Emergency since you were there,' the administrator interjected. 'You can't possibly expect them to remember every detail.'

'You must have those details recorded somewhere.'

'They would be in the post-mortem report . . .' the neurologist began.

'I'd like to see it.'

'They contain all sorts of medical details, some of which you wouldn't understand and others which as a mother you simply wouldn't enjoy.'

'I'm a journalist,' she reminded him forcefully.

'PM reports are confidential,' the administrator snapped. 'Especially to journalists.'

'I . . .' She was about to tell them about Benjamin, but stopped. She knew it would be of no use. A child's recollection set against their prejudice. They had closed minds and, anyway, Benjy's garbled words were scarcely intelligible to her, let alone to flaccid men such as these. It took a woman, or at least a better man than these, to acknowledge that simply because someone was less than forty – indeed, less than four – their opinions might yet carry weight.

The psychologist, too, had concluded that the interchange was going nowhere. The spectacles were already waggling at her. 'You must accept, my dear, that emotional doubts are absolutely natural in a woman who has been through a harrowing experience such as yours. They are to be expected. Quite normal. What we have to do is to enable you to release your anxieties, to come to terms with the tragic events. What I am going to do is to recommend that we arrange for you, via our excellent social services staff, to visit the scene of the accident. It will be painful, of that there is no doubt, but it will help act as some sort of . . . catharsis, a purgative for your doubts and emotions. Help to face up to the reality of your baby's loss. And we shall arrange for you to talk to some of those who would have helped take care of little . . .' – he glanced down at his notes – 'Isabella.'

'I've already done that. I talked to the mortuary technician. Didn't help too much, did it?'

Damn the woman and her intransigence! The glasses were rammed back on his nose. Already the bridge was beginning to shine brightly, to appear angry and sore, belying the fixed smile which split his features. 'And I suggest that we have a regular session, just the two of us, every other day while you are an out-patient here. Get to know each other.'

'And I'm sure we can prescribe something to help you sleep — if you feel you need it, that is,' Weatherup offered, trying to be helpful.

That's it, she mused, the traditional medical response. Surround and sedate.

The psychologist had dived into the pocket of his waistcoat and produced a small appointments diary. 'Let's start our counselling on Mon ... No. How about Tuesday?' His silver-encased pencil was poised ready to strike. She was about to be arranged, filed, written in and written off.

God, but she knew she needed help. An angry and insatiable dog was scratching away within her, a mongrel whose father was pain and whose mother was Izzy's own sense of guilt that somehow she had been responsible for her baby's fate, that she had let Bella down.

She would find relief only in facts, yet she knew there were no answers lying on this man's couch or sitting at his feet upon his undersprung chair. She had to accept the possibility that he may after all be right, that the neurotic and emotionally unstable woman reflected in his bespectacled eyes was deluding herself, clutching at illusions in an attempt to by-pass reality and create a hope and a world which simply didn't exist. Bella was dead, almost beyond a reasonable doubt.

But Izzy was a professional sceptic, trained to be unreasonable, to believe no evidence that couldn't be grasped with both hands and dragged out of shadows into the remorseless light of day.

She was also a woman who would bleed rather than be snowed under by the patronizing concerns of the male Establishment.

Be reasonable, they said. Yet how could a mother be reasonable?

They were looking at her, waiting, the silver pencil still poised. There were times to strike, times to dissemble, times simply to lie. She had their attention. She settled back into the foam-filled embrace of the chair, crossed her legs in a manner which raised the hem of her second-hand skirt to expose her knees, and smiled. If they insisted on a silly, simpering woman, that's what she would let them think they had.

'Of course. You're right. I'll telephone to arrange an appointment. Soon as I've settled in.'

The psychiatrist braced his shoulders in victory. He pushed his spectacles back up the bridge of his nose, put away his diary and silver pencil, relished his small triumph. He thought he had the measure of Isadora Dean.

Bloody fool.

They approached the Devereux home through a long avenue of dogwood, its blood-tipped tendrils reaching up through the decay of autumn like . . . What? The prospect of life and hope? Or flesh-stripped fingers piercing through a burial mound? Izzy couldn't decide.

Devereux's driver had been waiting for her; indeed, as a result of her foray into the mortuary and diversion amongst the medical profession at Weschester General he had been waiting some considerable time. He seemed gruff, taciturn, his manner suggesting impatience, or was it simply the innate reserve of country folk when dealing with strangers?

In any event conversation was impeded since, while he drove, she was left to sit in the back seat clutching Benjamin, who was petrified at the prospect of another car journey into the unknown. Not that the Devereux vehicle bore any substantial resemblance to the shattered Renault: a Rolls Royce Silver Cloud, nearly forty years old, a classic combination of blues and grey with original albeit cracked leather upholstery, of the vintage which set idiosyncratic yet enduring standards of design before luxury cars began their inexorable progress towards computer-induced anonymity. Devereux travelled in style.

The gardener-cum-chauffeur was named Chinnery, that much she managed to extract, but no first name. Around forty, hirsute, dark frown, short-cropped hairstyle with tattoos on his forearms, and working clothes which were well worn but practical and clean. Only his boots betrayed the slightest sign of soil, where the mud had been carefully scraped from around the sole leaving a damp tide mark. She guessed he was ex-military, other ranks, used to taking orders but no experience of socializing in the officers' mess. And the same weathered, suspicious face she had seen peering out at checkpoints and from behind barricades in every war zone she had filmed, where the hoe and sickle had all too frequently been interchangeable with a Kalashnikov and ammunition belt and where mounds of freshly dug earth betrayed anything but the beauty of an English garden.

The Devereux house, like his car, was large and superbly appointed. An old brick-and-sandstone farmhouse with a gently beaten face that had undergone many modifications over the centuries but which now settled under a thick and freshly trimmed covering of thatch that the winds of winter had as yet had no opportunity to bedraggle. The setting was magnificent, with views over many hundreds of acres of wood and farmland to the spires of the small town of Bowminster, nestling below in the protective embrace of gently sculpted hills. Beyond Bowminster, with its toy-like rooftops and smoke curling up from a dozen wood fires, perhaps some twelve miles away and through a cleft in the surrounding hills she could see the grey waters of the English Channel.

This was Hardy country, the very heart of it, beauty and timeless mystery that lingered in the rural shade. And personal tragedy, always in Hardy there was personal tragedy. Was there ever a happy ending? She couldn't remember.

As they had driven through the winding avenue of dogwood and into the cobbled courtyard surrounded by pleached limes, she had grown uneasy. The exclusiveness of the setting meant isolation and reminded her that she was alone. She was a woman used to the bustle of the DC Beltway or the suicidal rush of an autobahn, clouds of traffic fumes rather than scented sea breeze; the bucolic tempo of Bowminster encouraged introspection, meditation, relaxation. Not throttling out the truth about Bella.

As the Cloud braked gently to a halt she found herself drumming her fingers in impatience, but relief in the form of the outside, familiar world was at hand. In the courtyard was parked a black Ford saloon which, judging by the fresh mud thrown up against the bodywork, had come a considerable distance and in something of a hurry. It bore diplomatic plates.

The driver emerged, a diminutive but meticulously presented man with undersized shoulders and overtrimmed moustache who scurried over to open her door. His bearing, head high and chest thrust forward above awkward, spindly legs, reminded her of the strut of a chicken. From the cut of his suit and the length of his trousers, which showed altogether too much sock for European tastes, she guessed he was American. Kentucky Fried.

'Pomfritt. Harry Pomfritt, Miss Dean,' he introduced himself with diction slightly too precise. East coast. Private school. 'Consular Officer from the Embassy. Mr Devereux asked me to meet you. Delighted you're out and about.' He suffered a slight lisp that became more apparent when excited or ill at ease.

Hoping to be helpful, he reached for Benjy, who shrank back, in fear of being stolen away from his mother once more.

'Perhaps not,' the official agreed. 'May I help you with your luggage?'

'Hardly. I'm wearing it.'

Pomfritt stepped back and smoothed his moustache. This was clearly not his time to bat. He remained quiet until Chinnery, also without a word, had left them seated around the refectory table in the large flagstoned kitchen.

Pomfritt decided it was time to intervene once more. He clapped his hands enthusiastically. 'I could murder a cup of good English tea,' he contributed.

The implication was clear; instinctively, with neither conscious deliberation nor intention to offend, he assumed the woman would make it. It was scarcely a novel reaction. Camera crews around the world would conclude without debate that, as the token female, Izzy was the one to organize the wake-up calls, book the restaurant, act as secretary or social hostess. After all, it was only natural . . .

Men.

She recalled the time she had gained an exclusive interview with the newly installed President of Peru less than a fortnight after his military coup. He had sat magisterial and bemedalled behind the presidential desk, overshadowed by a huge oil portrait of himself, while she had stood asking the pointed questions about death squads and Opposition leaders who had vanished in the middle of the night. With great patience and considerable charm, he had answered all her questions by turning to face the three men who comprised her crew. Not once during the entire interview had he looked at her directly except to ogle her breasts; it seemed impossible for him to comprehend that she could be there for anything other than decoration. And to make the tea.

Izzy looked at Pomfritt and inclined her head. 'Thank you. I don't take sugar.'

The Consular Officer looked around the kitchen in considerable confusion, he'd never done battle with an Aga stove before. He hopped, flapped his wings, searching in vain for an electric kettle until, to his considerable relief, he was rescued by the arrival of a voluminous, tent-like apparition who turned out to be Sally, the housekeeper, and very good at making heavy-duty orange tea.

'I'm grateful you have come so promptly, Mr Pomfritt,' Izzy offered in truce.

Pomfritt put down his cup and with some care wiped his moustache. The grooming was a mistake; it only helped to emphasize the lack of anything resembling a chin. 'My pleasure to help, Miss Dean. Particularly when the request comes from a man such as Mr Devereux.'

'He carries a lot of weight with the Embassy?'

'With everyone right now.' His head bobbed forward, as though pecking at corn seeds on a farmyard floor. 'Confidentially – I'm sure I can trust you to treat this purely as background, Miss Dean – many of us think he has an excellent chance of taking over from the Prime Minister within the next couple of years. And even if that weren't the case, as Defence Secretary he carries a mighty big stick with us Americans.' He was lisping once more.

Izzy's nostrils flared. This one was typical State. Yesterday's cable news served up as today's confidential briefing.

'You mean the Duster?' she enquired.

'You're familiar with it? Of course, Miss Dean, your job. Well, it's no federal secret that the Administration values this project highly and there's quite a game of poker being played. Paul Devereux seems to be holding one damn' fine deck of cards, if you know what I mean. We want to be very good friends with him.'

She adjusted Benjy's position on her lap; in the warmth of the kitchen he'd quickly fallen asleep. She prayed he wouldn't pee himself. 'Tell me, why is it so important?'

'It's important in its own right, Miss Dean.' He had that irritating and unnecessary habit of repeating the names of those with whom he was talking, as though by constant emphasis he could persuade them of his integrity and good intentions. Straight out of Foggy Bottom via Dale Carnegie. 'It's important for our defence strategy; thousands of jobs are swinging on it. But there's more, much more. You see, it has great significance not just for impressing our potential enemies, but also our allies. If we can get our act together with Europe on this one, it could open the door to all sorts of collaborative projects. A new supersonic transport to take over from Concorde. Co-operative ventures in space – a new space station, perhaps.'

'Using our NASA shuttle, of course,' she added conspiratorially.

He appeared oblivious to her sarcasm. 'Even hold-

ing each other's hands on things like a new generation of fusion power plants and the reprocessing of
dangerous wastes. You see, Miss Dean, there's a lot
of heavyweight baggage piled on the back of this
particular pony, and right at this moment Mr
Devereux's got control of the reins.'

'I seem to have fallen into very powerful
company.'

'You surely have. But let me assure you we would
have come hotfoot out to help you in any event.
You've been through a lot and the American
Embassy is delighted to help.'

The moustache bristled and twisted as if imbued
with a life of its own; she realized he was trying to
smile.

'So, Miss Dean, tell me a little about your
accident.'

And it was very little. A few second-hand details,
large gaps in the narrative, she wasn't even sure
about date and location.

'No means of identification left at all?'

'None this side of Paris.'

'Could your husband help?'

'Could. But won't. We're divorcing.'

'A friend in Paris, perhaps. The cleaner. Someone
who has the keys to your apartment and can send
on some sort of documentation?'

Izzy sat there for a moment, lost in concentration.
'I'm sure I have a cleaning lady, Mr Pomfritt.
Trouble is, I can't for the life of me remember a
thing about her.'

'Your passport number. Can you remember your
passport number, by any chance?'

'My date of birth. I can remember my date of
birth.'

The Consular Officer's moustache was wriggling

with considerably less animation. She wasn't being a lot of help. 'I see. Well, it could take a couple of days for me to sort things out. I'll need photographs from you. Have to get confirmation from the local police about particulars of the accident, send to Washington for documentary evidence of your details, that sort of thing. We need that before we are allowed to issue a replacement passport. But in the meantime I have this for you.'

From the rear of his file he extracted an envelope which bore the eagle crest of American officialdom.

'It's a letter of introduction, a temporary ID which states who you are and asks anyone with queries to check them with me at the Embassy. It's a fallback, just in case you should need it.'

'Funny,' Izzy mused, 'without an official identity it's as though you don't really exist.'

'You exist, Miss Dean, I can assure you.' The smile began revitalizing. 'Trouble is, you can't prove it!'

'There's something else I'd welcome your help in trying to prove, Mr Pomfritt.'

'Name it, ma'am.'

'My baby. They said my baby died in the crash. I just don't believe them.'

The moustache stood frozen in mid-wriggle. 'My good Lord. What are you trying to tell me?'

She picked her words hesitatingly. 'I'm . . . just not sure. You see, I think someone may have made a mistake.'

'Who?'

'I'm not sure about that either. But I don't believe the baby who died in the hospital was mine.'

'Oh, I see.' He guarded himself, expecting imminent tears. Pomfritt was a bachelor, self-reliant, occasionally gay, one who had always been too unadventurous to allow the sensibilities of a woman to gush untrammelled across the emotional desert of his neat and orderly life. 'Why do you think that, Miss Dean?'

'The baby who died in hospital had different colour hair from Bella.'

'You asked them to double check?'

'Can't. They cremated the body almost immediately after the autopsy.'

'That's ... unusual,' he conceded, picking his words with great caution. He was treading on the thin ice of bureaucratic procedures. 'But you must realize, Miss Dean, there is almost nothing we can do. Or, indeed, should do. You know, I've been in many different parts of the world and Britain has the most reliable records system of anywhere I've been, better even than the States.'

'Mr Pomfritt, I too have been in many different parts of the world, and I know mistakes can happen.'

'But in this case how? Why?'

'That I don't know. That's why I need your help.'

Pomfritt attempted to suck his moustache with his bottom lip which served to make talking difficult. 'Miss Dean, apart from the colour of the hair, why else do you think a mistake has been made?'

Izzy remained silent for a moment. This was the difficult bit.

'My son told me that Bella had been taken away. By a blonde woman.'

'Your son. Benjamin.' He indicated the sleeping infant.

She nodded.

'And what else, Miss Dean?'

She took a breath. It had to come eventually.

'Instinct.' It wasn't enough. 'And I have dreams,' she blurted, rushing it.

'Instinct. And you have dreams,' he repeated pointedly, condemning her in her own words.

That was it, wasn't it, she told herself. All of it.

'Please, Miss Dean, listen to me carefully. I want to help you, believe me I do. But the greatest help I can be is to put it to you frankly: isn't it just possible that your accident coupled with your bereavement have, in some way . . .' – he hesitated, but couldn't stifle the lisp – 'misled you? Clouded your judgement? Made you believe things you want to believe, rather than what you ought to believe?'

'It's possible. But not certain.' She felt defensive, her logic as inadequate as her evidence.

'Step outside yourself for a moment, become the journalist again. If someone came to you with a story such as this, what would be your response?'

Her head began to drop. She knew what her response would be. Reassurance. Psychiatric counselling. Tranquillizers. Scepticism. Everything they had been thrusting at her all day. Her silence spoke for itself.

'Look, why don't you think about this for a couple of days, mull it over and see if you haven't perhaps twisted things a little out of proportion. When I come back we can discuss it again. That's a promise.'

What did she have to place against such good advice? Hardly any evidence. No more than a nagging doubt that things didn't quite fit. A fluttering inside. A hope, a mystical and entirely unsound hope, that Bella might be out there. Somewhere. Somehow.

There was no point in pressing the matter. She thanked him and quickly he had gone – flapped and flown, without waiting for a second cup of tea.

* * *

It took her no time to settle in; she had nothing to unpack that didn't fit in her carrier bag, the contents of which amounted to a few toiletries, one change of clothes for them both, a plastic racing car and a cuddly rabbit with a tattered ear.

Sally showed her to their bedroom, in the original wing of the house, a seventeenth-century farm cottage with undersized rooms and low ceilings, from which the rest of the house had grown southward like a vine thrusting towards the sun. From the outside it suggested a traditional country residence; inside Devereux had modified and enlarged so that reception rooms swept on one after the other, offering light and space while retaining the ancient charms of irregular beams and inglenook fireplaces. The fruit of this architectural vine was Devereux's office, a wide semicircular room set on the southernmost end of the house offering a panoramic view across the vale in the manner that a ship's bridge might view an approaching coastline.

The house was surprising, deceptive even. Behind the solid oak doors and traditional, rose-shrouded window frames she had expected to find olde English paraphernalia – a few warming pans, much polished brass and hunting prints, a couple of retrievers, perhaps, not the original and oriental pieces that so obviously interested Devereux. She particularly liked the life-sized Burmese dancing maiden which carried the scars of two centuries with grace and still retained much of the original gilding, and wrinkled her nose in captivation at the carved wood panel with its minutely detailed carving of a young woman servicing four men at the same time. It was an ancient temple frieze, from India, she assumed. God is Love.

And God is Death. God Is. But inside Izzy, where

He might have been, there was nothing. She felt like a gutted fish.

She asked for a telephone. Sally told her Devereux had insisted she use his office, already tidied and prepared for her — it looked sparse, meticulously appointed but not a piece of paper to be seen, everything presumably fastened away behind the security locks of the tall metal filing cabinets.

From the windows she gazed across the vale. The fields stretched like patchwork, the soil newly turned, the low-lying meadows rain-sodden and flooded, the surrounding hills green, understated, very English.

With a desperate sense of urgency she wanted to be back in her own world, the one she had been so much part of and which she had left a lifetime ago. This world, the world outside these windows, was a place of gentle themes and peace, a place to recuperate, to forget. But this was not her world. And she didn't want to forget, no matter how much pain the memories carried. She reached for the phone.

Her first call was to Katti, to tell her where she was and how she could be contacted. Katti had already started checking after Bella, dragging the details out of the system, and would be back in touch. Two days, she promised.

Then she called Grubb.

'God, Izzy, how the damn are you? We've all been so worried about you,' the voice gushed.

'Sure, Ed. You've all but buried me in your concern.'

'Look, Izzy,' the foreign editor said in a lower tone, cut by her sarcasm, 'I'm sorry about the letter. Hell, you know I'm up-front about these things, if I need to chew someone out I'll do it to their face, not with some miserable letter. But ... well, you know how it is. New management. New times. New instructions.'

'And you were only obeying orders.'

'Sure,' he said, the insult flying over his head. 'But it's great that you're gonna be back in action. We really have missed you. You're our best, you know that. Couldn't do without our girl Izzy.' He was gushing again.

'So you can give me another couple of weeks.'

There was a silence.

'Two weeks, Ed. I want another two weeks, that's all.'

'But you've already got a deadline, runs out in two weeks. You want an extra two? Two and two?'

'Makes four. I'll be back in four.'

'Two, Izzy.'

'Give me another two, for Pete's sake. Until New Year. Can that be too much to ask? I need a little more time.'

'Why? You sick? You told K.C. you'd be back by Christmas.'

'No, I'm fine, getting fitter every day. But there's some things I need to take care of, Ed, after Bella's death. And Benjy needs a little more time with me.'

'Your employer needs a little more time with you, too, Izzy.' He breathed deeply, inhaling the noxious smell of motherhood. 'The big bad world out there ain't gonna wait while you play nursemaid. Hell, if it were up to me, of course. But it's not. Head office have got their own problems, and they've put it on the line. Come back in two weeks or ... not at all.'

'Generous bunch, our bosses.'

'They think so. You stuck your rump in the air when you took off like that, and by rights they should have shot it off before now. Look, I know it's been hitting you from all sides; K.C. told me about the divorce. I'm sorry.' It was an inadequate word but the only one he could find; he was notoriously bad at the personal touch. 'But your disappearing act was damned unprofessional, Izzy, and you know it.'

It hurt. He was right and it hurt. How could she explain that she'd felt desperate for the chance to get away and clear her head, to escape from Grubb, from the phone, from Joe, from the deadlines, from the incessant pressure, and find out what really mattered to her? On a good day the foreign editor might understand, but he would never forgive. Pressure was part of the game, the stimulant, not the excuse.

She had always regarded herself as the ultimate professional who believed passionately in her duty to deliver news and to do it better than the next man. They had told her it wasn't a job for a woman, but she refused to accept that her sex was of any material consequence. Except when she was pregnant, of course. A Muslim cameraman in Yugoslavia had declined to work with her when he discovered she was several months down the road and, in spite of her anger and insinuations that he was more afraid of mortars than a miscarriage, he'd stiffly maintained his refusal.

And she knew he had been right. It did make a difference; it had to.

There had been Bulgaria. The frantic trip to the nuclear power station which seemed to have been constructed of sandbags and old drainpipe and had blown almost as badly as Chernobyl. Twenty miles from the plant, as they had entered an infants school which the authorities had still not evacuated, their Geiger counter had started complaining like a stuck pig. They had stayed to film anyway, no more than twenty minutes, and within a week of her report going on air the school and all its children had been moved to uncontaminated pastures many miles away. But it had given her a radiation dose equivalent to more than five times the recommended full year exposure.

No problem, the limits are deliberately cautious, the doctor had assured her – except when she missed her next period and they discovered she was pregnant.

'Not what we would recommend, but I'm sure there's nothing to worry about,' he had told her with the fixed, insincere smile which doctors practise on nurses before turning on their patients. The smile had grown considerably more relaxed and genuine when, a few weeks later, she had miscarried what would have been her first child.

'It's for the best, you know. Didn't want to worry you, but I was anxious about all those millisieverts you'd been hit with. Never can tell what will happen to a foetus after that sort of thing. Forget about it. Give yourself a rest for a couple of months and then start all over again.'

And she had, at the same time dispensing with the services of a condescending male doctor who couldn't bring himself to trust a woman with the truth about her own body.

She had found it considerably less easy to deal with the pain which the miscarriage had brought. Not just the trickle of blood grown to searing physical pain that twisted and tore and tormented her inside, leaving her lathered with sweat and utterly exhausted in a heap on the bathroom floor, but the emotional wounds that would never heal. The guilt that could never be erased. The baby that could never be reborn.

She had compromised, thinking of today, of

herself, trying to balance dreams of professional success against those of motherhood. She told herself that her work had saved the lives of countless children – at the school in Bulgaria, in the besieged cities of Yugoslavia, in the camps of Southern Africa and on killing fields around the world.

But it had cost the life of her first baby. The miscarriage was her responsibility. Maybe.

Now she was responsible for the death of Bella. Maybe.

There were beginning to be altogether too many maybes in her life.

There were no maybes with Grubb. He was unmistakably clear about her body. Have it parked back on location within two weeks, or not at all. Kiev or kids. Media star or motherhood. The balancing act was over, she was going to have to choose.

The ornate, hand-blocked wallpaper with its heavy Tudor motif gave the small room a gloomy aspect. Behind the palatial scrubbed stone exterior there were few Members' offices in the House of Commons with any style or hint of magnificence, and certainly this was not one of them. A desk, a couple of chairs, a filing cabinet that doubled as a lock-up for bottles, an undernourished hide sofa. Even swift and fast-improving steeds like Devereux had to wait their turn behind the old parliamentary warhorses, long ago put out to grass and living off cobwebbed memories of when it had been *their* time.

They should be shot, put down, out of their misery, he had long ago concluded. Not for him the lingering death of an elder statesman, waiting in desperation for the telephone to ring, for someone to remember. Devereux would go up. Or out. Up to the very summit decreed by his talents and ambitions, if his luck held, out to some new and well-grassed pasture if it did not.

He had made preparations. His diaries. Memoirs in the making and easy pickings at that. An advance of a hundred thousand in exchange for patronizing and poisonous reviews in the Sunday book sections, two hundred if he named names and times and treasons and revealed who screwed whom and how.

God knows, he needed the money after the destruction his father had wrought upon the family's fortunes, but memoirs were one-off, unrepeatable. There were other, more incisive ways to catch the financial tide, particularly with his newly established credibility on matters of defence. A few well-placed consultancies. A splicing together of contracts. A facilitator's fee of modest percentage paid into a bank account of indecipherable anonymity. Using what he was already learning and would continue to discover so long as he remained in post. Another reason for giving the Americans a damned hard time but, in the end, giving them what they wanted.

The Duster.

They would remember, and recognize his value, if the time ever came.

He wondered what she would remember. What was her name? – Rosalinde. The tall, elegant, tight-breasted wife of the Transport Secretary. Or, rather, the former Transport Secretary. She was a Westminster wife, more ambitious than he and infinitely more corruptible, utterly unforgiving that he, and therefore she, was now numbered amongst the living dead. 'Like wandering through the catacombs of Rome,' as she had put it, 'and never being able to find the door.'

Devereux had brushed into her along the Library

Corridor. She had been reeking of Givenchy and gin, drifting between receptions and anxious once again to be touched by the trappings of power. And he had touched her, there, on his parliamentary sofa as, in that grating Sloane voice of hers, she had whispered venomous disloyalties about inadequacies, political and physical, of her husband.

She had approached sex like an election-night count, rushing through the initial tally more rapidly than seemed possible only to demand an immediate recount. Incredibly dominant female, constantly wittering about his massive majority. It had been all but beyond him.

It was only after sex that her true seduction began, building from vows to be rid of her encumbrance of a husband through outpourings of her long-standing admiration for her new lover and climaxing in protestations of her desire to see more, much more, of Devereux.

He had told her of his suspicions that her tits were as false as her loyalties and had thrown her out. Almost invariably he had humiliated and discarded every woman he'd ever known. Yet still they came back; or, at least, a certain type of woman did. Those attracted to power, who could only reach orgasm on a front page.

He took little pride in such sterile passion, the adulation and easy conquests. He recognized his trait for what it was. Failure. His failure, though not his fault. Like father, like son, he heard himself mutter, tasting bile. He washed it away with a mouthful of Scotch.

He looked across the room to the dark oil painting behind his desk, the portrait of his father that had hung in every office he'd occupied since entering Parliament. It lied, like all portraits. The face was imposing, as was his father's, even if the artist had shaded the most unkind ravages of time and alcohol which had spattered his father's cheeks. But the eyes were not those of his father. The eyes depicted in the painting were clear, forthright, staring directly at Devereux in a way his father had never done. His father had never been able to hold his gaze or return the affection offered by the child. At first Devereux had imagined it was because his father had no love for him; only later did he realize that his father was too ashamed to face his only son and look him in the eye.

Perhaps it was because of the dog. Scarcely more than a puppy. A token – as it turned out, the final token – from his dying mother. And it had fouled the rug. His father had been looking for a target, that afternoon it was the dog, and the father's hunting boot had driven into the animal several times before Devereux's desperate lunge had placed his own body between boot and dog. And for a while the father had seemed not to notice the difference.

There had been damage to the dog, perhaps a dislocated hind leg, and the boy had been instructed to leave his whimpering dog in the stables. That cold night, in defiance of his father's explicit instruction, the young Devereux had crept out to comfort it.

Discovery had perhaps been inevitable; the consequences less so. As the child cowered amongst soiled straw, clutching his pet, pleading with his father, the animal had been wrenched from his terrified arms. Towering above him, the father had dangled the dog by the scruff of its neck. Then, accompanied by a savage snapping sound, the neck had been broken. A stifled yelp of innocence, a twitch. And a relentless, unforgiving anger that would wash away any future moment on which his father might be tempted to offer trust or love.

It had not been the only cruelty, but it had been more than enough.

The father disgusted even himself with his increasingly frequent and irrational outbursts of wrath that would send the son scurrying in terror from the sound of his approaching footsteps, but the rages proved to be beyond anyone's control. Particularly after the mother's death.

Living with an alcoholic father created many wounds, even a father who climbed so high. And fell so far. It had condemned Devereux to a life spent taunting his father's ghost, yet at the same time trying to escape from it. He hated his father with a fixity of purpose which, otherwise directed, might have built empires. He hated his father for not being what he might have been, someone to respect, to honour, to teach him love. There had never been love in the Devereux family, not after his mother had deserted him, opted out, by dying. After that it had been an expensive school, all male, where the only regular female contact was with matrons and cleaning women. Servants. Nothing to teach him respect for women, only for power.

Devereux knew his ill-formed emotions were a grievous fault, even as he indulged them. He had built a life in the mirror-image of his father. He drank, sometimes to excess, but not to dependency, and every time he put away a half-empty bottle was another little victory over his father's weakness. He had entered Parliament, where his every political victory mocked his father's failure. He had achieved his father's ministerial position. And now he would surpass it.

And he had his own family. Devereux had sworn

protection to his family with the intensity with which his father had offered only abuse. A childhood of fear, of being betrayed, was not what Devereux would inflict on his own child. His love might be imperfect but unlike his own father's it would be given without question, the new generation contemptuously rejecting the old.

Yet, as he had come to know, even in a father's unquestioning love there could be danger. And dishonour.

As he looked up, his father's lips seemed to sneer.

The bass guitarist stank. But to be truthful so did the entire band, a desperately fashionable post-heavy metal funk 'n' fuck affair which tried to drown its deficit of talent in an excess of volume. The bass guitarist was the worst. He had completely lost it in the middle of a complicated riff and, fumbling, had attempted to cover his ineptitude with the visual extravagance of throwing his guitar high above his head.

Perhaps it had been the glare of the lights, or the sweat in his eyes, or simply the head full of smack. In any event his coordination was way off. The tumbling instrument had evaded his flailing hands and struck him directly on the bridge of the nose. Practically killed the bastard. The audience screamed hysterically as the cameramen closed in for the full effect.

Michelini laughed, for the first time that day, a sound that implied no humour. He'd been flicking idly through the cable channels and picking at slices of belly pork from the Cantonese take-away, trying to fill the hole in his life. It had been one of those days. A cancelled meeting on the Hill, stood up by his date for dinner, time to brood and to remember.

It was one of those empty evenings when he could no longer hide behind the macho male frontage, and he felt very much alone.

It was her fault, of course, and somehow when the phone rang he knew it was she.

'Joe. How are you?'

He offered little beyond an indecipherable grunt.

'We have to talk, Joe.'

'I'm listening. But I'm busy,' he barked, commencing another attack with his chopsticks. 'What is it?'

'It's about Bella. There may have been a mistake, I think she may not be dead.'

There was nothing but silence, a crushing silence of incredulity and anger. She felt her confidence draining away.

'Benjy says she's not dead, Joe, that she was taken away by some woman. I know it sounds far-fetched but . . . The post-mortem. It was wrong. The hair colour. But we can't check because they've locked away the file and . . . Oh, Joe, I'm so confused.' She was losing control; it was so unlike Izzy. 'I need your help,' she added. That was unlike Izzy, too.

'How?'

She wanted to say that she needed his love and comfort because she felt hurt and so very much alone, and he wanted to hear it, but they both knew there was no point.

'Money. Send some money, Joe. Right away. I need to buy clothes, to look after Benjy, until I can get my credit cards and everything else sorted out. I need time, to find out what the hell is going on.'

If hearing her voice had made him smoulder, her demands turned him to incandescence. Savagely he pushed away the stir-fry. 'The only thing you'll get from me is the price of a one-way ticket back to the

States so I can be sure you stop dragging that poor damned kid of ours around. He needs to be back home, not dumped in some foreign backwater.'

'But Joe, there's something wrong. I know it, I can feel it. I can't leave here just yet, not until I know.'

'Then send Benjy back.'

'To you? And you'll let me have him back when I return.'

'You're crazy.'

'Joe, let's try and be reasonable about this. Put the divorce and everything to one side, just for the moment. Bella may not be dead.'

Her words were tearing at him. He ached for certainty, for the simplicity of bereavement. He could handle that, through his anger, but not this. Alive. Dead. Despair. Doubt. Hope. She was toying with him.

'What in God's name are you trying to do with me?' he responded plaintively, his anger for the moment blunted by confusion.

She told him what she knew. What very little she knew. And felt. As she spoke she realized how inadequate it still all seemed and how unconvinced he remained, like Pomfritt. And, yes, she had raised it with the doctors.

'What did they suggest?'

'Tranquillizers.'

That he believed. He sighed. 'Why don't you come home, Izzy?'

'I can't. Not until I know. I'm staying here.' Resisting him. As ever, stubborn.

'And where is here?'

She told him, and the name seemed to grow until it had filled all his emptiness inside. Paul Devereux's. *The* Paul Devereux's.

An image came into Michelini's mind. Of a plane.

In flames. Crashing. A plume of smoke and debris. Dust.

She had destroyed his family, of that he was sure; now, through her interference and neurotic behaviour, she could end up doing the same damned thing to his career.

'We have to find out the truth,' she was saying.

'The truth, Izzy, is staring you in the eyes. It's simply that you refuse to face up to it. Bella is dead. You killed her in a car smash, and now you're trying to concoct some unmitigated crap to explain away your guilt.'

'But they may have made a mistake . . .'

'For Chrissake! People like that don't make mistakes.'

'Benjy says . . .'

'Benjy's not even three years old. The poor kid might say anything after what you put him through. And mixing up bodies in a morgue – neurotic nonsense!' He snorted in contempt. 'Think, woman. Stop trying to fool yourself. Accept the fact. It was your damn fault!'

'Be reasonable.'

'You be reasonable. Put Benjy on a plane back home.'

'No.'

'Send him back.'

'Never!'

'Then I'll see you in court.'

And the phone went dead.

She sat alone in the night, her world wrapped in darkness, bewitched by her sense of guilt, her need for an excuse – any excuse, other than the obvious. A torrent of uncertainties emerged like demons from the mists of her overwrought mind: could they all be wrong? The psychologist? The mortuary technician?

Weatherup? The Consular Officer? Grubb? And Joe? How much more likely that they were right, that she was being absurdly emotional, distracted, deceiving no one but herself? Made distraught by grief and guilt?

Yet there remained one fragment of certainty that no one could refute. In the morning, when the first rays of sunlight and sense came to chase away the demons of the night, she would be there, alone. Without Bella. That certainty set against their doubts.

She tore herself away from the study and its morbid perspectives and began slowly to walk around the house, running her hands over the furniture, touching, feeling the need to stay in contact with what was solid and undeniably real. In the corner of the great hall stood a grand piano and she sat down on the stool, laying her fingers on the keys. She'd always loved the piano, yearned to play, yet suddenly she had no memory of whether she could. Had desire ever made contact with reality? Bizarre. She couldn't remember. That part of the brain which held those memories was still fumbling, dropping the pieces, creating confusion. She might not recall whether she could play, but surely she could never forget the art of playing?

She emptied her mind, allowing instinct to take over. She raised her hands high above the keyboard, prepared herself, let herself go, allowing her fingers to fall where they would.

The result was a discord of jumbled notes and noise.

For the first time since the accident she began to laugh. Of course she hadn't learned to play, never had the time. Bloody ridiculous. She was deluding herself. About the piano. About Bella.

And the laughter took hold and gripped her, and turned to tears. Of loss. Of guilt. Of pain and the anguish of bereavement. The tears turned to a flood of weeping as at last she began to submit to her misery and shame, to release her despairing grip on the false hopes and fanciful explanations, to come to terms with her folly.

She had lost.

It was many minutes before she could begin to compose herself, to dry the tears, trying to find comfort in the feeling that at last she had unshackled herself from the evil spirits of doubt that had so plagued her. As the mists in front of her eyes cleared, she began to see the real world again; her fumbling fingers, the keys, the piano in its dutifully polished walnut case and, on it, the decorative silver frames with their melody of family images.

A wedding scene with a younger Devereux and a statuesque but somehow vulnerable bride.

A baby wrapped in christening clothes.

A man who bore more than a passing resemblance to Devereux shaking hands outside Number Ten Downing Street with Harold Macmillan.

Devereux in court clothes bowing before his Queen.

And the photograph of a man and a teenage girl on a tropical beach, posing as any father and gangling daughter would in swimsuits and sun hats, looking overly pink and uncomfortably English.

It took her paralysed mind what seemed an age for the memories to stop passing by on the other side, to reach out and make the connection. The man, of course, was Devereux, ten years younger but the unmistakable lean frame and self-confident air. And beneath the shoulder of the doting father nestled the fledgling, soon to be of an age to fly the parental nest, the form beginning to fill and grow more feminine, the figure already setting aside the ungainly architecture of youth for the statuesque heights of early adulthood.

And, beneath the straw boater with pink ribbon, a cascade of shoulder-length hair glistened blonde in the sun and fell around a face that, though not yet flawed and drained, was nonetheless *that* face. The face infecting her dreams.

The skin, youthfully fragile, that would turn to dried parchment. The eyes, bashful before the camera lens, not yet tinged with fear. The lips, dried in the sun, that would one day grow thin and cracked and come to sneer at Izzy as she lay in her hospital bed. The long, thin fingers that would snatch at Bella.

Her nightmare had returned, and now she could almost touch it.

FOUR

Friday. Devereux was delivered home late that night by his Ministerial car and its Special Branch driver. Izzy had retired but was not yet asleep – how could she sleep? From a biographical dictionary taken from the shelves in his study she had identified many of the new pieces, for there are few private pieces in a public life.

Outside Downing Street, the father: *'Rt Hon Sir Francis Nugent Devereux, Kt, PC, MP; MC; b 1914, d 1966; o s of Patrick Nugent Devereux, qv; Educ: Eton; Jesus Coll. Oxford . . . Minister of Education (1955–57); Pensions (1957–60); President, Board of Trade (1960–62); Minister of Defence (Apr–July 1962).'*

After July 1962 there was nothing but his death. A beginning steeped in both privilege and prospects which had led to an end as sudden and complete as the progress had been glittering. Illness, perhaps.

There was a mother, too, bride of Francis Nugent, who had died young, with Paul no older than ten.

And under Paul Devereux's own listing a wife: *'m 1970, Arlene Fitch-Little (d 1980) . . . '*

Tragedy and early death seemed to run in the family, at least through the women. And he had never remarried. Only one child, a dau. *'Paulette, b 1974.'* It didn't state that she had blonde hair or large, frightened eyes and was last seen holding a baby, it didn't have to. She was the right age, early twenties, from the right family. A daughter named after himself, in his own likeness, the child an extension of the father. She wondered just how alike they might be.

Yet again she told herself that she was submerged in self-delusion, the daughter was no more than an image in a dream. But the dream was a nightmare, inextricably intertwined with her other nightmare centred upon Bella's death. Or disappearance. Somewhere, deep within the jumbled recesses of her mind, a connection was being made which she did not yet understand but whose message was unmistakable. Find his daughter; find her own.

Yet, if the Devereuxs were involved, why, for God's sake why, had he invited her into his home?

It was easier to believe in concealment than coincidence, but concealment of what? Shame? Guilt? His daughter? There were secrets in this family which hid the truth not only about themselves but also about Bella.

Yet what was she to do? To confront? To run? She had nothing to confront him with and, if he were concealing something, she had much more chance of revealing it by staying close than by leaving. So long as he did not know she suspected. Anyway, where could she run?

And perhaps he, too, was merely a victim of circumstance, a player trapped as innocently as she within a web that seemed to be enmeshing their two families. It was not a time for rushing to judgement.

She slept fitfully, uncertain whether she had accepted his hospitality or entrapment, whether his hand was extended in charity or restraint, and it was the following evening before she had an opportunity even to talk to him. Saturday was no day of rest for a politician; he had left the house early and was clearly wearied by the time he returned.

He disappeared into his study accompanied by a tumbler full of whisky, not reappearing for a full twenty minutes. When he did so, he seemed more relaxed, the tension gone from his shoulders, as though he had undergone some form of therapeutic treatment. Cleansed, almost. He noticed her inquisitive expression.

'My diary. I keep a political diary. Wonderfully invigorating. Like war. Loading the ammunition, aiming the guns at targets which don't even know they're in the firing line, waiting to blast them out of the water – when the time is right.' He adopted an expression of well-rehearsed theatrical gravity. 'In reality political diaries are a pathetic attempt by their authors to secure immortality, to record the lies they wish they had told at the time rather than the lies they actually told, to claim the triumphs of others for themselves and to distribute the fruits of failure as widely as possible amongst their colleagues.' His blue eyes lit with amusement. 'Helps keep me sane.'

The eyes lingered on her, longer than was necessary for the appreciation of the joke, still amused, challenging.

'How about I take you to dinner – unless you've made other arrangements, of course?'

He knew she hadn't.

'Sally will keep an eye on the sprog,' he offered.

She was exhausted, had no appetite, but Benjy was sleeping soundly and she did not hesitate.

Le Petit Canard was a small French-Canadian restaurant, an oddity in the back lanes of Wessex, situated in an old coaching inn at the ancient crossroads which bisected the village of Maiden Newton. She wondered who had been the Maiden Newton, and why they had named an entire village after her.

The plaster was old and crumbly, the beams low and the cedar wood fire filled the air with a musky fragrance. The cuisine was exceptional, a mixture of Pacific-rim creations, reflecting the chef's extended and adventurous youth spent dressing poultry and impressing waitresses in a dozen different ports.

The chef's wife, who was in charge of the liquid side of affairs, proffered a wine list, but Izzy declined. A fine vintage could achieve many wonders; repairing brain damage and unscrambling the mind were scarcely amongst them. So Devereux had agreed to split the bottle with the chef's wife, with whom he spent several animated moments discussing the merits of an '85 Vosne-Romanée, Suchots – 'lovely legs, lots of flesh, goes a long way', as the tasting notes pointed out – and an '86 Cabernet Sauvignon from the Californian Napa Valley – 'Nosegasm'. He chose the American wine.

'In your honour,' he revealed to Izzy. 'Oh, and a bottle of Dorset sparkling water,' he insisted. 'Has to be home grown, one of the Prime Minister's great passions. Water. Though on reflection, perhaps nowadays it's his only great passion,' he added in a tone that she took as almost contemptuous dismissal of his leader. He was confiding in her, sharing secrets, drawing her in. As the great cedar fire had diminished, he had grown mellow. And perhaps a little vulnerable.

In another corner sat a couple, he with wedding ring, she without, all eyes and ovaries. For a wistful moment Izzy reflected on how long it had been since she had been part of that chase, out to impress, to kill, to make herself irresistible. Too long. Quickly she thrust the thought out of her mind.

'Your new job must be exhausting,' she offered weakly.

'Exhilarating. More exhilarating than exhausting.' He poured another glass of wine, well over his fair share of the bottle, relaxing. 'And I've many family reasons for wanting this in particular. My father once held this same position, more than thirty years ago, and I feel as if I have to . . .' He was about to say 'bury a few ghosts' but instead chose to mutter some homily about finishing his father's work.

'How's the Duster?'

'Ah, at work, are we?' He raised a disapproving brow. The wine was getting to him, lending an exaggerated edge to his character.

'No, not at all. But more than idle curiosity. I, too, have family connections. My husband is deeply involved in the project.'

'Mmmm,' he considered. 'And tell me. Are you very deeply involved in your husband?' he asked bluntly. 'Or is that too rude a question?'

'Not particularly. And probably. In that order.'

'Small world,' he said reflectively. 'That your family and mine should cross paths so . . . A very small world.' He swirled the dark red liquid around his glass, lingering on its aroma before drinking deep. 'So, the Duster. To you professionally, Miss Dean, I offer an absolutely frank and forthright "No comment". But to you privately, Izzy . . . ? We're making progress. Nothing more, but certainly no less. It's now down to the politics of it rather than the finances, and since political positions come cheap, I'm confident the deal will be done. Your husband should be content.'

He had flattered her with a confidence, but Izzy struck him as being remarkably underwhelmed by the news. Her mind seemed elsewhere.

'Talking of family,' she asked, 'was that your father? Amongst the photographs on your piano?'

He nodded.

'And your wife, I assume.'

'My wife died. Many years ago.'

'I'm sorry.'

His mood had grown sombre; she felt she was intruding. But she could not stop.

'And your daughter?'

He became more animated, wanting to say more, seemingly unable to find the appropriate words. 'My daughter . . . lives away from home.' And no more until: 'Families can be a rock, Izzy, on which you build your life. Or on which your whole life is dashed.' There was a heaviness in his reply which discouraged further questioning, as though a great weight were about to topple and crush him. She did not doubt that his pain was genuine.

'You must be very lonely at times.' She didn't mean it to sound like a come-on, but she hadn't intended to feel sympathy for him, either.

'There are . . . compensations. My job, for one.' He made a conscious effort to lift his mood. 'And distractions. I'm well connected. A widower. My own house. Nice car.' He was mocking himself. 'Some women seem to find that . . .'

'Intriguing?' she suggested.

The blue eyes were looking directly at her now, searching, challenging; he was delighted when she returned his stare. She wasn't going to back down, run away. The point had been made, his interests registered; he changed the subject.

'Tell me, why did you choose your career? Unusual job for a woman.'

What a question. How could she tell him? She wasn't sure herself. A fascination with Man's folly? Admiration at his ambitions and achievements? Folly, it was more the folly, the soaring heights which leaders and nations coveted and the pride, the hubris which always brought them low. And her conviction that the world needed to know about it all, whether the world gave a damn or not. Usually not.

But it was more than that. She remembered it clearly. The day shortly before Christmas, 1968.

It was a time when America was preparing to set foot on the Moon and was about to reach its nadir in Vietnam. Richard Nixon had just been elected President, a man who would reach for unprecedented heights around the world, breaking down the doors of Communism, yet whose folly and false pride would bring him wretchedly low. A time of inspiration and involvement, of earthquakes which brought down political mountains around the globe.

But that was not what she remembered. Izzy was little more than ten, a schoolgirl living a comfortable but undistinguished life in an undistinguished suburb of Respectability, Mid-America.

It had been a quiet day. Too quiet. Izzy had known something was amiss, her normally tranquil mother was increasingly enveloped in agitation, but her gentle enquiries had been rebuffed and Izzy herself increasingly ignored, until shortly before the lunch hour. Izzy remembered being borne along, unnoticed, in the turbulent wake as her mother moved from the kitchen towards the dental surgery that Izzy's father had built on the side of their undistinguished clapboard house. Her mother had swept past the empty desk where the recently hired receptionist should have been, where files and dental charts lay abandoned, and through the door that led to the surgical inner sanctum – the mother, agitated, unaware that the child was following; Izzy, unsighted, having difficulty in seeing around the back of the large dental chair, able only to glimpse her father's bald head protruding above it, ruddy and flushed, his legs astride. The child had barely enough time to wonder why those legs wore only socks and suspenders. She was quite unable to comprehend why a separate pair of naked legs appeared to be hooked over her father's shoulders.

All that Christmas they had sat in silence, watching the tree and the marriage dying. By New Year it was separate bedrooms.

Izzy had adored her father, his smile, his laughing eyes, the enchanting and extravagant tales he told while seated on the end of her bed, weaving pictures of another world that lay beyond mundane Respectability. And she had never again trusted a man in authority.

'Jules Verne,' Izzy addressed Devereux. 'It was bloody Jules Verne who made me become a foreign correspondent. Loved his books. Read them all. Hated him because the only role he gave to women was to wave their hankies and wait patiently at home while the menfolk went off round the world in search of adventure.'

'He was a Frenchman,' Devereux responded, as if that explained all shortcomings.

'Are Englishmen any different?'

'Some are,' he mused. 'How many have you known?'

'My grandfather,' she replied, deflecting his innuendo. 'He was English. From this part of the country. That's why I came here. I think. Something about going back to my roots, trying to find out who I really am, and what matters most to me.'

'Perceptive of you. We can't escape our roots. Links in a long, unending chain, you know, one generation to the next. We can twist ourselves, change the shape a little, but in the end so much of us is what we were born. That's why we blame our parents; why we bear so much responsibility for our own children. They are what we have made them.'

His voice had grown very subdued, his eyes more watery and distant. For the first time, Izzy sensed he was revealing a little of his inner self. He carried his family obligations like a great load that had bent his back and, at times, brought him low. She had sympathized with him, now she could identify with him.

'You sound . . . almost as if you have lost your children.'

'I have only one. My daughter.'

Izzy could feel a coil winding within her.

'And our relationship is not what I would want.' He clenched his jaws, keeping tight rein on himself. Stiff upper lip. 'My fault, probably. Too busy for her problems. She needed a mother; perhaps I should have remarried, but . . .' He shrugged. 'Hasn't lived at home for a long time. Funny things, families.'

The damp blue eyes swam with pain and he reached out for support, to draw strength from her. She let his hand remain on hers; he had touched something inside her, too. They were two lonely people, sharing pain about something they had in common and cared very much for. Family.

She knew he wanted her. And she hadn't the slightest idea how she would respond.

'Tell me about your daughter.'

The question hung over them. He stared fixedly, remembering, struggling with something. Then a door closed inside. He sat up straight and withdrew his hand.

'No, not now.' He shook his head as though to clear it of sorrows. 'Perhaps later.'

He had taken control once more and she knew it would be foolish to press him, for the moment, at least. As he said: later.

'Later' came as he opened the creaking oak door which led into the great hall of his home. The long room was lit only by the glow of a banked fire in the inglenook. As they entered he took her wrist, turned her, brought her into his arms, and she did not resist, even when his lips sought hers. She wanted him, even though she could not trust him.

His body pressed into her, she could feel him hardening, his hands moving round from her back to find the softness of her breasts. No objection – how long had it been since someone had sought her like this, since she had smelt the heat of a man? She needed him, too. For all sorts of things.

But most of all for Bella.

Was his attention cover-up? Or coincidence? Her suspicions struggled with her lust.

'Paul . . .' She drew her head back, but his tongue still pursued her. She had to test him, not knowing how, confused by her own feelings. His body was still hard against her.

'I'm not sure I'm ready for this. So soon after the accident.'

'You're ready. I can feel you're ready.'

'Perhaps we should get to know each other a little better,' she whispered, but her body displayed no such caution, pressed into him, egging him on. He was right, she was ready. And he was on fire, youthfully impatient. He would have her on the nearest chair.

'I need a little more time,' she gasped as his fingers manoeuvred like scouts across a battlefield. Soon she would have let him go too far easily to stop him, if he insisted. 'I want to help you, Paul, with everything.' A button gave way and rattled across the floor. 'Everything, Paul.' Time to test him. 'Even with your daughter, Paulette.'

And against her she felt his desire ebb. The moment was gone.

'Izzy, we're both consenting adults, let's be realistic. God's sake, you're going home. Now *is* the time, the only time. Or was.'

He attempted a smile as she adjusted her clothing.

'Don't worry,' he added, 'I do understand. Hope I haven't embarrassed you.' The English gentleman again.

'Maybe there is time, Paul. I'm not sure I should rush anything. Even going back home.'

'What?'

'I might stay.'

In the darkness it was difficult to see the anxiety creep across his face, but she felt him tense. Then he drew back and there was no contact.

'I'm told you're making excellent progress. Surely home is the best place. Complete your recovery.'

'Home is where the pressure is. And the job. I could do with the break. Just a week or so longer.'

'I'm really not sure that would be wise, Izzy. The doctors know best, you should listen to them. Home for Christmas.'

'Maybe.'

His tone was moderate, reasonable, in no way threatening, but in the spitting embers of the fire his eyes seemed wine spilled, a little bloodshot, their liquid turned incandescent. The fire spat once more, casting harsh shadows across his face.

There was a silence, filled only by the scythe-like ticking of the great clock that echoed off flagstones and rebounded from hard plaster walls, counting down to the next move in what had become their game.

She moved her body back towards him, within his reach, offering. He did not respond.

She had to be sure.

She moved again, closer still. This time he retreated.

'Staying on would create difficulties, I'm afraid,' he was saying. 'I have house guests arriving in little more than a week; it would not be possible for you to stay on longer here. I'm sorry.'

'Of course, I understand. You have already been more than generous. Perhaps I could find a small hotel . . .'

'Unless you have sorted out your finances, that will be difficult. Sadly our social services couldn't help. Very restrictive rules. Surely the thing to do is to return home, Izzy, sort everything out there, rather than hanging on in this country without any visible means of support. Living in clothes which have been begged or borrowed, camping in a draughty seaside hotel. And over Christmas? Not what you are used to, I'm sure. Or Benjamin. I hear he's finding it difficult to adjust.'

He was as accurate as he was well informed. Inevitably Benjy had been badly scarred by the sudden disappearance of those he loved most, and the return of his mother had served only to increase his confusion and apprehension that she might desert him once again. His sleep was fitful, riddled with anxiety that she might leave; his waking hours were spent either clinging to her or fretting for her return. Every time she left the room he was anxious, when they parted he was in tears, at night he woke and screamed until she was there to comfort him. A hotel would be a terrible idea.

'Perhaps you're right. Let's see what the doctors say on Monday.'

'Of course. I'm so sorry I can't be of any further help to you.'

But, without intending it, he had. His conviction in urging her to return to the States had been as inflexible yet as persuasive and moderately argued as his original invitation to Bowminster. Confronted with the choice between her body and her departure, he had not hesitated. He wanted her gone. No man she had ever known would have done the same. Devereux was lover turned gamekeeper.

Locking her out.

He was a player in this game, trying to move her around like a pawn on a board. She knew none of the game's rules, didn't comprehend its objective, yet as long as the prize was the truth about Bella she knew there was no alternative but to play.

She also knew that, if he had taken the risk of offering her his home, it must have been because the risk of leaving her in Weschester was still greater. She didn't know what she was looking for but now, at least, she thought she knew where to look.

The inspector at Weschester Constabulary smiled as she and Benjamin were shown into his cluttered office. But men always smiled at her. The secret was to know when they meant it.

She had telephoned for an interview and it had been readily granted – one of the more productive calls she'd made that morning. Katti was uncontactable, no one seemed to know where she was. The credit card company had been difficult when she was unable to give them detailed information such as the number of her card, in any event the account was based in the United States 'and, madam, you really should have reported the loss at the time, not weeks later. That's your legal responsibility, you know.' The girl on the other end of the phone didn't seem to understand the meaning of the word coma, responding as if she were on the verge of one herself, but eventually informed Izzy that she might be held liable for any misuse of the card since its loss and could pick up a replacement tomorrow at a local bank. Izzy had been unable to get through to the editor of the local newspaper, who didn't appear to surface much before lunch, so she had left a message accompanied by her WCN credentials expressing the hope that he might have time to see her later that afternoon.

She had used the bus to cover the fifteen miles between Bowminster and Weschester; Chinnery's constant scowl depressed her, and she didn't care for him or others to know what she was about.

Along with the inspector's smile Izzy and her son were offered machine-dispensed coffee and Coke in plastic cups and a homily about how local authority cuts had denied the police vital investigative tools such as fresh tea and biscuits. The station had an air of Victorian gentility about it, no Yankee hustle, no chaos of suspects being dragged inside to account for their crimes, no wailing of sirens or protestations of innocence and, apparently, no kitchen. But, she had noticed, there was a brewery next door.

The inspector listened attentively, sipping tea in between his attempts to inflict further damage with his teeth upon the end of a much-mangled pencil. He did not take notes.

'I can't be specific, Inspector, but something is – I don't know how best to describe it – going on. I want your help in tracing the truth about my baby.'

'I see,' he mused. 'And you think Paulette Devereux may be at the bottom of it?'

'Of course, I have absolutely no proof, but . . .'

'That's right, you don't. Let me ask you a few further questions, about the accident. In fact, that's why I thought you were coming to see me.'

'I spoke to one of your constables in hospital.'

'Yes, I know. We were rather hoping your memory might have improved somewhat. After all, it was a serious affair, someone was killed.'

'That's what I'm not sure about . . .'

'But you are sure you were driving?'

She nodded hesitantly. 'I must have been.'

'How was the accident caused?'

'You know that already. Apparently the car went off the road. No one seems to know quite why.'

'No other vehicles involved, no collision?'

She shook her head. 'I simply can't remember.'

'You see, Miss Dean, I have a problem. A baby was killed in a car accident with no apparent cause in which you were the driver.' The pencil was pointing directly at her. 'That makes you liable to be charged with death by dangerous driving. Unless you can find some reason to explain the accident.'

'But what about my baby . . . ?' she gasped, taken aback by the suddenness of the assault.

'Let me put it to you bluntly, Miss Dean. You are faced with potentially very serious charges to which you have no answer, pleading amnesia. Instead you blame everyone else, from the doctors who saved your life to the hospital mortician. You even seem to accuse our local MP and his daughter of some unspecified crime which involves spiriting off the very baby for whose death you are alleged to be responsible.' The pencil snapped in two. 'By the way, aren't you staying at Mr Devereux's house?'

How did he know . . . ?

'Your accusations might strike some as lacking a certain gratitude, don't you think?'

'Inspector, I came to you for help in clearing up what has happened to my child.' She was flustered. The sudden tension in the office had caused Benjy, until then patiently sitting in his mother's lap, to start wriggling, and she lunged to prevent his drink spilling down the front of her dress. She was doing battle on two fronts at once; Clausewitz would not have approved.

'You have other responsibilities, Miss Dean, to your surviving child. Our law is very protective about impecunious parents subjecting children to unnecessary hardship, and overstaying your welcome in these parts might be deemed by our social services to be just such an unnecessary hardship.'

'I am not impecunious!' she snapped.

'No, I'm sure you're not. But I want to remove as much possibility for misunderstanding from this matter as I can. You have already caused far too much. Some might even deem your accusations to suggest a measure of instability on your part – temporary, I am sure, the after-effects of your medical condition, an understandable depression. But enough to cause good people concern about the welfare of little Benjamin here. They might feel it wise to consider taking him into care.'

'What are you trying to do to me?'

'It's what you are doing to yourself, Miss Dean. Can you not see that?'

'You won't help me search for my baby?'

'There is nothing to search for. Forgive me, but I have a hospital report, a death certificate, reports from the autopsy and the Coroner's Office, even a certificate of cremation, all testifying to the fact that your baby *is dead*. You refuse to believe it but haven't a single shred of evidence. The obvious answer is that your medical condition is adversely affecting you, and may therefore be endangering the welfare of your child.'

'You are not taking Benjamin away from me. Never!'

'The alternative proposition is that you are deliberately seeking to confuse matters in order to cover up your guilt and responsibility for the accident. That is what a court might conclude.'

'You are going to charge me with my own baby's death?' She could barely believe what she was hearing. Benjy had begun to whimper.

The inspector looked at her over the broken ends of his pencil, encouraging her to imagine the worst. When eventually he spoke, his tone was more conciliatory.

'I think, at this stage, not. I believe we have the *prima facie* evidence to charge you but I am not convinced, not *yet* convinced, that it would serve any useful purpose. To be honest I am more concerned with the welfare of Benjamin and also your own state of mind. I am sure that neither can be served by you staying on in Weschester longer than your doctors require.'

'What are you saying precisely?'

'You are in grave danger of abusing our hospitality. Go home, Miss Dean. I'm telling you to go home.'

Not until much later in the day did Izzy begin to wonder how, all of a sudden, the inspector seemed to know one hell of a lot about her plans to extend her stay.

*   *   *

141

She was considerably more circumspect with Barry Brine, editor of the *Wessex Chronicle*, when, eventually and after some considerable delay, she was invited into his office to share yet more machine-manufactured beverage. She couldn't get further than describing it as beverage; its identity as tea, coffee or oxtail soup remained heavily disguised beneath its frothy and swirling suds. To everyone's relief, including his own, after walking around the town for some considerable time Benjy had fallen fast asleep.

Brine gave her the physical impression of being foreshortened, as though a vast hammer had hit him from above and compressed all his features until it seemed as though he would burst at the seams. The top of his bald head was flat and square-edged, the neck thick, waist heavy, with legs simply not long enough to do justice to his top-heavy body. Perhaps, she hoped for the sake of her own endeavours, he had spent his life remorselessly bulldozing his way through locked doors and closed minds. Alternatively, banging his head against a brick wall. She would soon discover which.

She did not mention her fears about Devereux or his daughter, she stuck instead to the possible case of mistaken identity at the hospital and mortuary. Unlike the police inspector, Brine made copious notes with one of a series of coloured pens he kept in his shirt pocket.

'Have you raised this matter with the hospital?' he enquired, stretching the vowels in traditional West Country manner as though he were eating them for lunch.

'Oh, yes.'

'And what did they suggest?'

'Sedatives and a course of psychiatry.'

He arched an eyebrow but, before he could explain whether it implied scepticism of his visitor or her doctors, they were interrupted. He had not shut the door, a steady stream of disturbances was likely and, perhaps, on the editor's part, wanted. A young man, late twenties with the rain-softened brogue of a southern Irishman, required urgent decisions about photographs. The editor excused himself and disappeared. He was gone many minutes and, when he returned in the company of the young man, was apologetic.

'I'm very sorry, Miss Dean, but sadly we have deadlines approaching. And, as much as I would like to, I fear there is little we can do.'

It was the brick wall.

'Couldn't you simply ask? Make a few enquiries? All I want to do is to establish the facts.'

'I'm afraid that missing children are not really our diet.'

'Please . . .'

'You see – I hate to admit as much to another journalist, but I have to be up-front about it – people don't buy our paper for news and scoops. They buy it for the classified advertising, the news about the sales and what's on at the cinema and who's got arrested or died. Strictly hatches, matches and despatches, that's us. We've no call for investigative journalism here.' He threw his hands wide. 'Look around my office. Does it look like a hotbed of intrigue and insight?'

He slumped back into his chair, shirt buttons straining, shirt tail adrift. As he replaced the pen in his pocket he left a smear of fresh ink on the polyester. She could see what he meant.

'Your story touches me, more than I can say. I've got kids, four of 'em, I know what you must be feeling.'

She had been waiting for that one. She wanted very much to scream.

'I wish with all my heart I could help you, this gives me a real and deep sense of personal failure – it is not for us. I hope you will understand.'

And already she was being ushered to the door and a secretary was weaving her between the desks of the cluttered newsroom towards the far exit. Before the door closed on her she turned for one final look: Behind the protective glass walls of his office, the editor was hiding his real and deep sense of personal failure by recounting a joke which caused the whole of his heavy frame to wobble like a jelly.

That evening, as she travelled back to Bowminster on the bus, she clung to Benjy with all her might, burying her head in his hair, pretending to sleep. She wanted no one to see the tears.

'Did you see her? Practically falling out of her dress. Cut up to her knickers and down to her navel. Tart!'

The Prime Minister, the Right Honourable Richard Flood, as usually happened when he'd had one malt and mineral water too many, havered and gyrated between relaxation and aggression. What with reshuffles and rising unemployment and being bloodied at by-elections in Scotland it had proved a difficult parliamentary session, though underway scarcely a month, and everyone had grasped at the approach of Christmas with acute relish. And Christmas, it was commonly agreed, was getting earlier every year. The two other men nodded in understanding.

'I found her, you know, years ago,' the Prime Minister continued, 'when she was ... what? Opposition spokesmistress for Misery or Moral Decay or some such crap. In her little office at the House of

Commons overlooking Speaker's Court, with a parliamentary researcher half her age. Can't imagine what he was researching but she certainly wasn't providing very effective Opposition!'

The laughter was coarse. Devereux wondered what Flood, who at the time could have been no more than a junior Government spokesman himself, had been doing wandering late at night around the none-too-accessible corridors where Shadow Ministers had their miserably cramped quarters, and in particular inviting himself into the office of a woman whose widely discussed parliamentary reputation had been established as much on her back as on her feet. He tried to fashion an innocent interpretation for his colleague's motives, and failed.

'She was a remarkable sight tonight, I must admit,' offered the American Ambassador. 'Crimson dress, that eyeshadow. The pile of extraordinary yellow hair.'

'A parrot,' Devereux riposted. 'You know, in the Green Room, against the backdrop of that marvellous Japanese wallcovering you have, all that lush foliage and bamboo? She reminded me overwhelmingly of a parrot.'

'A bird of paradise, in her day,' Flood mumbled.

'Antique, you know,' the Ambassador added, a trifle vaguely. 'The wallcovering, I mean. Not the parrot.'

The locker-room laughter erupted once again. They were sitting in the private quarters of the Ambassador's residence, Winfield House, an elegant mansion set in the heart of London's Regent's Park. Half an hour earlier they had watched a fox slinking through the grounds in search of a duck dinner, but that had been a couple of stiff whiskies ago. And the Prime Minister had already exhausted himself after battling against the flood tide of Embassy hospitality that had flowed freely through the reception rooms downstairs. He was relaxed, amongst friends, vulnerable; it was a good time for the Ambassador to strike.

'So what do you think? You guys going to be able to help us on the Duster, Prime Minister?'

'The man never sleeps!' the head of government responded in a tone of mild rebuke, seeking inspiration in his glass. 'It's . . . looking good.'

'But not certain,' Devereux interjected flatly.

'I thought you'd made a lot of progress on your last trip to Washington, Paul. We've given a damn sight more than makes strict commercial sense. We've guaranteed you a massive chunk of the design and manufacturing spin-offs, you've got the funding arrangements you want, the specs have been adapted to suit you. Hell, we even twisted the arms of the Saudi navy to order a new destroyer from one of your yards. Sure is difficult to see what more you can expect from us to make it a good financial proposition.'

The Prime Minister looked to Devereux. Flood had been elevated by his colleagues for his capacity to listen and his willingness to heed their point of view, but what had been seen as a source of strength at a time of prosperity was increasingly regarded as indecisiveness as the pendulum swung back towards recession and retribution. The Prime Minister convinced himself he was standing firm; to others, including his colleagues, it appeared increasingly the stance of a rabbit before the headlamps. In any event he felt too relaxed to throw his mind around the Ambassador's questions; he was happy to leave it to his colleague.

'It's not just a financial proposition,' Devereux

began. 'You have to understand the political problems it causes, too.'

The Ambassador arched a thick greying eyebrow.

'We've had a difficult period,' Devereux continued. 'Jobless figures rising, miserable by-elections, media whining all the time. It could be said – *will* be said – that the country needs a multi-billion-dollar fighter project slightly less than a Government-sponsored arse-kicking contest.'

'You're not going to let a little whingeing deflect you, surely?'

'Of course not,' snapped the Prime Minister heatedly.

'Of course not,' Devereux repeated with considerably more control. 'We can ignore the whingeing, but we can't ignore the political realities.'

The ambassadorial eyebrow sank to form a frown.

'You scarcely need to be Director of the CIA to know we're not in the greatest shape,' Devereux continued. 'The reshuffle was not only desirable but absolutely necessary. The PM had been let down badly by some of his colleagues,' he added, sensing that the moment was right to bind rather than expose his leader's wounds. 'The Government needed a new start, a freshened image. That's as important as the financial considerations.'

The Prime Minister's pink eyes betrayed a wrinkle of uncertainty, unsure where he was being led, but the Ambassador harboured no such doubts. He poured more whisky – Devereux declined, holding his hand firmly over his glass – before picking up the thread which Devereux was dangling.

'What did you have in mind, Paul?'

'If we join in developing a new generation of fighter aircraft . . .' – the Ambassador noted, as was intended, the conditional – 'it will be in response to our view about Britain's role in the world – Britain's significant, some would say leading, role.'

'Sure,' the Ambassador nodded.

'But not certain,' Devereux continued, his tone cool, precise, in total control of his argument. 'And without that leading role the Duster's nothing but an expensive irrelevance.'

The American pushed his glass to one side. He had started this game, knew he would need a clear head to finish it.

Devereux leaned forward in his chair, head erect, the body language emphasizing that this was no mere post-prandial provocation.

'There is a view being spawned within your State Department that Japan and Germany should be invited to become new members of the UN Security Council. That means someone else making way. A sacrificial lamb. Britain.'

There was a long silence. The Ambassador would offer no denial. It is commonly held that diplomats are sent abroad to lie for their country, but on this occasion the transparent lie could serve no purpose.

'The lion is not yet toothless, Ambassador. There's not a hope in hell of the British Government accepting that. We'd be torn apart by our own supporters, and rightly so. The President can't have both the Duster and our Security Council seat.'

'You're making direct linkage between the two issues?'

'Political logic demands it. There's little point in Britain being a supersonic whipping boy.'

'I'm not aware the President has come to any conclusion on the Security Council. It's just a kite being flown by some of his advisers.'

'Precisely,' Devereux said, smiling thinly. 'We're not even asking him to change his mind.'

'Fair point,' the American conceded. 'I'll pass on the strength of your feelings. I can't promise anything, you know. But my suspicion is the President is likely to find your argument . . . persuasive.'

'We're very proud of our world role,' the Prime Minister contributed, a touch pathetically.

'Which is why we must insist on American backing in our dispute with Cyprus.' Devereux was at it again. 'We must hold on to the facilities at our base in Akrotiri. Without it we can't maintain any strategic position in the Middle East. Couldn't help you sort out the fuzzy-wuzzies.'

'You are remorseless,' the Ambassador exclaimed in jocular protest. 'You know we can't get involved in that. We're neutral, Paul.'

'Bollocks, Mr Ambassador.'

The Prime Minister started at Devereux's belligerence, spilt his drink and began pouring himself another. He still did not speak, had no inkling of what to say, precious little idea of what was being said. His colleague's assault continued.

'When you start being neutral between your allies and some upstart little nationalist who has fiddled his way to power and is intent on abrogating all his treaty obligations, then it makes one wonder what value America places on alliance and friendship.'

'You know we can't get involved.'

'You are involved, whether you like it or not, because *we* are involved. And behind closed doors your Under-Secretary of State is involved in it up to his tatty little hairpiece. That's what comes from letting a damned second-generation Greek loose inside the State Department.'

'Steady on . . .'

'He's been spreading poison every chance he has.'

'How do you know . . . ?'

'His words of incitement and support are plastered across the windows of every kebab house in the country. They're even being played out on Greek-Cypriot community radio across the whole of North London.'

'I've not heard it,' the American objected.

'You don't speak Greek.'

The Ambassador did not know what to say, so said nothing.

'Look, we don't want a declaration of war from you. What we require – insist upon – is a clear statement in support of international law and the honouring of treaty obligations; that the problem must be solved by negotiation between the two parties, not by unilateral initiatives and the beating up of off-duty British troops on the streets of Limassol. You can leave the rest to us. That bloody little pipsqueak president of theirs can't last long, he'll be gathered in before the next olive crop; we'll just bide our time. Oh, except for one thing. You can sit on that bloody Kostas of yours. Hard.'

'Michalides,' the Ambassador corrected sullenly. He stretched for his drink, cursing himself for his folly in starting this conversation.

'Finally . . .'

The Ambassador choked.

'. . . I feel sure the President would want to ensure that the Prime Minister receives a truly adulatory reception in Washington on his next visit. Probably late next summer. And you will find us the best of friends and firmest of allies.'

'Late next summer?'

'I can't pre-empt the Prime Minister,' Devereux nodded in his master's direction without diverting his eyes from his target, 'but next autumn might provide an ideal window for an election. With your help, the Prime Minister will be projected as a major figure on the international scene . . .'

Alongside flying pigs, the Ambassador mused.

'. . . his loyal and re-enthused parliamentary troops behind him, his international opponents put to flight. Throw in a little luck and the beginnings of an economic recovery. A fascinating and richly rewarding scenario, wouldn't you say?'

The American turned towards the Prime Minister in question, who had been nothing more than a pale spectator at this match. Devereux, with whom the American was relatively unfamiliar, was playing an extraordinary game, upstaging his leader, showing himself to be more adept at both tactics and strategy. And there could only be one master in any camp. But the Ambassador was no fool, either. He knew his Prime Minister, who, by morning, would remember only what had been achieved, not who had achieved it, and Devereux would be guaranteed full favour as the talisman, the lucky general. Commanders crave lucky generals. And Devereux would prosper, by Prime Ministerial preference and by his own craft. He was a man to watch.

The American felt emasculated, drained of strength and further resistance. Summoning up the last of his energy and the dregs of a smile, he raised his glass.

'Gentlemen, a toast. To the Duster.'

In the morning she had called Katti. She did not know what else to do, she had no idea where else to turn. Yet still Katti was not available.

'Her line is busy. Will you hold?'

Yes, she would hold, and she held, and held some more. And when Katti's line at last became free it was answered by someone else, who was new and who hadn't 'got no idea at all, love' where Katti was or even who she was, and could do nothing other than take a message and ask Katti to call.

Depression. It crowded around her like a fog bank rolling in from the Channel until she could see nothing. She felt as if she were slowly melting inside, her resistance, her energy, her hope, all but gone. They had told her she might feel depressed after the accident, a potential clinical consequence of brain damage. God, were the doctors right? About everything?

The phone rang. She sprang. 'Katti?'

'No, I'm afraid it's not,' the voice responded. She recognized it immediately. The clear diction of an extensive education melted into the soft tones of the Irish countryside, a voice that massaged, a voice confident and direct that held clarity both of meaning and of purpose, a voice that captured the rhythms of a bubbling stream slipping across pebbles rather than the prostrate nasal tones of the Mid-West prairie she had been born to.

The voice she had heard yesterday in the editor's office.

'My name is Daniel Blackheart.'

'Black-who?'

'Blackheart. Several centuries ago one of my ancestors owned a stretch of coastline along Blackheart Bay. West coast of Ireland. For some unfathomable reason the name hasn't died out yet.'

'You're kidding.'

'Quite serious, I'm afraid. It's not a name you carry around lightly.'

Laughter bubbled through the stream; he was mocking himself. The Irish did that, could be so understated, indirect, so very un-American.

'And how may I help you, Mr . . .' She hesitated, her lips puckering.

'Daniel. Just call me Daniel. And I think it's me who might be helping you.' His voice lifted a corner of the blanket of cynicism and depression in which she was cloaked.

'We've met.'

'But not been introduced. I heard a little of what you had to say to my editor, about your missing child. I'd like to help, and perhaps I can.'

The transparency of the editor's expressions of concern still stung and she expected nothing genuine from that direction. 'How do I know you're not setting me up?'

'The only person I may be setting up, Miss Dean, is me. I had to rifle the editor's notebook for your details. If he finds out, I'll be swimming around the old family bay with rocks in my boots.'

'I don't understand . . .'

'May we meet?'

'Do you do lunch?'

He laughed, a lilting scale which soothed her mind. 'I've *done*, as you put it, practically everything else. Lunch would be fine.'

And so they arranged to meet, outside the museum at Weschester, beneath its seventeenth-century gables with their wooden eaves where the deserted nests of last spring's house martins sagged and decayed, much as they had done at the time of the American Revolution. Life in this part of the world resisted rapid change; she found herself unable to decide whether she approved or not.

She was early, a free moment, an opportunity to phone Katti yet again. She had a growing sense of unease, wondering whether the social services worker was being deliberately elusive, another brick in the wall which this place seemed to be raising around her. The old reporter's maxim: if in doubt, harass. Yet it was as though Katti had vanished from the face of the planet, with successive voices on the telephone covering her trail in a sandstorm of professed ignorance and impenetrable excuses until it seemed she'd run out of voices to interrogate. She left another message, this time not asking but insisting that her call be returned, and threw the phone impatiently back into its cradle.

And he was there. She turned from the booth to find him staring at her, in a manner that suggested he had been staring for some while. He'd been early, too.

Daniel Blackheart gave the immediate impression of a buccaneer, a youthful buccaneer, slim with an unruly tide of thick black hair which flowed and ebbed across his brow and all but covered one eye, like an eyepatch. He had an earring and a slight limp that gave him the rolling gait of a seafarer, a lopsided grin and flashing mahogany eyes of exceptional darkness which, as she turned to face him, couldn't resist offering her an appreciative brush of inspection.

She resisted her impulse to respond; he was perhaps ten years younger than she and, anyway, this was business. But the image of a swashbuckler stuck, a wandering soul who left heartache and merriment in his wake. And none the worse for that.

'Daniel Blackheart. At your service.' He gave a brief nod and extended a hand which she half-expected would prove to be a hook or at very least callused by rope and salt water. Instead it was smooth and warm. She was surprised at the softness; she had become accustomed to the toughened palms of older men or the liquid skin of children, there was a gap between childhood and middle age in her recent experience and this fellow fitted right in between.

'I rather expected to discover a knight on horseback. Full suit of armour, at very least,' she commented wryly, examining his faded denims while trying, none too successfully, to ignore the sinewy elegance of the body within.

His face grew instantly serious. 'Vizors make a terrible mess of the Big Macs.'

Her cheeks ached. She had all but forgotten what it was like to smile; he had brought help, lifted her depression, even before they had finished shaking hands. Yet as he had come close and she had looked into those sparkling eyes of his, she had noticed more than she'd expected. He was too young for anything but the most thinly pencilled of creases when he smiled, but the eyes themselves had unnatural depth, a soul exposed, something burned away within. A sailor he may be, taking his chances with the winds of life, but there was also a sense that he had been blown about by them and badly bruised in the process. Damaged goods.

They were members of the same club.

'Izzy. The name's Izzy. And this young handful is called Benjy.'

The Irishman leaned closer to make a face at the child held in her arms and she smelt it, the clean, sweet smell of baby powder. The man was wearing baby powder! Perhaps that was why Benjy, startlingly, did not draw back in suspicion at the arrival of yet another strange man in his disordered and overcrowded life but gave a chuckle and offered a sticky hand, which was promptly accepted.

'We owe you lunch. But you'll have to be patient. First we need to make a small detour to the local bank to pick up a replacement credit card.'

'Then it is you who'll need the patience,' he suggested. 'If you don't mind, I'll wait outside.'

She saw what he meant as soon as she entered the bank, a lavishly panelled edifice of classic Victorian style crowded with lunchtime traffic.

'Waiting in line,' she muttered with impatience, 'the weapon of last resort which the English use against Americans.'

And she had waited, and waited, engaged in a struggle with her increasingly impatient child.

'Look at that little boy,' she encouraged, indicating a docile infant in the next queue clinging to the arm of his mother. 'See how good he is.'

Benjy took one look, decided he didn't care for the comparison, and let forth a piercing yelp that would have done credit to a raiding party of Navajo.

The old and graceful bank building proved to be a remarkable acoustic vehicle. The child's cry bounced off the marble floor and seemed to echo undiminished around the ornate plaster columns, rattling the ugly and invasive glass partitions that separated banker from banked, until it died somewhere amongst the bloated cherubs floating high above the tellers' heads. The assembly turned as one to examine. And to offer a collective sniff of disapproval.

At last she was greeted by the glass-smeared appearance and mechanically amplified voice of a young teller. Around the window trailed a selection of last year's recycled Christmas decorations.

'My name is Isadora Dean. I've come to collect a replacement credit card.'

The young girl rifled through a small plastic box of index cards, extracted one, read it, looked again at Isadora and without a word vanished into one of the farther reaches of the banking hall. She returned

a few moments later with a man, older, bespectacled, moist and fleshy lips, whose narrow frame
was lost within the shapeless folds of his off-the-peg
suit. In his hand he held a sheaf of papers and a
bright new credit card.

'Ah, yes,' he greeted, a puckered smile lurking
beneath a tired moustache. 'The lady with the
delightful young child. Mrs . . . ?'

'Dean. Isadora Dean.'

'Ah, yes,' he repeated, scanning the papers. Then
a frown. 'I beg your pardon, there appears to have
been some confusion. My instructions are for a *Miss*
Isadora Dean.'

'That's me. I use my unmarried name.'

'I see.' The banker's lips pursed slightly, disapproving. 'Well, everything appears to be here, *Miss*
Dean. I need you to fill out a few details, obtain a
signature from you. And, of course, some proof of
identity.'

She pushed Pomfritt's eagle-crested letter beneath
the glass, which he took and studied intently.

'Do you have a passport, Miss Dean? A driving
licence, perhaps?'

She explained the circumstances.

'I see.' The lips were pursing again, as though he
were kissing a mirror. Then it was his turn to disappear. She could hear the sighs of impatience grew
in the line of customers behind her; the English
unable to take their own medicine, she reflected.

After some appreciable delay the banker returned,
accompanied by another man. Older still, fuller
bodied, lips like a crack in china glaze, another off-
the-peg suit but better fitting and in pinstripe with
the additional embellishment of a waistcoat.

'What appears to be the problem, Miss Dean?' the
Big Banker enquired.

'No problem. I'm here to pick up my new credit card.'

'But as I understand it from our Mr Wheelright, you haven't brought any means of identification.'

'I have a letter from the American Embassy.'

'But no *proof* of identity.'

'The letter asks that you should telephone the Embassy if there are any queries. Mr Pomfritt.'

'I'm very sorry, madam, but we aren't allowed to accept telephone verification of identity.'

'It's the American Embassy, for goodness sake.'

'Particularly in the case of *foreign* identity.'

He made it sound like a disease; the shuffling behind was growing more intense.

'What's your problem? The credit card company seems sufficiently satisfied to have sent you a new card for me.'

'But, madam, it is the credit card company itself which insists we obtain sufficient proof of identity before handing the cards on. You'll be aware, I'm sure, of the huge increase in the fraudulent use of credit cards, particularly at the Christmas season.'

'That is *my* credit card you have there. *My* name on it. You have a letter of identity from the American Embassy. What more do you want?'

From behind her a querulous female voice was complaining in deep rural tones that she only had a forty-minute lunch break, was already late back and still had Alf's tea to buy. Izzy was beginning to feel marginally less acceptable than an outbreak of head lice.

'It's very difficult for us here to deal with these sort of problems. It would be better, much better, perhaps, if you were to attempt to sort this out in London.'

'Even better back home in America,' came the voice behind.

'What in God's name . . . ?' Izzy began, before checking herself. She was more than willing to raise her voice and lower the level of gentility if that helped, but in this case she felt sure it wouldn't. Another overwrought, hysterical woman, they would say. Just like the doctors. And Benjy, seated on the counter beside her, was sensing the tension and beginning to fret.

'Let me get this straight. You suggest I go to London to sort this out.'

'That would be best.'

'But without my credit card, how do you expect that I should get to London?'

'To my regret, we run only a bank, not British Rail.'

'This is ridiculous.' The blood was rushing now.

'Perhaps your husband could help?'

Izzy snapped, voice rising. 'Get me the manager!'

'Madam,' pinched lips offered in reply, 'I *am* the manager.'

She had run out of patience and perseverance, as had those in line behind her. Then Benjy was in tears, tugging at her. A bladder problem. Got to go. Their weapon of last resort had won.

'Is it because I'm an American, or a woman?' she spat, trying one last time.

Her only reply was a blank expression.

'You're a truly wonderful bunch of people,' was all she could manage to say as she swept up Benjy and left.

Behind her, someone sniggered.

As she disappeared, the banker smiled tightly, first to himself and then at his customers. He insisted on serving the next two himself, offering apologies as though it were his fault the irascible foreign woman had caused such a scene, before relinquishing his post to the teller. He retired to his office, where he closed the door and lifted the phone.

'Yes, she was here. Just as you suggested.'

A pause while he listened.

'Quite emotional, indeed almost aggressive. But then these American women are.'

Another pause.

'Of course. No need for thanks. As a banking official it was my duty. And as a friend, my pleasure.'

He replaced the receiver, straightened his uniform, pulled the gold watch from his waistcoat and decided it was time for lunch. Roast turkey. With seasonal stuffing. He felt he'd deserved it.

Izzy's mood, desirous of drawing blood, did not improve when she discovered Daniel outside the bank, stretching like a contented cat in the unseasonable December sunshine, sharing both a bench and his opinions with an attractive young woman who was in possession of a large, unavoidable chest.

'You're supposed to be helping me, Mr Blackheart, not helping yourself,' she muttered, even as she chastised herself for succumbing to the tug of – impatience? Jealousy? No, surely not jealousy, but he was the only thing approaching a friend she had in this hostile place and she felt in urgent need of his attention. She was grateful when the new arrival was promptly detached and his attention was hers once more.

'Do I need a drink,' she exclaimed. 'Trouble is, I can't afford to buy you one. Those slimeballs won't let me have my credit card.'

'A drink is the easiest problem in the world to

solve,' he said soothingly, and soon they were sitting in the gravel courtyard outside an inn whose cob walls were clad in ancient lichen and mosses. The Thomas Hardy were premises where the great writer was, according to the legend inscribed above the door, supposed to have slept and supped, but the original rutted cart track that ran alongside it had long ago been turned into a busy public road.

While he drank orange juice, she outlined her story. She held nothing back, not even her more lurid impressions about Devereux's daughter; she was too downhearted, too frightened to dissemble.

'Do you know Paulette Devereux?' she probed. But her hopes were quickly dashed.

'To be honest, I wasn't even sure he had a daughter, certainly doesn't feature in the *Chronicle*. But why would she, why would anyone, want to take your baby?'

'If I knew that I wouldn't be here. I keep hoping it's all no more than a mistake – perhaps even my mistake, that there is no mystery. But every time I ask, I feel as though they're building a brick wall around me. Every direction I look, another brick is dropped into place, shutting me in prison. Do I make any sense?'

'They're not shutting you in, Izzy, they're shutting you out.'

'What do you mean? And who are "they"?'

'"They" is this place, Weschester, and the people who matter here. You're an outsider, a foreigner. Even more of a bloody foreigner than I am. You're causing trouble, stirring things up, disordering their lives.'

He leaned across and touched her arm. He was a very tactile person; she was glad of the contact. She desperately needed reassurance.

'This is a fine place,' he continued. 'In the four months I've been here I've found the people warm and friendly, exceedingly generous. But they live life at their own pace, a pace they've been used to for generations. It makes them suspicious of pushy strangers. It can also make them seem insensitive, blind.'

His gaze was earnest and steady, almost uncomfortably so. She sipped her glass of wine; it was revolting, poured from a box.

'Look at it from their point of view. You arrive here, uninvited, accept their hospitality and their healing. Then you go and create trouble for the hospital, the police, the local newspaper, the social services, even the local MP. You're rocking their boat, and in a rural community like this they all row in it together.'

'So what are you telling me to do? Forget it?'

His grip on her arm tightened. 'Of course not. But you have to understand what you are up against. Know the opposition. And know yourself, too, Izzy. Know that it's possible – probable, perhaps – that there is no mystery. That, sadly, your child is dead. You realize that, don't you?'

'I also realize that if you were certain of that, you wouldn't be here. You're not just a Good Samaritan taking care of an emotional cripple.'

'Maybe I'm here because I was captivated by you as you swept through the office yesterday.'

'And maybe you've forgotten that I'm married with enough years behind me to be . . . well, at least be your considerably older sister.'

They exchanged a warm glance, grateful for the temporary distraction.

'I'm also a journalist,' he continued, 'like you. Not much of one, I admit, not here in Weschester, covering scoops like the development of cracks in the ceiling of the public library and the outbreak of rain at the Mayor's garden party. But . . . it wasn't always Weschester, may not always be Weschester for me.' His voice held a touch of wistfulness, the bruising behind his eyes momentarily more apparent.

'Why *did* you decide to help me?'

'Oh, many reasons. You needed help. Isn't that enough?'

'No. That's pretty much what Paul Devereux told me.'

'And because, shortly before you arrived in the editor's office yesterday, he received a telephone call. I don't know from whom, but it mentioned your name.'

'That's impossible! I told no one I was going to see him.'

'Nevertheless, someone was warning him off.'

'Damn.' She downed the dregs of the wine, lips pursing on acid. 'And it's not been just the editor. There was the hospital. The police inspector. Big Brother at the bank. The social services . . .'

'Male prejudice? People not willing to take you seriously?'

'Not in the case of Katti at the social services.' She was staring blindly into the distance, her mind swarming with fresh insight and innuendo, mentally scrambling up the brick wall they had built around her, starting for the first time to peer at what might lie beyond. 'And, dammit, the police inspector knew I intended to stay on. No one knew that, no one . . .' She caught her breath. 'Except Paul Devereux.'

'Your host.'

'Or maybe jailer.'

'But did you tell him you were going to see the police?'

'No, no, no,' she insisted. 'He couldn't have known.' Even from her new vantage point atop the wall, all she could see was a maze. Dead ends.

'Then perhaps all you have is rural insularity, a local community instinctively closing ranks.'

She shook her head emphatically. 'The police inspector knew about me even before I'd arrived. Your editor, too. Someone told them.'

Their conversation was temporarily drowned by the bellow of a passing heavy goods vehicle, its diesel fumes stinging their nostrils, their glasses vibrating. In the background a telephone rang, insistent but unanswered.

'That's it!' she exclaimed with fervour, diving into the maze. 'The telephone. Daniel, I arranged to see the inspector by telephone.'

He rubbed the cleft in his chin, ruminating, trying to catch up with her.

'And your esteemed editor,' she continued.

He was almost there. 'And I'll bet you arranged a new credit card – a card which all of a sudden you can't get – by telephone.'

'That's how I tried to get hold of Katti, too.'

'Which telephone?'

She had turned a corner and at last the way ahead began to clear.

'In Devereux's study,' she responded, 'The one he insisted I use.'

Suddenly the sun had lost its warmth.

'Could Devereux do it, Daniel? Stitch me up?'

'Stitch you up? That man could embroider an entire tapestry, so he could. The Member of Parliament. A power not only here but throughout the country. One of Wessex's most famous families. His father a Government Minister. Around here the Devereux name is the social equivalent of God. And it just so happens that Paul Devereux is a personal friend of my editor. Would be bound to know the police inspector. And almost certainly the bank manager, too.'

'But not Katti.'

'No, not Katti. Somehow she doesn't fit.'

'Sheeee-it!' The oath was drawn out, stretched to its limits, full of frustration. She pounded the wooden table, sending her empty glass flying and waking Benjy, who had been dozing peacefully in her lap.

He mocked her lack of restraint. 'I read somewhere that you Americans have at least thirty different ways of pronouncing that word . . .'

'Daniel, what have I done?' It was her turn to lean across and grasp his arm. 'The arrangement we made? To meet each other this morning? It was on the same phone. Devereux's.'

His flippancy subsided rapidly. 'That might be inconvenient. I told his good friend, my editor, I was going to interview the august chairwoman of the local WI about their forthcoming flower show.'

'Sorry.'

'Don't be.'

A breeze ruffled her hair and she pushed it back into place. Benjy, released both from sleep and her arms, slipped from her lap and began playing on the gravel, trying to fill her shoe with stones. She shooed him away.

'You seem . . . very detached about a lot of things, Daniel. Your job. Your life here. People.'

'Had a lot of practice. At times it's necessary to be detached, even from yourself. Particularly from yourself.' For a moment she thought she saw the bruised soul once more, twisting in the winds of memory, before he rescued himself with a shrug and a self-deprecating smile which lit his face. He had a very fine smile, she decided.

'Anyway, I hope you don't mind me attaching myself to you, Miss Dean?' His gaze was direct, upon her, more than the Good Samaritan, much more than a younger brother. She ducked.

'So fah, so very good, suh,' she mimicked in drawling tones.

'I'm glad. To work, then. What do we do next?'

'Figure out how Devereux knew who I was talking to on the phone.'

'An extension? A tape machine, perhaps, tapping his own phone? That's easy enough.'

'But Devereux's been hundreds of miles away. Yesterday he was in Scotland, visiting some nuclear submarine base. I saw him on the news last night.'

'So how does he keep his finger on the pulse?'

'. . . around my throat?'

Suddenly her thoughts were swamped by instinct, telling her all was not well, to be alert, that danger called. She could no longer hear the sound of Benjy throwing gravel. Instead there was traffic, the sounds of a country road abruptly grown busy, of heavy speeding tyres on tarmac. Of rapid, careless footsteps.

She turned to see a dust-smeared farm lorry, saw too the anxious and tormented face of its driver as he reached simultaneously for brakes and horn, and then she could see Benjy's heedless meandering from forecourt to gutter that led directly into the lorry's path. The noise of the horn blaring out its warning fused with her own cry as brakes protested and tyres left a smouldering path along the road. Benjy, at last aware of danger, turned, faced the oncoming juggernaut, transfixed.

Nightmares are made up of such pieces. The

tendency is to freeze, to cower beneath the bed-clothes in fear and impotence, to wait until the awful dream has passed. It is how many men and women have gone to their deaths, refusing to believe the testimony before their eyes, praying the moment will pass, unable to react, even to protest.

It seemed inconceivable that she could have beaten the lorry to the spot where Benjy waited, that in a stride she could have pushed him from danger's path and still been able herself to avoid the desperate advance of the lorry, but mothers possess a capacity to be more than mortal. As she stood, trembling, clutching her son in exultation, seared by the knowledge that she had let him stray and that she alone was to blame, she knew for the first time the true depths of her plight.

She knew, if she had ever doubted it, that she must persevere, that she would be unable to find peace without first knowing the truth about Bella. Simply, she could never live with her guilt.

Yet there were many sides to her guilt, other risks which she now had no choice but to recognize. She had just seen one of those risks, only by some extra-ordinary chance averted it. The risk was to Benjy, placed in peril while her attention was elsewhere. Even as she chased after the shadowy truth about one child, she was dragging her other towards danger. Could she live with that guilt? Was it to be Benjy? Or Bella?

There was something else she knew as she stood sucking the breath back into her lungs and soothing Benjy's alarm. For a fleeting moment before it disappeared back behind a protective curtain, through the window of a tea room which stood at an angle across the road from The Thomas Hardy, she saw a face.

167

The dark scowl of Chinnery. Spying on her.
Now she knew how Devereux had been aware of
her every move.

FIVE

The room was shrouded, lit only by a table lamp on the great mahogany desk and the reflection from the city lights which penetrated through the uncovered windows. It was how the Prime Minister liked to work, to concentrate in the solitude of his study in Downing Street. Richard Flood was gazing through the centimetre-thick glass, trying to scratch away a mark with his thumb nail, slow to realize the imperfection was buried in the multi-layered and mortar-proofed pane, when Devereux walked in.

'Paul, good evening,' he offered without turning round. 'You know, the garden looks a mess. I really must get it cleaned up.'

'Mmmm,' Devereux muttered, not sure quite why he had been entrusted with such crucial information and wondering whether the Prime Minister, who was gaining something of a reputation for his eccentric behaviour under pressure, was going to ask him to roll up his sleeves and fetch a spade.

'How's Bizzie?' he offered.

'Oh, Elizabeth's fine, the little lady's just fine. Never better, thank you,' Flood muttered distractedly, as though Devereux had asked after the time of day rather than the Prime Minister's wife.

Fool, thought Devereux. Three years in Downing Street had turned the man into a puppet of formality, a hive of hidebound inactivity who seemed even to have forgotten how much his wife hated her full name. He'd forgotten much else about her, too.

Flood spun on his heel. 'Paul, I wanted you to be here to share it. Remember, our evening at the American Ambassador's the other night? When I twisted his arm about the UN and Cyprus and things?'

'Ah, yes, Dick,' Devereux repeated, clearing his throat of the sour humour which the Prime Minister's words had caused. 'A wise move, I'm sure.'

'Not just wise, Paul. Brilliant! I heard this afternoon that they're going to agree. To everything. Absolutely bloody everything. Wonderful, eh? The President's due to telephone in a few minutes to put his personal seal on things and I thought you might like to share the moment with me. Couldn't have done it without your support, you know.'

Devereux shook his head in what he hoped did not betray his feelings of scorn but appeared more a gesture of self-deprecating denial.

'They've really crammed this deal through, the President must need it more badly than we realized,' Flood continued. 'Maybe we let them off too lightly. What do you think, Paul? Should we tweak 'em for a little more?'

'The cows have been well covered. Let's not exhaust the bull with too much pleasure.'

They were interrupted by the warble of one of the three telephones on the desk. Within seconds the connection was made.

'Mr President, good evening. Oh, you're in California and it's still morning? I want you to know I'm very happy for you. I also want you to know I have Paul Devereux with me, my Secretary of State for Defence. I hope you won't object if I put this call on the speaker so he can listen along?'

The Prime Minister punched a button on the

console and the deep Virginian tones of the American leader echoed into the room.

'Blessed are they that giveth, Prime Minister, and, as I guess you know, I'm about to be pretty damn' blessed.'

The American leader was known for his fondness of biblical quotation and analogy with which he cultivated the public image of a Southern gentleman and national father figure. In private, it was not unknown for him to conduct meetings with his advisers while occupying a toilet seat.

'That's most kind of you, Mr President. I trust your rewards will be plentiful and in this life.'

'Sure as hell better be. That's where I need a little generosity of spirit on your part, Prime Minister. You've got what you want. The financial deal on the Duster. The Security Council, Cyprus, and we'll put on a reception during your trip to Washington which'd make Walt Disney go green. But there's one other item I want your truly British help on.'

'Which is?'

'Well, see here, you know I have some little local difficulties with the Congress on this project. As the Good Book says, they have eyes that cannot see, ears that cannot hear and mouths that cannot stop. Or something like that. So I need to be particularly friendly towards the senior Senator for Wyoming, who just happens to be the chairman of the Senate Armed Services Committee, and who also just happens to have a grand-daughter desperate to get into your Oxford University. Now, if the kid had as much brain as the old man's got influence there'd be no problem, but . . . Could you fix it for me?'

The Prime Minister's lower jaw wobbled. 'Well, the Government doesn't control such matters, of course, and those intellectuals make such a fuss about academic freedom . . . But I'd be happy to look into it for you. Personally.'

'Goddamn it, I don't want it looking into, Prime Minister, I want it done. Isn't the Duster worth one little lousy place at Oxford, for Chrissake? I'd have thought it'd be worth an entire university.'

'I . . . I . . .' Flood's jaw wobbled once more, taken aback at the other's approach.

'Mr President.' Devereux stepped into the conversation. 'You have to understand the Prime Minister must ensure he is not seen trampling roughshod over academic freedom. It would do no favours to the Senator or his grand-daughter if there were a great public outcry over the matter.'

'Well, ain't that the truth.'

'However, I think there is a way round the problem. I'm sure the Prime Minister could find a British defence contractor, one closely involved with the Duster perhaps, who might be persuaded with the Prime Minister's personal encouragement to take a keen interest in endowing an academic chair at Oxford. An ideal and imaginative way of displaying his deep social commitment. A commitment which might lead him all the way to the House of Lords, eh, Prime Minister?'

'Well, yes, I'm sure . . .'

'I suspect that, in these very stringent financial times for them, the university authorities would be likely to take a very understanding and sympathetic view of any . . . minor conditions which might be attached to such a munificent gesture.'

'You mean you can fix it?' boomed the President.

'Yes.'

'Yes!' repeated the Prime Minister.

'Gentlemen, thou shalt become an astonishment, a proverb, and a by-word, among all nations. Know something, I believe our little baby has lift-off.'

'Bless you,' muttered the Prime Minister as the President bade his farewell and the line went dead. For the first time in weeks, Devereux saw Flood smile.

The Defence Secretary spent a further hour with the Prime Minister as the latter savoured the triumph over a glass of whisky. They set to resolving other problems, settling scores, planning initiatives which might lead to revival and electoral success. Flood was enthused and Devereux content to take a back seat, to listen, offer guarded suggestions, to let the Prime Minister pick up the ideas and run with them. He had to act with care. He could not outshine his leader yet must provide a sufficient measure of comfort and encouragement to ensure he maintained the inside track which was opening for him. Win or lose the next election, Flood was unlikely to last much beyond. For the first time in a purposeful fashion, Devereux began to consider the possibility that he might soon take his colleague's place.

Prime Minister. It was there, beckoning. Then the ghost of his father would most truly have been laid.

Flood, in generous spirit, accompanied Devereux to the front door of Number Ten where, at the moment the door swung open, the television lights for the nightly news broadcast were switched on, bathing them in the glow of national attention. The Prime Minister took Devereux's hand and shook it warmly, a gesture of endorsement which, even bereft of words, would be seen and understood by all who followed the uncertain tidal streams of political fortune.

'An excellent evening, Paul. Thank you. I suppose you are off to celebrate our success?'

Devereux returned the smile. 'Perhaps later. First

I need to call the American Ambassador. There are a couple of details that still need sorting out with him.'

He seemed to be everywhere. On television, in the headlines, all around the house, within her marriage, even inside her skull. She had woken in the middle of the night, pillow damp from the torment of the nightmare and mental effort of trying to break free, but to no avail. The face of Paulette had loomed once more out of her subconscious, the image clearer and more precise than ever. Except when the face of Paulette had melted into the features of Paul.

But what had inspired most terror within her was the fact that, struggle hard as she might, as the image of the girl gained in clarity so the other image seemed to dissolve. She could not recall what her own baby looked like. Bella was gone. The childish, half-formed features, the pitch of her cry, the face, the changing colour of the eyes and the special way the red hair fell across her brow, all blurred in her mind like the scorched celluloid of an old film. She wanted to take the easy way out, and panic.

She wiped her damp brow – hell, it wasn't damp, it was running with sweat – and lay back on her pillow to listen to the sounds of the old house. Such places were never still, constantly creaking, echoing with time. And time was not on her side.

Time passed, day by day, taking her further away from Bella. How long had it been? And her question gave birth to an insight, perhaps one last place to try.

She had burgled every room in the house, invaded every cupboard, inspected every corner in her search for some sign, evading the suspicious eyes of Sally who seemed to have been told she was up to no good. Most normal hosts would have thrown her out as soon as they discovered she suspected his daughter, perhaps even himself, but Devereux was normal neither as a host nor as an opponent. He obviously preferred to have her watched, to know where she was, what she was doing.

She, too, had resisted the temptation to move away from the house. There seemed little point. She had nowhere else to go, no money and, since the Devereux family had become a target, staying in the house somehow placed her nearer to her goal. It was intended as a prison, but the doors remained unbolted.

So she had stayed. And searched. But there had been nothing. Not even any locks, no pretence of trying to hide clues, except in the filing cabinets within the study, and they were Government secured, probably alarmed, unbreachable. And yet, perhaps . . .

As silently as she could, without lights, she crept from her bed through the darkened house, like a thief, catching her breath as every floorboard groaned like a coffin lid, her senses on edge, listening for the snap of a light switch, fearing illumination and discovery. There was only Sally, who slept at the back of the house, but in the dark the place crawled with a thousand ghosts. Devereux ghosts.

Then she was in the study, her eyes set not on the filing cabinets but on the word processor. Perhaps the one place which held secrets that Devereux had forgotten to lock. Unless he wrote his diary longhand.

As she switched on, she knew how great was the risk of discovery. The equipment began to whine and beep with a noise that would carry through the old stone house; she sat bathed in blue light which must have been visible right across the vale, and certainly as far as the cottage where Chinnery lived. She turned in alarm at a tapping on the window, but it was no more than a hawthorn bush, disturbed by the wind.

'Disk error.'

Damn. But delight. There was a floppy disk in the jaws of the drive. A button release, a flashing screen, an orchestra of electronic greetings.

'Microsoft Word.'

Great! The whole world knew this program. And she was into it. Probing. Ransacking. Revealing.

And there she found it, on the floppy.

'Diary.'

Just like that. Bloody fool. He'd forgotten, over-looked it – but didn't everyone?

It was not the full diary, only musings of the last months, since October. But that would be more than enough. Quickly she scrolled through, flashing past secrets both personal and political, the ammunition he had loaded.

'Oct 14. Cabinet. PM pathetic, wretched man. No backbone, no balls. D. is talking of a leadership challenge . . .'

She dared not tarry.

'Oct 20. Spent night with BL while PM off in Brussels. The fool. Being screwed on all fronts . . .

'Oct 30. New private secretary at Department. Rebecca. Divorced. Dynamite. Delightful prospect. . .'

And so it continued but she had no time to take it in, catching only fragments of the inner man, until she had reached the date of her accident.

Nothing. Nothing but a wine-drenched dinner party against which he had recorded the political indiscretions uttered by the host and the personal indiscretions he had been led to expect from the hostess.

She scrolled on. The next two days, and more.

And there it was. Cryptic. Scarcely incriminating, no proof, but enough for Izzy.

'P. My darling P. How could you? I have been so blind. God help her. God help us both.'

What had he discovered about his daughter so soon after the accident that had left him on his knees? The despair cut clean through. This was the real Devereux, or at least part of him, but she had no time for pity or any other judgement. She jumped in dismay as once again the wind scratched the hawthorn across the pane and, from the cottage that nestled in the lee of the house, a light appeared. Chinnery's light.

She snatched at the switch on the screen and the blue glow faded but the main drive still hummed, the computer was still toiling. Another light in the cottage went on and a dog howled; the world was waking. This might be her last chance.

More by memory than the pale light of a winter moon she found the box of computer disks at the back of the desk. Clean, empty floppy disks. Like sponges.

She couldn't risk any form of illumination. She sat in front of the console and typed, blind, two fingers.

The computer stirred, fell silent again. She extracted the original floppy and replaced it with a new one. More stirring, more silence.

She was desperate to switch on the screen, to check, but she thought she could hear signs of movement from inside the house now. Sally. She switched disks once more, leaving the original back in its drive.

Had it copied, had the sponge soaked up the information? No way of checking, not now. Clutching the new disk, she quickly retraced her steps back to her room.

So he had known, almost from the start. And had become part of it. For there could be no other interpretation, no other understanding of his diary entry. His reappearance in her life had been no coincidence. Now she knew the measure of her enemy, for enemy he surely was.

A parent driven by overwhelming obsession, and love, faith and hope, and perhaps guilt, to protect the child. No matter what.

It seemed all too familiar. Like looking in a mirror. She understood how determined he might be. As determined as she.

And that made Devereux a very dangerous man.

Daniel dropped them at the hospital. Only as she sat waiting for her check-up did she realize how little she had thought during the last few days of her medical condition. She had found enough strength to spring after Benjy, enough physical resource to see her through the days. No headaches. Her bouts of depression she put down to the loss of Bella rather than the clinical after-effects of the accident. She'd even begun some gentle aerobic stepping exercises to rebuild the muscle tone. No question she was getting stronger.

And Weatherup agreed. A slow, painstaking examination of her neurological signs, from the shape of her head and the reflexes of the retinas to the sensitivity of the soles of her feet, seemed to leave him well satisfied. Izzy Dean was working.

'You're a medical mystery, Izzy. A few weeks ago you were supposed to be dead. Now, apart from your spleen scar and that slightest nick by your eye, I can find no evidence of the fact that you were ever in an accident. It's as if you've found something within you which is repairing all the loose ends, retying all the knots, far more effectively than any drug I could prescribe.'

It's called hope, she told herself.

'Amazing what a few press-ups will do, doctor.'

'Now, don't you go overdoing things,' he chided. 'Any damage you received to the brain is irreversible and we simply don't know enough about such matters to tell you what, if any, difficulties that might cause. Just take it easy for the next few weeks; your brain and your body will let you know of any problem much more effectively than we can. But, as far as I can tell, so far, so very good.'

'You're telling me that the medical profession isn't omniscient? That it makes mistakes?'

He recognized her challenge. Cautiously he seated himself on the end of the examination couch, conscious of the fact that their last conversation had turned to confrontation.

'In my job we understand so little. We struggle so hard with inadequate tools, and we pray. If we succeed, we still don't know whether it's because of our skills, our luck or simply our prayer. But also there comes a point when we have no choice but to bow our heads to the inevitable. When the struggle has to stop.'

He held up his hand to stall the protest he knew she was about to launch.

'Please, Izzy, listen to me for just a minute. It's very common for mothers to have difficulty in believing they've lost a baby; it's not only natural, it's normal. You have the added problem of not having been there to say goodbye.' He licked dry lips, searching for the right words. 'But you see, there are too many steps in the system, too many people involved. A mistake simply couldn't have happened. You've got to find some way of letting go.'

She wanted to shout at him. What about mistakes of hair colour? What about babies in Bournemouth? But he was trying to be genuine, she could detect no trace of craft in him. She held her peace.

'Those ID bracelets are checked every step of the way, against all the medical records we make. For a mistake to have been made would take the entire hospital, every doctor and nurse who dealt with your baby. It simply couldn't happen.'

He took her silence as acquiescence; his frown turned to an expression of encouragement. 'Don't just take my word for it. Go and prove it to yourself. Talk to those who looked after your baby, find out how much care she was given. Then perhaps you'll find you can accept.'

Her shoulders dropped. He was right, not everyone in the hospital could have made a mistake, she had to accept that. Even more, it would have taken a mistake by the Coroner's Office, the undertaker, the police ... seemingly everyone in the country. No conspiracy theory could cover so many people. And what would be their purpose? Suddenly she felt tired, belittled. Her head fell forward, as though she no longer had the strength.

'I shall do as you suggest.'

'Good.'

'So, when would you like to see me next?'

'See you, Izzy? As far as I'm concerned, you're as strong as a horse and as free as a bird. A remarkable recovery. In a word, go. So long as you don't overdo it, listen to what your body is telling you, in my opinion you can leave. Fly back tomorrow, if you want. Spend Christmas at home. In fact, I would suggest it, probably the best recuperation you can get.' His voice softened to a whisper. 'Get away from here and its memories. Give yourself a chance to forget.'

People forget, but not systems. They are built to retain, to store the myriad details of life. And, as Daniel was discovering, of death.

After dropping Izzy off at the hospital he had driven to the Coroner's Office, with no idea of what he was searching for except, with the assistance of his press credentials, to test the version of events she had been given.

And for all the world it seemed to be correct. The Coroner himself was not available, it was not a full-time post, so the wizened clerk with the leathery skin and bottle-black hair informed him. But she offered her own help, delivered in a prim manner and pedantic voice which he later discovered was the legacy of half a lifetime of schoolteaching before her early retirement to the less stressful and considerably quieter enclaves of the Coroner's Office. On medical grounds, at her doctor's suggestion. She wore no ring.

'A baby girl,' Daniel explained. 'Unknown identity. Died in a car accident.'

She retrieved a slim manila file from a locked cupboard, wiping it meticulously with a bright yellow cloth although nothing in the office bore any trace of dust. 'You're not the first to enquire, as it happens. A lady from the social services just last week. Strange accent. Forin, I believe.' She pronounced the word with particular emphasis. Very English.

So Katti hadn't ducked out . . .

'Sad case. The baby had died in a car accident. Death certificate, after post-mortem.' She shuffled through the few forms in the file. 'All here, the paperwork . . . Cause of death, sub-dural haematoma – a nasty bang on the head. Here's the Coroner's "E" certificate, releasing the body for disposal.' She read. 'Cremated.'

'No trace of family?'

'It seems her mother was in the hospital, in a coma. Inquest adjourned. No other traceable relatives, all the usual enquiries were made.'

'But the body was disposed of even though the mother was still alive in the hospital?'

'In a coma, young man,' she insisted in schoolma'amly fashion. 'And not expected to live, according to the doctor's report. Little point in waiting.'

'Even so, it seems a little hasty, to dispose of the body only a couple of weeks after death.'

'Just what the forin lady suggested. So I took the trouble of enquiring from the Coroner himself. There's no mystery. Our mortuary facilities were simply overflowing with . . .' – she hesitated in search of a more delicate word – 'unfortunates. It's quite common for them to be stacked two to a tray, and sometimes even that's not enough. We really do need expanded facilities but, you know, the cuts . . .'

Cuts, the last resort of the bureaucrat, the eternal explanation for inadequacy. The same cuts that had produced the new A&E wing at the hospital, the indoor sports complex with Olympic-size swimming pool, and an additional primary school. But no new fridge facilities at the mortuary. The dead have no votes, he reflected.

'So on rare occasions the Coroner, most reluctantly, is forced to issue his "E" simply to make room, you see. Unless the police have questions or suspect foul play, which was not the case in this instance.'

'That's . . .' – he wanted to say convenient – 'understandable. And that's what you told the other lady?'

'Would have done. But she never called back, and that after I'd gone to the trouble of contacting the Coroner himself. Not very good for social services, is it? You wonder at times why they can't find local people to do these jobs, don't you, Mr Blackheart? Maybe it's the cuts again. Although you would have thought they could find room for such a tiny baby,' she added wistfully.

'You have to sweep out the mortuary very often?' His tone was deliberately casual which he knew she would find offensive.

'*Very* rarely. And I certainly wouldn't put it like that.'

'So you haven't had to get rid of a large number of bodies?'

'Absolutely not. Very few, in fact.' She was defensive. 'This was a most exceptional circumstance.'

'An unusual case, you'd say?'

'Yes, a most unusual case. Unique. Pity, really.'

'A great pity.'

He found mother and child seated on the plastic chairs in the corner of the hospital's main reception area, as though trying to separate themselves from the rest of the world as it bustled past. Izzy seemed deflated, grown smaller since he had dropped her off.

'You OK?'

'Fine. Fully fit,' she replied without enthusiasm, her hair in uncharacteristic disarray from lying on the examination couch. She looked her age. The skin around the eyes had a slight waxiness. For the first time he noticed the face appeared drawn, and it wasn't just the hospital lighting.

'They say I can go home.' She made it sound like a sentence.

'But you're not going.'

'I need . . . I need something more. There's still no reason, no motive for all this. I feel . . . Frankly, I feel ripped apart.'

He sat beside her, placing an arm around her shoulder. 'Come on. What's wrong?'

'Hell, I don't know. Because my hair's messed up, my clothes make me look ridiculous, the doctor all but convinced me there couldn't have been a mistake – how many more reasons do you want?' She paused. 'Because every time I close my eyes I see Benjy standing in front of that lorry. And because no matter how hard I try I can't remember what Bella looks like. And because . . .' For a moment she thought she might tell him that her hormones were conducting civil war inside her, that this was the first time since her coma and they were taking their revenge for all the months of oestrogenal regimentation which the accident had brought to an end, but men were so damned juvenile about such things.

She couldn't help herself. She felt the tear creeping down her cheek; normally she would have fought it, summoned up her professional self-respect to obliterate any possibility of them branding her as weak, of giving men the excuse to categorize her as another faint-willed woman. But Daniel was different. He had a manner about him that was entirely non-judgemental, uncritical, that encouraged others to express themselves freely and without inhibition – that suggested he had been there, too. With him she had begun to find her emotions once more; she'd smiled, even remembered how to laugh, and now felt the freedom to shed tears. Her head fell on his shoulder as though dragged down by an intolerable weight. Without wanting to, she noticed how firm and unfleshy he was beneath the shapeless stitching of his jacket, how unlike any other man she had known for a long time, unlike Joe had ever been. She found it a confusing thought, with her child at her feet – a child who refused to be left out.

'Mumee, Mumee,' Benjamin exclaimed.

'Yes, dear?'

'Danny huggling you. Danny nice.'

'Yes. He is, isn't he,' she mumbled, her face buried in his shoulder.

'You're a beautiful lady, Isadora Dean,' he whispered into her hair, 'but you can't sit round all day falling into the arms of strange men who bear nothing but lecherous intent. At least, not while you've got a job to be getting on with.'

Her head stayed down. He decided to try a different tack.

'Interesting news, Izzy. The disposal of the baby's body was completely in order, all the legal requirements taken care of, all their little forms present and correct. But what wasn't correct was the rush with which it was handled. It's almost unheard of to dispose of an unclaimed body so quickly.'

'You're not going to tell me that the Coroner is Paul Devereux's brother-in-law, are you?'

'Not as far as I know, but somebody is panicking.'

'You have the evidence?'

'That's the point, Izzy. All the evidence is being removed. The baby's body. They are trying to get rid of you. And they succeeded in getting rid of Katti.'

Izzy froze. Her head lifted, eyes red.

'Katti did begin making the enquiries she

promised you, but before she was able to find the answers she disappeared. Or rather, was removed. After leaving the Coroner's I called up the social services.' He smiled an artful smile. 'I have inside influence. A young lady. Former close companion. Blonde, no brains, just my type.' He was goading her.

'We were discussing Katti.'

'You told me she promised on Wednesday afternoon to start making enquiries. She did. Coroner's Office acknowledged as much. And by Monday morning she was out of the country.'

He watched as will-power alone dried the tears and forced the sparkle back into her remarkable emerald eyes. She ran a hand through her hair; it sprang back into order, back on parade. With reluctance, Daniel removed his arm from around her before continuing.

'They discovered something wrong with her work permit. Technically it made her an illegal immigrant, so they gave her a choice. Leave the country voluntarily for a couple of months while the problem was sorted out, or be deported and never allowed back in again.'

'But why have they been giving me the runaround? Why hush it up?'

'Be embarrassing for an official agency to be seen employing illegal immigrants.'

'The Establishment closing ranks.'

'Someone's running scared, Izzy. Someone with a hell of a lot of influence.'

'Paul Devereux.' Her voice was soft, no more than a whisper. She picked up Benjy and wrapped him protectively in her arms. 'Once you start a cover-up, that cover-up in turn has to be covered up, and so on. He covers up for his daughter, then he has to cover up for himself. It never stops, Daniel. And if the baby who died wasn't Bella, who was she? And how did she die? Someone out there must be pretty desperate. I'm already in their sights, Benjy too. You'll be next on the list.'

'Too late. They fired me this morning.'

'You're not serious,' she blurted.

He was.

'No worries,' he smiled. 'The *Wessex Chronicle* was never going to be more than a minor stepping stone on the way, so now I've been able to jump it considerably faster than I thought.'

'You sure?'

'Think of it this way. You want me, you got me. Exclusive and full time.'

He wanted her, suddenly she knew it without any doubt. It caused her alarm, confused her, invigorated her. There was no room in her life for complications, her emotions were still too raw to be exposed and, anyway, he was almost ten years younger. And he was exactly what she needed to restore her sense of self.

'So what's next in my life, Miss Dean?'

'Next, Danny Blackheart, is to get you as quickly as possible to Accident & Emergency.'

A&E was modern, well equipped and beplaqued as befitted a facility opened less than a year before by a minor scion of Royalty, and, on this occasion at least, quiet. No more than a split thumb from a nearby building site and a mild concussion from the local school sports field. The duty sister, on being told of Izzy's history, welcomed them with warmth and a cup of tea, while Benjy quickly became distracted in a wrestling match with a sizeable stuffed panda.

'Take me through what would have happened to me and my children that night.'

'You would have been brought here by ambulance, we would have been expecting you. So no waiting around here in the reception area with the grazed knees and sprained wrists, straight through for examination. Either in one of the cubicles or in the emergency room.'

'Which one in my case?'

'Depends. If there were no obvious signs of serious physical damage, no heart failure or the like, probably in one of the cubicles here.' She indicated a row of compartments, separated from the reception area by no more than a curtain.

'And my children?'

'Little Benjy was unharmed, you say? Well, probably we would have kept him out of the way, occupied him with toys in the waiting room like he is now. In the case of your baby, she would have been examined immediately, along with you. Look, if it's important, I think one of my nurses was on nights then, might remember much more than I can tell you. Would you like to talk with her?'

And so Nurse Ali Duffin was introduced, a slender, composed young woman with eyes which cared and were shaped like almonds and a figure which many male patients had expressed themselves happy to die for. And who knew Daniel.

'Hello, stranger.' She offered a wary smile. 'What brings you back into my life?'

Izzy sensed caution – genuine warmth, no hostility, but a guarded, almost professional approach to an old friend. There was a strong atmosphere of past pleasures and pains. Izzy suspected scar tissue.

Daniel offered both his hands, fleetingly accepted, and expressed his delight but offered no kiss. Definite scar tissue. 'Ali and I were once very good friends,' he explained to Izzy. 'Way back. In London.'

'Three and a half years,' Ali added. 'But who's counting?'

'I fouled things up.'

'How are you, Danny? Fully recovered?' She stepped back to run an approving eye over him, peeling layers of clothing off the body, admiring, reminiscing.

'I'm fine. My only problem is that I never found a chance to thank you properly. I had no idea you were bumping around in the same town. Why?'

'Got tired of London. Tired of living in debt and dirt. Watching too many of my friends jump in at the deep end and never come up. You know how it is, Danny.'

He turned to Izzy. 'Ali helped me during a long illness a few years ago; she'll always be very special to me.'

'OK, enough Blackheart charm. I've seen it all before, remember?' But the face had grown relaxed, the smile broader. She ushered them into the sister's office.

'I remember that night you came in rather well,' Ali explained to Izzy. 'It was hellish busy, there was not only your accident and the normal wear and tear of a Saturday night but also a cardiac arrest and some trouble with several Weekend Willies — drunken fans from a local football derby.'

'So it was pretty confused?'

'Very. Mind you, on a Saturday night it always is.'

'Humour me, Ali,' Daniel interjected. 'Perhaps confused enough for the identities of two patients to be switched?'

She first looked startled at the question, then shook her head firmly. 'No. We put on identity tags as soon as we start looking at patients. No chance of a mistake.'

'But couldn't someone deliberately switch the tags?'

'Not really. The patient would have to be unconscious or delirious —'

'Or babies,' Izzy whispered.

'And no one was going to go round cutting off ID tags and replacing them on that night of all nights. Not with policemen everywhere.'

'Police?'

'Place was swarming with them, what with your accident, the football match . . . There was even a burglar with a broken leg. That's one of the reasons I remember the night so well, our local constables can be as much trouble as the patients.'

'In what way?'

'Always asking you to assist them with their enquiries. And you know the only enquiries men are interested in.'

Both women looked at Daniel, who responded with a passable impression of choirboy innocence. Except Izzy had never met a choirboy with an earring.

'They're incorrigible, Miss Dean. One tried to ask me out even while we were both in the car park trying to deal with the fire alarm. Trouble is, I was dumb enough to accept.'

'The fire alarm?' Daniel's voice all but cracked as the words forced their way out.

'Yes. One of the drunks activated the fire alarm and so we had to empty the department of non-emergency cases, just for a couple of minutes while we checked. It happened just as you arrived, actually.'

'So much of A&E would have been left unattended?'

'Not entirely, and the disturbance lasted only for

a couple of minutes. We discovered it was a false alarm even before we'd got all the non-emergencies out.'

Izzy closed her eyes for a moment, imagining the scene, patients wandering, confused, disorganized, the hard-pressed casualty staff doing their best to restore order from the chaos, attention distracted. Perhaps even before they had time to put on ID bracelets. Before Bella had been given an identity.

'Ali, is it possible in the middle of the fire alarm that a patient could have been left alone, in one of the cubicles, while the nurse or doctor stepped out to discover what the commotion was all about?'

The nurse thought. 'For seconds, perhaps. Not minutes. The whole thing was over so quickly.'

Both Daniel and Izzy sucked up the information, the possibility that in the confusion there had been a mistake, perhaps even a deliberate mistake. After all, it was far quicker to swap babies than it was ID bracelets. The work of seconds.

'And do you remember my baby, Ali? What she looked like?'

'No, I'm sorry, Miss Dean. Babies are the most difficult patients to remember. They all have the same tiny, unformed features which seem to stretch and change every five minutes, and I didn't deal with your baby personally. As it happens I was dealing with another baby at the time and in all the confusion of that night I'm not sure I can even remember her.'

The world had stopped.

'There was another baby here? A baby girl?' Both Daniel and Izzy seemed to compete to get the question out first.

'Yes. The mother had dropped her and was terribly

anxious the baby might have suffered some damage, but she was perfectly fit. A quick check-up, then we let her go.'

'No ID bracelet?'

'No need. She wasn't admitted.'

'But she was here during the fire alarm? At the same time as me?'

'Certainly.'

'Ali, this is most important. Can you remember the mother's name?'

'No, I can't. And anyway I'm not supposed to give out information about other patients.'

'Come on, Ali.' Daniel's anguish was transparent. 'This could be more important than anything I've ever asked of you. Anything.'

'You're serious.'

'One hundred per cent.'

The nurse looked warily from one to the other, then back again. 'Well, I don't suppose names count strictly as medical records. Wait here a moment.'

She returned clutching a large manila envelope, from which she extracted its single sheet of paper.

'Smith. The name was Smith. Just a surname for the baby, no mother's name recorded.'

'You're kidding,' Izzy protested. 'Surely you can do better than that.'

Ali shrugged. 'It happens. A lot. People not wanting to give their full names to casualty. Anyway, the baby wasn't admitted, she received no treatment apart from a check-up. And in all that confusion . . . I'm sorry.'

Izzy and Daniel visibly shrank with disappointment.

'All I have here is an address.'

'An address will do very well, thank you.' Izzy's

hand trembled as she wrote down the details. Bilshay Crescent. 'One last thing. Can you remember what she looked like?'

'The baby? No.'

'The mother.'

Ali wrinkled her face in concentration. 'Young, I guess.'

'Thin? Blonde?'

'Mmm, think so. Why, do you know her?'

Izzy's body felt consumed by fire, comprehension spilling like acid through her veins. Yes, she knew the mother. And she thought she knew how Bella had disappeared, unidentified, in the midst of the confusion.

How she might have been left with the wrong, dead child.

After all, which baby was which came down to no more than a matter of paperwork, of officialdom.

Of Paul Devereux.

Bilshay Crescent, when they found it, backed onto the river. It was part of a long corridor of Victorian houses which snaked along the contours of the river bank. Red brick, ornately tiled roof in the fashion of the previous century, flaking paint and small front garden which had received scant recent attention. A smell of damp. It was locked and dark, with no sign of life. Curtains drawn, impossible to see inside, a broken bell-pull. No one answered their repeated knocking. They found nothing but a small brass plate beside the bell-pull which they read with difficulty by the light of a distant street lamp. It declared they had arrived at the 'Mission of Mercy'.

'We'll come back, in the morning. First thing,' she said.

*　　*　　*

The restaurant was modest: tired cotton table cloths, a tang of fried garlic in the air. The sort of place Grubb would take his wife. Scarcely the sort of place he expected ET to choose while they discussed the future of the news operation. Maybe Hagi was trying to make a point about economies.

'So long as that clown in the White House fails to squeeze any co-operation out of Congress, the economy's going to keep on sliding south, dragging the dollar with it,' the money man was explaining. Even by candlelight his face retained its unhealthy, unnatural cast. 'This Administration's an Enema Express. You understand the significance of that, Eldred.'

'Sure, Hugo,' Grubb lied through a mouthful of meatballs. 'But don't hide anything from me. Lay it on the line.'

'We're an international news-gathering operation, Eldred. Which means expenses abroad and revenues at home. The revenues are falling because of the recession and our expenses rising because of the devaluation of the dollar. Ten per cent of our annual budget, blown straight out the presidential ass.'

Grubb noted that Hagi's language was growing uncharacteristically flowery under the influence of the wine, their second bottle of a fine old Bardolino and thick enough to chew. Grubb relaxed a little, each bottle cost as much as the food, ET's mask was slipping.

'That's tough, Hugo.'

'Tougher for some than others. I need a ten per cent cut in wage costs across the board.'

A meatball slid down, unchewed. Grubb went red, unable to respond.

'Either salary cuts or redundancies, Eldred, but that's for you to sort out. I need your recommendations within two weeks.'

Grubb was rescued by the arrival of the waitress, a pretty if brassy blonde who set about her tasks with a youthful cheerfulness which compensated for her obvious lack of experience. Once more she refilled their glasses, leaving a trail of expensive wine across the table cloth. She apologized profusely, explaining that it was her first week, working her way through art school. For the first time he could remember, Grubb watched as the deadpan mask on ET's face twitched. ET was trying to smile. He showered the girl in forgiveness and ordered another bottle.

'So what do we do?' Grubb prodded.

'We cut. *You* cut, Eldred.'

'I'm a foreign news editor,' Grubb protested.

'You are also a senior employee of World Cable News. I assume it's a position you wish to retain.'

'Are you threatening —'

'No, simply stating a fact of life. We've got to find substantial savings or soon none of us will have jobs. Hell, the average American's view of foreign affairs stretches no further than the distance between Massachusetts and Minnesota. So buy in more footage from foreign networks, maybe; close down some of our foreign bureaux.'

'You mean Izzy Dean?'

'If necessary. No room for passengers.'

The waitress was clearing the remnants of their meal from the table, ET's eyes firmly clamped upon her backside.

'Tell me about Izzy Dean,' the managing editor mused. 'Is she one of us? A team player? Willing to make sacrifices?'

'What sacrifices?'

'The sort of sacrifices women have to make.'

'Naw, not her. She's never screwed around to get a promotion.'

'But will she go to the limit for us professionally? Has she ever got on her back to get a story? It's no more than we would expect of a male correspondent. The WCN Nightly Screws . . . Bedlines from around the world . . .' He was growing intoxicated, beginning to giggle. It was ET cast in a new light. 'I mean, does she have too many scruples to do the job properly?'

'Too many kids, that's for sure.'

'So don't let's go soft on her. She can't play both newsgirl and nanny. You get her little fanny across to the Ukraine by this time next week.' He sipped. 'Or it's bye-bye birdie.'

The waitress had brought the bill, which the managing editor thrust across at Grubb. While Grubb fumbled reluctantly for his card ET exchanged banter with the waitress, discovering where she lived, offering her a lift home. 'We pass your place on the way, don't we, Eldred?'

'We?'

'Sure. You can drive, give me a lift home too. It's not so far out of your way. Earn your huge salary for a change.' The alcohol and power thing had gone to his head.

'What's twenty miles between friends,' Grubb griped.

They drove in silence. ET had taken the back seat with the waitress, leaving Grubb to focus through a light drizzle on the road ahead. He needed all his concentration; too late he realized how much he had drunk. And he was worried about his future. And the foreign bureaux. It dawned on him that if there were no foreign bureaux, there was no foreign editor. No job. No Grubb.

'We need the foreign coverage, Hugo. Now more than ever.'

An uninterested grunt came from the rear seat.

'Look, the whole friggin' world's in the process of falling apart out there. Ethnic wars all over what used to be Commie-land, South Africa burning, the Saudi ruling family about to be flushed down the pan and take a million barrels of oil with it, the biggest civil war the world's ever seen threatening in China.' He grazed a kerb. 'Warheads from the old Soviet nuclear arsenals scattered everywhere. It's like fireworks on the Fourth of July. The touch paper's lit, we're just waiting for the big bang.'

ET offered no response. Grubb tried a new tack.

'We shouldn't be too hasty about Izzy Dean, either. She's the best we have. There'll soon be a bigger demand for foreign news coverage than at any time since Vietnam. You know, maybe we should be patient with her just a little longer and . . . Shit!' As he concentrated on his argument the car had begun to stray, edging too near the brow of the road and into the path of an oncoming truck whose headlights blazed out warning. Grubb swerved sharply, glancing in his mirror to mutter apologies to his passengers.

'Shit,' he repeated, this time in a restrained tone of irritation. As the beam of the headlights swept across the interior of the car, it illuminated the lurid and contorted mask of Grubb's boss, the pale and plentiful skin of a young girl working her way through school, and considerable dishevelled clothing. Christ, ET was human after all. And Grubb had been wasting his breath.

'Sorry, Izzy, I tried,' he muttered to no one but himself, rehearsing the call he now knew he could not avoid making. 'It's Kiev or quit.'

*   *   *

197

It was in the morning, almost before first thing, when Pomfritt arrived. Daylight had scarcely broken through the long winter night, the Consular Officer must have set out from London well before dawn, but there he was, bright, besuited, flapping his wings before the door of the Devereux house, clutching two passports.

'Miss Dean, I'm delighted. Even sooner than I'd expected,' he exclaimed as they sat at the kitchen table sipping large mugs of tea. 'It's a pleasure to be able to help, and to get you and your son back home. I'm sure you must be looking forward to it; don't hesitate to ask if you need any help with the arrangements . . .'

Bizarre, she thought. That within hours of her receiving permission from the doctor to travel she was receiving encouragement from the Embassy to do precisely that. But she had long ago given up clinging to any belief in coincidence. 'Thank you, Mr Pomfritt. I'm not going.'

The brightly scrubbed face seemed to freeze in mid-breath; the moustache drooped.

'My baby didn't die in the crash, and I'm going to prove it.'

'Oh, not that again, Miss Dean. Please, I beg you – don't punish yourself.'

As Izzy watched he actually wrung his hands.

'What assistance can I get from the Embassy?'

'Assistance? What sort of assistance?' he lisped, unable to get either tongue or mind around this new challenge. 'I'm afraid we can't help financially—'

'Assistance in tracing what happened to my baby. How she was switched for another baby. Where she is now.'

In agitation he rose from his chair and proceeded to pace about the kitchen, his heels clicking on the flagstone floor. 'This is so far-fetched, surely you must realize that, Miss Dean?'

He waited for a response, but none was forthcoming.

'Have you seen a doctor?'

'Yes. He says I'm perfectly fine.'

'Physically, perhaps, but inside . . . ? And who is supposed to be responsible for this alleged . . . babynapping.'

'Paul Devereux.'

Pomfritt came to a sudden halt. The tea dashed against the side of his mug like a winter sea and began dripping down upon his brightly polished town shoes. He didn't notice. All he could comprehend was that his Ambassador as well as Paul Devereux had taken a personal interest in this case, he had instructions to wrap it up quickly and without fuss, and his carefully plotted path to diplomatic preferment was now in jeopardy. Because of this woman. He had many interests in his life for which in appropriate circumstances he might consider endangering his career. His porcelain collection. The Tang grave statuary he had smuggled out of China in two pieces. Wagner. Tuscany – even the occasional man, although that only under the liberating influence of a few drinks and never in the country in which he was currently serving. But never a woman.

'I have to warn you, Miss Dean, that you are taking this nonsense altogether too far. It is possible to sympathize with a grieving mother, but such absurd accusations are altogether too much.' The hair above his lip was positively bristling. 'Paul Devereux is one of America's closest friends . . .'

'So was the Shah of Iran and President Diem of South Vietnam. We betrayed one and shot the other.'

'He has also been one of *your* best friends, if only

you opened your eyes. Good God, woman, we're sitting in his kitchen. Your accusations lack a certain logic, some might say. And what do you have as evidence – hard evidence, mind, not flights of feminist fancy?' The sibilant alliteration posed a challenge with his lisp – too much of one, as it proved; he wished he hadn't used it.

'I am an American citizen, Mr Pomfritt.'

'Since when did being an American citizen ever change things for you? Dammit, you media goons travel halfway round the world trying to show up America, criticizing and denigrating everything we do. Yet at the first hint of trouble there you are waving your passports and shouting for "good ol' Uncle Sam". I tell you, Miss Dean, there are some parts of my job and some of the people I meet in it that make me feel physically sick.'

'Aren't you taking this a little personally?'

'And you are not, I suppose?'

'Cut the crap, Pomfritt. I'm an American citizen, you're a public employee and it's your damn job to help me!'

His jowls bulged as he chewed over his reply. 'Your husband, too, is an American citizen, with just as much right to ask for our help. And your son, Benjamin, is also an American citizen whom we have a duty to protect.'

'What?'

'Your husband, Miss Dean – or, rather, his attorney – has been in contact with the Embassy expressing concern that the boy's interests are being damaged by your erratic and irresponsible conduct, in particular by your refusal to return home, which is subjecting him to unnecessary hardship. It seems to me there are good grounds for that concern, and my report will reflect as much.'

'I can't believe what I'm hearing. You're spying on me?'

'Reporting, not spying. On Benjamin, to be precise.'

He threw the remains of his tea into the sink and turned on her, cheeks mottled and burning like bush fires at the ends of his moustache.

'Look, can't you see how much damage you are doing to yourself? How irrational you are making yourself seem? Your husband is suing you for custody, and I can think of no better way of persuading a court of your husband's case than doing precisely what you're doing: running around a foreign country, subjecting your child to unreasonable hardship, making quite preposterous claims against a leading member of the Government. It's utterly outrageous, woman. If you have the slightest interest in retaining custody of Benjamin you *must* return home immediately. You have your passports.' He threw two, mother and son, onto the table. 'If you want to keep the kid, use them.'

She sat in silence. She had known it would come. Benjamin, her weak point, her vulnerability. Everything came down to Benjamin. Her reason for marriage, even the failure of that marriage. The custody proceedings. Her inability to pursue singlemindedly the trail left by Bella. The lorry.

Since the lorry, what had been no more than an uneasy feeling had become firm knowledge, that she could not both pursue Bella as well as protecting Benjamin, not all at the same time. His demands, his needs, were too great. It simply couldn't be done. Weighed down with Benjamin, she would in all probability never be able to catch up with Bella, and by seeking Bella she might end up losing Benjamin, too. Lose them both.

She felt cold, too cold to shiver. She had fought with her conflicting responsibilities for long enough to know that she couldn't keep it up forever, that the pain, far from becoming customary, simply grew worse. The missed anniversaries. The children crying for her down the phone, being unable to comfort them. Arriving late for Joe's business dinners, or not at all. The death of desire. Losing the connection that would have flown her home in time for her mother's funeral. The grease put under her professional heels every time she told them she was pregnant. Cutting that vital final half-hour from the edit, the time which turned a good piece into a great one, in order to make it home by Benjy's bedtime.

She had flown to Ethiopia that last time, to visit the hunger camps, carrying a cold which Benjy had brought home from kindergarten. She had returned home wondering how many starving children she had infected – condemned to death, perhaps, for the sake of that story.

The juggling act was over. She had fumbled her marriage, her career, now the kids. It was time to decide. She knew what had to be done.

'You make a persuasive case, Mr Pomfritt.' The voice was subdued almost to a whisper, the eyes misted. 'The whole world seems set against me, even my own Government. Very well, I'll return home, as soon as I can. Sadly I have no money but I'll get in touch with my husband. Today. Get him to send the money for the tickets. Back home to the States. Should only take a few days.'

'A wise decision, Miss Dean.' The moustache wobbled in imitation of a victory salute. 'I'm sorry it came to this.'

'Yeah. Me too.'

*   *   *

Frostbite, frostbite of the heart; it was scarcely a new sensation with her. How often she had fallen into bed while on assignment, between clean, starched Sheraton sheets, exhausted, afraid of the world she had momentarily left and would visit again in the morning. You never got used to it, no matter how many times you were there. A few hours' tormented sleep before climbing out of bed and into stale dungarees and yesterday's knickers, swapping the security of the hotel for the sewage of war which lay beyond the front door. To save yourself, you tried to stop feeling.

Izzy cared, how much she cared, but in order to go on caring and doing her job she needed to freeze her emotions, place them in cold storage, until she got back home. It was the only way. Forget about your own life, your own children, because as soon as you started equating the mutilated carcasses and tiny corpses which lay around in the flowing gutters and rat-gnawed piles of rubble with your own children, it was the end. You would never go on. So you froze inside.

She was frozen now, she must allow nothing else to matter. Close off the heart so that nothing else penetrated.

She was solid ice by the time Daniel arrived to pick her up, shortly after Pomfritt had flapped his way out of her life. Daniel noticed the change, but said nothing.

They set off in his smoking Volkswagen Beetle, coughing across the cobbled courtyard and past the stable door behind which she knew Chinnery was lurking. They headed for Weschester, through the December rain that clung in the air and which the primitive VW wipers moved inefficiently around the windscreen, mixing with the road spray until it had formed an opaque mask of rural muck. She couldn't see where she was going. She felt vulnerable, exposed in this noisy, rudimentary metal box with its battered springs and sagging fender. She preferred the Rolls, and wondered if it were following.

The 'Mission of Mercy' burned with light. There was life. At their knock the door was opened by two tiny figures, old ladies, with bright faces and chirping voices who hopped excitedly from foot to foot, but whose garb, by contrast, was unostentatious and even dull. Grey and brown cardigans, oversized and out of shape. They reminded Izzy of two rain-drenched sparrows.

'Welcome to the "Mission of Mercy". Come in, come in.'

They were led into a large room, once used for dining, with views over an unkempt garden down to the river, and high shelves along the walls which sagged with assorted paperwork and files. There were long cracks in the plaster ceiling and signs of damp, with flower-embossed wallpaper which wilted in several places. Yet the room, like its occupants, was impoverished rather than uncared for; the window glass was clean, the floor swept, the two oversized desks polished and neat. The two elderly women appeared to share one desk, the other stood unattended.

'Sit you down, my dears. Now, how can we help you here at the Mission?'

'We are interested in your work,' Izzy responded cautiously.

'Oh, pardon my rudeness. I'm Sister Agnes. This is Sister Faith.'

'Nuns?'

Sister A nodded cheerily. 'And you are Mr and Mrs . . . ?'

'Appleton,' Izzy responded quickly. Instinct told her the truth would only complicate matters. 'And Benjy.'

'Mr and Mrs Appleton. And Benjy. Lovely,' chirped Sister F. 'You're foreign, Mrs Appleton.'

'Canadian.'

'Doesn't matter. Doesn't necessarily make a difference. The Mission provides quite a few children for adoption abroad.'

'Adoption . . . ?'

'Yes, of course. The "Mission of Mercy for Children's Aid and Adoption". You want to adopt another child, that's right, isn't it?'

'Yes.' She felt her chest rising and falling as she sucked in the air. 'Tell me, please. A little about your work. The children you have available. For adoption.'

'Well, my dear, as you probably already know the Mission is the official adoption agency for this area.'

'Official?'

'That's right. For the last few years the local authority has contracted out all their adoption work to the Mission. The cuts, you know,' she whispered, as though invoking the Devil. 'The Mission has been operating since Victorian times – only in a small way, you understand, but when the council discovered that as a charity we were able to handle the work much more cheaply than they could, they closed down their own adoption office and gave us all their business and an annual subsidy. And still saved money.'

'Ah. The cuts.'

'Terrible. Terrible,' twittered Sister F.

Izzy's lips felt heavy and ponderous as she formed her next words. 'Do you have many children? For adoption?'

'Quite a few nowadays, yes, really quite a few,' Sister A responded. 'A lot through the convent network, you know. Good Catholic girls, in other parts of the country, in Ireland, on the Continent, who've got themselves in trouble. Our Order spends a lot of its time trying to persuade them not to have abortions. So they come here – it's lovely near the coast, isn't it? – where they can have their lovely babies in peace and quiet—'

'And privacy,' Sister F added.

'Yes, and privacy. And we help them have their babies, then help place the babies with good families. Just like yours, I expect.'

'You know, it's terrible, terrible,' Sister F interrupted again. 'So much ignorance. So many back-street abortions. Babies born in the fields and abandoned. This way we can give both the mother and infant the love they need.'

'And, of course, there are children from the local community around Weschester. Babies who've been neglected, or whose parents aren't capable of looking after them. But there aren't many of those, of course, not in these parts. This isn't London, you know,' Sister A squawked.

'Not London. A terrible place, terrible.'

'How many children do you have?'

'In the course of a year? About twenty. Wouldn't you say about twenty, Sister Faith?'

'At least. At least twenty.'

'You know, there's never a problem finding a good home for them. Not nowadays. It was different when I was young but now . . . oh, dear, what with contraception and abortion and the like, there are just too few children to go round, it seems. They're like gold dust.'

'Sister Agnes, how would I . . . how would we go

about adopting? Another child? I don't seem to be able to have any more . . .'

A touch belatedly, Daniel reached over to grasp Izzy's hand.

'Would the fact that I'm Canadian count against me? Do I have to be local? Would it be a problem already having one child?'

'Well, my dear, that's not exactly up to me or Sister Faith. There are guidelines, of course, but at the end of the day at the Mission we are allowed to use our common sense in each individual case to decide what's in the best interests of the child. So what the Adoption Officer is looking for is a couple who will be good parents. That's the main thing. Don't have to be local, not all the time. The right parents for the right child. Although normally there's a cut-off age of forty.' She peered at Izzy. 'That's not a problem, is it?'

'No. Not yet,' she responded tightly.

Daniel squeezed her hand once more.

'And which of you is the Adoption Officer?'

'Oh my, not either of us. Dear me, no. We're just here to help.'

'So who is the Adoption Officer?'

'Miss Paulette Devereux. Her name's Paulette Devereux.'

'I beg your pardon?'

'Granted, I'm sure. Paulette Devereux is the name. She's responsible for handling all the adoption matters in this area. Lovely girl.'

Daniel was squeezing her hand until she thought it might crack.

'And may we see Miss Devereux?'

The two nuns exchanged glances and looked towards the empty desk.

'You might have to be a little patient, Mrs Appleton. I'm afraid Paulette is rather unwell just at the moment.'

'Not for very long. She's never been away for much longer than a couple of weeks before,' Sister F encouraged.

'May I ask what's wrong with her?'

'Oh, it's her nerves, I think. Don't you, Sister A? Paulette never complains, says she's not sick at all, but you can tell just by looking at her. Under a lot of strain, poor thing. Terrible, terrible. Works so hard, we couldn't do without her. It *must* be her nerves. She can't concentrate, can't sleep, so she gets into the office late. It all builds up until she has to take a little time off.'

'She's away now?'

'We're simply filling in for her, holding the fort until she gets back.'

'My wife and I . . . we're so keen to get things moving. Could you let us know where she is, perhaps we could visit her, gently get the ball rolling? I have to go abroad on business very shortly.'

'Oh, I'm sorry, young man, she's not here. In London, I think. But I'm not sure.'

'No address?'

'None. And there's no one else who can really help. Paulette is responsible for all the paperwork, both for the children and the parents. She's the only full-time staff the Mission can afford.'

Izzy's disappointment was palpable. The good Sisters took pity on her.

'Look, my dear, I know how impatient you young things get. If you're really in a hurry, perhaps you ought to have a word with the Chairman of the Mission Trust. He's a local person, lovely man, buries himself in good works while he's here but spends quite a lot of time in London on business. That's where he is now, I think. Here's his card. Wonderful, wonderful man. His name is Gideon Fauld.'

The bones of Izzy's hand cracked painfully in Daniel's grip. She turned to protest, but cut herself short when she noticed the taut, censorial expression in his eye. He uttered not another word until after he had all but physically dragged her from the Mission, the blessings of the entire angelic community floating in their ears, and they were seated back in his car.

'Daniel, what on earth's wrong with you?'

'It's Gideon Fauld.'

'What about Gideon Fauld?' she demanded. 'You know him?'

'Only by his other works. Gideon Fauld is the Coroner who had the baby cremated.'

Her hand was shaking, she couldn't control it. At last she forced herself to pick up the phone and the number connected. It had barely passed six in the morning on the East Coast, but Joe was an early riser. He worked damned hard, she had to give him that.

'Michelini.' His voice was gruff, still full of sleep.

'Joe, it's me. Listen, don't hang up.' A catch in her voice. 'I want to bring Benjy home.'

A silence.

'You still want him, don't you?'

'He's my son. Of course.'

'Then I want your help in bringing him back home. I need you to send me the money for the fares, Joe.'

He considered for a moment. 'OK. But don't misunderstand me, Izzy. I still want custody.'

'I hear you. But maybe we can talk about this more

sensibly when he's back in the States, rather than shouting at each other down the phone.'

'I'll telex the money straight away. It can be with you close of play this afternoon, tomorrow latest.'

'Fine. There's one more thing, Joe.'

'Why is it with women there's always one more thing?'

'Listen, if we're going to argue about custody —'

'We sure as hell are.'

'. . . then I think it's important we don't do so in front of Benjy. Let's not get at each other through him.'

'What are you saying?'

'I want you to be at the airport, Joe, so that when he gets off the plane he sees his father. Not a lawyer, not a writ, not a dogfight, but his father. I'm still going to be his mother and you his father, no matter what we manage to do to each other. Let's not tear up his life along with the marriage.'

'Sounds too reasonable. What's the catch?'

'No catch, Joe. I love my son too much to start playing games with him. Just be at the airport to greet him like a normal father.'

'OK, Izzy. When?'

'Friday afternoon. British Airways flight 223. Gets in around four thirty in the afternoon. Take an early break from work.'

'Sounds good.'

'Just be there, Joe. Be there.'

And inside the ice melted a little beneath tears which fell without restraint. She vowed they would be her last.

Within three minutes she had booked the tickets, to be paid for on arrival. Everything was completed.

She looked out from Devereux's office across the valley, a scene of great beauty and peace, a tranquillity she could not share. For this place had cheated her of her child. She tried to tell herself for the thousandth time that it was the only solution, yet no matter how insatiably the frost gripped her soul she could not persuade herself that it was any solution at all. She was going to turn her back on her child.

It had taken her less than a minute to pack, to throw her miserable collection of belongings into the bag. She had spent the rest of the time before dawn sitting on the end of Benjy's bed waiting for him to wake. She washed and dressed and fed him with little fuss, slipping into their conversation the mention of an aeroplane. She didn't want him agitated. Even at his age he was a sufficiently experienced traveller for the prospect to cause neither alarm nor undue excitement; rather he looked forward contentedly to being fussed over by men and women in uniform who would thrust colouring books and his own special tray of food at him and would smile rather than scold if anything spilled.

Even mention of his father did not perturb him; the man he called Daddy had passed in and out of his life on enough occasions for it to be but part of a familiar pattern, and there was relief for the child that the familiar patterns seemed slowly to be returning. A mother. Now a father. Talk of home. The nightmare fading.

Daniel had arrived to take them to the airport. She went through the formality of thanking Sally for her help; of Chinnery there was no sign. Then they were gone, past the bloodied fingers of dogwood which led away from Devereux's house, throwing up a trail of oil smoke as they left Bowminster and Wessex behind, until through the window Benjy was pointing at the lumbering nose-up aircraft coming in to land. She guided Daniel to Heathrow's Terminal Four by the back doubles which on a busy day could save vital minutes. They weren't in a hurry but old habits die hard. Daniel dropped them at the Departure level, not even switching off the engine but climbing out of the car to give Benjy a small model aeroplane as a farewell gift in return for a kiss, willingly exchanged, Benjy failing to notice the tight smiles carved on the faces of both his new friend and his mother. He accepted Danny's hug of goodbye with equanimity, as he had done every day since they had met. Then Danny was gone.

They had but one bag, a small vinyl grip, and they threaded their way through the controlled confusion of the pre-Christmas exodus to the ticket desk. The briefest of paperwork, Joe's money in exchange for two tickets. A short walk with the infant to the Customer Services counter. A check of the passports. Everything in order. And already they were being shepherded by a stewardess towards the departure area and its milling crowds.

She had to struggle with a barely resistible urge to look round. She knew he was there, *he* was there, could feel his presence, the watery blue eyes, had suspected, rightly, that he would be unable to forgo the temptation of confirming for himself that she was fulfilling the arrangements she had made over the telephone. To savour his triumph. Driven by the need to know she was finally gone.

That was why, after booking the seats, she had amended the arrangements from a payphone.

And now it was time. They were at the departure area, she had deliberately left it late in order to reduce to a minimum the opportunity for Benjy's tears – or for hers, come to that. The area was a sea of waving hands and weeping relatives, and had become a battlefield as overdue passengers fought with overloaded baggage carts, as fond farewells collided with frantic dashes for departure gates. The three of them – Izzy, Benjamin and stewardess – pushed their way towards the far line, squeezing through the crowds. Izzy wanted to get as far away as she could from prying eyes behind, put as much confusion as possible in between.

Once more she explained in a matter-of-fact tone to Benjy that his father would be waiting for him at the other end. They had arrived at the narrow departure channel, almost at the point where a security officer would check boarding passes, where passengers would be separated from those they were leaving behind. The moment had arrived. She handed over the little vinyl bag and two tickets, one for Benjy and one for the stewardess, the airline 'Auntie', who would accompany him. Izzy smiled encouragement. And smiled and smiled until she knew her face would explode in protest. She had dosed the child with Calpol to help him remain calm; there was no means of release from her own torment. Yet even as she screamed inside and cursed all gods, she gave thanks that Benjy was not protesting or imploring – she couldn't have taken that.

Now the Auntie had him in her arms, was presenting the boarding passes – a face over her shoulder, a face being carried away in the crowd, a face with a growing look of doubt, of accusation, a face coming to the realization that once again she was deserting him. The lip wobbled, eyes rimmed with tears of uncertainty as his faith in her fought with the evidence before him. But he didn't cry; he could still see his mother, the mother he loved, the only thing he loved, or trusted, and she was still smiling encouragement. Perhaps it would be all right.

And his hand had come out, a small, perfectly formed hand with five tiny outstretched fingers, beseeching, wanting his mother.

She had screamed at herself not to but couldn't control it and she found her own hand reaching up, stretching out towards him, to grab him back, to protest, to stop the pain, the feeling that something deep within her was being torn by its roots from her womb. And she stretched out to grab him back but instead she was waving, still smiling, and he was biting his lip and believing in her, burying his fears beneath his trust. God, he was a fighter, that one; would he ever forgive her?

And then Benjy was gone. Back to his father. Out of her life. And she had ducked beneath a barrier and fled in despair.

She could not tell what the future might hold, what her husband or any court might decide, what the world would think of a woman who could give up custody of her child so brutally and later seek to claim him back, as she had and would. Yet she knew she had no choice. As much as she was unable to live with the possibility of losing Benjy, she had to set that against the certainty of losing Bella. A doubt weighed against a certainty.

Torture beyond reason, to give up one child in the hope, however forlorn, of regaining another. She might end up losing them both.

There were no tears, no longer any place in this new world of permafrost emotion for tears, merely an overwhelming numbness as she found the far exit of the terminal without once looking back.

The crass Volkswagen with its rusted paintwork

and sagging fender was waiting in the car park. She climbed in beside Daniel.

'Could this car go as far as Kiev?'

'I doubt it.'

'Didn't think so. OK, let's go find Bella.'

SIX

They had stopped on the M3 motorway into London for petrol. Daniel came back from the cash kiosk rubbing his wallet ruefully.

'By my reckoning, if we eat nothing and sleep in the park, we might have enough money to get us through, oh – at least until the weekend.' He smiled thinly. 'We need to figure out a plan.'

'Already have.'

'I must seem a pretty pathetic excuse as a noble knight come to your rescue. I've no job and practically no money.' He thumbed through the few notes in his wallet. 'Sorry.'

'At least we're swimming in it together, Daniel.'

'Meaning?'

'I've no money. And I have no job – at least, I won't have when I fail to turn up in Paris or Washington next week.'

'Bother.'

Her eyes lit in amusement at his understatement, but he failed to see the humour. He was troubled, her buccaneer becalmed.

'I'd sell the car, but who'd want it? Never mind, we'll think of something. I'm afraid we'll have to slum it.'

She shook her head. 'That's not on. We have a lot to do and very little time.'

'What do you suggest? A dawn raid on Harrods?'

'If you like.'

'And I assume we'll take a suite at the Ritz?'

'At The Stafford, in fact, a very exclusive hotel just off St James's. It's already booked.'

He began to laugh, then stopped. 'You're serious, aren't you?'

'Deadly. We need to open doors. No one is going to invite us in if we tramp around London dressed like Orphan Annie.'

'Orphan Annie found a millionaire.'

'It needn't cost that much. What we need is the right image. You know, on assignment my most precious piece of luggage is a twenty-dollar waterproof holdall that stays zipped up until five minutes before air time. It's got nothing in it but a silk blouse, flash earrings, cosmetic wipes and a brush. I can be dressed in rancid jeans, standing up to my crotch in swamp and reeking after a week without a bath, but as long as I look good from the waist up, no one cares. Image is everything. Truth to so many people is only skin deep.'

'To Americans, perhaps.'

'No, Daniel, the English are the worst! Everything with these guys is external – the suit, the old school tie, the way they speak, the long aristocratic noses which keep their mouths as far away as possible from their brains. The English are all first impressions. We can't handle them looking like refugees from an Oxfam bring-and-buy.'

'My mother and me, we lived in an old tumbledown manor house overlooking the Bay. Lots of rooms, running water when it rained, no money. So when she wanted to create a fresh impression she'd move the furniture around from room to room.'

'So what are you suggesting?'

'Maybe we could swap earrings?'

She laughed. 'Oh, Danny Blackheart, but you'd

look weird in my blouse.' Slowly she ran an experienced eye over his ill-clad torso, jeans, sneakers, faded ski jacket. 'I wonder what you'd look like in a well-cut suit.'

'Pretty good, actually. There used to be a time . . . But that was in a different life.'

'I mean this life. Today.'

'Izzy, be real.'

'Daniel, the whole bloody English Establishment is out there trying to squash me. We have to fight them on their own terms, we can't do it from the gutter. They'll find out I haven't gone back, sooner or later. Then they'll start looking for me. And you. But they won't start looking for Mr and Mrs Daniel Franklyn living at one of London's most exclusive addresses. Not for a while, at least.'

'But how . . . ?'

'Daniel, just drive.'

So he did, and as they entered the heart of the capital she felt her energies returning, her batteries recharged by the electricity of urban life. She no longer felt isolated and exposed. Here the traffic confronted every intersection like a bull attacking a cape, while pedestrians risked life and limb by mimicking matadors and swerving between the angry vehicles, each audacious pass accompanied by an ovation of horns. This was the city, impatient, angry, anonymous. At last she was fighting on her ground again.

They drove until she directed him to stop in a side street off Piccadilly in the heart of the fashionable West End, drawing up outside the main London branch of Thomas Cook, the country's biggest travel agency, into which she disappeared. Less than ten minutes had passed before she returned.

'And now?' he enquired.

'First things first. Underwear, I think. Marks & Spencer.'

'Come on, Izzy, what game are you playing?'

'Same game, Daniel, only now we're making some new rules.'

She pulled up the flap on her coat pocket. It was stuffed with fifty-pound notes.

'Fifteen thousand pounds. Enough to be getting on with, you think?'

For a moment his lips offered a remarkable impression of a feeding perch. He started to frame the next question but the words failed him. 'How . . . ?' he croaked, then subsided.

'The brave and bold folk we call the corps of foreign correspondents are constantly racing off round the world at a moment's notice armed with nothing more than overnight bags and our editors' unreasonable demands. And in the sort of places we go credit cards are often useless. You can't bribe or barter with plastic, sometimes can't even get a hotel bed. Many of the places we stay aren't likely to be around in thirty days' time to collect on Amex. So WCN has this little arrangement with Cook's to provide a cash float to anyone who's on their list of accredited employees. Up to fifteen thousand pounds. And I'm accredited.'

'But you said they were just about to fire you.'

'That's right. I imagine there'll be one mother of a row.'

'It's, it's . . . theft.'

'Not technically. I intend to give it back.' She shrugged. 'Anyway, at the moment my need is considerably greater than WCN's.'

'Neither WCN nor the police might see it that way.'

'I'll take the risk.'

'At very least it could ruin your reputation. It's scarcely ethical.'

Green is a colour of varying charms that can reflect the warmth and intrigue of an emerald or the enchantments of an ancient forest. It can also petrify the spirit like ice-bound wastes beyond the Arctic Circle. As he gazed into her eyes, eyes which for him held so much charm and grace, he thought he'd never seen the colour so remorselessly glacial.

'Daniel, I've had one child taken from me. This morning I gave up my other child. You want to stop and talk ethics?'

He touched her arm; she flinched as if brushed by a burning iron.

'OK, Izzy. What's your plan?'

'Simple. Open a few doors. Find Paulette Devereux, find Bella. Any ideas?'

They were interrupted as a young police constable stared suspiciously at the mobile rust wreck anchored alongside some of London's most exclusive retail property. Izzy flashed an enormous, on-camera smile. The policeman nodded, impressed less by the insincere gesture than by the fact that terrorists didn't usually ignite car bombs while still sitting in the front seat. He motioned them on, staring disapprovingly at the plume of oil smoke coughed out by the exhaust.

'Tell me a little more about Paulette,' Daniel demanded as he nosed his way back into the thick West End traffic. 'What she looks like. Not from the photographs you've seen, but from what you can remember.'

She closed her eyes to shut out distractions, sucked in her breath to chase after a memory and entered a deep, forbidding cave, a world of darkness and putrefying damp that made her flesh creep and that whispered abhorrent thoughts of decay, and of death.

'She's tall. Blonde. Shoulder-length hair. Pretty at first glance but then you look more closely and see an old hag trying to climb out of a young woman's shell. Difficult to tell precisely what age. The hair could be beautiful and has a professional cut but is ragged, unwashed, the flesh on the face seems to have shrunk away, almost anorexic. Pencil thin lips. Don't know about the teeth, she doesn't smile, seems almost incapable of expressing emotion. The features are somehow empty, as if she's drained of feeling inside and been repacked with rags and cotton wool. And up really close she's . . . dirty. The skin – oh, the skin is appalling, greasy, clogged pores. A sore on the upper lip. You get the impression that it wasn't always like that, that once she was beautiful. But the eyes are the worst, the very worst part. So haggard, exhausted. Cursed.'

She opened her eyes, relieved to let the image fade. 'But it's what I felt rather than what I saw which left the strongest impression. Those eyes have no depth, as though made of frosted glass so you can't see the real person inside. Makes you wonder if there *is* a real person inside. I start asking myself if she really exists, if this Paulette has any being beyond my mind.'

'She exists, all right. But she'll be a bitch to find.'

'She must be somewhere.'

'Yes, but not the sort of places you are used to looking in, I'll be bound.' The light in front of them turned red. Daniel sighed and put on the hand brake. 'The description you've given me – physically flaking away, ruined beauty, empty – and so unreliable. Remember what the nuns said about her, couldn't sleep and then could never get up and into the office, often floating off for days at a time? She's on something. An addict. Probably smack. Heroin. Heroin addicts hate to wash, hate the feeling of water. That's why their skin can be so bad. And if I'm right and she's come to London on a smack binge, she won't be staying in The Stafford, that's for sure. You won't need any pretty clothes where we'll have to go.'

'Devereux's daughter? An addict?'

'Why not?'

It made sense. Izzy had little experience of white drug addiction, most of what she had seen first hand had been black or brown or yellow, and often dead, scattered around the slums and decaying ghettos of the Third World or the American capital. But she recalled the anguished tones of Devereux's diary. How he'd been so blind. Not seen it. Until it was all too late. And now Paulette had fled to London. Sin City.

'So we're looking for a needle in a haystack.'

'And in a haystack of needles, just to complicate things a little.'

'But there's one part of the package which is altogether more difficult to hide. Mr Coroner Fauld. He's a public figure.'

Daniel cursed as at last they pulled away from the light only to be cut up by a motorcycle messenger displaying suicidal tendencies. 'But if Fauld's involved—'

'He is.'

'He's scarcely likely to volunteer information.'

'True, but we have one advantage. He's blind. We know who he is, yet he won't know us. Even if he's been warned he'll be expecting the sad and single Miss Izzy Dean. Not this odd couple, Mr and Mrs Franklyn. I think I shall call myself Fiona.'

'Izzy, you seem to have thought this all through in considerable detail. You're way ahead of me. So one question.'

'Shoot.'

'This odd couple, Mr and Mrs Franklyn, who have the suite in The Stafford.' He risked taking his eyes off the traffic long enough to look round at her. 'Their . . . body space. Are we talking single or double beds?'

She laughed.

'Don't mock me, lady, I'm serious. I'm no master with words and I can't afford roses. And I daren't tell you how much you frighten me—'

'Frighten you?'

'Course you do. You're a very powerful woman, Izzy, you don't operate like most other women. You seem so very much in control.'

'Oh, Daniel, if only you knew . . .'

'Your age and experience intimidate me, to be honest. But . . .' He smiled, an expression completely lacking in guile. 'But you will always find me honest. And I would very much like it to be the double bed.'

'Daniel, stop the car.' The laughter had disappeared.

'Izzy, forgive me—'

'Daniel, stop the car. Now.'

He pulled over, defying the bleating protest of the car behind.

'Daniel, you have offered me friendship, your job, most importantly you've given me back hope. How could I refuse you anything? As far as I'm concerned, you can have my bed, my body, and anything else I'm capable of giving, whatever you want. Willingly. If that's what you want. But . . . not me, not the woman inside. Not now. Not yet. There's too much guilt and confusion, too much fresh scar tissue. For the moment I'm an emotional cripple, I've got nothing more to give in that department. I can't share, Daniel, not while I have this job to do. No distractions.'

'Forgive me, I'm a slow, thick Paddy, Mrs Franklyn. Let me get it clear. That was American for "no", was it?'

'Be patient, Daniel. Please.'

He jammed the car into gear and pulled out without looking, to be greeted by an orchestrated protest from behind.

'Bugger it,' he said. 'I guess timing's not my strong point.'

'Neither is driving,' she whispered.

The day was turning to triumph.

Devereux had arrived in a crowded Chamber to defend his decision on the Duster before his colleagues, friends and foes in the House of Commons. He permitted no one to mistake the importance of the occasion.

'With the collapse of the Soviet Union and the power blocs that had been frozen in place by what we called the Cold War, we have been launched into a world of great flux, great uncertainties,' Devereux had intoned, every inch the statesman. 'The decisions we take today will shape the world of our children and our children's children. Indeed, it is not too great an exaggeration to say that it might resolve whether they have a world at all.'

Weighty stuff, but words which would not shift the Opposition Defence Spokesman, a dour Lancastrian called Stubbins, a man of such considerable girth that he had inordinate trouble shifting himself. A man who had 'terrorized tailors all the way from

Blackburn to British Home Stores', as Devereux had once mocked to great effect.

But it was not the Opposition whom Devereux had to convince: the Duster's future – his future – lay in the hands of a small cohort of sceptics within his own ranks who doubted one or other aspect of the deal. Small in number they may be, but it would take only a handful of deserters to swamp the battalions of a Government whose majority numbered less than two dozen.

So he had reverted to the basic tactic of parliamentary debate: unity through abuse, of either editors or Opposition. Devereux's moist eye had roamed across the green leather benches before him in distaste; the Opposition comprised a mongrel collection of interests and ideologies, utterly lacking in breeding or distinction, fit only for snapping at the heels of those with greater stature. Those like Devereux. Yet there was danger when they hunted as a pack.

He pointed directly at Stubbins, while addressing his own troops. 'The Honourable Gentleman was once against this project – as a matter of principle. But when he realized that the deal I had negotiated might bring hundreds of new jobs to his constituency, he changed his mind – as a matter of expediency. Then his so-called colleagues got to him, and twisted his arm, so now he says he's not sure – as a matter of intimidation.'

Devereux shook his head in a theatrical gesture of disbelief. 'He doesn't know what to think, Madam Speaker, but I for one wouldn't condemn him.'

Devereux turned to wave a hand of admonishment at the jeers of derision which he had manufactured behind him.

'No, I wouldn't condemn him for admitting that

he doesn't know what to think. Why, it's probably the most honest political statement he's made in his life!'

The jeers aimed at Stubbins turned to cheers of support for his tormentor, accompanied by the animated flapping of Order Papers. Devereux was providing a lead, staring straight into the eyes of the enemy, and his parliamentary troops were rallying.

Yet of itself, abuse was not enough. Sceptics from his own side required much more considerate handling. Alternately he gripped and pounded the Dispatch Box in front of him – the same polished buriti and bronze piece on which his father had leaned and eventually sagged – pausing on occasion to rest one elbow upon it in order that he might turn and face those to his rear, those who should be backing him, those who might yet overwhelm him from behind; arguing, disputing, cajoling. To those who had feared an excessive concentration of defence options into one weapons system, he had shown a remarkable grip of technical detail; to those who questioned the financial prudence, he had argued a carefully prepared case emphasizing the greatly improved terms he had wrung from the Americans.

'In our hands lies the future of the trans-Atlantic alliance,' he had told one doubter. 'Today we in Britain are the linchpin of the democratic world, the bridge which brings the two halves of freedom together. Yet if we desert our American allies at this late juncture, they will surely turn to others in Europe for friendship and reliability. We would find ourselves alone, a small island drifting somewhere between Europe and the Americas, a part of neither, untrusted, unloved. And largely undefended.'

The performance was impressive. In a Chamber

deprived of the rhetorical skills of the past by the ever-expanding pressures of parliamentary business and sound-bite television, Devereux's words and confident mannerisms were refreshing, gathering ever more doubters to his banner.

But it was not enough, not yet. There was still the Chairman of the Defence Select Committee, a Cockney, elevated largely through his own elephantine persistence and the excruciating ineptitude of his rivals, and whom it was so easy to dismiss yet so dangerous to underestimate. And he was still not satisfied. The man sensed the omissions, knew there was more, parts of this deal as yet unexplained and which he wanted laid before the House. Yet how could Devereux reveal that he had badgered and brow-beaten the Americans into offering up the United Nations, stuffing that little Cypriot upstart and fixing a vote-winning propaganda visit to Washington? These were deals done behind closed doors which could not bear the light of public scrutiny, which would embarrass both allies, which could be written into no accord or memorandum of understanding. They were triumphs for a future day. And his diaries.

They were secret, and the Select Committee Chairman hated secrets. He had longed to be a Minister but had consistently been denied – no one could or would say why. One of those things. No justice, no reason. Politics. Nothing to do with his unfashionable East End background, they assured him, let alone his inability to tell Burgundy from best bitter. But the injustice rankled and, having failed to gain entrance to the club, he had instead established his parliamentary reputation by playing the Jacobin and dragging the club's members out from behind barred doors for public inquisition. If not a man of power, then he would be a man of the people.

He rose from his seat three rows behind Devereux and in high-pitched Cockney tones addressed the tight waves of hair on the back of the Minister's head.

'Well done, yes, very well done. So far, so good. But, Madam Speaker, we so often find on these occasions that we've only been given half the picture. Can my Right Honourable Friend give the House his personal assurance that there are no – well, what you might call "knots" – no intertwined strings, no hidden commitments, nothing tucked under the pillow which might influence the judgement of the House on this vital issue?'

Turd, muttered Devereux, and smiled.

'All too often in such matters we've learned only long after the event of clandestine conditions and undertakings – bar-room deals which this House would never have accepted – well, it's precisely why over the years Governments have been in the habit of making them clandestine. But is my Right Hon Friend aware that he won't be forgiven if at a later stage we find out he's dropped us in it, has deceived the House, if not by lying – no, God forbid any Minister should lie to this House – then at least by concealing the full truth?'

Devereux rose, turning a full 180 degrees where he stood to look directly at the Chairman. You miserable worthless East End excretion, he chanted inside, you sanctimonious little shit, he sang to himself, before smiling more broadly still and returning to lean on the Dispatch Box.

'What can one say? On such occasions there is no evidence, no proof that can be offered to satisfy my Honourable Friend's enquiry. All I can do is to tell him that I have examined every part of this project personally, studied every spigot and specification, read and rewritten every line of the relevant agreements, and then read them all again. I came rather late to this project, as he knows, but in all modesty I now regard this project as being my own. I can assure him that nothing has been hidden, and that everything has been considered. I can give him no proof of that which does not exist, I can only give him my considered and strongly held judgement, and my word of honour. I hope he will feel able to accept both.'

Devereux and the Duster. Or neither.

And with a short nod of consent from the now-sedentary Chairman, he was free. He had shown skill of both negotiation and explanation, and mastery of detail; it was an all too rare combination which had impressed even his enemies. And as editorial after laudatory editorial would confirm on the coming day, by cementing his own fate to that of the Duster he had made it probable that both would soar.

It did not need the Father of the House, the Member of Parliament with the longest period of continuous service, to rise unsteadily from his place below the central gangway in order to confirm Devereux's personal victory, but nevertheless he did. The octogenarian caught Madam Speaker's eye and the House hushed, out of respect and of necessity, to catch the quavering voice.

'May I say to my Right Honourable Friend that I was a member of this House' – the old man's tongue ran across cracked lips as he pointed an unsteady finger – 'when at an earlier time his father stood before that same Dispatch Box? He has done honour to his family's name today. May I say – and I think

I can say without any danger of contradiction – his father would have been well pleased with the way he has handled not only himself and his departmental brief, but also this House?'

Intended as a fulsome accolade, it was recognized as such by all around.

The words were still ringing in his ears as Devereux reached the privacy of his parliamentary office and hid behind the closed door, losing track of time and diary obligations as he stared, transfixed, into the lying eyes of his father.

'Pleased? Are you pleased?' he whispered. 'How could you be? I've not only matched you, I've beaten you. I've won, don't you see? Standing there, in your shoes, in your place. But not mocked and derided, not like you, not throwing it all away. At last I'm free, free of you. Rot in hell!'

There was no pleasure in the invective. No conviction, either. Somewhere within, a wire was cut. As he slumped into the chair at his desk and his watered eyes turned from father to ornately framed portrait of his daughter, he let out a fearful sob of despair. Because he could never escape his father. Chains beyond the grave.

Was it not his father who had instilled in the young Devereux the belief that women were objects to be used and if necessary abused, be they wife, housemaid, nanny or any other he met in an alcoholic fit? Who had stretched out his hand only to chastise? Who had deprived the son of any tolerable concept of family, of mother and father, of life within the walls of a home bound with love rather than barbed wire? Who had taught him to inflict sex as a matter of punishment rather than pleasure? And who thereby had led the son's wife to despair and degradation, and ultimate suicide?

The family's influence had ensured the inquest recorded a verdict of accidental death, a stumble on the cliff top, but Devereux knew better. She had walked with purpose, not so much jumped as been pushed.

By him.

By his father.

It had enabled Devereux to act out the role of gentle widower, loyally clinging to memories, but – *God!* – it was the memories which clung to him as leeches sucking blood and stifled any chance of normal human relationships and happiness. Behind the facade of public acclaim there was nothing, nothing but shame and suffering, utter loneliness, nothing but the hypocrisy of public esteem covering a private agony, the corrosive legacy of his father. *Nothing.*

Except for Paulette.

And it was through his beloved Paulette that Devereux knew he had not won, could never win. For he cared, cared too much, perhaps, had covered his eyes to her faults just as his determination to succeed may have covered his eyes to her needs. Her faults were his faults; she was the only thing he had, he could not blame her. Blame his father instead. Blame himself. Make any sacrifice, take any risk. So long as it might save Paulette. Whatever she had done.

As he held the photograph of his daughter in front of him, he could see reflected the image of his father and, in the reflection, distortion. The eyes carefully painted in sincerity seemed to glint with malice, the lips in smile now seemed to scorn, to shout that you have not beaten me! It is I who have beaten you! In the only thing you have ever cared about, the raising of your beloved daughter. You loved her as you have hated me, the only two sincere emotions of your life. Yet it is I, a womanizing drunk, a man in whom you could find no credit, who did a better job of raising you, miserable wretch that you are, than you have done your own daughter.

'Look at her!' the reflection seemed to cry. 'You vowed you would never be like me, never lose your grip, would always be in control. Control!' the image mocked. 'You cannot even control your own daughter!'

A more worthless father than was ever his own. As the reflected image mocked, Devereux buried his face in the photograph of Paulette.

'You bitch,' he wept.

Children. She wondered what made them such a force. Objects so tiny, so weak and pathetic, yet of such irresistible might. Who, before they were born or even conceived, could bind together relationships. Or tear them apart. And whose tiny fingers somehow never let go, even from beyond the grave.

She might no longer be able to recall clearly what Bella looked like, but she could remember the smell, like malt, with a clinging pollen of sweet powder. She could not escape the smell, it was the scent of all young infants which seemed to linger in every place she went. In queues for taxis, amongst the clothes racks at Selfridges, at the cash till in Bally's and in the corner of the coffee shop behind Marks & Spencer where they paused for breath during the effort of spending so much, so quickly. She would turn sharply as she caught a glimpse of a waddle that was Benjy's or a tuft of red hair that was Bella, but always it was a deception, someone else. From the corner of an anxious mother's eye all young children appeared the same.

The Stafford flowed over with English understatement; it all but cascaded down the Regency wallpaper and echoed from graceful cornices. Not an air-conditioning unit in sight. The entrance hall was diminutive, some might say cramped, scarcely a hotel foyer, redolent of a private house which, indeed, it once had been.

'Just like home,' Daniel muttered.

'Yeah.' She felt an ache. She no longer had a home, indeed it seemed as though she'd never had a home. Not since the day her father had been caught with his dental receptionist and the family had cracked and frozen like a pond in winter. As her own had now done. Seasons turned full circle.

They were greeted with dignity and discretion, if also with a half-raised eyebrow when it was indicated they intended to settle the bill with cash, but Mrs Franklyn was, after all, a foreigner, Canadian, and they did things differently. Anyway, they had booked in for two weeks rather than a couple of hours, they weren't going to use the hotel as a knocking shop. The Stafford wasn't like that. Here one had affairs, *liaisons*, arrangements, not leg-overs.

One guest, an American, now in her mid-sixties, had been coming every year for a week with a man nearly twenty years younger than herself, to occupy a room where with the window open one could hear the changing of the guard at Buckingham Palace, just across the park. The sound of the military band helped keep rhythm and maintain stamina. Percussive passion.

Daniel was not to be so lucky. They took a suite in the Carriage House mews to the rear. Cobbles. Character. And two beds, Daniel noted with a look of disgust. He took himself off to the bathroom as she sat and dialled.

'Joe, it's me. How's Benjy? Did you get the letter I sent with him?'

It took a moment for him to respond, in a tone more conciliatory than she remembered. But why shouldn't he be conciliatory, he had Benjy. He'd won – and in winning had discovered that looking after a child by himself could prove to be more of a social constraint than endemic halitosis. The free time, the orderly apartment, the periods of peace that had been his were no longer his own. Like trying to screw in front of spectators. Distraction. Constant interruption. The bitter-sweet fruits of victory had taken the edge off his aggression, leaving puzzlement.

'What are you up to, woman? We're in the middle of a custody battle and you send the kid back, free, gratis, no charge, with a note saying you'll want him back later. One of us has tumbled out of our tree, and it sure ain't me.'

'I'm the mother of two children, Joe. Bella as well as Benjy. I had no choice.'

'You had the choice of facing reality. Bella's dead, Izzy.' He groaned, genuine anguish. 'Lord, I don't want you to suffer without cause, really I don't, but . . . Grubb called me yesterday, asked if you were back, were coming back. I know what's going down there. You've thrown away your kid. You've thrown away your job. You're throwing your whole world away, Izzy. You'll have nothing. *Nada.*'

'That's not how I see it.'

Stubborn damn woman; still, it was her problem, at least he'd tried.

'Is that how your new friend Danny – that's his name, isn't it? – is that how Danny sees it?'

She bit her lip. Benjy was obviously recovering his ability to talk, fast. At least it meant he must be comfortable. 'How is Benjy?'

'Fine, great. Staying at my sister's while I sort things out. But you can forget him, Izzy. I don't want to see you hurt any more, that's not my objective, but there's no way I'm giving him back and you're gonna get creamed if you take this to court. The woman who lost one child and abandoned the other . . .' An edge to his voice. 'Off with a man who's not her husband . . .'

And money that was not her own, she added silently.

'. . . who doesn't even have an income. It's a real pissy mess. The lawyers'll make hamburger out of you.'

He didn't like this other man, a man whom his son talked about with smiles and affection. He felt the need to retaliate.

'And me? Well, I've got a huge promotion on its way. The Duster's really coming through and they're giving me an extra piece of the action. More salary. More status. Security for Benjy, everything you can't give. If you fight I've got the custody hearing sewn up tight as a duck's ass.'

She didn't respond; his analysis was persuasive.

'Don't fight, Izzy. Don't hurt yourself more than you need. Stop running away from the truth.'

'I'm running *after* the truth, Joe.'

'What truth?'

'I'm . . . not sure yet, but it stinks. Bella was taken, I'm sure. They're all hiding something; the local police and press, the bank manager, the Coroner —'

'And the American Embassy,' he offered sarcastically.

'Maybe them, too. Certainly Paul Devereux.'

'You're kidding,' he stammered, incredulous, his head ringing with the sound of his future crashing in flames.

'Daniel's another journalist and he's helping me track down—'

She failed to notice the changing tone, his feeling that she was accusing him of parental neglect, of lacking concern, that she was screwing around with his Duster. And it was a mistake to mention another man.

'Stop! Stop this shit!' he cried, male pride tangled with impatience. And remorse. He had to shut it out. He couldn't accept any suggestion of Bella being alive; Bella was for him a corrosive mixture of guilt and personal failure, and Izzy its catalyst. 'Why am I wasting my sympathy on you? This is no more than another one of your assignments. That's it, and that's all of it. Izzy Dean, correspondent *extraordinaire*. You don't give a damn about the kids, only your story. You're not a mother, just another half-baked journalist who can't hear breaking wind without smelling a conspiracy. Who'd pass up on anything for an exclusive – her marriage, even her kids.'

'There *is* a story here, a huge one.'

'Get off this nonsense, get real, woman. Get laid for all I care. But just get out of my life.'

'Joe, I'm serious.'

'Me, too. Damn you. So see you in court.'

Then the phone went dead.

She stared at the receiver in her hand for long moments until it started to warble in complaint, as though offering her warning – *Danger! Go no further! Do not proceed beyond this point.*

She silenced it, slowly held it up again, and redialled.

Connection. Response. A woman's voice.

'Hello. My name is Fiona Franklyn. I'd like to talk with Mr Gideon Fauld, please.'

*   *   *

236

Daniel came into the room naked to the waist. There was no flesh on him, just sinew, muscle, unblemished skin – never Mr Universe, but . . . young. She tried not to look too hard, to notice the firmness, the dark brown nipples, the ripples of tightness across his abdomen, waist so much narrower than his shoulders – territory which with Joe had been not so much forbidden as forgotten – all capped by an irreverent grin and cascade of freshly washed hair which he was towelling dry. As the towel flapped back and forth, the action presented his torso like a well-tuned keyboard begging to be played, to have hands laid upon it.

Pity. A waste. Like a vegetarian at a lobster bake.

She tried to disguise her attention by adjusting her hair in a mirror, but he had already noticed her furtive stare.

'It's not just physical, you know.'

'What?'

'You. For me. I want you to know that. I feel very strongly about you.'

'Thanks.' She looked sheepish, out of practice at dealing with sincere emotions. 'It's on. Tomorrow afternoon. Around twelve thirty,' she added, changing the subject.

'Fauld? That's great,' Daniel responded. 'At least, I suppose it's great. How do you reckon we handle him?'

'*We* don't handle him. I do it. On my own.'

'No way.'

'The only way.'

He looked hurt. 'Impossible. I'm there. We go as a team. A couple.'

'A rather odd couple, don't you think?'

'Why, for God's sake?'

'Our nationalities. Our ages, for a start.'

'Are you trying to suggest you and I would be unnatural or something?'

'Daniel, you don't even know whether I take sugar in my coffee. Or even if I take coffee. We don't have the right body language for a married couple. He might spot the deception in a hundred different ways. We can't afford the risk: I've got to go alone.'

He took this badly. The towel flew angrily across the room and sulked in a corner. 'Don't start shutting me out. Don't take it out on me just because I asked you to go to bed.'

'No, Daniel. You've got it all wrong. You didn't insult or offend me, I was ... flattered.' And flustered.

His scowl remained distinctly sceptical.

'Daniel, take your mental processes out of your underwear and put them back where they belong. Fauld runs an adoption agency. So we talk to him about adoption. Babies. I'm a foreigner. But if I take you along and pretend we're just another happily married couple, even if you know everything about me, how on earth do we explain why we've come more than three thousand miles just to adopt? Why not do it back home, on our own doorstep? No, if I'm to get him talking, trying to find the wrinkles in his operation, I've got to pretend that there's something wrong with me. Some reason why I can't adopt legitimately. A medical problem. A criminal record.'

'Perhaps you could suggest you're too old,' he offered sullenly.

'Thanks a bunch!' She was about to laugh until she realized he might have a point. The laughter drowned in a minor panic tremor. 'I go on my own. A single woman. With some reason why no legitimate adoption agency in the world will look twice at me.

238

Daniel, it will be much more convincing if I'm on my own. You recognize that, don't you?'

'And much more dangerous.'

'How do you figure that?'

He sat on the edge of the bed. 'Look, Izzy, I hadn't wanted to ram the point home but . . . If Paulette Devereux is an addict, she won't have been working at the Mission out of charitable instinct. Addicts need supplies, supplies cost money. Lots of it. She will have found some way of making money, a large amount of it, out of the Mission. And the only asset the Mission has is the babies. Like Bella.'

'What are you trying to say?'

'Bella could have been sold.'

'You think that's possible?'

'I think it's probable.'

'Sold? For adoption,' she whispered, the tone begging reassurance.

'Presumably.' But he had hesitated, his eyes dropped, the response lacking conviction.

Fear seemed to have stopped her heart, fear of the unknown. She walked across the room as though in physical pain and sank down on the edge of the bed beside him. She stared blankly at the wall, suddenly wanting to hear lies, not wanting to confront the truth she knew she would find in his eyes.

'What else might a baby have been sold for?'

'Izzy, I'm really not sure. I'm sorry. But you mix drugs, criminal baby bartering and a whole pile of money, and you've a mess that I don't want you walking into on your own.'

She sat silently, bowed, lashed by imagination. She was back in Colombia, in the car, being driven along dusty roads and dilapidated streets towards the airport, remembering how on a bright sun-filled day the window beside her had suddenly shattered and left her staring into the flaming barrels of three Uzis. She had thought she was going to die at that moment, felt the bullet slicing through her breast, the warm-sticky flow of blood dripping into her lap. She recalled the only words she had found as they had sped away. 'Those bastards have ruined my favourite blouse.'

She had discovered it was possible to fight shock, and pain. At the hospital, as paramedics and nurses crowded round, she had waved them away, climbed across the fragments of shattered glass and out of the car, head held high. She hoped that from a distance some of her assailants would be watching. They might try again, might even succeed in killing her, but never in cowing her. Not Izzy Dean. She wanted them to know that.

Yet that was Colombia, by herself; now, with Bella, she was finding it altogether more difficult to be brave.

'Don't worry,' she assured him. 'I'm pretty good at dodging bullets. Only ever been caught once . . .' She was about to wave lightheartedly at the scar on her breast, but decided it would not have the right effect on Daniel.

'Aren't you frightened?'

'Of course,' she responded quietly. 'Frightened I might discover nothing from Fauld. And terrified I might discover all too much. All the more reason I have to go on my own – my baby, my risk. Whatever it takes to find the truth. That's the only thing that matters to me right now.'

'Let me share the risk.'

She shook her head, said nothing. It had all been said.

'I'm in this with you anyway, whether you like it or not. Whether I like it or not.'

'You're a very fine person, Danny Blackheart.' In the circumstances her compliment was not enough; she had meant to say more, but the words eluded her. She sat as though in prayer, her body bent under the weight of the thoughts and fears crowding in upon her.

'Just one thing, Izzy. How do I know you're not simply using me?'

She couldn't see his face, didn't turn. The words were squeezed dry of emotion, but there was no mistaking their importance to him.

'You don't, Daniel,' she responded without looking up. 'And you won't know. Until later.'

'Why?'

'Because I won't know myself. Until later.'

He deserved her honesty; it was the least she could give. Yet they were words of indecision she would grow to regret for the rest of her life.

Devereux sat in the study overlooking his beloved vale, his relief so evident he could taste it. The awful dream was over, Izzy was gone. From his home, the country, his life.

Yet his mood was tinged with tragedy. He'd played the game for all it was worth, gambled, and won. But he found no joy in victory, no virtue for him to extol. Only shame. He had sat debating with himself what to record in his diary, the diary that one day would reveal to the world the man in his full glory – as statesman, wit, raconteur, and yes, as lover, too. And as father?

Through its revelations and rigorous honesty the diary would ensure that the Devereux name and his accomplishments would endure; he would not be forgotten, like his father, drowned in the vat of history. But . . . honesty could be taken too far. Particularly when it came to Paulette. He had no right to damage her, even to record the damage she had done to herself, and others. The memories of that last, awful confrontation with her, when he found himself no longer able to deny her problem with drugs and had discovered the terrible truth about the baby, still burned inside him like hot coals. They were memories to quell, not to record.

It had to be that way. Isadora Dean would merit no mention, not even a footnote in his history. Not the means by which he had outwitted her and protected Paulette. The police inspector, a member of his own Lodge. The editor whose scalp he'd saved by extricating him from a ruinous libel battle. The bank manager with whom he played Sunday tennis, the hospital administrator who owed to Devereux his job, even the Embassy of the United States of America, beholden because of the Duster. None of them had known why he had asked for their help in dealing with this deluded woman, a troublemaker, and foreigner to boot. They were pleased to offer their support nonetheless, to him, to Paul Devereux, out of respect. But the story could not be told.

His diaries would record the truth, but not the whole truth. There was nothing here of which he was proud, nothing he wanted ever to be repeated. He felt only shame; it was not an emotion he was used to or wished to share.

Instead, he sat and wrote late into the night of his triumph with the Duster. Of the low-life Chairman of the Select Committee. Of how his skills had fixed the Germans and the Japs, and that little upstart Cypriot shit, of how he had helped manufacture an election victory. Of how he, Paul Devereux, had changed history. And he wrote, too, of his victory over that tarty wife of the former Transport

Secretary, whose name he still had trouble recalling. And the others.

Paul Devereux. A man amongst men. And one day it would all be revealed, his conquests. But not yet, not until the truth could no longer damage him. Not until time had lent perspective so that his bending of the rules of politics, of marriage, of public and private life, could be seen as the great achievements they were. Historic achievements.

Achievements he would gladly have sacrificed, every one of them, in exchange for Paulette.

SEVEN

Daniel stirred, opened a tentative eye, and focused on Izzy sitting up in the next bed. She had spent an uncomfortable night, sleep ground away by brooding thoughts.

'We need to know more, Daniel. About children, what happens to them. Who buys, who sells.'

'Mmm.'

'Before this afternoon and my meeting with Fauld. I need to prepare the ground. Make sure I know what I'm talking about.'

'Right.'

'Let's stop kidding ourselves. You know as well as I do that a baby can be sold for much more than adoption. We need to know facts.'

'We?'

Her eyes flashed in reprimand. She was already becoming accustomed to the fact that the fewer clothes he wore, the more he seemed driven to talk with her, while the fewer her clothes the more he seemed incapable of much other than laconic grunts. She pulled on a bathrobe.

'Yes, we, Daniel. You and me. Remember? So put your thinking cap on and anything else you propose wearing today and find someone we can talk to before twelve thirty this afternoon.'

He shook himself. 'The police? Scotland Yard, perhaps?'

'That's right. I'm not supposed to be in the country and I've got fifteen thousand pounds of someone else's money in my bag, so you want me to walk straight into Scotland Yard?'

'OK, OK. I'm a bog brain. I'll find someone else.'

'And I take no sugar in my coffee,' she threw over her shoulder as she headed into the bathroom.

When she returned, fully clothed, he was sitting beside a partially demolished jug of coffee and looking smug. 'Your wish is my command, O mistress mine,' he said ambiguously. 'In ninety minutes. Catholic Concern. The other side of the river, behind Waterloo.'

'Thank you, slave,' she said and bent to kiss his forehead. She smelt wonderful.

They were ten minutes early but their contact greeted them with an uncomplaining smile and dark, statuesque looks which were highlighted by a 'Save the Forests' T-shirt tucked into tight-fitting jeans. She introduced herself as Judi Wasserman in a voice that carried a faint trace of East London. They meandered through the entrails of a large and somewhat dilapidated building whose paintwork could most politely be described as stoic, whose walls bore a kaleidoscope of postered appeals for environmental disasters and Eritrean coffee ceremonies, and whose occupants, mostly women, squashed themselves into crowded offices where the battle against a rising tide of literature seemed to have ended in abject surrender. Judi's office was in the building's converted attic where the sloping eaves allowed few shelves, causing the paperwork to rise in great piles from the floor like stalagmites thrusting roofwards. Judi stepped carefully over one pile, swept clear two stools which had been similarly infested, and invited them to perch.

'Welcome to the God Squad. You want to know about kids? I'm your girl. How can I depress you?'

'We want to know about babies for sale,' Izzy said softly.

'Sold? For what purpose?' she asked.

'Does the purpose make any difference?' Daniel interjected.

'A hell of a difference if you're the baby,' Judi responded. 'For babies in most corners of the world life is a short, sharp battle against disease and brutality which the majority of them will lose. So selling babies is perfectly legal in many countries, particularly Asia and Latin America. And the lucky few will get sold for adoption to good, white, middle-class Western parents.'

'The lucky few?'

'Five, maybe ten thousand a year. Depends upon the fashion. Get a TV camera into a decaying Third World orphanage and the would-be mums and dads waving chequebooks won't be far behind, looking to buy one and maybe take a second if they can get a good discount. "Heir and spare". Naturally they'll convince themselves they're contributing to the welfare of the child's family; sadly, it doesn't work like that.'

'How does it work, then?'

'It works because someone, somewhere, is making money, usually a large amount of it and never the mother. Often a lawyer who charges a very modest fee but then discovers a pile of unidentifiable expenses.'

'You disapprove?'

Judi pushed the dark hair back from her face. 'Completely. Buying babies for adoption only encourages other forms of exploitation. The market's worth millions every year; I just wish that money were put into keeping families together, not tearing them apart. The West has stripped these countries of their natural resources, why take their babies too?'

'You talked about other forms of exploitation,' Izzy pursued.

'For every child who goes for adoption, maybe ten others are sold for different purposes. I spent a number of years in the Far East, in places where children were treated like television sets, to be bought and sold in the marketplace or to be thrown away when they were no longer of any use. In Thailand you can rent boys or girls by the hour or buy them outright. For cash. Four hundred pounds. Sometimes much less. Parents will sell their children for as little as it takes to buy a fix or a refrigerator. Much the same in the Philippines, South Korea, India and a dozen other countries. In China they give away baby girls, if you can find a way of smuggling them out.'

'Who? Who buys?'

'If the kids are lucky they'll be bought by some Western couple desperate to adopt. If they're not, they are bought for child prostitution, organized crime, helping to run the drugs rackets. You stuff a child full of packets of heroin and you can smuggle it almost anywhere undetected. Unless, of course, the packets burst, in which case all the authorities have is a dead child who nobody claims.'

Izzy felt winter invading her system.

'In India they recently found a Bihari group who were selling kids' organs for transplant,' Judi continued.

'You're not trying to suggest they were . . . killing, sacrificing children just for their organs?'

'Not suggesting. Stating. There's an international market for children, just like TV sets. Some people buy the whole set, others just buy the parts.'

Izzy sat quietly for a moment, struggling as a mother to reject the concept of children as a commodity to be bartered or butchered. Yet as a correspondent she knew what the charity worker said to be true, she had seen as much in Colombia and other parts of Latin America. She had arrived at Bogotá airport, a soulless concrete mausoleum, to find it packed with German couples arriving with bundles of US dollars or leaving with bewildered-looking infants and screaming babies. Parents and children, with not a single word of common language.

'What about nearer home? Europe? Here? Tell me it's different.'

'Sure,' Judi responded. 'The difference in Europe is that the price goes up. You can wait for five or six years to adopt a baby the official way and then be told you're too old. In some countries there are twenty sets of parents chasing each local child. So people pay more. To buy from abroad. To jump the queue. To find someone who will get round the rules and regulations.'

She looked at Izzy, grown pale under the onslaught of the story. 'You're upset. Would you like a cup of tea?'

Izzy shook her head.

'I can't apologize for upsetting you. Things won't change until people start getting upset. It's not a story you can cover in saccharine.'

'I don't want apologies, only the truth,' Izzy replied. 'In Europe, in this country, are children sold for reasons other than adoption?'

'It can happen. Not in the sort of numbers you get in the Third World, of course, but Europe does have one thing the Third World can't offer.'

'What?'

'White skin. People will pay more to adopt a white

baby. I still have trouble understanding it, but people will also pay more money to have sex with a white child. There are paedophile rings which make pornographic videos involving children. The police occasionally find the videos, rarely the ringleaders and almost never the children.'

'What happens to them?'

In answer Judi rifled through the papers on her desk and plucked out a press cutting. Of a paedophile ring in Amsterdam which circulated videos of a man torturing two girls, the younger of whom appeared to be scarcely eighteen months old. Izzy and Danny read the report, drawing closer together with each fresh detail. Of the police raid on a country farm, of the discovery of video equipment, of instruments for inflicting sexual pain. And a barrel of acid which according to the article appeared to contain pieces of dissolved flesh. Pig flesh, the arrested man claimed.

'In Europe the stakes are higher, so the price of babies is higher. There's even reverse racism. Reports from the Lebanon of Arab traditionalists purchasing white baby girls so they can be brought up in the harem, white women reared to know no better. A suggestion that one sheik in Yemen had purchased two white girls for his young son, like laying down vintage port for his coming of age. I'm not trying to suggest it's widespread. But you did ask.'

Izzy nodded in pain. 'That's in Europe. What about here, in Britain?'

'Britain is Europe. There's no difference any more, no checking of passports, no customs posts, nobody to ask questions about the identity of the small boy or girl in the back of the car. Doesn't matter where you are in Europe, it's all the same. Just one big happy family.'

The discussion appeared to have affected Judi, too. Her lips had drawn thin, her jaw set, her manner grown fierce, almost aggressive.

'How did you get into this job, Judi?' Daniel asked gently.

The mask on the charity worker's face cracked for a fraction of time before it was reassembled with practised speed. 'I had a baby sister who disappeared. Accident? Crime? Kidnapping? No one knows. Not a single trace. We never did find out.' She exhaled as though expelling demons. 'Somehow I keep hoping that this job might one day help me find the truth, bring her back. And bring other babies back.'

'Wasserman,' Izzy whispered, her voice chafed with emotion. 'A Jewish name, isn't it?'

Judi nodded.

'What are you doing working for Catholic Concern?'

'Babies aren't Catholic, or Protestant, or Jewish or Moslem or Hindu. They're just babies. And a dead one is no good to any god.'

She reappeared from the hotel bathroom shortly before noon. Daniel rubbed his eyes, making sure. He'd expected something demure, discreet but very fashionable, probably Italian. Not jogging shoes.

'Mother of God,' he gasped, lapsing into brogue, 'and just look at you.'

'Didn't I tell you?' she responded coquettishly, spinning on her toes so that he could get the full effect of her designer tracksuit. 'He couldn't see me for ten days. Too busy, his secretary said. No free appointments. No lunches, either, because he always goes jogging in the park. So I thought I'd try to short-circuit the system.'

'You're going to run him down?'

'Something like that. His office is only a stone's throw from St James's Park. I'm betting that's where he does his work-out.'

'And if not?'

'What have I got to lose?'

'Apart from a few pounds . . . ?'

For a moment she wanted to kill him.

Twenty minutes later she was hovering on the southern side of the park, at the edge of the pelican lake, as the lunch hour approached. She was perturbed at the number of masochists who began to emerge in all shades of running gear to brave the chilly December conditions, but most were young – too young, she guessed, to be a Coroner. She was looking for someone in his forties, at least.

And then he appeared, on the stroke of the half hour, clad in a sweatshirt declaring him to be a supporter of the Weschester Hospice Fund. He began a well-practised if ungainly circumambulation of the lake, more of a rapid shuffle than a run, scattering the pigeons and raising a cackle of protest from the Canada geese in search of crusts. She fell in beside him.

'Mr Fauld? Mr Gideon Fauld?'

He looked at her but said nothing, his stride pattern not faltering. He was in his mid-forties, of medium height and build with steel-rimmed glasses which covered sharp-witted, darting eyes. The hair was thick but slightly receding and swept back, giving him prominent temples and lending him an almost donnish air. He also had a prominent stomach which obtruded alarmingly; whatever his lunchtime restraints, it appeared he managed to stoke the fires forcefully at other times of the day. His jogging habit also suggested that he lived in constant regret of his indulgences.

'Mr Fauld, my name's Franklyn. Fiona Franklyn. I'm sorry to appear so impatient but your secretary said you couldn't see me for over a week. And I'm desperate for your help.'

'What do you want, Mrs Franklyn?'

'To adopt. You . . . were recommended.'

Already she was discovering that it was difficult both to jog and communicate in anything more than short bursts.

'You're not English.'

'Canadian.'

'Then try there. Your adoption regulations are much less restrictive than in Europe.'

'Yes, but . . . there are complications.'

'What sort of complications, Mrs . . . ?'

'Franklyn.'

They were forced to swerve in order to avoid the stubborn progress of an old derelict, a woman wearily pushing her way around the park behind a shopping trolley piled high with bulging plastic bags of rags.

'What sort of complications, Mrs Franklyn?' he repeated, slowing for the first time in order to look more directly at her.

'I can't adopt in Canada. It's my husband – there's no easy way to put this . . .'

'If you don't feel you can trust me, there's not much point.' He quickened his stride.

'He's serving a long prison sentence. He'll be inside for many years. Fraud. And I'm already thirty-seven years old. I can't wait, Mr Fauld. But no one's going to allow me and my husband to adopt, not with his track record. So I've come to Europe. I want to be treated on my own merits, not those of my husband.'

The explanation was beginning to leave her

winded, and conscious of her lack of fitness. Her breasts were feeling unpleasantly heavy.

'It's even more difficult to adopt in Europe,' he responded, beginning his second circuit. 'There are very few babies available nowadays, what with contraception and abortion. We've a declining population, the number of babies up for adoption is dropping sharply.' Even he was beginning to breathe more heavily. 'So the authorities can afford to be very selective. It means they normally rule out single parents. Or families with difficult social backgrounds, like you. And you're getting very near the upper age limit for an adoptive parent.'

She was beginning to feel that her physical stamina was not what it once was.

'I'm desperate, Mr Fauld.'

He stopped suddenly, looked directly at her as though reaching a judgement.

'I don't think I shall be able to help you,' he said, and began stretching exercises.

'But why? Are the rules so rigid?'

'It's not so much that. There are strict guidelines, inevitably, but within those guidelines every case is judged on its individual merits.' He stretched towards his toes, obstructed by his stomach, several times before rising to face her. 'To be frank there seem to be few merits in your case. And you a foreigner into the bargain.'

'Are you telling me it's impossible for a foreigner to adopt a child in Britain?'

'No, there are always a few exceptions – highly individual cases, you understand. I make no apologies for being blunt, Mrs Franklyn. If you are that desperate for a child, there are many easier ways than adoption. Get a divorce. Get artificially inseminated. Get naturally inseminated by a man other than your husband. There are many women who come into my office who decide to do exactly that.'

'But I can't, Mr Fauld. My husband's sentence is especially long because he refused to locate the money he'd embezzled. I'm a rich woman, so long as I remain married to him. So I must adopt. I can afford to give my child the best, the very best. Doesn't that count for anything?'

He had stopped his stretching activities, his hot breath clouding in the cold winter air.

'If money is no object . . .'

'It isn't.'

'. . . then why not find a baby from one of the developing countries. Almost anywhere. Fifteen to twenty thousand dollars, including air flights. Join a queue, or pay to get to the front of it if that's what you want.'

She shook her head repeatedly, her voice rising with emotion. 'No, that is not what I want. Mr Fauld, I want a child I can call my own, not something plucked from the gutters of the Third World. I want a baby with two legs and two arms and without any mental disabilities who looks enough like me so that he doesn't have people smirking for the rest of his life when I introduce him as my child. Is that too much to ask?'

'Almost. There's a pecking list in the adoption world; it's supply and demand. At the bottom of that list are the children who are available but who no one wants. Black and brown, disabled, mentally handicapped, children who are above the age of five and already formed in their ways, often with deep social problems. Children who will never be your own. Even in your difficult circumstances you could probably arrange something along those lines.'

'But I don't want those lines, don't you understand? I want a baby, and I want it white.'

'Precisely. But so does everyone else. And it's the white babies that aren't available.'

'How much money would it take?'

They had been standing still for some time in the chill.

'Come and have a cup of coffee,' he suggested, guiding her in the direction of the lakeside tea house. But it was crowded so, in spite of the conditions, they sat outside trying to catch the pale winter sun. His eyes passed over her, probing, calling her to account. He seemed very analytical, almost academic in his interest, reaching for a judgement as though in court. With an air of casualness she did not feel inside, she unzipped her tracksuit, not provocatively but enough to reveal the lycra-clad breasts beneath. The result was inevitable. Assailed first by the heat of extended exercise and now by the blast of winter air, the nipples exploded in protest. He noticed, and she knew he approved. His attentions were not confined to the academic.

'Why did you come to me, Mrs Franklyn? Who recommended you?'

'I came because I was told you were someone who could help with problems like mine. That you were . . . imaginative. Resourceful. Not a narrow-minded interfering agony aunt like those I've had to deal with back home.'

'And who told you this?'

'A girl, young woman. Called Paulette. I met her in a pizza parlour, she seemed down on her luck, we got chatting. I got the impression she has worked in this field. Blonde hair. You know her?'

'I think so. She . . . has been useful in the past. Been unwell recently.'

'She said it would cost money, but I have money. This is the only chance I might have in my life to become a mother, Mr Fauld. You can't deny me. I'll do anything.'

He looked across the lake and into the tumbling water of the great ornamental fountain, seeking inspiration, calculating the odds. 'I must explain something to you, Mrs Franklyn. I agree with you entirely about the interfering do-gooders. All too often they have no judgement, no imagination. There are vast numbers of would-be adoptive parents and a limitless supply of needy children, yet it seems beyond the authorities to bring the two together. They strangle everything in red tape and bureaucracy, terrified they might make a mistake. So, they do nothing. And as a result, couples are left bereft while children starve and are brutalized.'

A sparrow flew onto their table and hopped around in search of nourishment. Disappointed, he flew off in the direction of a squabble over crusts that was developing between two eider ducks, hoping to benefit from their distraction.

'Do you know that in Romania, after the Communists were thrown out, they discovered tens of thousands of children in state institutions which were little better than concentration camps?' he continued, his thin lips tightening, his tone betraying anger. 'You must remember the television pictures, they touched the conscience of the world. But not the conscience of the authorities. Thousands of couples went to Romania to adopt these poor children and, amongst those thousands, there were a few problem cases. A handful of couples who changed their minds, who perhaps should never have become adoptive parents. A few weeds amongst the harvest of happiness. So the outcry at the discovery of the children was followed by a fresh outcry about how unsuitable parents were buying these children without any safeguards. TV reports can be so wretchedly moralizing and distorting.'

She knew.

'So what happened?' he continued. 'The authorities shut the whole adoption business down. For months. No . . .' – one hand became an axe, chopping across the other palm – 'not the Romanian authorities. The British authorities. Protecting their reputations. So afraid of criticism for what was going on they decided that nothing more should be done until they had set up a vast, cumbersome machinery to handle matters.'

'What happened to the children while this was being done?'

'They died, Mrs Franklyn. In their thousands. They couldn't afford to wait for rule books and regulations. Sacrificed in order to save the reputations of a few cowardly bureaucrats from a little ill-informed criticism.' He shook his head in despair and disbelief. 'It seems to me an extraordinary way of protecting the best interests of children.'

'But can you help me, Mr Fauld?'

'I have connections with a charitable adoption agency. I'm a firm believer in the laws governing such concerns, Mrs Franklyn, but I also believe the overriding need is that of the children. It's their concerns which should be paramount, not those of unimaginative social servants. So, under the law, my agency is afforded considerable flexibility in the way we operate within the rules and guidelines, and my interpretation emphasizes the welfare of the children. And above all else, children need parents who are committed to them. I believe you may display just the right sort of commitment.'

She smiled encouragingly while he wiped his glasses on his tracksuit.

'Such matters are not inexpensive. There are many overheads we are forced to incur in order to make our judgements as individual and as reliable as possible. For every parent we are able to supply with a child, there may be a dozen or more who will not qualify, yet who nevertheless involve our operation in considerable cost.'

'How much?'

'A white baby is top of the range, Mrs Franklyn.'

'How much?'

'Twenty-five thousand pounds.' He let the condensing words hang in the air. 'That is not a price you understand, but a suggested contribution which includes, I might say, a sizeable donation to children's charities.'

He was a master, she mused. Even if she had a tape of this conversation there would be nothing directly incriminating. Indeed, in black and white he might sound almost heroic.

'However, I must say that your case would still be exceptionally difficult. I have to ask myself what the public reaction would be if it came to light that I had assisted someone with such a *difficult* background to adopt one of my children. I run a very discreet operation, Mrs Franklyn, for obvious reasons.'

'Hey, I understand. The money is fine, no problem.'

He had replaced the glasses, refocused on her, probing once more, making up his mind. Trying to catch another glimpse of her breasts.

'It's not just money, however. I need to be sure that you are completely committed to the sort of operation I run. No doubts, no hesitations.'

'I'd do anything, Mr Fauld.'

'All too easily said . . .'

'How can I prove it? You name it.'

He smiled again, and the eyes flickered. He thought he might have found what he was looking for. 'Look, there's still a long way to go before I can be sure it would be appropriate to help you. We need to get to know each other better. Much better. Informally. Person to person. I'd like to suggest we meet again elsewhere in more relaxed surroundings. Dinner, perhaps? I do need to know so very much more about you. You understand, don't you?'

She understood perfectly.

'I'm free tomorrow evening. Let's start then, shall we? Where are you staying?'

She told him.

'Then let's say eight o'clock. The Wilton Towers? It's very convenient for you. I'll meet you in the reception area.'

She had offered the bait, he was nibbling. It was time to strike.

'This is the most important thing to me in the whole world. I can't tell you how grateful I am.'

'I'm sure you'll find a way.'

Her mouth had run dry, bile burning the back of her throat. 'I want to find some way of saying thank you to Paulette, too. She opened your door for me, I'd like to offer some token of how much I appreciate it all. Where might I find her?' She tried to make the enquiry sound casual but the taste of bile had made her suddenly hoarse, the words squeezed past dried lips.

'I'm sure that's not necessary,' he said slowly.

'Oh, but I'd like to. I'd like to help her in some little way, show my appreciation. Some money, perhaps. I got the impression she might need it.'

'That's incredibly thoughtful, Fiona – I may call you Fiona, may I? – but . . . really, she's fine. Moving about at the moment. I'm not quite sure where she is, to tell the truth.'

Don't push it, she screamed at herself. Don't blow it all away by showing unnatural curiosity.

She was trembling, knowing she was so close to touching Paulette, knowing the information would not come free. She knew she must take her time, be unhurried, and willing to pay whatever price was asked.

'I see. I rather got the impression she worked for you.'

'Oh, she does, has done. She's taking a little time off at present. Tell you what, leave her a note. I'll make sure she gets it.'

So he does know where she is. But already Fauld was inspecting his watch, rising, waving his arms to restore his circulation, preparing to return to his office. And snatching one last look beneath her tracksuit top.

'I *am* looking forward to tomorrow night, Fiona.'

The eyes opened stiffly, laden with sleep and pain. The light blinded, confused her, and it was minutes before any form of coherence began to creep past the shutters of her mind. The sun burned angrily in the sky, beating down on her, slicing her lids apart, forcing the dreams from her head until she woke to find it was no more than a street lamp shining through the winter drizzle, and the earth beneath nothing but another stinking doorway. The street cleaners had swept through the Portobello market hours earlier, taking all the detritus of another market day with them, save her. They had passed by on the other side, leaving her in the doorway with her eiderdown of discarded vegetable leaves and rotten tomatoes.

She had tried to make it home, and failed. It had been beyond her, she'd been too impatient, too much in pain. Again. And now the pain was already returning, twisting at her as though being sliced by a blunt knife – no, worse than physical pain, for this was not isolated, could not be cauterized. If she could have, she would long ago have grabbed the iron and burned it out herself.

Her head slumped forward, seeking shelter from the light burning into her brain and the breeze of dank decay that brushed her cheek, too disorientated yet to move from beneath the street lamp, even to identify the noxious fluid which dampened the doorstep around her. She tried to climb back inside herself, hiding from the terror of the world outside yet knowing she would be betrayed once more by the horrors she found within.

Emaciated fingers covered her face. She'd lost a lot of weight this time, more than the times before. Her periods had stopped; a relief. She was having to turn an ever larger number of tricks – no, not tricks, tricks were for whores and she was no whore. She only did what she had to, and even if that meant fucking an ever larger number of punters to find the money she needed, getting pregnant was not part of the plan. Or wouldn't be, if she had a plan.

And it was getting worse. A squall of December rain hit her and she started shaking again; she knew it was coming back, the battle she couldn't win. It tore at her, the guilt and the pain ripping her in different directions. She could never work out which tormented her more, but while she couldn't cure the guilt, she could always submerge the physical pain.

So the guilt could wait. Until tomorrow. Just one more time.

She swallowed with difficulty, the back of her throat felt like cooked liver. She would need to find another man quickly, several men, perhaps. No point in trying to steal from stores any more, they spotted her as soon as she walked through the door. Perhaps she would try going back to her father, but she'd already done that and even he seemed reluctant to give in to her any more, now that he had found out. It would have to be men, and even that was getting more difficult as she trembled and stank and found that they would screw her, any part of her, abuse her and beat her, then leave her in a doorway without paying.

Like this.

It was why she was being forced to take the risk, buying on the street, stuff of unknown quality from people she didn't know, suffering if it did not work, suffering even more if it worked too well. Like the last fix, when she couldn't make it back to her own bed.

The last fix. The very last fix . . .

It would be better . . .

She would get herself home, clean herself up, find better punters, just once more, grab the strength to get herself back into shape, confront the guilt, give it all up. Just this one last time, she pleaded.

But it would pursue her, as it had done before, like a hawk. Every breath of wind would be as the beat of the hunter's wing, every shaft of sunlight the glint of stretching talons, every burst of children's laughter the screech of triumph from a gorged craw, every dawn bringing anew the agony of being torn alive. Only in darkness, in the corners and crevices of the world, in dark stinking holes and doorways, did she seem to find respite from her fears, where she could bury herself in a different world.

Her world. A world in which pain was transformed, blotted out. Smack. Where the mind was released to roam free. Smack. Where every flower became a needle and every needle, salvation. Smack. Every vein a river of release and every breath a demand for more, where the hours could be stopped so that time no longer bore down like the lash of thorns.

Smack. Smack.

Where twisted love and memories dark were drowned in numbness. Smack. Where the hate for her father could be transformed into love of all mankind, where tears would be dried and agony end. Smack. Smack. Where she could reach out and be gathered in the gentle arms of a mother so cruelly torn away and regain a childhood so abruptly destroyed.

Smack.

Where nothing, nothing, not life nor death nor time nor Judgement Day nor her father, particularly not her father, would matter ever again.

Smack. Smack. Smack-smack-smack.

'I don't want you to go, Izzy. Not without me.'

They were sitting in the American Bar of The Stafford beneath its cross-Atlantic memorabilia, a thematic mayhem of ties, baseball caps, pennants, helmets and stag horns which hung down from the ceiling like ripe grapes from a vine. She had sought refuge in the corner beneath the framed aircraft carriers, feeling in distinct need of a drink – no more than a glass of Chablis, she would need her wits, though it had dawned on her that he never drank alcohol.

'You know I can't take you, Daniel. My husband's supposed to be sewing mail bags somewhere the other side of the Rockies.'

'But you don't know what you're taking on.'

'I've got a pretty good idea,' she muttered. Too good an idea, she thought.

'He's a Coroner. A man of importance. Of power. He'll fight ruthlessly if he thinks his position is threatened.'

'But it's more than that, isn't it?' she responded quietly. 'I've been wondering why on earth a Coroner would get involved in an adoption scam. OK, it seems pretty safe. You run the system yourself, it relies on subjective judgements about suitable parents so you can always be seen to be playing within the written rules.'

'What if people start asking questions?'

'Who's to ask? The kids aren't in a position to complain. And who would doubt the integrity of the local Coroner? The facade is so drenched in respectability it's practically perfect. But it's more than that, has to be. So I've been putting two and two together, and it comes out in six figures.'

'How do you mean?'

'Remember what the nuns at the Mission told us? Maybe twenty babies a year. Say only half of them, less than one a month, were involved in his scam. At twenty-five grand a time. That's a quarter of a million pounds passing through his fat hands, tax free. A nice little earner, wouldn't you say?' She leaned forward. 'That's why we have to do this right.'

Her action in bending forward had served only to remind him of his other feelings for her. He looked wistfully into his Virgin Mary. 'You look stunning. I wish you could stay.'

She had taken considerable care. An hour in the hair salon trying to regain some of the lost style, another hour soaking in suds and highlighting eyes, a dress of bright green which complemented her eyes and was supported by the thinnest straps that left no need to guess at the flawless skin of her shoulders and tops of her breasts, decorated with a trailing scarf of embroidered silk. She was down to a size eight again, cradle fat vanished, melted in the ferocious heat of her pain and fears. She looked good, her best, for Fauld, and hated herself.

'Why is it,' he said in a voice soaked in Irish charm, 'that I want so much to tear every shred of clothing off your body?'

'What's the matter, you don't like the dress?'

'On a hanger, perhaps.'

'Trouble is, Danny Blackheart, I know you say that to all the girls.'

'True, very true,' he grinned, 'but I don't go falling in love with them all, now, do I?'

'I'm sure you only want me for my money.'

'You know, my family used to have a lot of money, least by Blackheart Bay standards. Lost it all, so long ago that no one can truly remember why. But my dear mother used to tell me, beware of wealthy women. Their money can disappear, along with their looks. Then you're left with nothing but misery and might-have-beens. So she told me to stick to women who make you laugh, with their clothes on or off.' He winked. 'I don't know yet what makes you laugh, Izzy, but I'd like to learn. On or off.'

'I don't know if I shall ever be able to love you the way you want me to.'

'I'm a gambler, I'll take the risk. But if you pick me up, be careful. Don't ever drop me. If I slip from your hands I'll probably shatter. I'm a terrible

Humpty Dumpty when it comes to emotions, and there are already far too many cracks in my shell. Another tumble and you'd better call for the omelette oil.'

There it was, the bruising again. Even though covered with a wry smile the words weren't idle. Unhealed wounds. But from where? Of what sort?

'I know so very little about you,' she whispered. 'I've been taking you for granted, haven't I? Forgive me.'

'Forgiven. You've enough problems, I don't want to add to them. Just treat me gently.'

'Even as you tear the clothes from my body?'

'Especially then.'

'Soon, Daniel, we'll have the time for each other. The maiden and the Irish buccaneer, a voyage of discovery. I'd like that very much.' And meant it.

He raised his tomato juice.

'Fair winds, Izzy.'

The foyer was crowded. Airline crew and piles of leather baggage. A Japanese businessman gesticulating at two bored women, over-dressed and under-age, chewing gum. A fat St Nicholas leading a small choir of siliconized reindeer women whose dress struck a peculiarly unbiblical note. Scatterings of artificial snow. Christmas spirit laid on with a plastic trowel.

He was there, waiting for her, wrapped in smiles and a well-cut mohair suit. As he advanced to greet her the eyes behind the steel-rimmed spectacles were like magnets, clinging tenaciously to her breasts. They never made her ankles, nor her own eyes until he was almost beside her. In spite of the hotel's extravagant overheating, she shivered.

He offered banal compliments and a strong trace of men's perfume, leading her by the arm through the confusion of revellers and scurrying concierge staff, away from the protection of numbers, into the lift. The crush forced them closer together, the difficulties and doubts crowding in, corrupting her confidence; already she felt dirty, soiled by association and the simple act of standing next to this man. Yet each passing floor, she reminded herself, led closer to Paulette, to Bella. She hoped.

They were not headed for the rooftop restaurant as she supposed; at the twenty-third floor he led her out and produced a key.

'I have retained a suite,' he explained. 'More privacy.'

Of course.

The view was spectacular, overlooking Buckingham Palace, the Royal Standard snapping in the glow of floodlights while the brake lights of London's nightlife danced around the Palace perimeter like a river of volcanic fire. The elevated panorama distorted perspectives, reducing the world they had just left to pygmy proportions, its associations and laws shrunken, discarded. He had chosen the territory where the gods peer down from the clouds and mock. Hunting territory.

He took her coat and she could feel him pause, ponder, his breath upon her shoulder; she felt her skin quiver. A table was set for two in the bay of the window. She knew what he wanted, but not when: before, after eating? Both perhaps?

He opened champagne and spilled it, standing above her to serve and gaze down upon the curves of her body.

It had started with the *hors d'oeuvres*. He had probed and she had revealed the pieces of her carefully prepared story, like Penelope weaving her tapestry, deceiving, for love, and he had made encouraging noises while rejecting all attempts by her to discover more about his own operations. To her every question he responded by pouring more wine. 'You are the adoptive parent, not me. I am of no interest.' But he drank deeply, his temples beginning to glow, intently, and small pieces of his resistance flaked away like scales from a rotting fish. She discovered he was unmarried, had never been married, parents ardent Baptists, hence Gideon. Hints of an overly starched childhood. Two years of his twenties in Riyadh as the contracts executive for a Saudi ports project. Constant reference to his physical pursuits, most of which seemed to be dated, hints that he was/had been a marathon man. Undue emphasis on his stamina. Innuendo. He was turning out to be a slug.

He poured and drank, and his eyes grew more bloodshot as the evening progressed, the high forehead beginning to melt, a line of sweat appearing above his upper lip. The carefully trimmed hair was starting to dampen and sag, the fires stoking inside. He opened a third bottle but she declined, covering the crystal with her hand.

'Enough. I must keep sufficient wits to finish your questions before I have any more to drink,' she insisted.

'Questions? I think I'm done. You've told me all I need to know, Fiona.'

'And do I pass? Will you be able to help me?'

His tongue seemed to have thickened, getting in the way of some of his words. 'I believe I can. On certain conditions.'

'A baby? New born, no more than six months. That's possible?'

'Difficult. Easier with an older child. But possible.'

'How soon?'

He chuckled defensively. 'You're remorseless.'

'No. Determined. As you know.'

'I'll have to make some enquiries. Let you know.'

'Look, for twenty-five grand I don't expect to be kept hanging around London like a call-girl on a street corner. Babies don't suddenly appear with the stork, they arrive pretty much when expected. So I'm asking. When is the next one expected?'

'Feisty, I like that,' he nodded. 'But, my dear, you're not the only parent looking to adopt such a child. There are others.'

'You must have some idea,' she protested.

He raised his hands. 'I surrender, I surrender. Very well, let's see if I can give you some idea.' He rose and, feet floundering, walked unsteadily across the room to the bed, beside which he had laid a black document case. He fumbled inside and produced a wallet-sized object.

'My little toy,' he explained. 'My travelling office. My world.'

It was a businessman's electronic organizer.

'Reminds me to pick up my clean shirts . . .' he was mumbling.

And meetings, anniversaries, addresses. Contacts.

For the first time her spirits revived. A link to Paulette. Perhaps.

'Mmmmm. Look, I can't guarantee it,' he muttered, 'but I might be able to lay my hands on one in no more than . . . two months?'

She was mesmerized by the small plastic case he held. The sight of it refreshed her hopes, her mind floating across the room and attempting by sheer naked will-power to invade the organizer, to drag from it the information she needed, to open the door to Paulette. To avoid paying his price.

The jaws of the alligator snapped shut. He closed

the organizer and placed it on the table beside the bed.

The bed. She knew – had always known – that the answers she sought would be found on or around his bed. She could prise loose the information she sought – from him, or from his organizer. Two chances, two doors waiting to be forced, both here, beside the bed. No painless route.

He returned to his seat. 'Two months. If all goes well.'

'I can get a baby? In two months?'

'Oh, no. Not immediately. The baby must be under the care of the adoption agency and its local managers for at least ten weeks. For assessment and recommendations, you know the sort of thing.'

The local managers. Fauld. And, of course, Paulette.

'And then?'

'The papers go before the Fostering and Adoption Panel. A dozen or more people. Respectable. Upright. Honest.' He leered. 'So you understand that the paperwork must be in perfect order.'

'What about the baby? And the mother?'

'Good God, no. Do you really expect a meeting of the great and the good, of retired vicars and women in silly hats, to be disrupted by a bawling, incontinent child and overwrought parents? No, that's for the adoption agency to deal with.'

'And the panel trusts the advice of the agency? And its local managers?'

'Wouldn't be any point in having an adoption agency if it weren't trusted, eh?' He sank a long draught of wine. 'So then we hand the baby over to the adoptive parents. Another three months, perhaps. More reports, paperwork. We must be very careful, you understand.'

He lusted at her, his eyes bathed in wine and mauling her body.

'Then the Adoption Order is approved,' he continued with thick tongue. 'Court hearing in front of a local judge. On the recommendation of the adoption agency.'

An agency, she realized, run by a fellow member of the judiciary. Fauld and Paulette controlled the whole process. The paperwork. The reports and recommendations. The panel of the good and utterly gullible. Where the child went. The court hearing. Everything rubber-stamped. Above board. Beyond enquiry. Not that anyone would make enquiries.

With the identity of the child known to no one, except by means of paperwork. Just like the mortuary.

'So you *can* let me have a baby!'

'It's . . . possible.'

'What is this "possible" crap? You've just told me it's possible.'

'Trouble is, there's a queue. Many people waiting. Others ahead of you.'

His red eyes slithered across her once more.

'What would it take,' she asked quietly, 'to get right to the head of the line?'

He leaned across the table, getting closer to her. 'My dear, you are asking me to take a tremendous risk. Not many people would accept your right to adopt a child, not in this country, at least. If a word of this leaked out I would be lost. Utterly lost.'

His whole face was aflame, fuelled with alcohol. She refilled his glass, hoping desperately that he might imbibe and simply expire, but his was a body practised in punishment and the wine was serving only to bring the first traces of feeling to his eyes. She did not care for what she saw.

'You want me to take the most desperate personal risk for you,' he continued. 'In return I must insist you show me at least as much commitment, prove that this is not some mere whim . . .' His sour breath stung her nostrils.

'What is it you want?'

'I have given my life to this work. Enabling women to attain fulfilment. Endless hours. A lonely life . . .' His eyes were roving across her chest, his hands would soon follow. 'I ask in return only a little comfort, a brief companionship. A few moments in exchange for what will be a lifetime of happiness with your new baby.' His words came in breathless spasms; he had reached across to brush away the straps of her dress, knocking over the bottle as he did so, his clammy hand pawing down to her breast. 'And with your husband so far away . . .'

Then he led her to the bed.

She did not protest, slipped off her shoes and dress and scarf while he ogled in a form of weird rapture. He was panting, tugging at his own clothes down to his underwear, his food-extended belly flopping absurdly downward, then he was tearing at her tights and all the rest until she was standing naked, trembling.

Her mind and soul were entombed in ice; she made no objection as he laid her on her back, grasping at her breasts and forcing her arms upwards above her head until her wrists rapped against the bedhead. Then he had her scarf, was tying her wrists, securing them to the bedhead with vicious knots that tightened still further as she struggled while he gazed down upon her, slavering, and pounced.

She did not resist, was unable to resist as his body lay across her like a great slab of whale flesh. He fell upon her like waves upon a shore, penetrating, withdrawing, to return again, and again, beating down upon her in a fury of wringing, sweat-soaked flesh which pounded incessantly until she thought he must certainly have expired. She had known what he would demand and what she must offer, had persuaded herself that it was a tiny price, a necessary price, for Bella, that he was claiming the most unimportant part of her body, and not her soul. She was a mature woman, no virgin, what did it matter?

It came as no consolation when she became aware that he was diminutive, minuscule. But as the pressure of his body forced its way relentlessly inside, so did the feelings of anger, of frustration, of rage that the world should conspire to rob her of the only part of her body that truly mattered, her children. *Think only of Bella*, she told herself in distraction, and suddenly she could see Bella again vividly in her mind's eye, every detail, the curling hair, the bright eyes, the soft pursing of tiny lips, in front of her. She was reaching to meet the baby's outstretched fingers, that satin touch of skin, together once more . . .

And then she was falling, uncontrollably, into the depths of an endless pit, tumbling over and over, with the image of Bella receding from her, falling away, vanishing, going. Was gone. Nothing.

From deep within Izzy let forth a long cry of fury and despair, a cry of pain that only a mother might know.

'Pretty good, wasn't I?' His face poured sweat and self-congratulation just inches above her. 'You seemed as if you really enjoyed it.'

'Untie me,' she whispered.

He leered at her before flicking at one cord until it was loose, leaving her to untie the other. 'God, I need another drink,' he exclaimed, rolling off her onto the side of the bed and modestly replacing his underwear. She groaned as the weight lifted from her body.

'You were fine, really fine,' he congratulated, slurping wine. 'I was all right, too, wasn't I? We'll do it again in a minute. Something different this time.'

She forced a mouthful of wine past her lips to take away his taste. It failed. She tried to wipe away his sweat from her body with the back of her hand.

'I suppose a man like you has many girls. Is Paulette one them?' she asked, trying to sound indifferent.

'Paulette? Good God, no. Couldn't. She's a friend of the family, so to speak. Used to be a pretty girl but ... it would get too involved.' He swallowed more wine, relaxing, lowering his guard.

'She gave me the impression she didn't spend all her time in London, that she was really only a visitor.'

'S'right.' The words were beginning to slur a little. 'She's a silly bitch. Comes to London to hide.'

'Where would someone hide in London?'

'Be buggered if I know. She moves about a lot. I just phone ... Look, what's all this about bloody Paulette?' There was suspicion in his voice; in her heart she heard one of the doors slam.

'Nothing, not a thing,' she reassured.

'Not jealous of a younger woman, are you?'

'Yeah, maybe a little.'

'Look, I didn't come here to talk about bloody Paulette. I came here to have a bit of fun, which is exactly what I propose to do. Again. In just a minute.' He drank again, ran his hand up the inside of her thigh. He looked at her for a while, and then moved once more for the scarf. She beat him to it.

'My turn, lover. Your chance to relax for a change. You mighty man.'

His face flushed with apprehension but he did not object, inhibitions of inadequacy overwhelmed by alcohol, and he lay submissively on the bed, arms raised. She tied them severely to the bed head; he winced but uttered no complaint.

'I want the full works,' he insisted. 'Use your imagination, not your hands. Don't want you scratching me to pieces with those filed fingernails of yours.'

'You're not going to know what hit you,' she said, smiling. She reached for a linen napkin from the table. 'It's what I call blind man's buff.' And she placed the napkin over his eyes, securing it tightly around his head so he was completely sightless.

'What's going on?' he demanded.

'Wait for it.'

And there was the organizer. She scooped it up as she headed for the drinks trolley from which she took a bottle of a popular cream liqueur. Irish liqueur. Blackheart country, she thought, and it hurt even more.

'What is it? Where are you?'

'You will never have tasted so sweet,' she reassured, unscrewing the bottle. She ripped off his underpants and proceeded to drip the creamy liqueur, spot by spot, from his eager lips slowly down his chest to his navel. The effect was electrifying. He tightened, not knowing where the next drop might hit, feeling it cool and trickle upon his hot skin, every part of him growing tense, rigid, his excitement extreme. He proceeded to cry, utter low moans of pleasure, alternately to complain and congratulate as he waited, blind, bound, helpless, for the next tantalizing drop.

And she flicked through the organizer. It took her a while, one-handed, divided attention, flickering screen, trembling body. Dashing between hope and hell. At one point she dropped it on the bed, but he was aware of nothing except the sensation of cream liqueur being massaged gently with the tip of her small finger into many parts of his body.

There was no record under 'Paulette'. With climbing anxiety she searched under 'Devereux' but Fauld was growing more demanding, insisting she be more physically explicit.

And there it was. 'Devereux'. With Paul's details. And then, separately, Paulette. Nothing but a telephone number. In London. She had it. *She had it!*

'Come on, woman, don't drown me in the bloody stuff.'

But she was busy sweeping her underwear and tights from the end of the bed into her bag. She rose from the mattress.

'What . . . ?'

'Don't worry, lover. I've got to disappear to the bathroom for a second. Another surprise for you. And have this to keep you going.' She dribbled more liqueur onto his lips and the pink tongue reached out to capture every drop. 'You wait right here. I may be a little while.'

She replaced the organizer exactly where she had found it – he must never suspect her real motives – and in a stride had retrieved her shoes and dress. In the bathroom it was the work of less than ten seconds to towel away the dampness and climb into dress and shoes, the rest could come later. Her coat, a hand through her hair. One last glance at the trussed and blindfolded body. Then she slipped out the door, pausing only to hang a sign on the handle requesting early room service.

Her whole body dripped with fury and disgust; she resolved to put Fauld out of her mind forever. But as she fled through the hotel foyer, one further thought insinuated itself into her mind. She picked up a pay-phone and dialled.

EIGHT

Devereux spread himself across the green leather of the Government Front Bench, his feet propped languidly upon the Clerks' table, enjoying himself. It was a debate on the economy, the Chancellor of the Exchequer was up batting for the Government and he was building a minor monument to the fact that most things in politics conform to the cock-up rather than the conspiracy theory. Conspiracies involve a meeting of minds; there was none here. Fuelled by good dinners and the heady atmosphere of the crowded late-night Chamber, the Opposition were being merciless in taunting the Chancellor by resurrecting his many optimistic but ultimately erroneous prognoses of the last election campaign, when he had spied many a green shoot bursting through the arid economic wastelands.

'Green shoots?' one loud Welsh voice derided. 'What sort of trip was the bloody man on? If there were any green shoots around he must have been smoking 'em!'

Devereux hid his mirth behind a sombre expression. Must support the Chancellor. In public. Even as the man dug his own political grave and removed himself from the lists of 'the man most likely to . . .'

The House of Commons attendant appeared beside the Speaker's Chair and passed a green message slip along the ranks of Ministers crowded onto the bench. From hand to hand it was carried, until it had reached its destination, Devereux. He opened it, irritated that he should be disturbed in the middle of such fine entertainment, the irritation turning to exasperation and anxiety as he read. His daughter was waiting for him in Central Lobby. What on earth? With a curt bow in the direction of Madam Speaker, he immediately vacated his seat and the Chamber.

He found her lurking beside the statue of Gladstone. Devereux gasped. In the weeks since he had last seen her she had grown emaciated and unkempt. A pallor had invaded her face and the skin had roughened, signs of wear which she had attempted to cover in excessive layers of cosmetics. The result was a garish, scarcely recognizable mask, slashed across by two brightly rouged lips. They appeared to be moving.

'I had to see you.'

This was not the place. Central Lobby is the busy crossroads of Parliament where politicians and public congregate; it offered Devereux no chance of privacy. But few places within the Palace of Westminster offer privacy – he had to get her to his room, even though that lay on the other side of the building and entailed a long walk through corridors bustling with colleagues. Many cast a jaundiced eye in his direction as they saw him hustling along a young woman who was clearly remarkably rough trade.

Ahead of them, in the Library Corridor, he could see a group gathered around the news service printer, swapping gossip and ribaldry, their spirits and volume high. In mid-sentence their exchanges ground to a halt as their attention turned upon him. And the girl. He knew what they must be thinking and flushed with embarrassment. That they should think that of him. That they could think that of her.

He pushed her into his room and slammed the door closed.

'In God's name, Paulette . . .' His voice bristled with anger.

She stood, head down, and wouldn't meet his eye. And as he saw her misery, his voice fell, flooded with concern.

'Look at you! What on earth has happened?'

'I need help.'

Not 'please', not 'Hello, Father' – she rarely called him 'Father' or used any other form of address, it had all grown so distant; he got a more personable greeting from the professional beggars in their doorways up the Strand.

And she always wanted, always took, never gave. Now he had discovered why she took and what she used it for – he should have guessed much earlier, should have known, but a father is always the last to know when it comes to his own little girl.

'What sort of help?'

'Money. I need money. Just a few hundred pounds.'

'A few hundred. On top of the few thousand.'

'I've had a difficult time and—'

'No more,' he interrupted sharply. 'I told you last time that there would be no more money, Paulette. Any other form of help that it is within my power to give. But no more money.'

'But I need some cash. Can't you see I'm starving? At least give me enough to eat.'

He stared at her, what she had become, struggling to find any trace of his child within this ghastly apparition, tearing at himself inside.

'No.'

'But why? Just when I'm getting better. You told

me to sort myself out and that's just what I'm doing. Honest. But do you think it's easy? I'm in agony, cold, hungry. I just want enough to live on while I'm getting my head straight.'

And he wanted so much, so desperately, to believe her.

'No.'

'Just a hundred, a measly hundred, that's all I'm asking.'

'I'll pay for a private clinic anywhere in the country, everything you need there, but not a penny in cash. I told you before.'

'You told me lots of things before.' For the first time the two charcoal eyes that were burnt into the mask turned directly to him; they had a vicious edge. 'You told me that you loved me.'

'I do.'

'I bet you told mother that you loved her. Is that why she killed herself?'

'Stop!'

'You drove her to it, now you want to turn your back on me, too. Is that it?'

'For pity's sake, Paulette—'

'A hundred bloody quid. That's all. And you want to moralize with me?' The tongue sprang forth like a cobra's. 'You cheated on her, cheated on her like a dog. All I can remember of my mother is her crying herself to sleep, every night, alone. And now you want to cheat me, too.'

'I don't! I want to help. I love you.'

'But not enough to give me money to eat.'

'It's because I love you that I say no!'

'But that's always your version of love. Saying no. To me. To mother.'

'I'll not help you destroy yourself.'

'I'm starving, for Chrissake. Can't you see?'

He could see, but he could find no words, could do nothing but look on in bewilderment.

'I wonder what all those other bloody politicians were saying as they saw you and me. Another one of Devereux's women? Going down-class a bit, isn't he? But he did always screw anything in sight, even when his wife was around, didn't he? Didn't she even find him giving it to her best friend? In her own bed?'

He collapsed on the sofa, burying his head in his hands, sobbing.

Then she was on her knees beside him. Touching his hand. Sobbing too.

'Sorry. I'm so sorry,' she gasped. 'Didn't mean to hurt you, please forgive me. It's just so hard for me right now. Say you forgive me, Father.'

He looked up through swollen eyes. 'We have a lot of forgiving to do in our family, Paulette. Of course I forgive you. I love you. I want to help you.'

'I promise, on my mother's memory, I'm clean. No more nonsense. All I need is just a little time. And a little money —'

'No!' he cried, and with a sweep of his arm had hurled the side lamp across the room where it smashed into the far wall. 'Because I love you – No! Can't you see it would be so easy to give you the money, to stop this persecution? But it would be wrong. I may have done so little for my family of which I am proud, Paulette, but I would rather die than watch you harm yourself still further.'

She had sprung back to avoid the flying table lamp, and now she stood by the door.

'So what do you expect me to do? How do you expect me to live?'

He had no words, simply shook his head. She opened the door to leave.

'Do you know what I'm going to do?' she shouted in a voice which echoed along the corridor. 'I'm going to get the money from a man. Lots of men. Whatever they want, so long as they pay for it. Just like I've got money before. I'll use my body, just as you have. Like father, like daughter. Except there's one big difference between us . . .'

He looked at her as though he had seen his own corpse rise from the grave.

'You fuck for power, I fuck for money. Hard cash,' she screamed. 'And my way, dearest Father, is one hell of a lot more honest than yours. I feel filthy just having been associated with you!'

His hand stretched out to restrain her, to bring her back, but she was gone. In her place at the door stood a colleague, immediately joined by another, drawn by the commotion. They took one look at him and, with mumbled apologies, left.

Devereux sank to his knees. And towering above his head, just as on that night in the stables with the dog, his father's face was laughing at him.

Barely daybreak. Inside, the cathedral was gloomy and ill-lit, light sufficient only for the handful of passing souls who had come to pray beneath the soot-encrusted roof and the droning passage of a cleaning woman polishing the floor of wooden tiles. It was a place of heavy atmosphere, of unfulfilled dreams: the vast domed ceilings had been intended for lavish gilt and mosaic, not bare brick that displayed only the ravages of time and a century of corrupting candle smoke, and which leant in one corner upon a buttress of polythene-clad scaffolding. The time span of God is eternal; not so His roofs.

It was cold. Daniel shivered as he entered,

unshaven, unbreakfasted, hurriedly dressed, summoned by her message. It had been many years since he had entered a place of worship, yet he found himself instinctively making the sign of the cross. Couldn't help himself. Conditioned.

'Never knew you were a Catholic,' he greeted, slipping into the place beside her in one of the rearmost pews. It smelt of fresh polish.

She offered nothing in reply beyond a shake of her head.

'Why here?'

'Nowhere else to go,' she responded eventually.

'I've been dying a thousand deaths, waiting, imagining the worst,' he told her, his own sleepless night lending an edge of accusation to his voice. If he had been hoping for sympathy, even an explanation, he was doomed to disappointment. Nothing.

She had changed, aged, the vitality gone, the cheeks hollowed as though with a sculptor's knife. The fingers twitched in agitation as if passing rapidly over some invisible rosary. The eyes were dark and starved of sleep.

She had withered, like one of the beshawled women who huddled devotedly at the far end of the nave before the great altar. She was not the woman who had set forth the night before.

'I got a telephone number,' she uttered eventually in a small voice. 'Paulette's. I thought.' She raised eyes filled with reproach to the huge painted crucifix that hung suspended above the congregation. 'But it's not. No one's number. A public telephone in a coffee shop. Never heard of any Paulette.'

'You sure?'

'Don't be bloody stupid, Daniel,' she bit. 'Of course I'm sure.'

Towards the front of the cathedral a bell sounded

the call to morning prayer; people bobbed in their seats and devotions began.

'What do I have to do, Daniel? Even Abraham got a break. I've given everything; how much more am I supposed to give? My career. My son . . .' Her eyes fell from the cross to her lap, the thought unfinished.

'Yourself?'

She turned towards her friend, her eyes brimming, and nodded. 'Everything. I'm fresh out of things to give.'

She failed to notice the lines of his face slowly turning to stone.

'All I want is Bella. My child. What's so bloody unreasonable about that?' She was trembling, gazing at the crucifix, alone with fractured hopes and beliefs. A low chanting of responses rose from the other end of the cathedral as the crimson-cloaked priest, diminished by the distance, began pacing his way through the ceremonies. An old man propped on bent leg shuffled towards them with an offertory bag, hesitated, then passed by, conscious of grief.

She was back with him. 'What do I do, Daniel?'

'Carry on.'

'I'm not sure I can.'

'Of course you can, you've got to.' His tone was abrupt, strangely dismissive.

'You OK?'

'No.'

'What's wrong?'

'What could possibly be wrong, apart from the fact that I'm sitting here feeling about as useful and as used as last week's toilet tissue.'

'What on earth — ?'

'It'll sound a little selfish, I know, thinking about my problems rather than yours for just a fraction of time, but have you any comprehension of what it makes me feel like, to sit here and have you discussing the loose elastic in your underwear while you've got me playing the white man, taking cold showers back in the hotel room. Jesus, if only I'd known you weren't coming back last night I could have gone out and maybe got lucky myself.'

'Daniel, I never even thought —'

'Precisely. That's what is cracking my nuts. That you so obviously never even considered what it might mean to me. You took me so much for granted you didn't even spare me a passing thought.'

'That's not true. Why do you think it took me so long to call?'

'Because I assume you were otherwise occupied.'

The ornate chalice glinted in the candlelight as the priest raised it high above his head. The churchgoers queued for the sacrament, coming together in fellowship, sure of support and strength. But not Izzy. Suddenly she was falling into the darkness again through a swirling fog of incense, watching helplessly as the final knot tethering her to reality unravelled into pathetic strands. Panic bit through her misery, but also there was anger. Not a single man would have thought twice about doing what she had done, least of all Daniel. Done it? They would have bragged about it. She'd be damned if she would allow him to make her feel guilty.

'Stop being so bloody juvenile! I had to make a choice last night. Between you and Bella. So I chose Bella, and not you. For what it's worth, it hurt me, hurt like hell. And I knew how much it would hurt you, too, so much so that I didn't feel I could come back last night. Can't you see?'

'What I see is that you chose to sleep with him, but not with me.' His eyes welled with pain, battered rather than bruised. 'I asked only one thing of you, that you tread carefully with me. Don't go rocking old Humpty, I said, don't go wobbling his wall. Instead, you drove a sodding bulldozer through it.'

'And what would you have done? Washed your hands? Beforehand or afterwards, Daniel?'

Her rebuke stung him into silence.

'Don't turn your back on me, Daniel. Not now. I need you.'

He sat like granite, grey, impassive, unresponsive. It seemed an age before a tremor ran through the block of stone.

'Had a schoolmistress in the Bay, a Miss O'Donnell. Very particular about hygiene, she was. Insisted that we wash our hands at meal times, after digging potatoes and dissecting frogs. And before we left for Mass. But I don't recall her ever mentioning sex.'

'A misspent youth, Danny Blackheart.'

'So I guess I'd better stick. I'm committed to this, Izzy. To finding Bella. And to you. Oh, God and Miss O'Donnell help me!'

She reached over and took his hand.

'I'll make up for it, Daniel, and that's a promise. Not just to you, but to myself. I think I deserve someone like you. Just give me a little more time.'

'We've got time, I suppose.'

'All the time in the world.'

The bruising in his eyes had cleared, as though sprinkled with healing water.

'Bloody odd place you've chosen, Miss Dean, if that's a proposition.'

'Let's say it's more of a reservation than a proposition.'

'Don't tell me. First, there's work still to be done.'

'Yes, Daniel. If only I knew where to start.'

'With a cup of coffee, I would suggest.'

*   *   *

They found the coffee shop with little difficulty after a phone call mentioning a delivery and mutterings about a scribbled and indecipherable address. It was located close behind the fashionable shopping precinct of Kensington High Street. Tolman's.

They had returned to The Stafford and changed their clothes; their roles had also perceptibly changed. Daniel had taken control of proceedings, insisting that he dress down while she dressed up, even over-dressed. He was on edge, mysterious and uncommunicative, perhaps still smarting from her night-time exploits, instructing her to put on high heels and too much make-up.

'I feel like a vamp,' she complained.

'Great,' was all he would offer. 'And we'll need to take some serious money.'

Tolman's was a scruffy emporium, located on the intersection of quiet back streets and out of keeping with the bustle of the fashionable main thoroughfare barely fifty yards away. It was an unambitious, make-shift place, formerly a shoe shop which had failed to float in the backwash of the High Street, with large windows, a small serving counter and potted plants that appeared exhausted in spite of the fact they were artificial, with mirrors along one wall that would have made the shop feel brighter and less cramped had any recent attempt been made to clean them. It was the week before Christmas, yet the only sign of Yuletide decoration was a large bowl on the counter entreating tips. There were no tables, nothing but a narrow ledge that ran all the way around the shop; customers were not expected to linger.

Harassed mothers perched their bags and babies on tall, scratched stools while trying to tell the owner that tea should be brewed and not stewed, only to be met with shrugs of contemptuous indifference. He had little time for women with their bags and baggage who took up too many seats and spent piss money on piss tea and whose noxious infants pissed on his floor. They weren't to be encouraged.

Izzy and Daniel arrived around three thirty and tarried over their coffee, ignoring the impatience of the owner. They had hit the right time, for around four o'clock as December dusk fell the character of the shop seemed to undergo a transformation. The rush was over. Women shoppers had left to pick up their children from school or to begin preparations for dinner, workers on early shifts were hurrying home, tourists headed back to their hotels for recuperation before the onslaught of evening. A new clientele had arrived. Male, five of them, all under forty, a majority in suits with wide lapels and fashionably shapeless trousers, none ordering anything and accepting without comment or thanks the beverages the owner brought across for them. A youth was loitering by the door, pretending to read a newspaper, eyes patrolling the long stretches of approach road that led to the coffee shop.

'This is it,' Daniel muttered beneath his breath.

'This is what?' she snapped, grown frustrated with his lack of communication.

'The dealers' drop,' he whispered, motioning her to keep her voice down. 'Watch. Listen.'

There was a warble and from inside his jacket one of the men produced a mobile phone, conducting a muttered conversation in heavily accented English.

'No more than ten minutes,' Daniel whispered.

It took less than five. A woman appeared, thin to the point of anorexia and dressed simply in black trousers and chain-belted smock, ordered a drink from the counter and returned to sit beside the man. She placed her bag on the ledge, open, facing the man.

Izzy watched the switch. Crumpled notes for sachets. From bag to suit pocket, and back again. A moment's flurry of activity, not a word spoken. The girl immediately abandoned her drink and the shop.

Other mobile phones were appearing, deals being done. The next two exchanges were conducted at the front entrance, both with young men in smart business suits who appeared too nervous to enter, their oversized company cars parked illegally and blocking traffic.

'The dealers will stay no more than fifteen, twenty minutes. This is the happy hour. Good location. Can see trouble coming from way down the street, able to disappear into the shopping crowds.' He sounded analytical but tense.

'Then why are they paying no attention to us?'

'Simple. I told the slimebag of an owner that I was new in town and looking for some action. And you were on my staff.'

'Your staff?'

'Yes. As a hooker. Drugs and hookers often make a tasty sandwich. I'm supposed to be your pimp. They think we're playing the same game as them. Love the lipstick, darling,' he smirked in a deep Mayo brogue.

'You bastard,' she exclaimed, watching another deal go down.

'Yes, but a totally and blindingly brilliant bastard. Come on, they're beginning to drift away. Time to move.'

He took her arm, not gently, he seemed very pre-occupied, and guided her towards the counter where the owner, an oversized man with an upper and lower stomach separated by the cord of a grimy apron, was emptying coffee grounds.

'Bugger off,' he greeted. 'You've been sitting around here too long for my liking.'

'Just inspecting your palace of entertainments. Looking before we leap, and all that.'

'Well, it's fifty quid a week for the seats whether you crap or get off the pot. In advance.'

'Sure. But first I need to check you out with one of your referees. A friend of mine who's in this game, used your shop. Paulette.'

'I told you already, bugger off.' The words reeked aggression, but the glance over his shoulder in the direction of the woman washing dishes in the rear of the kitchen suggested a vulnerable flank.

'As I was saying,' Daniel responded in a raised voice, 'this girl Paulette —'

'Keep your sodding voice down!' he whispered hoarsely. The woman had raised tired eyes from the soapy dishes and was looking at the back of the owner's head in a manner which suggested she was planning a lobotomy.

'I could always enquire of the lady wife, if you preferred,' Daniel taunted.

The owner took a deep breath, fury filling his eyes. He smeared at the surface of the counter with a damp rag, calculating the odds. No contest. This was a battle he had no wish to fight.

'Look, I did have a girl, Paulette. Worked here for a couple of weeks. She was ... helping out, while the wife was away by the seaside at her sister's.'

'Helping out, was she? And not just washing dishes, I'll bet.'

'She was a dirty little tart, pulling tricks behind my back ...'

'You didn't think she could support a drug habit on what you gave her, did you?'

'Look, I didn't know about any of that, not when I took her on.'

'Yes,' responded Daniel contemptuously, glancing around the shop, 'it's amazing what a blind eye you have to those sort of things.'

'You're not Filth, are you?' the owner demanded in sudden alarm.

'You were telling us about Paulette.'

'End of story. The wife came back early – didn't take to the weather or the welcome in Clacton – took one look at the girl and gave me the bollocking of my life. Anyway, Paulette was getting really weird by then, bombed out of her bleedin' skull. Started bringing some strange people into the shop. Had to throw her out.'

'When was that?'

''Bout two weeks ago.'

'And where is she now?'

'Don't know and I don't bloody care. Nothing but trouble, that one, with all her airs and graces and grubby habits.'

'You must . . .' interjected Izzy for the first time. She had felt scarcely able to breathe as the figure of Paulette had been dangled tantalizingly in front of them once again. 'You must know,' she protested.

But Daniel silenced her with a reproachful wave of his finger. With painstaking care, he extracted from his shirt pocket a twenty-pound note and unfolded it beneath the owner's nose.

'You ain't Filth, are you?' the owner pleaded, bloodshot eyes fixed on the money.

'No, but I can arrange for them to come calling. Although I'd much prefer to be clean away, out of this sewage farm you laughingly call a coffee shop. And I will be, as soon as I find Paulette.'

The proprietor smeared at the counter once more with the rag, weighing a twenty against a fading and not altogether pleasurable memory. 'Try Endeavour Road,' he spat, snatching at the note.

Daniel's reactions were quicker, moving his hand just sufficiently for the owner to end up pawing the air. 'Endeavour Road's a mile long. You can be a bit more precise than that. Where on Endeavour?'

The twenty was dangling once again.

'I don't bloody know, do I,' he seethed, making sure his back was turned towards his wife. 'But you could try one of the pubs. Seemed to spend a lot of her time there.'

'Now that didn't hurt, did it?' Daniel mocked, allowing the note to flutter to the floor on the other side of the counter, forcing the owner to stoop in order to retrieve it. 'And isn't that where you belong,' he continued coldly. 'With the scum on your floor.'

She hadn't seen him like this before. The Daniel she knew – or thought she knew – was good-spirited and patient; the one standing beside her cut like a serrated knife. She took his arm, it was trembling as though wanting to lash out, the bruising in his eyes had turned to blood and she was frightened for him. And a little frightened of him, she thought.

'Let's get out of here, Daniel,' she insisted, tugging at his sleeve.

They'd had enough. He had opened the door – more kicked it down, and she wanted desperately to jump through it before it closed upon her again. Light had entered her life. She felt alive once more, the stirring of hope begun within her, like the first stretchings of a new child.

She turned to find a knife flashing inches in front of her nose.

It wasn't much of a knife, as knives go. The blade, flicked forward from the handle, was less than five inches long and looked unimpressive. For a knife. Mass-produced Taiwan. As though the blade might easily snap with a sharp twist. At very least make an unsightly mess.

'G'day, sports.' Behind the waving blade and Australasian accent stood one of the men in sharp suits with mobile phones, waxed blonde hair brushed straight back, his fair, almost transparent eyebrows casting unnatural emphasis onto the eyes. They were small, pink, and too close together.

'I don't want no trouble in here, Mo,' protested the owner.

'But we've got trouble, mate,' Mo responded. 'Muscling in on my manor. Trying to carve up a little bit of my business, are we? Could prove difficult. With damaged goods.'

He drew closer to Izzy until she could smell his peppermint breath and after-shave. She could no longer see the knife blade; he had laid it flat against her cheek, the sharpened point an inch from her eye, applying pressure, forcing her head back, exposing her throat. She had stopped breathing entirely; felt herself rising onto her toes, desperate not to move or flinch, even more desperate to get away from the blade. He could see the fear in her face, smell it. She wanted very much to be sick.

'Steady on, Mo. Lighten up.'

But the eyes never flickered. Slowly he ran the blade down towards her lip. No blood, nothing more than an angry pink weal and a feeling of terror which trickled all the way down her spine.

'I think there may have been some misunderstanding,' Daniel said softly. Nothing in the coffee shop moved.

'No misunderstanding. You wanna play the big boys' game, you need to learn the rules. Which are these. First time I see you round here, you get a free taster, like an ice cream parlour.' The point of the blade pressed still more firmly into her cheek beside the base of her nose; she tried to move away but her back was against the wall, nowhere to go. She felt the point pierce the skin and as the skin gave way a rivulet of fresh blood crawled its way down over her lip.

'For God's sake, Mo, you crazy bastard. Not in my place!'

'Just a taste of things to come, pretty girl. Next time I'm gonna stop being a gentleman and start playing Australian rules. Understand?'

'You make your point very well,' she whispered.

'Enough, Mo,' the owner pleaded. 'We can't do with trouble in here.'

'No drama. Just wanna make sure they understand.'

But the drama had been all too intense, too captivating. It had grabbed the attention of everyone in the shop, including the look-out at the door. He had been slow, hadn't seen them coming, driving without lights the wrong way up the short one-way road leading from the High Street. Before anyone had a chance to move, they were outnumbered two-to-one. A fight broke out in one corner. Screams. Stools were overturned, cups smashed, curses hurled. The owner cowered on the floor while his wife screamed abuse, first at the world, then at the customers and, finally and most ferociously, at her husband. Distracted from Izzy, the Australian turned with the knife in his hand but was felled with a vicious kick to his balls. A heavily booted foot stamped on the hand which still held the knife, leaving Mo writhing, retching, unsure which part of his body to clutch with his one remaining good hand.

Then they turned to Izzy and Daniel. She was pinned to the wall as he was lifted bodily, turned and spread-eagled across the counter, knocking the breath from his body. Only when he bent his neck and saw his assailant produce a pair of handcuffs did it begin to make sense.

'We're journalists!' he moaned, trying to manipulate his tongue, which he'd bitten. 'ID's in my wallet. Back pocket.'

They held him pinioned, but displayed no more aggressive intent while they searched for his wallet and checked twice that he was not concealing anything resembling a weapon. A tray of cutlery that sat on the counter with its piles of bent and soap-stained knives, forks and teaspoons was swept to the floor, out of harm's reach. The Christmas begging bowl went with it.

'It's here, Sarge,' one of his assailants acknowledged, flicking through his wallet. 'Daniel Blackheart. *Wessex Chronicle.*'

'Never heard of it,' Sarge snapped suspiciously, but reluctantly nodded that Daniel should be allowed to rise.

'And the lady, too,' Daniel added, sucking air back into his lungs.

'Doesn't look like a journalist. Or a lady,' Sarge muttered, inspecting Izzy.

'I hope I look like a tart,' she responded. 'That was my cover, which you've just blown.'

'Didn't look as if you had much cover left when we came in, miss,' Sarge said, nodding at the prone figure of Mo. 'Here, better clean yourself up.' He produced a handkerchief.

'Thanks. You got here quickly.'

'Not really,' Sarge responded. 'This is a Drugs Squad raid, planned for about three months. Had no idea we'd find a damsel in distress.'

'We cynical members of the media aren't supposed to believe in coincidence.'

'Believe it. If we'd known these bastards were giving members of the media a hard time, after the treatment we normally get at the hands of the press we might have been tempted to leave it for another three months.'

'OK, I believe in coincidence.' She smiled unsteadily, still shaken. She liked Sarge. She wanted to throw her arms around him and smother him in kisses. Or burst into tears. So she smiled.

'And I'll need to know who you are, miss. I'll need ID. And a statement.'

The smile faded. The police. British authorities. Her airport subterfuge blown.

'Is this your bag, miss?' One of the policemen picked up her bag from the floor.

'Thank you, Officer. Let me get you that ID.'

She hoped it didn't seem as if she were snatching back her bag in too much haste. She'd only just remembered what it contained. But now she had no choice. 'Isadora Dean. I'm the foreign correspondent for WCN in Washington.'

'Yeah, I think I recognize you,' another policeman joined in. 'I've got cable, you know,' he added enthusiastically.

'Makes up for his lack of a social life,' Sarge derided.

He took the passport she offered.

'Wait here while we check things out, if you don't

mind, Miss Dean. Then one of my men will take a statement.'

'Of course, Sergeant. But . . .' – she dabbed at the wound on her face – 'do you think we could have a little fresh air. It's not every day I dress as a tart and get mugged in a drug den.'

'Sure. Collins will look after you.'

What Sarge meant, of course, was that Collins would keep a close eye on them until the matter of their presence amidst the dealers and pimps was sorted out. They perched on the bonnet of a squad car, ignoring the damp December wind, while Collins sat in the driver's seat, door ajar.

'Devereux's going to hear about this, Daniel,' she said quietly.

'How so? He thinks you've flown.'

'Think. What would you have done in his shoes, with his contacts? Made sure as sunrise that if ever I came back into the country, if my name appeared on anyone's computer, if I used a credit card at Tesco's, he or his tame inspector would learn about it. And fast.' She bit her lip. 'He'll know we're here. In London. And he'll know why. He'll get to Paulette before we do.'

'We've got to get away from here,' he agreed.

'They take one look in my bag and it's all over. They're never going to let us go.'

'What's with your bag?'

'Apart from a couple of thousand pounds in cash which I can't account for? Only my soiled underwear wrapped around the private address and unlisted telephone number of the Secretary of State for Defence. Try explaining that lot away.'

'I'd rather not.'

'Sorry.'

'Not half as sorry as you're going to be in about a

minute, as soon as they finish checking my name on their computers.'

'What do you mean?'

'This isn't quite how I planned to break it to you, Izzy, but you've got to know.' Even in the darkness of a winter's night and with the street lights draining all colour, she could see the bruising. 'I'm an addict. Been clean for almost a year, but I've got a record with these guys which will send sparks through their computer. I told you, there are a million cracks in this old Humpty.'

She stood silent, stunned. Then a breath. 'Damn it, I should have guessed. You knew altogether too much about this scene. About Paulette.'

'Disappointed?'

'Only in me, Daniel. I should have asked. Should have known more about you.'

'I am clean, Izzy. Working my way back. I'm going to be OK.'

'Problems?'

'Of course. Especially since I met you.' And she knew he meant it. 'Getting stuck emotionally in a one-way street isn't the greatest thing for a recovering addict. Everything starts hurting again. The Devil sitting on your shoulder. You learn to take it one day at a time.'

'And you brought me to this place, knowing what we'd find?'

'I had a pretty good idea about the coffee shop. Less sure how I'd do. Bit like a chain smoker taking a bath in petrol. I did all right, though, didn't I?' He looked a hundred years old. She hoped it was only the street light.

'And you did all this for me?'

'No, not just for you. For me, too. To test myself. To give me something to believe in again. You hide from drugs because they are stronger than you are. You loathe yourself, loathe your own weakness. Then there comes a time when you feel you might just be able to stand up to it, not to run away any more, when you have something to believe in which is stronger even than drugs.' He ran a weary hand through his hair. 'It's been a long time since I felt anything other than disgust for myself. But tonight . . . I reckon I did fine.'

'You made only one mistake, Daniel.'

'What was that?'

'About the one-way street.'

And she took him in her arms and kissed him in a way she thought she'd almost forgotten.

It was while they stood embracing that the boys loaded Mo into the van, and he didn't want to go, really didn't want to go with these guys who'd crushed his balls and his fingers, and he kicked out hard and savagely. One officer went down clutching his kneecap and Collins thought he'd go and help. Daniel saw.

'We really ought to get out of here,' he whispered.

'Not playing hard to get, are you?'

'Izzy, I think we should both be playing hard to get.'

And they had burrowed into the Christmas crowds of Kensington High Street even before Collins knew they were gone.

When they had finished running they walked, grateful for the fresh air and the anonymity of darkened streets, two miles, directly north, ignoring the drizzle that floated in the air and made the pavements shimmer and their feet damp.

They both felt exhausted, drained by their collision with the forces of law and lawlessness, yet they hurried on, drawn inexorably forward by what might lie ahead, pursued by what they had left behind. The pretence had vanished, their identities discovered and Devereux would soon hear, might already have heard. They knew they had little time left.

There were five drinking establishments along Endeavour Road, four pubs and a low-life wine bar. They found what they were looking for in the fourth, beyond the graffiti and the dog crap and the primary school; the Battle of Trafalgar, a gloomy Victorian edifice with dark panelled walls and wrought-iron supports around the bar, whose original ornate mouldings were all but hidden beneath oppressive generations of paint. Much of the miserable interior lighting came from the bank of slot machines and video games which obstructed the entrance to the toilets, and a television that flickered above the bar – the type of pub where the licensee chose not to see and the customers not to be seen.

'Jesus, what a dump,' she exclaimed. 'Looks like they never got round to cleaning up after the Battle. You sure you guys won it?'

'The *English* won the battle,' he corrected, a trifle testily. 'I can only conclude that the French died laughing when they saw that Lord Nelson had a blind eye and his rifle sleeve tucked into his waistcoat.'

'Not much to laugh about in here. What do we do?'

'You sit down and look around while I buy us both a drink, like any good pimp.'

She caught a glance of herself in a mirror and gasped – she looked appalling. The eyes drooped through lack of sleep, her hair had frizzled in the damp evening air, her face was pale and the make-up stood out in all its hideousness. The wound on her cheek had dried, leaving an angry red weal. She had forgotten she was supposed to be a tart; she looked every inch the part.

He returned with a Coke and glass of putrid white wine; his hand was trembling to the point that the drinks all but spilled.

'You all right?' she enquired anxiously.

'Brilliant.' He sat down heavily. 'They tried to peddle me some dope while I was waiting at the bar. Just like old times. And I wanted to say yes, Izzy.' As he tried to drink his Coke spilled down the side of the glass and dribbled onto the grimy table. 'There's a voice inside me telling me, screaming at me, that it's all right. That just a little won't hurt. That I can handle it, no problem. It was there in his hand, wrapped in a little twist of paper. And I wanted it so bad.' He banged his glass down before it slipped from his shaking fingers.

'I thought you said you were over it.'

'You never get over it, Izzy. It's not like the bloody measles. It's there the whole time, offering you an easy way out of your problems, like climbing into a suit of armour to protect yourself against the rest of the rotten world. Except you discover you've climbed into a coffin. I can't go back to that again, Izzy, it'll kill me next time.'

'Then let me help.'

He relaxed a little. 'You already have. You've given me something stronger than drugs. Just make sure you don't turn your back on me.'

'Never.'

She reached to kiss him but he moved away. 'Izzy, a pimp's not supposed to go round drooling over his hooker. It's bad form.' He managed a smile. 'I'll take a rain check.'

'Payment on demand. With interest.'

302

And he was better; the Devil moved from his shoulder.

They looked around the crowded pub, examining through the smoky atmosphere those who had begun to settle in for the long night ahead. There were old-timers and past-timers, occupying the stools and chairs they had sat on most nights for a lifetime, who could remember the Trafalgar in more glorious days when brassware had gleamed and pumps had been primed and the pub had appeared less of a war casualty.

Also there was another crowd, younger, that had a uniform all to itself. T-shirts that protested and gaudily coloured trousers that screamed, dreadlocks and bleached hair that appeared torn rather than cropped, all clothes casual and crumpled and much tattered, swaddled around bodies often painfully thin. Rings and chains seemed to be the fashion, rings that hung from ears, on fingers, through noses and several through lips, and chains which hung from these rings. Everything to excess. It was embellishment become defilement, a protest, like self-immolation. These kids didn't like the world; even less did they seem to like themselves.

The door across the pub swung open, complaining on unoiled hinges, and a newcomer entered dressed in an ankle-length leather coat and broad-brimmed fedora. A cigarillo protruded from between carefully trimmed greying whiskers. The teeth were appallingly stained and twisted. He did not cross to the bar but stood by the door, gazing carefully around. Immediately, a young man rose from his stool and crossed to greet him, slapping hands in a perfunctory ritual before both disappeared past the video machines and into the toilet.

Daniel nodded. 'Sixty seconds and one of them

will be out again and off. The other will be shooting up inside.'

She found herself feeling nauseous. 'Which one is the pusher?'

'Who knows? They might both be, buying for themselves and selling to others so they can buy for themselves again. Often there's little distinction. Whoever leaves first will be the one pushing tonight.'

And it was the leather coat, as Daniel had said, who was out and gone before most people were aware he had even arrived. Five minutes later the younger man emerged, slowly, relaxed, greeting a couple of the old-timers as he made his way back to his chair. He said very little for half an hour, not participating, before he became more animated and once more part of the group.

'He's our man,' Daniel muttered.

'What man?'

'The man who can find Paulette for us.'

'I thought we might ask the barman.'

'We could try, but there's a good chance he wouldn't know, or if he did wouldn't tell us, or if he told us would also warn Paulette before we got to her.' He shook his head. 'Too much of a risk.'

'And that guy there in his army-surplus shirt and semi-coma is less of a risk?' she asked sceptically.

'He's an addict and he needs money. And in order to get it he'll trade his grandmother to cannibals without thinking twice. He'd sell Paulette without thinking at all.'

'Or Bella,' she whispered.

'I sold everything I had when I needed to.'

She turned her eyes from the youth back towards Daniel; he was trying to tell her something.

'Don't be too harsh on Paulette, Izzy. There's no point. But try to understand. When you are in that condition there are no limits, no shame or feelings of guilt which can stop you doing what you have to do. You have no conscience, and no control. You can't help it.'

'Can't help selling babies?' she protested.

'I sold everything I had, Izzy. Everything I owned, everything I could steal. My father's war medals. The few paltry heirlooms my mother had struggled so hard to hang on to. Burgled from my own brother's flat. I even sold my own body.'

'You what?'

'Sold my own body. Just like you did last night.'

'That was different!'

'Of course it was different. And you sold your body only once. I sold mine time and time and time again.'

She trembled, backed away a little; he noticed.

'You have to know. I'm not going to hide the truth from you.'

'It did that to you?' she whispered.

He nodded sadly. He could see the confusion eating away at her. It seemed a long time before she spoke again, and suddenly he was vulnerable and very afraid. He wanted to jump back into the suit of armour, to shut out the fear. Her lips were moving but she was having trouble mouthing the words.

'It did that to you?' she repeated. 'Yet you would risk it all again. For me? And for Bella?'

'For myself. You see, I'm hoping you'll prove to be the best detox treatment any man could find.'

'When I get you back home, Danny Blackheart, or wherever it is we end up, you're going to need treatment.' A smile broke across her face and she looked suggestively through her glass.

'You working girls are all the same.'

She reached for his hand but the moment had already passed, his attention wandered. The youth had stood up from his seat and was meandering across to the bar, intent on ordering another drink.

'Time to get to work,' Daniel muttered grimly, preparing to follow.

'No,' she insisted. 'My turn, Daniel. You've bathed in enough petrol for one day.'

He struggled to find the spirit to protest but already she was on her feet, moving across to the bar. She squeezed in beside the youth, her breast rubbing purposefully against his arm as she did so.

'Hi, honey,' she greeted.

He looked around in surprise, eyed the breast that had attacked him, then looked once more towards the barman. 'Sorry, sister. That's not my game,' he responded in an accent smothered in the mud of the Thames Estuary.

'I don't think you understand. I'm not selling, I'm buying.'

His curiosity was immediately sparked. 'What you after? Pills? Grass? E? Summink a little 'eavier, perhaps?'

'Something much heavier. Information. And I'm willing to pay for it.'

Curiosity turned to suspicion. 'You're not—?'

'Do I look like Filth, for Chrissake? Funny type of policewoman you must have in this country.'

'What sort of information? And 'ow much?'

'I'm looking for a girl called Paulette. Been around these parts recently, probably this pub.'

'Why d'you need to know?'

'None of your damned business.'

'Never 'eard of her.'

'Ever heard of fifty pounds?' She had withdrawn a tightly folded note from under the strap of her wristwatch. She had his undivided attention.

'How's the memory job coming along?'

'I've . . . 'eard the name. Comes in 'ere once, twice a week maybe. Not seen 'er for a few days though.'

Paulette. Here. His words hit Izzy like exploding mortar shells. She found she had stopped breathing; in her hand the note had begun to tremble.

'You know where she lives?'

'No.'

Despair!

'Bu' I can find out,' he added hurriedly.

'I need to find her without her knowing I'm even looking. Quietly. Very quietly.'

'You don't wanna scare 'er off. No' my problem. Can be done.'

With great care she proceeded to tear the fifty-pound note in two. One half she clenched in her fist, the other was placed under her hand on the sticky counter. His spot-encrusted upper lip wobbled furiously like a squirrel at a nut.

'You get the other half if you can give me her address. Noon tomorrow. Here.'

He laid his hand upon hers. 'And a free fuck?' he sneered.

'The only thing you'll get for free is the feeling you've just blown the easiest fifty you ever made.'

He snorted. 'Cow.'

She removed her hand and he grabbed the torn half.

'Noon tomorrow.' She reached up and tweaked his unshaven cheek savagely. 'And you know what? I like you. Something about your smell. Tell me where she is, where I can find her tomorrow, without her knowing, and there'll be another fifty in it.'

'I'll be 'ere,' he spat, eyes red with resentment. 'Anyway, who'd want an old scrubber like you? Even for free?'

*   *   *

They did not return to their hotel, they didn't dare take the risk on any hotel, not if Devereux and his Establishment were already searching for her. She had slipped away too often and wouldn't be allowed another chance. In any event sleep was beyond them, carried by a surging tide that swept aside exhaustion and lifted them off their rock of doubt.

They sought refuge in an all-night café where, beneath strip lights and a vapour cloud of cooking fat, they drank coffee and soup and watched as the bleary-eyed owner abused with uninhibited Serbian partiality the patrons he decided were chemically, alcoholically or socially unfit to grace his meagre table. The night was punctuated by frequent rows and bouts of cursing as unwanted visitors were dispatched as promptly as they had arrived back onto the freezing streets, the splintered glass door bearing witness to the fact that more than abuse was occasionally hurled back by those he had offended. Strips of tape stretched across the damage, crudely disguised as a Christmas star. But at least it was warm, and she rather liked the *chorba* cabbage soup.

'How did it happen?' she asked.

They had been talking for several hours, exchanging verbal snapshots of their earlier lives, allowing the other to touch and share the moments and memories upon which a man or woman is built. And which sometimes cause them to crumble.

'It was my first week at university. I'd bought myself a Norton, 500cc of chromed mechanical beast. To celebrate. And to pull the girls. Damn successful, too, even in the first week.' He smiled mischievously. 'Until I was so busy enchanting a rather wonderful classics student named Anna through the university park that I completely missed the bend. Ended up wrapping the bike around a maple, front and back ends of both me and my beast meeting around the other side of the tree. The Norton was a write-off but they were able to glue me back together, over time. Took them several attempts at getting my leg right and I spent the next two years on painkillers.'

A bellow came from behind the counter and another would-be refugee from the cold night slunk back into the shadows.

'I was so proud of myself when I finally threw the crutches and the pills away,' Daniel continued, remembering, still hurting, 'but when the excitement had died down I found that nothing was quite right. Something was missing, something very important to me and my body, but I couldn't tell what. So I tried everything – a new Norton, snowboarding, parachuting. And a lot more sex. But nothing got rid of that empty, nagging feeling inside. Nothing. Except drugs. A girlfriend gave me some pills to settle me down before exams and my body told me right away that was it, that's what I'd been missing. Like a fur coat on a freezing day.'

He wrapped his arms protectively around his body. 'And, of course, I could handle it, couldn't I? It was the accident, after all, not my fault; I wasn't a junkie or anything. Even when I'd gone through popping and sniffing and snorting and was all the way to shoving needles into my arm, I could give it up any time I wanted. It was just to get me through finals, then through the bit where you're supposed to get out and find a job, and then, when I didn't, to cope with the disappointment and the rows I began having with everyone around me. Every problem I had, my body told me that heroin was the answer. It made a complicated world so simple. Everybody I knew was doing it; of course they were. No normal friend would put up with my abuse and lying. And so it went on.'

'Until?'

'I was in Salford, I think. I'd sold everything I owned, I'd even started renting out my girlfriend. Then I woke up one morning – or whatever time of day it was; scarcely capable of telling the difference – and she was gone. And I felt awful, and I threw up, and I desperately needed a fix but I had no money. I had only one thing left to sell. Myself. So I did.'

The implication shimmered uncertainly between them.

'That was me, Izzy. All of me. There was nothing left of me apart from drugs. Then I had a stroke of luck that saved my life,' he continued. 'I went back to the Bay to see my mother. Even as an addict I suppose I had some sense of shame left, because I'd avoided her for months. After I'd stolen my father's medals, I didn't want her to see me, what I'd become.'

'You went back to her for help?'

'No. I went back for the sole purpose of stealing from her again. She had long before thrown me out, told me I wasn't welcome under her roof while I was still "sorting myself out", as she put it. So I went back for coffee and lied and told her that I was off it all, and while my mother was busy I stole her purse and a necklace my father had given her. Not much, costume gems, but about the only thing she had left of any value.'

'So how was all that lucky?'

'She called the police. Then, when the good men of the Garda tried to brush over it and call it a family dispute, my mother caused a riot and insisted that I be arrested and locked up.'

'Your mother? Had her son arrested? She must have been extraordinarily bitter.'

'My mother loved me more deeply than I could ever imagine. She saw me killing myself. She knew that unless I was forced to face up to what I was doing she'd be getting another visit from the police, and soon, to tell her I'd been found stiff in some gutter with a needle in my arm.'

Up to this point Daniel's account had been delivered in a flat, almost academic manner, recounting dispassionate facts. Now emotion seeped through, a passion rekindled, a new flame flickering through the bruising.

'She visited me in the cells that night and listened to me ranting and raving. How could my own mother shop me? I screamed. For a few pounds, which she knew I would pay her back? I lied. So she told me she was dying of cancer, had but a few months to live, and didn't want to see me dead before she was. That if I took any more drugs she would never speak to me again, she loved me too much to co-operate in my own suicide. Then she walked out. That's when I knew I might never see my mother again. And I have never known a moment in my life when I felt more utterly destroyed.'

He held her gaze fiercely, locked in combat with the memories, his face grown gaunt and his voice shrunk to a hoarse whisper. Then Izzy watched as slowly a flush of pride began to glow inside and fill his cheeks.

'For the first time in months something other than heroin began to get through to me. And, by the time she died three months later, I was able to stand with my brother and the rest of my family to say goodbye properly. She asked that I read the lesson at her funeral. She was one hell of a mother.'

'I wish I could have known her.'

'In a way you do. You're very much like her. No half commitments, no going back. You remind me very much of my mother, Izzy.'

She bit her lip, finding no words.

'At least, in some ways you do. I never had an irresistible urge to tear the clothes from my mother's back.'

'I guess it's these little things that make the big differences in a relationship.'

They spent the rest of the night talking and sharing, grateful for the tug of discovery that was distracting from the tension rising inside. Yet it was an uneven battle. As dawn began to pick its way through the winter sky they decided they could sit no longer. The warmth of the café had begun to stifle, the caffeine eating away at their control, so they had stepped into the morning air that had an edge of ice and revived their spirits.

They found a public washroom and freshened their bodies, Izzy at last able to remove the mask of coagulated make-up that remained smeared around her face. For a long time she stared intently in the mirror above the bowl of ancient, cracked porcelain, looking into the eyes. There she saw Bella, in the colour, in the shape, in the soul behind. She reached out to touch, to grab back; the mirror smudged, the image blurred and faded. Her heart stopped. Would this be all she ever had left of her child? A haunted image, every time she looked into a mirror? Quickly she splashed more cold water over her face, lest people think they were tears washing down her cheeks.

By ten they were in Endeavour Road, unable to contain their impatience. A cold front had passed across the capital during the night, taking with it the rain and leaving a day crisply cold but bright with a few high clouds from behind which the sun frequently ventured. Even in winter, life on Endeavour was lived on the street, spilled out from within the dark terraces: shouted greetings and insults that flew across the street, double-parked cars and delivery vans that choked it, school kids who littered and loitered, mothers who tried to shield their eyes and their infants as they forced passage along cluttered pavements. They were black, white, dark, with accents of Celtic fringes and Caribbean isles, the peninsulas and outposts of Europe, and some that were incomprehensibly Middle Eastern.

The noise of rasta and rock and the protest of car horns mingled with the smell of fish stalls and curry houses, and dry cleaners, and bakeries, and things that smelled less sweet. Of ageing anchovies, and worse.

Basement England.

A middle-aged man in three-piece suit and scruffy shoes stumbled by, yesterday's button hole drooping from his lapel, demanding in broad Scottish dialect to know why they – whoever 'they' might be, he didn't specify – couldn't pronounce their fucking consonants properly. A one-man revolution against Estuary English. This was not so much a melting pot, more a pot that simmered and occasionally boiled.

And at the end of the street, like an architectural exclamation mark, stood Triumph Towers, an alien creation from another world come to invade and enslave. A brown concrete fortress thrust for twenty-eight storeys towards the sky, blocking out the light and casting a shadow on those who lived around and within it. A self-contained city of many hundreds of people but a home only to diseased urban pigeons and abandoned dreams, a towering monument to bureaucratic expediency that had been raised by planners in the sixties only to be targeted by their sons thirty years later for demolition. Except the money had run out. The bloody cuts. And, anyway, who cared?

Then it was twelve o'clock and they were in the Trafalgar.

He was three minutes late, arriving harassed, wearing his clothes of the previous night. He was breathless as he approached her, his chest heaving; she found she could not breathe at all.

'Mine's a large Scotch,' he demanded.

She nodded at the barman.

'And two 'undred pounds.'

The squeeze, as expected.

'Forget it.' Izzy began moving away.

'For the address you can find 'er at right now.'

Izzy stopped, turned, looked him directly in the eye in search of any hint of sincerity. Not a trace.

'All right.'

'Money up front.'

From within her bag Izzy removed the torn fifty, then three more fifties. Slowly she laid them on the counter, the half on top of the whole, and carefully tore the whole notes in two.

'What the f—?'

'My guarantee you're not just another pimple-squeezing creep,' she responded.

'I don't bleedin' like you,' he spat.

'But you like my money.' She pushed the three new halves across to him. 'And you'd love a full set.'

He snatched the scraps of notes and glowered at her, bluff called, his game lost. Then the whisky arrived, he downed it in one and with it seemed to swallow his aggression. He started laughing.

'The address,' Izzy demanded, fear suddenly smothering her.

Still nothing but a coarse laugh.

She needed to be strong, desperately wanted to stand firm but inside she felt herself melting like a wax doll in Hell. Her resistance and confidence were evaporating, she began wobbling and surely he could see?

The pimple-sore lips kept laughing.

'Where is she?' she demanded, waving the notes.

'In 'eaven,' he spluttered through a sneer.

'Where?'

''Eaven. In 'eaven. With a haitch.'

'Heaven. Heaven, you mean. She's dead?' Her knees began to buckle.

He was laughing all the more, the lips curling in contempt. 'No. Not dead, you stupid cow. Not yet, at least. In 'eaven. Where people crawl off to die and kiss an angel's arse. Up in the clouds. Look out the bloody window. There,' he said, demanded, pointing with a broken nail. 'In Triumph Towers. The nearest most of us are gonna get to bloody 'eaven.'

'She's there? But where?'

He smirked, looking closely at the half-notes in her hand. She threw two of them on the counter. 'There must be three hundred apartments in that building. Which one?'

He smoothed the two crumpled halves. 'Twen'y-fifth floor.'

Another half.

'Which apartment?'

His smile had disappeared. 'Look, I dunno. I swear to you she's there, but I dunno which apartment. You told me not to get too 'eavy. Christ, lady, there's only ten doors on each bleedin' floor, surely you can figure that bit out for yourself?' He picked nervously

315

at his teeth. 'And if I don't get that other 'alf I'll be up there screaming before you even get a chance to start asking.'

But he was wasting his breath. The note was already fluttering towards him. Izzy was running out the door.

NINE

They ran the three hundred yards, forcing their way through the flotsam of polystyrene wrappers and pock-marked derelicts that blew about in search of a leeward corner or crevice. The sun had disappeared behind the clouds, the grey fingers of winter settling upon the street and around Izzy's heart. Cold wind drew tears to her eyes, making them moist to the point of flooding. Like Devereux's. Something inside kept insisting she was running straight into his grasp.

The gates to Heaven were ajar, the intercom system and huge electronic lock broken, the doors creaking in the wind. A vandalized reception desk stood inside and from behind it St Peter, in the shape of a harassed old man with grey face and straggly beard, tussled with the demands of a family group consisting of shawled women who were all talking at the same time while two infants idly kicked the doors to the lifts. In the small office behind the reception desk a telephone rang, unanswered. As Izzy and Daniel strode past St Peter waved a restraining arm in their direction.

'Paulette. Twenty-fifth floor,' Izzy shouted over her shoulder, not wishing to catch his eye.

A second telephone started ringing; a child, ears boxed, started wailing. The jabbering of foreign tongues lashed around his ears and the old man subsided, resistance withered. He rather wished someone would steal the entire building instead of just the TV sets and electrical fittings, but who would want it?

Beside the lifts stood a great concrete urn, positioned there for some plant long since ripped out by children and replaced to overflowing with rubbish and refuse. The lift was all steel. Soiled. And slow. The count up to twenty-five seemed to take forever.

They sprang out into a corridor of pebble-dash, along the right-hand side of which painted doors stretched into the distance. On the other side, through pigeon-smeared double glazing, they found a view of the city that even at a moment such as this caught her breath. Beneath them stretched London, a mosaic of patterns built from the blocks of urban life, the roofs and roadways, the lines, the circles, crescents, parks and parkways, everything in miniature, tussling for supremacy and reaching out to the rural suburbs that lay through the winter mists beyond.

The corridor stank.

'Which one?' whispered Daniel.

They worked their way along. The doors were little more than flimsy barricades separating occupant from outside world. Through the first came the shouts of an exasperated mother screaming at children; through the second a snatch of the lunchtime television news. Daniel shook his head. Addicts don't give a toss about wars or weather reports. The third was enclosed behind a huge steel shutter on which kids had scratched obscenities and offensive remarks about each other, and around which spiders had spun dust-filled webs. The fourth had an angry black scorch mark creeping up from the letterbox; a woman was singing in Portuguese within. The fifth was silent. They both placed ears against the woodwork but caught no trace of movement or occupation. Izzy shrugged. Try again later.

As they stood before the next door, they could hear the unmistakable sound of coughing. Harsh, raking fits of expulsion, desiccated fragments of pain. A woman's pain. A young woman. Who was also whimpering.

Daniel raised his hand, motioning Izzy to stay while he ran down the corridor to conduct a fleeting inspection of the remaining doors, but within seconds he was back, shaking his head.

'This is it, isn't it?' she said. Inside her something was twisting, something sharp was scraping at her, causing her heart to pound and her head to swim.

Daniel stepped back from the door, took a deep breath and prepared to launch himself at it. 'Why do I always appear to be throwing myself at chunks of solid tree?' he enquired mournfully.

'Because you're too damned impatient,' she whispered. She pushed the door gently. It gave. On the latch.

A hallway. Cramped. Darkened. The only light came from an open door at the far end, through which drifted the sound of more hacking coughs. They crept forward, making as little sound as they could.

The room was small, scarcely more than twelve feet square, with stain-spattered vinyl flooring and walls covered in floral-patterned paper that had all but faded to invisibility. Some of the paper sagged away from the ceiling and had been torn, elsewhere a desultory attempt to paint over the years of damage had been abandoned before the butter-milk emulsion had reached the first corner. One of the walls was stained for several feet of its length towards the door by something which from its sight and stench they could only take to be vomit. Recent vomit. Although the sliding door leading to a balcony was ajar, the sour smell still hung heavily in the air, mixing with the stale aroma of food, some of which still infested the jumble of dirty plates that had been pushed into one corner.

There was no form of decoration on the bare walls, no TV, a naked bulb hanging from the light fitting, a rusting radiator. Anything of use was gone. Stripped away. Sold.

A low coffee table and two dilapidated chairs provided the only formal furniture, supplemented by chunks of foam rubber over which had been thrown old blankets. On one of these pieces of foam rubber squatted the young woman.

She was bare-footed, emaciated, clad in black leggings and jumper that served only to emphasize the unnatural paleness of her skin. The hair, which might once have been blonde, was now too filthy for anyone to be sure. One arm of the jumper had been pushed up several inches beyond the elbow and around the upper arm had been twisted the cotton cord of a bathrobe. One end of the cord was in the woman's mouth, her teeth exposed like a dog at a bone, tugging to increase the pressure. The crease of the elbow was blotched and scabbed with a series of angry holes which the woman was slapping with her free hand in an attempt to incite a vein to break through the covering of scabs.

On the table in front of her lay a small square of paper, a bent spoon. Alongside them was the cigarette lighter with which she had reduced the heroin to liquid form in the spoon, dissolved in the acidic juice from a mangled lemon that lay squashed on the floor. A razor blade. Chewed cigarette filter. And a syringe.

'Paulette?' Izzy gasped.

The woman glanced up: the same glassy, haunted eyes that Izzy remembered, but instead of exhaustion now ablaze with energy, frightened, hyperactive, like a player tensed up before the Big Game. That same face, more corpse-like even than Izzy had pictured in her nightmares, vacant, lifeless wax. It was she.

Paulette ignored them and returned to her search for an injectable vein.

'Paulette!' Izzy exclaimed more sharply.

Something crept into the girl's eyes, a spark, a glowing coal of anger, yet again she said nothing, the arm band clenched firmly between her teeth, her irritation at being disturbed expressed only in the still more violent slapping she inflicted upon her circulatory system.

Izzy was the first to react. She sprang across the room and before the girl could respond had snatched the plastic syringe.

'Where is my baby?'

'Give it back!'

'My baby? What have you done with my baby?'

With an animal's screech of rage Paulette threw herself after her syringe but the low table was between her and Izzy; she stumbled and fell sharply on her exposed arm. For a while she lay there, whimpering with pain.

'Give it back to me,' she pleaded in pathetic voice.

'Not until you tell me what you did with my baby,' Izzy responded from a safe distance.

'Who are you? Why don't you leave me alone?'

Paulette's eyes were focused on nothing but the syringe. Izzy held it behind her, placing her body between the girl and her desires.

'Look at me. Remember? The hospital!'

Paulette's eyes blinked in exaggerated pain. Everything was blurred, her needle had disappeared, and through the mists emerged a face. Something about a hospital. And she remembered.

'You!' she exclaimed involuntarily.

'Yes. And my baby. You stole her, didn't you? Where is she now?'

'Let me have the bloody works. I need it.' Paulette's frail arm stretched out. 'I'll talk later.'

'You'll tell me now.'

And Izzy had produced the syringe, waved it towards Paulette and depressed the plunger. A narrow stream of liquid sprang from the needle and splattered like rain across the table in front of Paulette. The girl uttered a primitive, wrenching cry. From behind her Izzy scarcely noted the groan of anguish from Daniel.

'Please . . .' the girl sobbed.

'First, my baby. Then you can have it. If there's any left.'

'I know nothing,' she lied.

A fresh fountain of heroin arced across the room. The girl stared at Izzy, hatred twisting her features, but in the other woman's eyes Paulette found a craving, an anger almost greater than her own, and a strength that her lies and deception could never match. Her needs grew, and her resistance crumbled.

'All right, all right,' the girl pleaded. 'No more.'

'What happened to my baby?'

She wanted to lie, to deny, but her ability to invent had been diluted in pain. It took Paulette many seconds to fight for control of her shattered nerves and shaking limbs before she began, in halting words, to tell her story. To trade the truth, just as she had traded everything else.

'I had . . . a baby,' she stumbled. 'Not mine.

Someone else's. A little girl, for adoption. Her foster mother had fallen ill, couldn't cope, so I had collected the baby to take to her new foster parents.' She was shivering all over. 'But I dropped it. I must have blacked out or something. Stumbled. Next thing I knew it was at the bottom of the stairs and its eyes were closed. It was hurt, very pale. I couldn't wake it. Didn't mean to harm it,' she sobbed. 'So I took it to the hospital. I wanted to help it! Don't you understand?'

'Get on with it,' Izzy demanded. She was trembling too.

'I got to the hospital. The baby was in my arms. And everyone was running about, there was no one to pay any attention to me.'

'The fire alarm,' Izzy prompted.

The girl nodded. 'I was wandering around looking for a nurse. By this time I think the baby had stopped breathing. I was so scared! Then I went behind a curtain and there you were. Blood all down your face. Unconscious. And your baby. Just about the same age. Smiling.'

'She's . . . alive.' Izzy scarcely dared breathe the words.

The girl nodded.

'Bella's alive,' she whispered. 'Alive . . .' Her voice faded away in a feeble, choked cry as the passion of release rushed to her throat. For a moment she was unable to fight through the tangle of emotions – to laugh, to exult, to shed tears, to shout or succumb to the feeling that someone had cut the wires holding her together inside. She felt light-headed, but through it all she clung fixedly to the fact that there was more, much more, still to be done.

'You bitch!' Izzy had turned cold with fury. 'You swapped them, didn't you? My baby for yours.'

'What else was I supposed to do? There was no one around. You looked as if you were dead anyway. I couldn't admit to harming the baby. They would have found out everything.'

'About the drugs. About how you and Fauld were farming babies through the Mission. Selling babies to the highest bidder.'

The girl hung her head in exhaustion and shame.

'And how your father was covering up for you.'

The girl's head sprang back. 'My father! Help me?' she spat incredulously. 'Damn him, don't you see this is all his fault? The big man who was supposed to be so much better than everyone else. The pillar of the community. The statesman everyone respected. But while he was out playing bloody God to the country, where was he when I needed him? When my mother needed him?' She clutched her stomach in agony.

'He's fought ruthlessly to cover up for you.'

'Guilt. Nothing but guilt. The bastard.' And she sobbed, a cry of more than physical pain. 'Please, let me have my needle.'

'Not until you tell me what you did with my baby.' Izzy lunged aggressively forward, barely conscious of the restraining hand from behind.

Paulette's eyes had begun to blur. 'Please,' she whimpered.

More droplets spattered onto the floor.

'What did you do with my baby?'

The girl drew in a huge gulp of breath that shook her gaunt frame as though it might break. 'I took her from the hospital. Nobody noticed. I came with a baby, left with a baby. And I gave a baby to the new foster parents, just like I was supposed to.'

'So where is she now?' cried Izzy in frustration, raising the syringe above her head as if to hurl it to the ground.

'No!' Paulette screamed, hiding her head in her hands and cowering like a dog. She remained in that position, whimpering.

The silence stirred nothing but hatred within Izzy. This woman had ripped Bella from her, stolen her child and with it Izzy's life, had inflicted evils that all but surpassed comprehension. Now she was pleading for sympathy.

There was none to give. Izzy had no resources for sympathy. She thrust the hypodermic at Daniel, scarcely aware of the tormented hand that took it, then turned to face the cringing woman once more. She would not allow Paulette to cower from the truth. She lifted the girl's shoulders, expecting to find tear-soaked eyes but to her surprise found not weakness but eyes that burned with malice. And action.

Paulette pounced, her fury lending springs to her feet. She hurled herself at her tormentor, intent on gaining by strength what she could not extract through sympathy. Two women, two lives, collided, one touched by evil, the other by innocence.

As she saw Paulette leaping for her, Izzy drew back her hand and crashed it full into the other's face. Paulette flew across the room, her head crashing into the wall, blood spurting from a badly split lip. Without respite, Izzy was upon her, shaking her, forcing reality back between the closed eyelids.

'Where is she now? Where?'

Paulette mumbled, Izzy propped her against the wall, the girl's eyes tightly closed.

'With one of our fosterers, don't know which. Waiting to be handed over to the new owners.'

'Owners?' Izzy flared, brutalized by the language. 'Bella's not some piece of second-hand furniture.'

But of course, for Paulette, she was.

'Owners?' Izzy repeated breathlessly.

'Foreigners.'

'Foreigners? From where?'

'Abroad.'

'Where abroad?'

Izzy slapped her cheek hard and Paulette's eyes flashed open. They were soulless, empty.

'Somewhere in the Gulf. Not sure where.'

'Why on earth would they want a baby like Bella?'

There came no answer, but Izzy thought she knew. Judi had told her, igniting a bonfire of fears. White flesh. The ultimate status symbol. To be raised in the traditional way. And even if it were for some other reason, it scarcely mattered. They had sold her baby.

She wanted to crush Paulette's head against the wall, to scatter her brains and her life across this stinking drug den of hers, to inflict agonies to compensate in some small degree for the pain suffered. But even as she held Paulette up, ready to strike, to pound her head and life into oblivion, she knew there could never be any compensation, that she could never make Paulette suffer enough. Not like she had suffered. And the real enemy was not Paulette, but time. Once Bella was taken from the country, obliterated behind the mysterious sandstorms of the Middle East, Izzy knew the door would be closed on her baby forever. The thought numbed every muscle.

Thank God she still had time. Bella was still with foster parents. Here. Close.

'Where is Bella?' she insisted once more.

'Waiting to be delivered,' the girl repeated. 'A

326

nurse will fly her out to the Gulf. Hand her over there.'

'But that's not possible,' Izzy protested, remembering Fauld's words. 'The parents are supposed to be here. For reports.'

'Supposed to be,' Paulette agreed hollowly. Reports. Another deception. Like so much else in her life.

'But they can't do that . . .'

'Paperwork,' came the fumbled reply. 'All paperwork. They paid extra. Door-to-door delivery.'

'The court hearing. The judge . . .' Izzy protested.

'The new parents might fly over for it. Or not. Probably not. Why bother, for a two-minute hearing? Maybe pay someone else to do it for them, like a driving test. Fool of a judge would never know.'

'So, when is the handover?'

'Can't remember.' She was mumbling badly now.

'Then throw that rubbish out the window, Daniel,' Izzy snapped, not taking her eyes from Paulette.

The girl beat her head, protesting, trying to clear the haze and sickness that enveloped her mind. 'Gideon wanted it to be when everyone was busy. No time for questions. Just rubber-stamp and run.'

'So when, woman? Remember! You must remember. Remember. Then you can have what you want.'

The girl's eyes were far away, as though in trance. Then she shivered, clutched her stomach once more, her lower lip bitten almost to blood.

'Christmas shopping,' she whispered.

'What?' screamed Izzy, fearful that Paulette's mind had gone completely.

'Christmas. When everyone was busy, he said. Rushing to do their Christmas shopping. Rubber-stamp and run . . .' She was panting now, exhausted by pain and effort. 'Friday. Exactly a week before Christmas. Fly her out to the Gulf. Abu Dhabi. From Gatwick when it's choked with charters. Friday before Christmas.'

The truth dawned slowly upon Izzy. For weeks she had been preoccupied, distracted, dates no longer meaningful. But Christmas is a date impossible to ignore. And it was precisely a week away.

Today. Today. Today. TODAY!

She had no more time. Her mind rebelled at the coincidence; the truth was beginning to fall in on her like a collapsing wall of hope, burying her alive.

'I've let you have what you want. Now my stuff,' Paulette demanded. Her eye had at last caught the syringe in Daniel's hand.

'Give it to her, Daniel,' she cried, 'and for God's sake let's get out of here.'

But even as she began to move for the door she saw that he was incapable of responding. His face had been transformed into a lurid, fear-wrecked mask. The hand that held the syringe was trembling, uncontrollably, and had been ever since his fingers had closed around the hypodermic. His head was shaking.

'I cannot give it to her,' he whispered. 'Not this.'

He stood frozen, but not so Paulette. With astonishing agility for a body so badly abused she had once again flung herself across the room, this time at Daniel. But he was too far away; she fell short and he backed off, towards the balcony door, as though to hurl the drug away.

'No. I can't let you,' he whispered.

To Izzy it would always remain the most mournful sound she had ever heard.

Through her pain Paulette could see nothing but the syringe. Every fibre of her body and mind was set upon it; it had been held from her too long and nothing else mattered in her world. It was her life-belt, her oxygen, her saviour. Survival. For she felt as though she were swimming in a pool of molten lead and someone had leapt upon her, forcing her down. Unable to breathe. Choking her. Panic. Syringe. Survival. Daniel. Needle. Now!

With the ferocity of a pouncing cat she had flung herself at Daniel, clawing for the hypodermic, her full weight meeting him in the chest.

She was not heavy but he had flung his arms wide to keep the syringe from her, placing himself off balance, and he was propelled backwards. As he staggered, the bottom of his heel hit the lip of the open balcony door. He tripped, fell back, his shoes scrabbling for purchase on the raw concrete floor of the balcony.

But they found nothing but fresh ice. Christmas frost.

His body slammed into the railing, his hands held above his head, centre of gravity high. As Izzy looked on, impotent in disbelief, his body performed a slow cartwheel around the railing.

Momentarily he seemed to hover, like a kestrel testing the winds, wings outstretched. Quivering. Reaching for her.

Their eyes met. He whispered her name.

Was gone.

Too late she had reached the balcony. Noise assailed her. Noise from the rail shunting yards, from the traffic that rumbled along an elevated section of motorway, from the pounding of a pile driver on the banks of the canal that ran close by. Above her, through the clouds, came the scream of engines from an airliner hitting the flight path into Heathrow, its undercarriage lowered. Drowning her own scream.

As she gripped the balcony rail and looked below, the sun burst through the cloud. A shaft of sunlight split the sky and travelled down, a stairway of celestial brilliance against grey winter, hitting the ground and glancing off a rail track into Izzy's eyes. Like the opening of a great door.

Then it was gone.

And twenty-five floors below, on a dilapidated parking area, lay a crumpled form.

In the room behind her Paulette cursed once, then again, and fled. Through the door, pursued by demons — as Izzy was now and would ever after be pursued by demons. Daniel had asked only that he be allowed to love her. Yet she had demurred. Not now. Later. Tomorrow.

Never.

As Izzy looked once more to the scene below, there was sudden activity. Bouncing into the parking area came two police cars, lights flashing, screeching to a halt. Officers swarmed like termites around the body. Then another car drew up, a black limousine, the rear door opened and a man stepped out. He straightened, looked up.

Even from twenty-five floors up she knew him. No question. Below, beside the body of Daniel, her lover who would now never be, was standing Paul Devereux.

The car was forcing its way through the tumble south of the river, headed for the motorway and the airport. Gatwick was a bastard by road. Even with the screaming lights and sirens of the police escort it was proving slow progress through the early evening rush hour. Particularly on the Friday before Christmas.

Devereux sat composed. He knew what he had

to do. It took only seconds to reach the Divisional Commander of the Gatwick Airport police divisions on the phone.

'A problem, Commander. Not too many details, not on a car phone, you'll understand. But it's possible we may have an incident on our hands at the airport. A potentially violent incident. May be a complete hoax, you understand, but I've been contacted personally by an American woman, recently released from hospital and known to be in a highly disturbed state. She's believed to be on her way to Gatwick now, making threats of bloodshed. Mid-thirties, red hair. Possible Middle East connections. Wouldn't normally have taken her too seriously, but it seems she is after all highly dangerous; already left one body behind her just an hour ago. Looks like a drugs-ring murder. Can't afford to take chances, not with the holiday crowds. She's disguised as an American correspondent called Isadora Dean. Dean is genuine but is known to be in America; the imposter may be on your doorstep any minute. I'm on my way there myself; if it's a hoax we can clear the matter up the moment I arrive; if not . . . Yes. I agree. No point in risking a tragedy. Full security alert. Watch the Gulf flights in particular, is my advice. Anything you have to do. Stop her, Commander, don't let her get near a flight and turn it into a Christmas hijacking. You'll have my full personal support.'

He sat back in his seat, the influence of his position having won police co-operation yet again. Their questions would wait. And, once the flight had left, taking the baby beyond reach, their questions would be so easy to answer.

Beside him, curled like a foetus, slept Paulette. His daughter. The wax mask where once had been a smiling face, the body, now withered, which he used to swing about his head on summer days, the scabbed and pus-pocked arms that every evening would fling themselves around his neck, the sore-infested mouth that once had launched laughter throughout the corners of his world. The wreckage of a life. Her life. Of all their lives.

'For pity's sake get a move on!' he pleaded.

There was no time for subtlety. Scarcely any time left at all. Her taxi had been submerged in the same congestion as Devereux's car; she had no telephone, nothing to allay her fears, no means of information or solace, nothing with which to fight back. Brake lights taunted. Intersections jammed. Car horns jeered. She had no thoughts. Every time she disengaged her mind from the numbness she felt only pain, remembered only Triumph Towers. It was safest not to think.

She did not think, therefore, about the open display of side arms and sub-machine guns and Heckler & Koch semi-automatics with laser sights that greeted passengers as they decanted into the terminal; after all, it was Christmas, the traditional season for terrorism when airports in many parts of the world automatically switched to a heightened state of alert. She did not remark upon the warnings issued at double the usual frequency about unaccompanied packages, or the squad of maintenance men removing the litter bins which could so easily be turned into bomb casings. The thought never entered her mind that running heedlessly through an overflowing terminal and causing throngs of pre-Christmas travellers to scatter like butterflies would attract undue attention. She did not think. But she heard. Above the voices of carol singers with their songs of joy and Christmas nigh, above the rattling of coins in bright plastic buckets, above the chorus of hand-bells that rang out in praise, above it all she heard the announcement for flight KR 432. Boarding. London Gatwick. Direct to Abu Dhabi.

Her run became a sprint, her objective the Departures area, her progress devoid of thought for any other than Bella, ripples of protest swirling in her wake as she thrust aside all in her path – shouts of anger, bruised shins, a trolley turned over, the cries of a startled child – and she could see the huge board with lights flashing. KR 432. Final Call. She was almost there. One last surge.

She was swung violently around. A hand had stretched out from behind a pillar, grabbed her, the momentum of her chase almost knocking them both off their feet.

'You!' she gasped.

It was Devereux. Her eyes flashed from him to the Departure board, back again, as she sought to wrestle herself free.

'Don't worry. Your baby is fine. I've already sent instructions to have her brought here.'

His words left her reeling, her breath drawn in gasping rhythms, unable to respond.

'You've won. Don't you realize you've won?' he continued. 'She's being brought from the gate right now.'

She shook her head trying to fend off what she thought must be trickery and lies, her head swivelling in every direction, desperately seeking some sight of the child.

'It's over,' he shouted at her, grabbing her by the shoulders to force her attention. It did. He lowered his voice. 'A few minutes, that's all it will take.'

She stepped back, repulsed by his touch, but his

words sank slowly in. She began sobbing. Bella. Bella was here! Could it be? It was over! The release flooded around her, threatened to sweep her away, her head ringing to the echo of his words and she felt herself buckling. He reached out again, this time in support, his arm on hers, and did not move. She searched his watery eyes, attempting to find the truth; they were subdued.

'They'll bring her back out through the Departure lounge. Any moment now. Try to be patient for just a little while longer.'

She had known she might have to confront him, had counted on aggression, threats, violence, but not calm reason.

'Apologies will count for nothing with you, Isadora, although as a father I feel devastated for what you have been through. I am sorry. Truly. I had no idea what was going on with the adoption ring, please believe that, not until Paulette told me everything on the way here. I thought you were a troublemaker. I was wrong. I can make amends in the only way I know how, by returning your daughter to you. I only wish I were as fortunate.'

'Fortunate?' she spat, struggling to find the right words of abuse, but her mind was numb.

'You are getting your daughter back. And she's fine. I'd give everything I possess to share that privilege.'

'Paulette . . . ?'

'God, you've seen her, what she's like.' His voice had a bitter, defeatist edge. 'I've tried, so damned bloody hard, but I don't think I will ever get her back. Not now. After everything she's done I still want her back. I don't know whether you can understand that.' The watery eyes seemed to be on the point of melting completely, and suddenly he was no longer the arrogant politician but a parent in great anguish. And she knew all about that.

He fought back the welling emotion. 'Sorry. But . . .' He looked despairingly at Izzy. 'Let me explain. Please? She's not as evil as it must seem to you. It's . . . not completely her fault.'

'Forget it, I'm not in the forgiving mood.'

'I don't ask forgiveness. At times I find what she has done difficult to forgive myself, but . . . she is my daughter. My only child.' He swallowed hard, fighting for self-control. 'Her mother died when she was eight. Committed suicide. What are the words people use on these occasions – a tragedy? A family blighted? A loss without reason, no one to blame? But to a little girl of eight who couldn't understand why her mother was gone there was only one person to blame. Herself. Paulette never recovered.' He braced his shoulders. 'And I don't believe she ever will recover. It's too late for her.'

His emotion was infectious, contaminating her judgement and her anger. 'You're not trying to suggest I should turn a blind eye. Forget all about it.'

He shook his head as if every muscle in his body ached. 'I turned a blind eye, for years. Persuaded myself there was nothing wrong with her, that it was a passing phase. You wake up every morning and hope that this is the morning when it will all be fine again, when she will be there at breakfast, smiling, loving, once again your daughter. But. . . . how do you show your love for a child intent on torturing herself? I thought by protecting her. I was wrong.'

'You covered up for her.'

'I did. I denied the drugs as vehemently as she did. And I was wrong and now I will suffer the consequences. I was weak. I love my daughter, she's the only thing that matters to me and I wanted to fight for her, to stop her being destroyed. Surely you of all people understand that?'

'I understand that your daughter was destroying the lives of many others.'

He nodded. 'I still find that unbelievable, but . . . yes, and now she will destroy me. But believe me, I knew nothing of what she was doing with Fauld, not until just now. How do you face up to the fact that your daughter . . . ?' He struggled to put it into words.

'Sells babies.'

'It will stop, has already stopped. Apparently Fauld, on top of everything, is a pervert. The Vice Squad got an anonymous tip-off, found him in compromising circumstances in a London hotel . . .'

So her phone call had worked.

'It seems it was not the first time he has been caught at sexual misconduct. Nothing criminal, but he will have to resign, I shall ensure it. And if I have any power or position left after this mess I shall use it to ensure that Fauld and everyone like him engaged in these barbaric adoption practices is stopped and the system utterly destroyed.'

'Bit late for a conversion, isn't it? An hour ago you brought a posse of police to arrest me.'

He uttered a choked, hollow sound. 'Good God. I was not pursuing you; I had no idea you were even there. I came with the police in pursuit of my daughter. To arrest Paulette. Don't you see, my years of excusing her and always bailing her out have been a disaster. That wasn't the way to love her, it has all but killed her. But can you imagine what it takes, as a parent, to hunt down your child with a pack of police hounds?'

She thought she could. She remembered Daniel's

mother. Devereux was beginning to make sense.

'I've learned a lot of lessons recently about parental love. Many from you, Isadora. In some ways we are very much alike, you and I. Parents who would give anything for their child. Only I gave blindly. A great pity my education came too late.'

She felt sorrow for him. She could never have imagined it up to that point, but the anger and bitterness was stifled. She could sense and share the loss he must feel. He stood before her amidst the ashes of his pride, a charred and broken husk.

And suddenly she realized what he was at.

'Bella. My baby. She's the only evidence there is. Against you. Against your daughter.'

He stiffened as if slapped in the face. And suddenly she was disengaged from his entrancing tale, her senses back in the airport. The minutes had ticked away, the final call for Abu Dhabi long since expired.

'You're not bringing her back at all. You bastard, you're here to make sure she's put on that plane and there's not a trace of evidence left for what your daughter's done. What you've done. Damn my blindness!'

And Izzy leapt for the departure gate.

The security arrangements leading air-side serve a number of purposes. The central search area is intended to examine passengers for appropriate authority to travel and their baggage for hazardous contraband. The checking procedures are usually sluggish and methodical as befits a slow-moving column of travellers, the various checkpoints for boarding cards, passports and baggage generally close together. The arrangements therefore provide a distinct albeit short-lived advantage for those who have neither boarding cards nor passports nor baggage but who meet the security gates at the charge.

Izzy had brushed aside the security guard checking boarding passes before he'd even looked up. The archway metal detector could do no more than buzz in impotence as she ran through, leaving behind the flailing arms and reproachful shouts of baggage inspectors, while the immigration officers who handle passport control are neither trained in nor encouraged to use martial arts. She was through the lot before they had time to do anything other than raise their voices and activate a variety of security alarms. But alarms warn, they do not stop. And by the time the Search Control Officer had begun lowering the metal fire shutters to secure the area, she was already well past.

Izzy ran down the long glass-sided walkway leading to the gates. On either side she passed faces full of bewilderment. To the front of her people drew back in concern in the attempt, not always successful, to avoid her onward rush. From behind she could barely hear the sound of heavy-booted pursuit. Hope collided with terror, blotting out all sense of danger. Panic lent extraordinary speed to her endeavours. 'Bella!' she screamed, 'Bella!' until her lungs could cry no more and she forced herself onward.

From corridors to her side and through the gateways she passed came other pursuers. They were armed, intent. The shouts and alarums of pursuit were growing louder, drawing unmistakably closer. A dog barked. She thought she heard the sharp metallic rattle she knew so well from other battlefields: of activating gun mechanisms, breeches being loaded, safeties being thrown. She knew they were gaining, tried to look behind, stumbled, almost fell, careening into a large stuffed Santa bear which was sent sprawling across the walkway along with the pile of gaily wrapped cartons and parcels that surrounded it. And from up ahead, beyond the crowds milling around the Duty Free, she could discern the dark blue uniforms of armed police, waiting for her, spread across her path like a human net. Three of them were down on one knee, both arms raised, combat position, guns pointing directly at her. From somewhere close came shouted commands for her to halt and for others to get down. Screams. Travellers in the long avenue began throwing themselves to the floor, like felled trees in a forest. She seemed to be the only one left standing. And more guns had been readied, were pointing at her. She could not stop.

Then she had reached the departure gate for KR 432 and had flung herself around the corner and into its waiting area. To the side stood a policeman, flak jacket, nervous eyes bulging in apprehension, side arm unholstered and being raised to its firing position, safety catch slipped, a warning shout on his lips.

And at the far end, walking out of the hall through the exit that led directly to the aircraft, was a woman dressed in a white nurse's uniform, and holding something in her arms. Arms which Izzy, on the charge, had seized, had twisted round, had forced with demonic strength to release their charge.

'Bella!'

The pursuit had caught up with her. The far end of the hall had been stormed as though by a charging herd, policemen spilling in and around until there was a solid wall of blue flak jackets from which protruded shafts of grey steel, aimed, ready for an order to fire.

Time travelled as slowly as melting wax. Barrels wavered, like the heads of snakes preparing to strike. Eyes fastened onto her, unblinking. The officer in charge filled his chest, seemed to hesitate and freeze. And the expression on the baby's face changed like the phases of the moon. From alarm, to the suffusion of pleasure, and finally – triumphantly – to the glow of recognition.

Isadora Dean clasped her baby in her arms and let forth a shattering roar of triumph.

Then Devereux was there – God, he was always there, like slime she could not scrape from her shoe, like the stench of death in the charnel house – whispering in the officer's ear. Guns were lowered, he stepped forward. His face had become grey stone, the watery eyes ice. Then he was beside her. She could restrain her feelings no longer.

'I would gladly shoot you myself, but others will save me the trouble. You're going to roast and I shall enjoy turning the spit. I'll sing for joy every time they carve a new slice. I shall destroy you.'

He found a thin smile. 'I think not.'

Izzy was shaking her head in contemptuous dismissal, but he continued.

'If you try, you will lose your baby.'

She taunted his suggestion. 'Not again. No one can ever take her away from me again.'

'Oh, but they can, Isadora.'

He appeared so arrogantly confident that the smallest rivulet of apprehension ran down her back. She clutched the infant more closely. 'What do you mean?'

'Simply this. Within five minutes of the first sign that you are causing trouble with your wild accusations about baby rings, I shall ensure that a warrant is issued for your arrest.'

She laughed in his face. 'On what charge?'

'Take your pick. Drug dealing? After all, you have been consorting with known drug dealers, and fled after being apprehended by police in a coffee shop notorious for its drug deals. Or would you prefer murder? Based on Paulette's evidence. Of Daniel Blackheart.'

She found her lips stammering. 'But that's ridiculous. The charges won't stick. Anyway, I shall be out of this wretched country.'

'But you see – and listen carefully, this is important – the charges don't need to stick. Merely be laid. For within a further five minutes of the charges being laid I shall ensure that your husband is informed of all the details. You are trying to fight him for custody. You've already abandoned one child, no court in the world is going to give you custody of a second with accusations of murder and drug dealing hanging round your neck.'

'But . . . you can't.'

'But I can. And will. Look, you have your daughter, that's what you wanted all along. Don't throw that all away with ridiculous ideas of revenge.'

'This is monstrous,' she exclaimed, vainly trying to find the flaw in his argument.

'Utterly monstrous,' he concurred in supercilious tone. 'But effective, wouldn't you agree? The slightest sniff of trouble from you and you will lose the baby once again. This time entirely legally, by court order.'

'People will listen to me . . .'

'They haven't up to now. Why should they change? My dear, you grossly overrate the credulity of your audience. Put an hysterical American woman against a solid English statesman, and the American will lose every time.'

'What on earth are you suggesting?'

'I'm suggesting that I go over there to the commander of this little posse and tell him that it has all been a dreadful mistake. That you are not the dangerous terrorist we all thought you were, but a distraught mother, the victim of a domestic dispute. They'll accept that with very little persuasion after your performance with the baby. Then you get a plane out of the country. Immediately. Tonight. Forget about Britain, forget about everything you've seen here and never come back.'

'Forget about what you and your daughter have done?'

'Yes. Unless you are willing to forget about your own daughter.'

'You expect me to forget what you've done to God knows how many innocent children?'

'The adoption nonsense was none of my doing. What I told you about Fauld is true. He's finished, it's over.'

'Forget about Daniel?' she whispered through clenched teeth. 'Never!'

'Look, you have two simple options. You can have your baby. Or you can have me. Revenge, or Bella. But not both. Simple as that. So what's it to be?'

She stood dumbstruck. Madly her mind was trying to puncture the scenario he had conjured up, but every one of her arrows seemed to bounce off an impenetrable shell.

'Look at your baby, Isadora. Look at her closely. You see, you really have no choice.'

No choice. No choice. The words burned into her brain as he sauntered over to the police commander and began gesticulating vehemently. They seared away truth as she was led back land-side beyond passport control, back to the world full of real people. But not Daniel. They befogged her mind and bewitched her emotions even as she stumbled through a brief period of police questioning, ably prompted by Devereux, while she clung to Bella and cried.

They let her go. With a warning. Dismissed by these men as just another overwrought, unfathomable female.

And Devereux had smiled. She had so wanted to lash out, to disfigure his smirking face, to smash away the condescending sneer, but she could not do it without letting go of Bella. And she would not, would never, let go of Bella.

She had Bella and she had thought that was all she had wanted, but it was not enough. She could not forget what she knew, leave behind what she had seen, ignore the children who had been abused and who might go on being abused. She could not stop loving Daniel, even though she had only just started. She would never stop hating Devereux. And she raged at her own impotence, and felt ashamed.

No choice!

TEN

This time Devereux took no chances, not for one moment taking his eyes off her. He watched her all the way: onto the plane, out to the taxiway, up into the air. On her way home.

It was over. He'd won.

Izzy gone. Paulette, stunned and inwardly stirred by the realization of all that she had done, at last repentant and clinic-bound. Fauld, resigned and headed for obscurity, his silence secured by his guilt, his foul trade finished – for so long he had fooled even Devereux, one of the few misjudgements Devereux had made.

The police were puzzled about Daniel's death – no dope in his system – but satisfied. After all, there was a drugs record as long as a perforated arm, and he died with a needle in his hand. Misadventure. No one to blame but himself. It might have seemed confused, a mess, this tangle involving a Cabinet Minister's daughter, drug addicts and a demented mother, but who wanted to enquire too closely? Doubt the word of Devereux? Anyway, it cleared up the paperwork.

A charmed life, Devereux thought. An ability to surmount the tribulations that would destroy any ordinary man. A purpose.

And Bizzie had just called; the PM had finally resolved to retire – not now, not immediately, but definitely, in the summer.

His purpose seemed set to be fulfilled. And soon.

Life was good, thought Devereux. In fact, it was great.

She had stumbled through the hours as though in a dream, the anger tightening around her stomach like a band of steel, her senses paralysed, blinded by shame. Manipulated. Left no choice.

She had Bella, at least, safe, loving, well. But it was not enough.

No choice. It burned inside her, like acid.

If only she could be content simply being a mother. But it had never been enough, so she had played the game of men, and lost. Kicked around between Devereux and Joe and Grubb and all the rest of the boys' brigade.

And even high above the clouds they were still rubbing insult into injury. That miserable little producer of hers – *ex*-producer of hers – was leering from the in-flight video, not even attempting to fill her job, not hard news about hard facts but some vacuous piece about celebrity gossip. Is that what it had all come to? Crap about the Prime Minister's wife christening a cross-Channel locomotive named after herself? The boys playing at trains?

She had fought all her professional life for integrity, but now she knew it had been an utter waste of effort and tears. She felt her composure and resilience ebbing rapidly – damn it, she would not cry! – and began scrabbling in the overhead locker for the tissues in her bag. She couldn't even do that properly; the bag fell to the floor where it lay, disembowelled, its contents strewn.

She sank to her knees in humiliation, hiding her face, burying her futility as she attempted to retrieve her few pathetic possessions.

'The Bizzie Lizzie,' the video intoned, revealing

the face of the Premier's wife who waved and looked so proud.

And as the champagne broke across the locomotive's bows, beneath the seat she found not only the tissues and hairbrush and other oddments but also a computer disk. Devereux's diary. And the parts at last began to fit.

'*Spent night with BL while PM off in Brussels. The fool. Being screwed on all fronts . . .*'

Bizzie Lizzie? Elizabeth Flood . . . ? Only now did it make sense. Devereux had been bedding the boss's wife! Not definitely, not absolutely for certain, but probably, and as soon as she got home she would make sure, damned sure, by reading the rest of the disk.

And then what? No publisher or editor would touch it. She couldn't prove the contents of the diary were anything but an elaborate forgery, there are no fingerprints on a computer disk. These things could never see the light of day.

But perhaps they did not have to. All she had to do was to ensure that they fell into the right hands.

The Prime Minister's hands. And with her contacts she could ensure that.

He wouldn't have to know, for certain. Only suspect. Devereux wouldn't need to be convicted in court, only in Flood's mind. And the suspicions of a cuckolded husband ignite like sulphur on brushwood. In the diary there would be too many indiscretions, circumstances, confessions, dates, too many private and political details which could only have come from Devereux, for Flood to be left in any doubt.

It was said the PM was not long for this world, that he would soon jump or be pushed. Whichever, he would make sure as hell is hot that he took

Devereux with him. To have slept with the Prime Minister's wife may not be the worst crime in politics, but to have bragged about it in a diary was a hanging offence. Devereux would be dismissed. Disgraced. Hanged. Very publicly.

She was crying openly now. Through her tears she could see in front of her the weapon with which she could destroy Devereux and all his works, without in any way involving Bella or herself. Destroy Devereux and *all* his works.

Which would include the Duster.

Even Joe.

And Joe's custody case. Her chance to win back Benjy.

On her knees she began to laugh. To roar. To exult in her triumph.

She had a choice after all.

To Play the King
Michael Dobbs

The No. 1 bestselling sequel to *House of Cards* that was made into an enormously successful and controversial BBC TV series.

Francis Urquhart is back! After scheming his way to power in *House of Cards*, the newly elected Prime Minister Francis Urquhart faces a crisis that could bring down his government. But as he plots the drastic measures that could save his political future he finds one determined man standing in his way – the idealistic new King.

Urquhart will stop at nothing to cling to power. As he prepares to expose the scandalous activities of certain members of the Royal household, he threatens to bring down not only his Royal opponent, but also the Monarchy itself . . .

'Rattles along from scandal to scandal . . . excellent entertainment.'   *Mail on Sunday*

'Michael Dobbs has an uncanny knack of forecasting the future. A fascinating read and a conclusion that would send a chill through Buckingham Palace.'   *Sunday Express*

'A model of its kind and impeccably timed.'   *Daily Mail*

ISBN 0 00 647164 1

Wall Games
Michael Dobbs

BERLIN – BEFORE THE WALL CAME TUMBLING DOWN

The dawn of *glasnost*. The thaw is slowly beginning as leaders in both East and West set out tentatively to build a new era of peace.

Yet the people of Berlin are in no mood for diplomatic caution. Across the heart of their city still stands the monstrous construction of the Wall that has split them apart for a generation. They will fight to have it torn down, and to reunite their city – just as there are those in Washington and Moscow who will use them to kill off the new flower of *glasnost*.

Into the troubled city of Berlin comes Harry Benjamin, a young and irrepressible CIA agent. He hadn't planned on falling in love – even less on that illicit love casting him as a pawn in this latest battle for Berlin. But Harry will not be anyone's pawn. He is determined to reveal the treachery, even if it means destroying the most powerful men in East and West – and his love – in the process.

'The account of vacillation and in-fighting at the top levels of politics is vivid, and credible enough to be disturbing.'
Evening Standard

'An expert on erring political shapers of public destiny. He undoubtedly knows where all the bodies are buried. Dobbs is the sort of operator who seems to be precisely where the action is at various moments in history.' *The Australian*

ISBN 0 00 617691 7

Last Man to Die
Michael Dobbs

Spring 1945. The final weeks of the war. One man holds the secret that will decide the fate of post-war Europe: Peter Hencke, an unlikely hero, a German POW on the run.

Refusing to wait for peace and the freedom it will finally bring, Hencke is fired by a personal mission that drives him to risk everything in his lonely, treacherous journey across wartime Britain, back through the battle-torn remnants of the Third Reich – to the very heart of encircled Berlin.

One man faced by the mightiest armies ever assembled, pursued by the most powerful and ruthless men in Europe – and helped and loved by two of the most extraordinary women. The secret of Peter Hencke will be hidden until the very last moments of the war.

'Truly the great escape . . . quite simply, a good old-fashioned adventure that rattles along to a cataclysmic finale.'
Daily Mail

'Thrilling escapism . . . what a corker, with a cunning twist in the tail. After this, the last moments of the war will never seem the same again.'
Daily Express

ISBN 0 00 647097 1

☐ TELLING THE PICTURES Frank Delaney	0-00-647924-3	£4.99
☐ VIOLENT WARD Len Deighton	0-00-647901-4	£4.99
☐ WITHOUT REMORSE Tom Clancy	0-00-647641-4	£5.99
☐ PROVO Gordon Stevens	0-00-647632-5	£4.99
☐ NAME OF THE BEAST Daniel Easterman	0-586-21088-1	£4.99

All these books are available from your local bookseller or can be ordered direct from the publishers.

To order direct just tick the titles you want and fill in the form below:

Name: _____

Address: _____

_____

Postcode: _____

Send to: HarperCollins Mail Order, Dept 8, HarperCollins *Publishers*, Westerhill Road, Bishopbriggs, Glasgow G64 2QT.

Please enclose a cheque or postal order or your authority to debit your Visa/Access account –

Credit card no: _____

Expiry date: _____

Signature: _____

– to the value of the cover price plus:

UK & BFPO: Add £1.00 for the first and 25p for each additional book ordered.

Overseas orders including Eire, please add £2.95 service charge.

Books will be sent by surface mail but quotes for airmail despatches will be given on request.

24 HOUR TELEPHONE ORDERING SERVICE FOR ACCESS/VISA CARDHOLDERS –

TEL: GLASGOW 041-772 2281 or LONDON 081-307 4052